The Twelve Sisters

The Twelve Sisters

A Novel

Don Gordon Pierson

David Thompson Dorris

Dresher Plains Press

USA

Printed in the United States of America
Dresher Plains Press, USA

ARInfo@dresherplainspress.com

ISBN 979-8-9865347-0-1

1. Thriller—Fiction 2. Mystery—Fiction 3. Renaissance Art

Dorris, David Thompson, 1953 -

Pierson, Don Gordon, 1953 -

The Twelve Sisters

3   5   7   9   10   8   6   4

First Edition, September 2022

For Valerie and Thea

Thanks for holding your questions until the end.

"Those who profit at my expense shall find evil in their midst."

- Giuseppe Antone

Table of Contents

Copyright   iv

Dedication   v

Epigraph   vi

Table of Contents   vii

Chapter 0   1

Part I – The Legend   3

Part II – The Family   23

Part III – The Angel   209

Epilogue   324

The Story Behind the Story   326

Acknowledgements   328

About the Authors   329

CHAPTER 0

Every story is a mix of truth and fiction. Well, here's the truth about this story. Two years ago, I threw a big Derby party. A lot of people came, including Darcy Cummings. I'd not seen her in years and was surprised to learn that she was at George Washington University wrapping up her master's degree in Renaissance Art. She pulled me aside and said she had a favor to ask. As I was the only author she knew who also had a bit of expertise in art, would I mind "taking a look" at the final draft of her thesis.

I agreed, but ended up doing more taking than looking.

During her research, Darcy had come across a handwritten manuscript in the antiquities section of the National Gallery of Art Library in Washington, D.C. The carbon/gum ink was miserably faded, but she deciphered the medieval Latin and painstakingly translated it into English. Portions of her translation, which she characterized as an oral history from the early 1500's, appears in an appendix of her thesis.

Those singular pages are what I took, and that antediluvian lore became the genesis of the book you are now reading.

Myths and legends are fascinating in and of themselves, but when one is fortunate enough to glimpse the actual origin of an ancient tale, the real allure becomes that boundary between fact and fiction. Were those few crumbling sheets of Fabriano paper a reliable record of a factual oral history, or were they largely the product of an overactive imagination and too many retellings?

I'm still unsure. You can decide for yourself after reading Part I of this book. It is, in fact, Darcy's translation (used with her permission) plus a bit of creative license to patch some of the lacunae.

Part I - The Legend

1484 A.D.

My mother, Angelina di Fabbro, told me a remarkable story on the night she passed from this world. She was old, more than forty years I think, and confused at times, so I cannot swear the truth of every detail. But one part I know is real; I found the evidence, hidden where she said it would be. And so, having been taught to read and write as my father wanted, I have faithfully preserved my mother's history as she remembered it. May she rest in eternity with Jesus and the Holy Virgin.

The Story of Angelina

I was a meretrix. From the age of fourteen, during the time of His Holiness Innocent[1], I lived and worked with twelve others.

My first night at the lupanar, my purity and innocence were sold to the highest bidder. It was a celebration for the patrons that filled the house, but for me it was pain, sweat, and stink. I was smothered by a fat swine of a man pressing down. I closed my eyes. The next customers enjoyed a first night experience at an extra charge. Those hours paid for my room and keep for the next seven days. It would never be that way again.

During those first weeks, I began to understand the sacrifices that were set in motion the day I was born. While my father worked hard providing for us, the choices were limited for a girl from a large family with moderate means. My brothers apprenticed with masters

1. Pope Innocent VIII, 1484-1492

in Florence and set their paths. My oldest sister married well and was supported by an acceptable dowry. By the time my middle sister was of age, my father was able to make payment to the Church for her life in the nunnery. The choices were fewer for me. Without money for a dowry or the convent, life in a brothel was the best plan, a plan I was too young to question.

I remember the tears in my father's eyes as he held our last embrace. He placed his precious boxwood and bone rosary in my palm and closed my fingers tightly around it. He tried to speak but words could not make it from his throat. It is a difficult last memory, but that and the rosary are all I have left of him.

My mother had negotiated my place in advance and traveled with me to a tall stone house on the southern edge of San Russo, the nearest large village. After a silent coach ride, she held my hands in hers and looked deeply into my eyes as if she were watching me grow up. She kissed my cheek, and then delivered me to kind and gentle Reina, the matron who would soon shape my world and my life. From that day I never heard from my family again, but that is how I came to be in the place where I met the man who would become your father.

The summer of my second year at the lupanar, a young man knocked on our door seeking work. He was tall and muscular with a full head of dark hair and penetrating blue eyes. Even his name was beautiful. Giuseppe Antone. Everyone in the house took notice. Reina told him we were doing fine by ourselves but promised to seek him out if needed. Strangely, maybe through Providence, several projects past our expertise appeared over the next few weeks. True to her word, Reina got a message to Giuseppe requesting his services. He arrived with his modest bag of tools ready to work. Evidently his skills and price met Reina's requirements. She came to rely on his services and soon his advice as well.

Giuseppe was poor. He lived somewhere in the hills outside of town. He picked grapes and olives at harvest and found odd jobs other times. When winter came and work disappeared, he bartered small paintings for food and pieces of used clothing. Many times during exchanges in the village I had seen a shopkeeper's portrait prominently displayed and wondered who had painted it. Now I knew.

The man who would become your father was a kind, gentle soul. He made a point of learning our names and treated us with respect.

From time to time, Reina invited him to share our mid-day meal while he was working in the house. We enjoyed the conversation and news of the outside world. It was a welcomed reprieve from the night talk of braggarts and drunks.

We learned that Giuseppe was the son of a highly skilled apothecary, but he was reluctant to give more details. As we moved on to other topics, I could see Reina's eyes fixed in deep consideration.

As the season changed, one of the girls fell ill. Reina was overheard asking Giuseppe questions about his father's business. His answers were soft and unheard, but that afternoon he appeared at the door and presented a small, corked bottle to Reina. His instructions were delivered with precision and he nodded when she repeated them back to him. The girl was restored to full health in no time.

Soon, everyone in the house was smitten by our craftsman and healer. Even old Reina's eyes lit up when he came around, but it seemed he saved his best smiles for me.

When the cold air returned that year, Reina offered the old stone wellhouse downhill from the lupanar as a place for Giuseppe to sleep. It was not free, Reina ran a business after all, but it did include a mid-day meal and an unobstructed view of the olive trees beyond the river bend to the south.

Giuseppe felt at home in the wellhouse. It was a welcomed change from sharing a shallow cave with the occasional wild animal or sleeping in fields at harvest time. His new home had a small south facing window near the roof. It lit the stone room, kept out the rain, and provided an escape for the smoke from a good night's fire. The thick rock would heat up during the day and pass the warmth inside at night. Plus the ground stable air from the dry well shaft kept him cool in summer and kept the frost away in winter. In addition to the dry well, the wellhouse contained a shallow cistern no longer in use. He adjusted the pivot point of the heavy stone cover to keep the cistern open and filled it with deep piles of straw. With a final layer of bartered sheep fleece, his bed was complete.

Our house seemed a little brighter with Giuseppe in our daily lives. Knowing he was around made the daytime chores pass more quickly. He was there to assist with work or repairs and would sometimes accompany us when we shopped. Most of the shopkeepers knew him and engaged him in conversation. With him by our side we felt less outcast than when we entered a shop by ourselves.

Our health improved, especially our business health. Before Giuseppe, even with Sunday's rest, our recovery was never complete. His daily treatments of herbs and minerals changed that. The day-to-day fevers and aches left us more quickly because of his care. And most importantly, not one of us was ever with child.

No longer did Reina have to threaten us to get out of bed. We looked forward to sharing meals with Giuseppe. Over the next few months I noticed him stealing glances at me when we sat across the table. Then it became more of a study, which I took as a prelude to courtship.

The courtship did not happen. But a gift, wrapped in paper, tied by a string, soon appeared at the door of my room. Fighting the urge to tear open the paper I carefully untied and unfolded the wrappings to find a portrait of a young, partially clothed woman in a flirtatious but confident pose. Tingles covered my body. I had seen my reflection before but I never let myself think I was beautiful. There was something in "my" eyes that pulled me in, as if an intimate conversation was about to continue. The tingles turned to blush; looking down past the crimson cloth over my shoulder I saw my breast exactly as I know it, right down to the imperfect mole hidden in the under shadow. If I had been in another life I may have felt violated, but nakedness was the nature of my business. So many had seen and touched my flesh, more than I could count. But there was only one who truly knew my face and the parts not traded for coin.

Later in the day I made sure to be alone in the kitchen with Giuseppe. I looked at him and smiled hoping he would betray his actions, but he simply returned my smile. Gaining courage, I mentioned something about a gift, wrapped in paper, tied with a string. He answered, "Gifts are enjoyable from all sides". I saw a sparkle in his eye as he left the house.

I hung the painting in my room. Reina and the girls were captivated. Each felt they were invited to join the girl in the image, a feeling they could not explain. They asked who painted it and although I had no real confirmation, I suggested it could have been Giuseppe. The next day Reina placed it in the downstairs gathering room, saying it would be good for business. And it was! Over the next few weeks I was first choice for almost every man who walked through the door. I was exhausted. Reina raised my price to even things out with the others. I was ahead of what I owed to the house for the first time since my introduction.

Giuseppe remained silent about the painting, but Reina paid a visit to him in the wellhouse to ask if he was the painter. When she entered his room, the question was answered. She found brushes and pots of dry colored powder, a makeshift easel and sketches of me covering one of the walls. Reina struck another deal and by the end of the year each of us had our place on the walls of the main room. Reina called us her Twelve Sisters.

As talk of the paintings spread, we became more than a local afterthought. Men came from far and wide. Business was so good that on occasion Reina would close the house. We would spend a day in the countryside, playing in the fields and cooling off in the river. Spring was my favorite time for these adventures. There was something about the way the sun warmed my winter virgin skin that stirred thoughts of Giuseppe. I often pondered his reaction to being with thirteen naked women lying side by side in the sun along the river's edge. Some wondered aloud why he never accepted their offers and invitations for intimate relations.

Your father changed my life forever, and having him so near saved me. One late night, a drunken mercenary traveling through San Russo decided his coin allowed him to beat me. When I cried out, the regulars wanted no part of going against a Condottiere. Reina's efforts to pull him away ended in her physical dismissal onto the hard floor.

Surprised to hear screams of terror, and not those of invented passion, Giuseppe rushed in through the kitchen and up the stairs. He found me covered in blood, trapped under the mercenary's weight. As the attacker raised his fist for another blow, Giuseppe seized the soldier's right hand and pulled back with all his weight. With a mighty twist, the bones snapped. The mercenary cried out in surprised agony and turned to see the rage of a giant man protecting his adopted family. He reached for his knife but in one motion Giuseppe picked him up and threw him headfirst into the stone wall.

The soldier stopped moving. Giuseppe sat beside me on my bed and gently touched my face. The world instantly slowed. Reina, my sisters, and the useless patrons faded away. I felt no pain. Giuseppe shouted orders of hot water, soap and clean cloth. There was no argument. He pulled up the blanket to cover and warm me, and then whispered calming words, saying this would never happen again as long as he lived. It was as if the sun washed over me on a winter's day. I was in love.

When my wounds had been cleaned and bandaged, I could hear

Reina and Giuseppe speaking in low tones as my sisters helped me dress. When Giuseppe reentered my room, he bent

 over me, caught my gaze, smiled. Without a word, he lifted me, blanket and all, and carried me to his bed in the wellhouse.

Your father nursed me until I healed, but the wounds left scars on my face. I knew, as Giuseppe and Reina knew, my price would go down. I would no longer be first choice. The night of the attack, he and Reina had made a bargain. Giuseppe would make his presence known every work night, taking care of any rowdiness, and I would manage the daytime cooking and cleaning. In exchange the wellhouse was ours to use. We would share meals in the main house and Giuseppe would still be paid for his apothecary and odd jobs. Best of all, my days as a meretrix were over. It was an odd family and it worked beautifully.

During my time of healing, Giuseppe proved his love. He stood silent watch or slept beside me at night, he kept me warm and washed my wounds, but he never touched me in a sexual way. He understood what I did not yet know. I needed to be the one to want him inside me. It's a choice I had never made before. From the age of fourteen, I was told to smile, collect the coin, and spread my legs. His instincts were true. I needed time to heal on the inside.

Each day together was a gift. I had never been this loved before. It was unconditional. The thousands of physical encounters while I was at the house were never mentioned. Your father knew it had been a matter of survival. And as his story unfolded over the days ahead, the depth of his compassion became clear.

Giuseppe's Story

During long walks gathering herbs and minerals, he answered my questions with patience as I learned about his remedies, how to match symptoms and cures. Some days we spoke of times before we met. I told him about my childhood with Mother and Father, my brothers and sisters. I told him the loss and confusion I felt when adapting to the life of a meretrix and how that grief began to lift the moment I saw him at our door. His smile and his confidence filled me with an unexplained faith in the future.

The story your father told of the journey that led him to me was much different, beginning in a life of rare privilege, but ending, like mine, in poverty. This is his history, a story I quilted from pieces he shared during the time we had together:

He was born in Florence, and he was given the name Nicolò. His mother attended court and his father was Apothecary to the Medici family, respected throughout the region as a Guild Master.

From an early age, Nicolò, or Giuseppe—the name he came to call himself—showed high intelligence. He was like a dry sponge. He discovered that the best way to learn was to be present and keep quiet, saving questions for those things he could not decipher himself. His father supported Giuseppe's desire to learn the trade, and whenever they were without customers, he would speak his actions aloud as he worked the recipes for medicinals as well as for artists' pigments. By the time he was ten, there was little that Giuseppe did not know of his father's vocation. He knew the origins of all the herbs and minerals and when and where to find them. He knew the mixtures and proportions, the doses for healing, and the conflicts they could cause.

The Guild was a world of status whose doors opened wide for the Master's son. In addition to apothecaries and surgeons, painters were also allied with the Arte dei Medici e Speziali. Most of the painters knew young Giuseppe by name. He was seen in his father's shop and when he delivered pigments to their studios. Most were content to let him linger in the shadows, observing the earths and pigments being pounded into colors and mixed with oils, or the wooden boards being plastered with lime.

One painter in particular took a special interest in Giuseppe. Domenico Ghirlandaio, from the Verrocchio workshop. He noted his knowledge and interest in the technical aspects of painting and encouraged him to visit, to observe and ask questions. From the age of twelve, he was allowed to spend all his free time in Ghirlandaio's studio. Soon he was being called upon to prepare plasters or mix pigments for Ghirlandaio and his contemporaries Leonardo, Botticelli and Perugino. Ghirlandaio told him soon he would be mixing color for his own brushes.

Before Ghirlandaio's prediction could come true, everything changed in Florence. During a Sunday Mass, one of the Medici brothers was assassinated. The bloody coup d'état failed[2] and the conspirators either fled or were killed. But that night, an angry throng of soldiers dragged Giuseppe's father from his bedchamber, simply because he had a business association with the bank owned

2. Pazzi conspiracy, 26 April 1478

by the family at the center of the conspiracy.

Giuseppe had heard the breach of the door and the heavy footsteps moving through the house. He ran to his father's aid, only to be beaten unconscious by the intruders. When Giuseppe awoke, the crowd had moved on and his father lay motionless in the blood-covered street, his heart no longer beating.

Fearing the crowd would return, Giuseppe raced up the stairs to find his mother naked and bleeding, lying face down on the edge of her bed. He dressed and comforted her as best he could. He left her to gather warm clothes and collect the few valuables that had not been discovered and taken by the violent swarm.

They fled the city in darkness and followed the river, avoiding the large settlements, and stopping only to eat and rest. At the end of the second day, a small hillside village appeared. It was safely beyond the daily trade routes to and from Florence, and his mother was unable to travel farther due to pain and exhaustion. They had no one to turn to for aid as their family members were all suspect, likely dead or in hiding by now. This would be their new home.

Giuseppe found food and water then made his mother comfortable in the shade on the north slope of the hill. The next morning, they faced their situation. They needed a permanent place to live and some sort of income, as the small bag of valuables would raise questions impossible to answer.

Only fifteen and already taller than most, Giuseppe easily passed for someone years older, something his knowledge and confident voice tended to confirm. In his search for work, he learned that the village had a small apothecary near the base of the hill. When he entered the damp stone building, the sights and smells seemed to welcome him, but the apothecary greeted him with caution. Gino was not accustomed to strangers. He was intimidated by the visitor, but after pleasantries were exchanged and the conversation steered by Giuseppe toward advanced trade topics, Gino relaxed.

It was soon clear that the stranger possessed knowledge well beyond Gino's. When he asked where he learned the trade, Giuseppe fabricated a vague but convincing history that kept his ties to Florence hidden. Gino relished the idea of advancing his own skills but did not wish to insult Giuseppe with an apprenticeship offer, nor did he have the means to pay him. Giuseppe sensed the thoughts rushing through Gino's head and never mentioned his need for a job. He asked if Gino knew of a place he and his unwell mother could reside. Gino smiled and told him he owned such a dwelling and led him down the hill to a small stone structure.

The hovel sat a dozen paces from the edge of a rocky ravine. A lovely creek splashed and bubbled over smooth rocks and pebbles many feet below. Giuseppe could imagine the sound of the water soothing his mother to sleep each night. Without turning to face him, he admitted he could not afford such accommodations. After a pause, Gino proposed that they could use the dwelling by the creek and share his food in trade for help in the apothecary. Giuseppe accepted the offer. Both men smiled, happy to have made the deal of deals.

After a life of relative luxury in Florence, Giuseppe's mother was not used to such basic living arrangements. But compared to sleeping on the ground and traveling on an empty stomach, finding food, shelter, and a job so quickly was a blessing. As her body healed, she began to make her place in her new home overlooking the creek.

Gino and Giuseppe were a curious pair, opposites connected by the healing arts. They learned from each other and enjoyed the company. After a few months Gino's confidence in Giuseppe increased to the point they shared duties as equals. From time to time, Gino would press a bright coin in his assistant's hand as a bonus for the increase in business.

Giuseppe and his mother had an open invitation to Gino's house in the village, and though they visited on several occasions over the years, they chose to have few social contacts. It was too difficult to hide his mother's noble upbringing with just simple clothing. If news had reached Florence of a young apothecary and mother springing up two days' journey away, and so soon after the assassination, their story would be compromised.

Over time Giuseppe noticed a change in his mother. Too often he found her at the edge of the ravine, perched on the rocks high above the creek, watching the dancing contradiction of the moving water. She had come to accept her new life but still had her eye in the past. The small, unspent bag of gold and jewels was her touchstone to her life in Florence. Just holding the red coral necklace of childhood or her mother's jade pendant made her feel warm inside. But of all her treasures, the pearl necklace with a gold encased emerald pendant was her favorite. Her husband had given it to her on their wedding night. She had worn it often, bringing compliments in all of Florence. "There are great memories in objects," she loved to say.

To cheer her, Giuseppe would sketch her sitting by the creek in the morning or by the fire at night. She smiled whenever he brought out his stylus and paper. With time, his skill improved.

Behind the apothecary, claiming to be working extra hours, he began her portrait as a surprise. He'd seen it done many times, but this was his first attempt at painting. Putting her image on the plaster did not go as fast as he recalled from the studio. He wanted it to be perfect. On the third try, with no ideas to improve the things his lack of skill revealed, he deemed it finished.

On the anniversary of her birth, Giuseppe presented the portrait to his mother. The smile that flooded her face soon turned to tears, and then she laughed at her own reactions. She marveled at how young and beautiful the portrait made her look and proudly pointed out his dedication on the back. "To Mother, Always Nicolò". She said the image had given back the years that time had stolen, but he told her, "I can think of no one to rival your beauty."

In fact the likeness was from his Florence memories of her, dressed in the fashion of the day, complete with her pearl and emerald necklace. He could almost picture his father by her side, descending their staircase. It was a good day for her. Sadly, it was her last.

The next morning began like most others, but that day the bright and sunny sky was a reflection of his mother's smile. Giuseppe had not realized the depth of her depression until he saw her restored. He was infected with her happiness as well. After a brief conversation, a tender embrace, and a kiss in the middle of her forehead, he left her smiling in her morning spot, watching the sun flicker in the rippling water below. He promised her something special upon his return, and then set off on his weekly day of gathering in the valley beyond.

Giuseppe's foraging was more successful than usual. He did not return until mid-afternoon and his sack was overflowing. He went directly to the apothecary to unpack and sort the day's gatherings. With Gino's help, it did not take long to wash, separate, and dry the day's findings. Once this task was complete, Giuseppe tied a string bow around the ginseng surprise for his mother and walked down the hill, whistling as he approached the house.

His mother was not waiting for his return in her usual creek-side perch. The door was open and he entered the darkened room. She was not there, but someone else had been. Their meager clothing and all of their food were gone. Holes had been dug in the dirt and the straw bedding scattered. The small leather bag that held their valuables and their history was gone. So was the portrait of his mother.

Outside he found three sets of heavy footprints, and one lighter than the others, that had approached from upstream, toward Florence. Bandits? Mercenaries returning to the city? Certainly no one from the village.

Gino heard Giuseppe's cries and raced down the hill to find him wild-eyed.

"Mother. Have you seen Mother? She is not here. We have been robbed of everything we own."

Gino tried to remain calm. "She may have run to the village seeking help."

"No, she would never go there alone."

"She could have gone up into the hills."

"No, no, no! Not without telling one of us!"

"She must be hiding then. Where would she go?"

They called out to her again and again. The only sound was from the moving water below.

Gino asked, "Would she climb down to the creek?" He peered over the ledge and gasped. Giuseppe followed his gaze, then flung himself down the steep embankment. His mother lay unmoving by the edge of the creek. The color of her skin and her cold touch confirmed his fear. A single blow to the base of her head had ended her life on earth.

Did she fall? She would not have jumped, not today, not when her face was filled with sunshine! Was she pushed? Why would bandits harm an old woman?

Giuseppe and Gino gently and lovingly carried the limp body up the hill to the apothecary where they laid her. In silence, they washed and prepared her for burial. They found signs of a struggle. Gino blamed himself. Had he not stopped to talk during his deliveries, he would have been at the apothecary, he would have heard her cries for help. He wondered aloud, "Why would anyone do this?" Giuseppe was afraid to imagine the answer.

They buried her with prayers, just up the hill under her favorite tree as the moonlight reflected off the creek below. Exhausted and numb, Giuseppe accepted the embrace of his friend and retired without words. Piling the straw back in the corner, he hugged himself tightly to endure the long, cold, and empty night.

It came in his darkened dreams, the realization that a bag of his family's history and a portrait of his youthful, well-known mother, signed with his birth name, would be like a signal fire in Florence. A reward to her killers in exchange for information would no doubt bring soldiers. Although Florence was in different hands now, the wealthy are never out of power.

Giuseppe found Gino in the garden beside the apothecary, weeding the herbs. While Gino expected to see the grief in his friend's eyes, he saw something more. After several minutes of silence, Giuseppe spoke with soft, measured words. "Gino, you are like an older brother to me. You took us in when we had nothing. Your trust and confidence have empowered me all my days at your apothecary. You not only saved our lives; you made our lives worth living."

Gino seemed to know what was coming. "Giuseppe, it is a blessing to have you here. Your knowledge and easy ways continue to make our apothecary indispensable to the people of this village."

"Thank you, Gino. That only makes this more difficult to say. I must leave this place in the morning."

Gino was crestfallen. "Is it because of your mother?"

"My mother's death is a part of it, but I need to extend my reach and discover what the rest of the world offers. First Venice. After that, perhaps the Silk Road."

Giuseppe did not wish to mislead his friend, but the less Gino knew of his plans, the safer they both would be when men of arms came to the village in search of a young apothecary from Florence.

At sunup the next morning Gino said his goodbyes, offering a strong embrace and food for the journey. He also placed a share of profits in Giuseppe's palm. Giuseppe bowed his head for several moments in respect. When the tears had drained from his eyes, he smiled at his champion and took his leave. Gino watched until the tiny dot on the horizon that was his friend disappeared into the green.

Giuseppe left Gino with no hint as to his plan. He would never set foot in Venice or travel the Silk Road. He could have thrived in either environment, but knew that someone on the run would disappear into the melting pot of a city seaport.

On the northern side of the last hill beyond the village, Giuseppe turned left off the path and kept out of sight. He did not wish to be observed walking west toward the sea. He moved at night, and slept during the day under the trees high along the hillsides. The food from Gino lasted him three days, enough to reach the low hills snuggled close to the sea somewhere between Pisa and Genoa.

He kept his head low and his face in shadows as he traveled between villages and small settlements. Gino's coins served him well, buying warm clothes and food, but they were soon scarce in his purse. He found those who were willing to trade a meal for a drawing and sold plants and herbs to apothecaries at bargain rates. He was careful not to draw attention to himself and knew it was time to move on when he encountered familiar smiles or nods of recognition.

As winter after winter passed, your father grew weary of being a ghost on the road. He had covered his tracks and had heard no rumors of a bounty on an apothecary's son from Florence. It was time to settle, and he was drawn back to an area he remembered from his early days of travel, a fertile valley on the Magra river flanked on two sides by rolling hills. Nestled between those hills was the small but charming town known as San Russo. It was off the main trade route and the nearest apothecary was a half-day's walk. This was the place that beckoned to your father's heart, the same small part of the world where I had worked for three years.

Giuseppe, now aged twenty-two years, found his way to the hills above the town. He slept in a shallow cave overlooking the place that soon would become his home. The next morning, he walked into San Russo just as the townsfolk began to stir and shops began to open. He held his head high, boldly greeting all he encountered. The days of hiding were over. With his charm and confidence and valued skills, Giuseppe quickly found work that paid in coin, or merchants willing to trade food and supplies for a sketch or an oil portrait. Each day, with the setting sun, he would slip out of the village and return to his cave in the hills.

Here my mother paused in her story and asked me to close the shutters. Darkness had fallen and she was sensitive to the chill. I lit the lamp and brought her a cup of water for her thirst. When she continued, she said:

I have told you how the fates brought your father to me, how he made himself invaluable to Reina, and how he rescued me from the drunken soldier. Now I will tell you how the fates took him away.

After my time of healing from the hand of the mercenary, we often ended our day at the entrance to Giuseppe's old cave, sitting silently, wrapped warm, watching the sun pull colors into the sky. This was the spot where I first knew that I wanted your father's love inside my body, not just my soul.

After all that I had been through, we did not dare to hope for a family. But you were a gift that grew out of our boundless love for each other. It was a surprise beyond our dreams when we discovered you were growing inside me.

One season after we learned we had been blessed with the promise of you, Reina woke one morning to the persistent pounding on the lupanar's heavy wooden door. She dressed and made her way through the darkened room, cursing the hour. The sunlight blinded her as she unbolted the door, "Come back tomorrow. We rest on Sunday." The door swung wide as they pushed past her. "What is the meaning of this? We are a licensed house. We pay our taxes."

The girls woke to the sound of boots falling heavy on the stairs. The soldiers broke through the doors and those cowering under covers were pulled from their beds and told to come downstairs. Wrapped in coats and blankets they joined Reina in the front room.

A young boy in a tattered uniform ten years too large for his frame spoke in a breaking but official voice. "Nicolò Matteo of Florence is hereby charged with witchcraft and the assault of La Forza. He is to be taken into custody and tried before the Podestà."

"There is no one here by that name!" Reina cried.

At that, a darkened figure appeared in the doorway. Reina studied him; he had been in the house before. She held her gasp when she saw his right hand hanging by his side; it was wrapped in leather, forming a permanent fist. The soldiers' search of the lupanar found nothing, but they left with promises to return.

Reina was out of breath when she knocked on the wellhouse door to awaken us. "Angelina, the savage mercenary who scarred your face has returned. He came to our door flanked by soldiers with charges against someone named Nicolò Matteo.

Giuseppe froze upon hearing his birth name. My mind raced to plan an escape, but our choices were few. We knew our lives were trivial tokens that the Condottieri would brutalize until his lust for revenge was satisfied. When Giuseppe declared he would turn himself in, I screamed and buried my face in his shoulder.

He held me and said that in the moment of rescuing me, he had been granted the greatest happiness a man could hope for. If that gift now meant his death or life in prison, he would accept the will of God. "I would do it all again for the joy of the time we have shared together." His only regret was that he would never hold the child I carried. There was so much he wanted to tell you, so much to teach and share. He made me promise to keep you close and safe and show you the ways of the world. He wanted you to learn to read and write so you could make choices based on truth.

The next morning, bathed and clean-shaven, Giuseppe walked alone to surrender himself.

The Young Soldier's Story

There was no word about Giuseppe for two days until Reina brought the soldier boy to me in the kitchen. I gave him something warm to drink then sat across from him as Giuseppe's last hours spilled out.

The prisoner was stripped, searched, and then led naked up the narrow stone stairs. He was pushed onto the cold, hard floor of a tiny cell. I was left to guard him. He passed the hours alone except for an occasional mouse scurrying across the floor. I was instructed to give no food or water. When the sun set and emptied his cell of light, he tried to sleep without success and sat quietly with his back to the far corner.

At first light the torture began. And for what reason? Giuseppe had freely admitted to crippling the soldier. He confessed to providing healing to many villagers, and that his methods were from God. But Marco was not looking for confession; he wanted revenge on the one person who bested him, and he took his revenge until exhaustion forced him to stop.

The rest of the day Giuseppe fell in and out of consciousness. His right eye was swollen shut, a broken rib pierced his side, and he lost much blood. He was asked no questions, but was kicked and beaten each time he revived.

He woke near midnight moaning in pain from abuse that would have killed most others. It was quiet. Everyone had gone to the watch room except me. As I stood in the shadows, I saw Giuseppe attempt to clear his head and to focus his good eye.

As his senses returned, he found that he was tied only loosely. After some effort his hands and feet were free. He trembled as he stood. I could hear bones scraping when he moved. Gasping for water, he shuffled slowly to the door of his cell. The lock was not engaged. The door creaked open and Giuseppe crossed the threshold. I had been instructed to remain in the shadows if this occurred.

He crept toward a sliver of light coming from the watch room at the end of the passage. He turned toward the muffled voices and quietly advanced. Across from the watch room he found the stairs that led down and out. Following behind, I saw him pause, unclear if he was escaping or simply looking for water.

Suddenly, light filled the stairs and a boot propelled Giuseppe face-first down the steps. As Marco pulled him to his feet, I could see the clarity in Giuseppe's expression. He chuckled through his agony, and said, "The path to escape was all part of your plan."

Marco pushed him out the door and then again to the ground. "You think you can beat on me without return? Now is your chance, you filthy trader's son of Florence. Start running."

With what little strength remained, Giuseppe rose slowly to his knees, keeping his back to Marco. Then a calm washed over his face. He closed his eye and crossed his breast with open palms. A smile parted his lips as he whispered, "We three will be together in Heaven". Those were his last words before he heard a match strike and a sizzle. Giuseppe escaped on his own terms.

The pistol shot brought the watch into the courtyard. Marco gave one order: "Hang him from the gate!" He flicked his hand in the air and walked away. I don't think Marco ever knew I was there, but my expression made the others laugh. They said get used to it, this won't be the last time.

I fretted all the rest of the night. What should I do? I want to be a soldier, not torture and shoot people in the back. I snuck out just before first light and came here, making sure I was not followed.

The boy's words painted a picture my mind could never erase. I tried to focus but found myself trapped in a dark tunnel that narrowed around me. Reina's lips moved, but I could no longer hear. My breath was gone. I was empty.

I woke in the wellhouse. Reina and some of the girls sat by my side. My thoughts slowly cleared and brought a heaviness I had never felt, never imagined. I was lost. But Reina had a plan. She spread the word that the house would be shut due to illness. She knew it would be the first place Marco would search when he discovered that Giuseppe's body was missing from the gate. During the afternoon we packed all our belongings and divided the food and our share of coin.

That night, six of us moved along the city wall and waited near the town gate until the watch moved inside. When the soldier boy signaled all clear, we carefully lowered Giuseppe and retraced our steps to the wellhouse. Reina helped me wash his body and wrap him in clean white linen. Using the rope and pulley, we moved him to the bottom of the dry well and gently covered him with everything we could find. Remembering his last smile, knowing he was thinking of you and me, helped to ease the irreplaceable loss. There would be time to grieve, but it was not then. I had first to secure our safety.

One by one, the girls placed their portraits on the straw that lined the cistern. We embraced, knowing it was the last time, and they left in the night to find a new life far away. When Reina and I alone remained, we unbalanced the stone and covered the cistern. Taking my hands in hers, she told me I would survive to do great things; she kissed each cheek and then my round belly. "You will always be with me," were her last words to me. She left with her portrait clasped tightly under her arm. Yes, Giuseppe painted her as well, but as a woman of nobility rather than of purchase. I watched her as she walked away, realizing she was the one who had shaped me for the world.

In my final moments alone with your father, I said my last words and then disappeared into the night, carrying both of my Angels— you, and my portrait.

I've often wondered what would have happened if there had been no assassination in Florence, if your father had taken his rightful place as Apothecary to the Medici when your grandfather passed. You would not be alive, and I would have traveled the fate of a short and very lonely path.

Her story finished, my mother closed her eyes. As her breath slowed and finally ceased, a look of peace spread across her face, a countenance I had rarely seen there. During the telling, her voice had been strong and her spirit never wavered. Still, wishes and fever dreams can muddle the memory, and I questioned the perfection of what she recalled. But the portrait is real, found hidden where she had promised, a testament to the beauty she radiated during her youth.

Now, as my oldest child, you must keep this document together with the portrait. You must pass them both to your children. The story of The Angel must live until the end of time.

SOURCE ACKNOWLEDGEMENTS

Bellina Giuseppe	Lucca, Italy 1511, Original, Tuscan
Caterina Marconi	Florence, Italy 1637, Latin translation
Darcy Cummings	George Washington University, 2019, English translation

Part II – The Family

1975

Chapter 1

Like her papà would say, if it's worth having, it's worth fighting for. *Especially a glass of Champagne.* Madeleine took a deep breath and wedged her way into the bar, into the horde of Formula One fanatics who were packed shoulder to shoulder. Her only option now was to move in sync with the glacial flow of bodies. At this rate it could take hours to get a drink. *Better get two glasses once I get up there.*

After jockeying to within shouting distance of the barman, she caught his eye and held up two fingers. At that instant, the lead cars screamed by outside and a cheer erupted in the room. The crowd surged behind her. She was slammed forward. As she crossed her arms to protect her face from the massive wooden bar, someone grabbed her from behind. Like a pillow, she was tossed up and toward the bar top. By pure instinct, she made a half-twist in mid-air and landed neatly on her butt.

Madeleine, stunned, clambered to her feet on the bar. The barman whistled and led a round of applause, then handed her two brimming glasses of Champagne, the national drink of Monaco. She lifted them and shouted how much. He shook his head and pointed to a man in the crowd, a bear of a man who was grinning up at her. She nodded thanks and looked away.

A quick scan of the room confirmed what she knew; exit options were non-existent. The big man smiled and patted his shoulder. Then he shrugged, palms up. What do you have to lose?

Indeed. He was handsome, he looked fearless and harmless at the same time. She took a gulp from each glass before draping herself over his shoulder.

He turned with her. The crowd parted.

Madeleine could take care of herself—her father had made sure of that—but an effortless ride through an unruly mass of humanity was the kind of perk she could appreciate. She was carried through the doors and to a curbside table. A cast of rowdy strangers, crammed together under an oversized Cinzano umbrella, greeted them with cheers. The man lowered her into the only empty chair and took a corner of it for himself.

He shouted something. She shook her head. He leaned in and with an index finger swept her long black hair over her shoulder.

"I'm Bruno."

She felt his lips graze her ear, like it was unintentional.

If he thinks that will phase me, he doesn't know me. Yet.

As a young girl, Madeleine Costanzo had loved the Monaco Grand Prix. She'd attended it multiple times, hanging on her father's arm and absorbing every word of his insight and analysis. This year, all grown up, she was at the prestigious Formula One race alone. But by the twenty-fifth lap, her favorite driver, the Welshman Tom Pryce, had dropped so far behind she had lost interest. That's when she'd gone inside for Champagne and ended up sharing a chair with a stranger.

"Hello Bruno, I'm—" She waited while the number five car shrieked past. "I'm Madeleine. Maddie. Thanks for the ride."

Did he blush?

Four dripping bottles of Champagne arrived at their table and were soon dispatched. The noise from the packs of cars flying by was nearly constant. Monaco is the slowest race on the Formula One circuit, averaging one hundred sixty kilometers per hour. Still, they scream at over one hundred ten decibels, indoor rock concert levels. Introductions and conversations were reduced to lip-reading, smiles, and gestures as Bruno's gang of friends gamely tried to welcome the new member of the party.

Bruno soon lost patience with the forced charades; he waggled a finger between himself and Madeleine, mimed a duck quack with his hand, then thumbed over his shoulder. She understood—let's you and me find a place with less noise—and nodded. The big man paid everyone's tab and left a healthy tip. Then he took her hand. They bowed to an ovation of whistles and cheers. He led her up the hill to a quiet little bistro, well out of tourist range.

Madeleine was twenty-one, back in Italy after four years of non-stop study abroad. She deserved the big week she had planned. Expensive seats at the race, an evening to blow a wad of her father's money at the casinos, and some sun time on a yacht catching up with her girlfriends. Today though, she would squeeze in coffee and whatever else developed with this attractive guy. It's always good to be flexible.

Chapter 2

Bruno smiled as the sun cut the morning fog. It was perfection, driving the coastal highway back home to Genoa, hearing the fine-tuned pitch of his father's new 1975 Dino Ferrari echo off the cliffs. Was there any place he would rather be?

Yes, in fact. He would rather be driving somewhere with the girl he met yesterday. They had only talked for a few minutes before business called him away. She was somehow different from other girls he had dated; more independent, less easily impressed. He barely knew her, and she was stuck in his head.

But his weekly Monday breakfast at the family villa was not optional. It was a mixture of business and pleasure—business for his papà, who continued to cram his fifty years of work experience into Bruno's hard head, and pleasure for his mamma. She seemed to need nothing more than to feed Bruno and to catch up on whatever slim life he led outside of the family business.

Bruno was grateful for the opportunity to learn. His papà, Mario Porcelli, had been enormously successful and had done it all on his own. The imports, exports, and shipping earned more money than they could ever spend, and yet it was *Mario's*, his eponymous fine dining establishment, that his papà was most proud of. He would correct you if you called it a restaurant. From the food to the staff to the crystal and linen tablecloths, it was *fine dining*.

Bruno drove through the massive gates and up the palm-lined hill to the Porcelli family compound, Villa Gazza. He was exactly on time, 7:30, but he could see his mamma peeking out from behind the lace sheers. On time was late in the Porcelli family's world.

As if he had just returned from a world cruise, his mamma wrapped him in a long welcome-home hug, her hands barely meeting around his back. Then she held his head and gazed, as if searching for evidence of wear and tear.

Her assessment was instantaneous. "Bruno, you look so tired, but your eyes, they are smiling. Please tell me it is a girl. I want my grandchildren while I can still enjoy them."

He kissed her cheeks. "Good morning, Mamma. It's good to see you. You are well?"

"How was your weekend? The Race, eh? Your papà and I, you know for years we were regulars. Dinner guests of Laura and Enzo. But your father doesn't travel well these days."

"He's doing great, Mamma, but he is seventy-two. And you, you are getting up there also, no? Soon to be thirty?"

A bright smile lit her face and she patted his cheek. "My boy! You keep saying that. Come. Your father is on the terrace and your food is getting cold. I made your favorites."

Mario was sitting at a round, granite table with his back to the villa. "My son. Welcome." The handshake was formal but the smiles were warm. "I heard the Dino drive up. How did she do? She's yours anytime you want to take her out."

"Thank you, Papà. She is a fine machine. I think their little auto business may have a future."

"Sit, sit. We have much to discuss. First, you eat."

Bruno's mother served two cups of cappuccino and left the men to their discussion.

"Your mother's frittata, a masterpiece. Hear that my Tesoro?" *My treasure.* "We will put you to work in Mario's Fine Dining one of these days!"

"Ha, like you would ever let me out of this house." They could hear her chuckling from the kitchen as her voice bounced on the marble floors and twenty-foot ceilings.

"Every day I praise the gods that such a woman, almost thirty years younger, married me." Mario leaned closer to his son. "Now to business. Speak to me."

"Yes, sir, Papà. We have had a good week. Demand is up, supply is steady, payments on time. No surprises. Dante did mention some potential territorial spats with two of the families. He suggests you call a sit-down to hear their grievances."

"Perfetto! Exactly the way to handle this. Quash the problems while they are small. How is your time with Dante? You are learning?"

"It goes well sir. Dante has a quiet way, but when he speaks, everyone listens. I am only beginning to understand the scope of his responsibilities within The Collective."

"It is that way by design, and the bottom line, he gets results. Dante has always been loyal, from the time he started to work for me. Just after the war, I gave him a job on the docks as a favor to his father. I trust him completely. He is smart and knows our business now, maybe better than I do these days, so listen to him, learn from him. It will not be long until the business, everything," he swept his arm in a wide arc, "will be yours."

"Papà, don't talk like that. You're stronger than most of the twenty-year-old—"

"Bruno, stop. I do not ask for a health assessment. In our business you learn by doing. It is imperative that you know by heart every job. Orders, sales, importation, managing the profits. It is why I move you around in the organization. And you must learn judicious retribution when it is necessary. A sound business decision is not a sign of weakness. Del Coltello must never be seen as weak."

"Grazie, Papà. Your confidence gives me strength."

Mario clapped his son on the shoulder and shook him playfully. "All this talk makes a man hungry. You will take another pastry? Guendalina, my love! Two maritozzi!"

Bruno's mind drifted. The woman he had met yesterday seemed, at the moment, more interesting than maintaining order in The Collective, growing profits, and expanding international reach. Would he ever have his father's passion for the family business, the devotion his father expected of him? He was twenty-two years old. He prayed his papà would live another thirty years.

He lifted his cup and tilted it slightly. "To your health!"

Chapter 3

"Ahoy Captain, permission to come aboard?" Madeleine stepped from the top of the gangway into the oil-slick arms of a bright-haired twenty-something beauty in a dark knit bikini.

"Permission granted. Get your little butt on this boat right this minute, Miss College-Grad Costanzo!"

"Bella, Bella! How are you? You look fantastic. What's new?"

Bella swept both arms wide and grinned.

"You?" Madeleine asked.

"No, the boat. First time I've taken it out alone."

"Ah. Someone's dad having a mid-life crisis?"

"You got that right. New boat, new mustache, new wife. Not that I'm complaining, she's more like a younger sister."

"That's creepy." Madeleine faked a shiver. "Sweet bikini, by the way, what there is of it. The navy blue makes your tan pop."

"Well take a good look, 'cause once we anchor down up the coast it's coming off. It's a no-tan-line excursion! Ship rules."

"Is it too late to go back ashore?"

Bella laughed. "Not if you want to walk the plank."

"Who's here? Did everyone make it?"

"Absolutely. Rosa, Caterina, and Lucia were all below changing last time I saw them. There's a drink with your name on it on the sundeck. I'll join you once we clear the harbor."

"Aye, aye Captain."

With a crisp salute, Bella headed for the helm.

Madeleine shook her head. So much had changed since she had last spent an entire day with these girls. Before she "defected" to America, the five teens had been inseparable. Fingers on a hand. Same age, likes, dislikes, even the same boys at different times. And best of all, same shoe size. What were they called? The Fab Five? The Five Musketeers? Their European History instructor had called them the five best reasons to give up teaching. They had kept in touch as best they could, which amounted to an occasional postcard or life-event letter, but so much had changed. They had four years of catching up to do.

She headed for the sundeck and found the other girls hovering around the bar.

"There she is! Maddie!"

"Look at you, Madeleine Fayechesca Costanzo! Give us a spin."

"Lucia, I can't believe it! Caterina, Rosa, I've missed you all so much."

"Group hug!"

Rosa handed her a glass. "So, Maddie, tell us, degrees in art and business, you must have found a man by now, no?"

She laughed, "Still one-track-mind Rosa. That's what we love about you. But, now that you mention it, this weekend—"

"Mention what?" Bella slipped up behind the group and put her arm around Rosa.

"Maddie's found a man!" Rosa shrieked.

Bella arched her back and pulled down her top for a second. "Yobetter be glad he's not around today."

"Oh, what money can buy." Caterina rolled her eyes.

"Stop it, you vixen. Tell us, Maddie, your fancy education actually paid off?"

"Well, if this weekend is any indication, it was money well spent."

"Spill it! Don't leave out a single fact."

Madeleine set her glass down. "It was more like a fairy tale than any facts." She took a slow breath. "During the race, in the bar, this guy literally swept me off my feet." She told them about being saved from the crush and then carried away by this tall, extremely handsome gentleman with the darkest eyes she'd ever seen.

"It was so crowded, we shared a seat, sitting with his friends. Had a couple of drinks. Maybe it's me coming home after suffering through four years of sappy American boys, but this guy got my attention. It's early, but I see definite possibilities."

"Does he have a name?"

"Bruno."

"Do we know him?"

"Is he from Monaco?"

"Does he have a last name?"

"Wow, I'm getting third degree burns. No, I don't think *we* know him. He's from Italy, and yes, I'm pretty sure he has a last name. He might have said it, but with all the race noise on the veranda it was impossible to hear anything. Later, I was too embarrassed to ask."

"Later? Details, we need details."

"So, we left his friends and went for a coffee. He works in shipping or imports or something. He grew up in Genoa, still lives there."

"Boring."

"And he says he's into art, but we'll see. He might have said that to score points. I know family is important to him."

"Does he know about your family?"

"You mean about my father? No, I just told him the basics about myself. Hometown, study abroad, looking for a career. Finding a man was way down on my list until yesterday. Hey, enough about me. Bella, what's in these?" She held up her empty glass.

"Something new I stumbled on in Tenerife last year."

"It's so good. I don't even taste any alcohol."

"Yeah, well, you noticed I said 'stumbled on'? It only takes a couple."

"I'll have another Stumbled On, please."

"What else did you talk about?" Rosa was not ready to drop the subject of Bruno.

"Not a lot. We didn't get too much past our CV's when a guy came up and whispered something to him. He excused himself and they had a very animated conversation by the front door. Then he headed for the pay phone and made five or six quick calls."

"Ouch."

"That's a red flag."

"That's what I thought, but he came back and apologized so nicely. Said something about being on call this weekend, some issues that needed his immediate attention. Then, get this, he said order anything you want, enjoy yourself, you have an open tab."

"That's crazy."

"He'd just met you."

"Who does that?"

"Wait, it gets better. He said, take your time, whenever you're ready my driver will be outside. He'll take you anywhere you want to go."

"No way."

"This is like a Cary Grant movie."

"End of story?"

"Almost. He planted a quick kiss on my cheek, then hurried away. It all happened too fast. I sat there stunned until the waiter brought me a menu. He had this sort of grin, like maybe he knew something I didn't."

"You walked out, of course. Right?"

"You didn't get in that car, did you?"

"Slow down. I thought about walking out, but you know me, I was starving. Why wade through the tourists and wait in line for some overpriced 'race day' food. So, I ordered. Limited choices, but everything was amazing. This guy knows quality. Points for Bruno."

"Was it there?"

"Was what there?"

"The car, his car."

"Yep, after an hour and a half. I couldn't resist the chocolate mousse."

"At this point I'm guessing you *did* get into the stranger's car."

"Yeah, well, after his driver opened the door and said welcome Miss Madeleine, Bruno asked me to take you anywhere you wish to go, I thought, what the hell."

"They didn't teach you anything in America!"

"Where did you go? Nice? Cannes?"

"You know me better than that, Lucia. He took me back to my hotel."

"So, that's it? No Snow White or Cinderella ending?"

"I didn't say it was over. Middle of the back seat, there was an envelope with my name on it. 'Madeleine, I enjoyed your company very much this afternoon. I'm sorry business called me away. Let me make it up to you with dinner this weekend. I'll be in touch. Sincerely, Bruno.'"

"Oh my God, Maddie. That is so romantic."

"We'll see. I don't know how he's going to find me. He doesn't even know my last name. And even I don't know the address of my new apartment yet. If it happens, it happens. I'm not counting on it."

"Hold that thought," Bella said. "I'll be right back."

The anchor was dropped, suits came off, tales of loves won and lost were spread around like spiced olive oil on warm rolls. Among the four girls, Madeleine lost count after the ninth or tenth boyfriend was described and then written off. With each story, she felt herself drifting further away from the camaraderie. She loved them, but something no longer fit. These girls had not changed, while for the past four years she had carved herself into something different. They were still a tight social circle, but she was no longer a round peg.

Chapter 4

Madeleine felt like she had hit triple sevens on a ten-dollar slot. That's how rare it was to find an affordable place to live in Monaco with an unobstructed view of the water. Bella had been right: Beausoleil was the perfect district, close enough for the sea breeze, high enough for the views, and just beyond the inflated prices of downtown. And living over the line in France left her free to play with papà's pizza money at the casino—locals were forbidden from gambling in Monaco.

Unpacking was a simple affair as she had accumulated little during her years abroad. Too many all-nighters, what she called close encounters of the study kind. One PAFA tee shirt (Philadelphia Academy of the Fine Arts established 1805 thank you very much), one frat boy's John Deere cap, and two knockoff Disney beer mugs. Beyond those, she had little to show for her experience that was not in her head or spilled out in a thesis or two.

For the immediate future, she planned to make up for lost time in the most irresponsible but legal ways possible. A few hangovers and walks of shame were in order before her career came calling and put an end to all that. She had earned the right to unwind in the best of ways, starting right now with the radio loud, the windows open, and the titillating smell of sea salt in the air.

When the phone rang, she flinched. So far, she had given her new number to exactly no one. She traced the cord from the wall to the bottom of a pile of clothes waiting to be refolded.

"Pronto?"

"Hello. Is this Madeleine?"

"Yes, it is."

"This is Bruno."

"Mm, Bruno who?" She held her breath.

"Porcelli."

"Okay. Can I help you?"

"We met at the race."

"I'm afraid you'll have to narrow it down a bit."

"We had coffee at the bistro."

"Ah, the big guy who kidnapped me from the bar?"

"You're angry because I had to leave suddenly."

The laugh she was holding twittered out. "Relax, Bruno. I'm very happy you called. But how in the hell—? My phone was just turned on this morning."

"I guess I have my ways."

"I guess you do."

"So, you found my note about dinner on Saturday?"

"Oh. Saturday? Let me check my schedule." She gripped the pillow in her lap. "Well, it happens I just had a cancellation. I could be free by, let's say, eight o'clock?"

"I'll ring your bell at eight sharp."

"You have a pencil?"

"Uh, no."

"For the address," she said.

"Thirty-one boulevard du—"

"Never mind. See you then."

"Ciao."

Damn! He's either psychic or incredibly well connected, she thought. I wonder which of my girlfriends won their bet? This could be an interesting weekend.

The antique Swiss clock on her mantle was striking eight when she heard polite taps on the apartment door. *Punctuality is next to cleanliness.* She glanced in the mirror. Hair, check. Makeup, check. Her nerves were half anticipation, half uncertainty. Something in his naiveté felt off, almost dangerous. On the third and much louder knock, she swung the door open with a flourish.

"Bruno, what a surprise," she said, breathless. "I was just heading out for the evening."

He glanced aside, questioning his mental day-planner. "But, I, uh…."

"Yes?"

"Didn't we, um, make dinner plans for tonight? I made reservations."

Easy to tease could mean he's genuine, rather than just dumb, she thought. "Indeed, we did, and I'm starving. Are those beautiful flowers for me?"

"Oh." He held them out, like he'd never seen them before.

"Come in while I put these in water. They smell fabulous." She kissed him on both cheeks.

"You're not like most girls."

"My one goal in life. Hold my jacket?"

"Sure." He blew out a breath. "I'll have you figured out by next time."

"Don't count on it." She turned toward the kitchen.

"Don't count on what?

"There being a next time. Or figuring me out." She laughed and wrinkled her nose.

"What am I getting myself into?"

"Probably nothing, Mister Presumptuous." She locked the door and headed for the stairs. He hesitated, then caught up and cupped her elbow.

The air was clear, and the evening star hovered near the dusky horizon. They took the sidewalk to the right. She expected to see a dark Mercedes and a driver. Instead, Bruno stopped at a bright red sports car. He bent low and opened the passenger door.

"Wow," she said. "What kind of car is this?"

"Dino." He closed her door, went around, and slid into the driver's seat. She was laughing.

"Are you kidding? You named your car after the Flintstones' dog?"

Bruno stiffened. "No. Dino is the model, it's a Ferrari, and it belongs to my father. Enzo gives us a different one each year to try out."

"Oh my God. You know Enzo Ferrari?"

"And his wife. My parents have been friends with them since before I was born. He's sort of a, you know, like a godfather."

"Well, Bruno Porcelli, what other surprises do you have up your sleeve?"

He smiled, like he finally had the upper hand. "I guess you'll have to hang on and find out."

He hit the gas and drove a bit outside the city before turning around. The road-hugging Dino was a perfect match for the double-back curves into Monte Carlo. Madeleine noticed he pulled the right turns extra hard at the last second, the force slinging her toward him. Childish, but she liked it.

It was fully dark by the time they slowed. He steered along endless rows of drab, seemingly abandoned four-story buildings.

She frowned. "I didn't know Monaco had a warehouse district. Are we lost?"

"Nope."

"What's the name of the place?"

"I don't know the name."

"You said you made a reservation."

"I did, but—"

"But what? You can't make a reservation if you don't know the name of the restaurant."

"There is no name. Only a phone number. You call two days before, leave your info. If you're approved, you get a call back within twenty-four hours with the time and the address."

"If you're approved?"

"Well, the first two times I called there was no call back. Since then, I've gotten in every try, and the actual reservation time gets closer to my request."

"That is bizarre. I supposed they only serve blue food or something."

"No, they serve all colors."

"Ha."

"Seriously, this is a night you'll never forget. I've eaten with them three times and it's never at the same location." He handed her a scrap of paper. "Here's tonight's address. Help me navigate."

"I have to warn you, I have the well-deserved reputation of being a bad navigator."

They found the address. It was on the only street where a line of parked cars stretched around the block. A large real estate sign leaned against the window from the inside: THIS SPACE AVAILABLE. There were no lights visible inside or out.

 "What, no valet?"

"I think that defeats their business model. We'll have to walk. Can you make it two blocks in those shoes?"

"I was born on my tiptoes." She smiled, with everything that implied.

Chapter 5

The meal was finished, and they were greeted with nippy air on the sidewalk. Without being washed away, any uncertainty Madeleine harbored about Bruno was, for the moment, submerged by the flood of good food, wine, and laughter. Was his artlessness a put-on? Why was he illusive about his background? And the seedy neighborhood he had taken her to for a first date? Who cares!

"That was, no exaggeration, the strangest dinner I've ever experienced. And maybe the most delicious. How did they create six courses for me, just by asking a few stock questions? What's my favorite flower? What's my sign?" She was tipsy, elated, and babbling. "Absolutely amazing! Great choice, sir!"

She latched onto his arm and his chest swelled. Mission accomplished. "Thank you. I deserve one hundred percent of the credit."

"Right." She giggled. "It's too bad we didn't park further away. I need to walk this off."

"Want to race me?"

As they rounded the corner, Bruno slowed. A couple of teenagers were messing around the Dino. He felt Madeleine brace, prepared for him to rush them, or scream something. Instead, he walked up casually and smiled.

"Cool car, gentlemen. Real beauty. Did you lock your keys inside?"

The taller of the two boys stammered. "Th-th-thanks. We're awful proud of her. No, we did something stupid."

If he only knew, Bruno thought.

"We were walking down at the harbor and dropped the keys in the water. It's too deep to reach them."

"Maybe I can help. My father is a locksmith. He taught me a little secret to open a locked car. Can I show you?"

"S-sure, that'd be great. Thanks, Mister."

Bruno had the two would-be thieves sit above the wheel wells on the driver's side, one front, one rear. "Okay, just bounce up and down in rhythm. Get the car rocking good, and I'll spring the passenger door. One, two, three...." He whispered to Madeleine, "When I open your door, take the keys, get in quietly, and lock it back."

"Almost there, fellows, just another sec."

When Madeleine was safe, Bruno moved to the street. "Got it! You can stop now."

"Thanks for your help mister— Hey, w-what's going on? What's she doing in the, uh, our car?"

"Let's be honest. This isn't your car, is it?"

"Course it is. What are you talking about?"

"Game's over, boys. The car belongs to me, and it would be in your interest to turn, walk away, and count your blessings."

"We don't think so." The taller boy snarled. "There's two of us and only one of you, old man. Get her out of our car." He flashed a nine-inch stiletto, and the other boy slid one out of his boot.

Bruno shook his head and let his eyes sweep from their feet to their greasy hair.

"What are you looking at?"

"Not much. I've got twenty centimeters and thirty kilos on you. More on your little brother."

"Yeah, well, who's got the blades?" He flicked his wrist.

Bruno slowly rolled up his shirt sleeves. "That's your plan? Fine. Me, I got options. One, you lunge, I grab your wrist and turn it against your thumb, you drop the knife, I break your outstretched elbow. Snap. Or, I sidestep your lunge, grab your neck and crush your windpipe. Not like I haven't done it a hundred times before."

 "Yeah, but there's two of us. Now!"

The larger boy got in one running step before Bruno spun into a roundhouse kick, connecting leather loafer to left ear. Blade and boy both scattered across the pavement.

"Then there is option number three. I guess you didn't see *Billy Jack*?"

Little brother was nowhere to be seen by the time Bruno lifted his attacker with one hand and set him on his feet. The fear in the boy's face overshadowed any embarrassment—his eyes were fixed on the knife tattooed on Bruno's left wrist.

"Del Coltello?"

"Born and raised," he said.

"I-I-I'm sorry, I didn't know it was your car, I would never do anything against Del Coltello. Please don't kill me!"

"You're in luck, little friend. I'm on a date with a beautiful woman who doesn't need to see anyone die tonight. Now, here are your options."

The kid nodded to everything Bruno said and answered yes sir more times than he took a breath. As he let go of the boy's collar, he heard the driver's side window whirring down.

"So, Sal, is it? You understand what I'm saying to you? Are we clear?

"Yes sir. Absolutely clear."

"Okay then, have a good life. I won't be seeing you around."

"No sir. Thank you, sir."

"Walk away slowly. And smile. You and baby brother get to live another day."

Bruno stooped and looked into the car. Madeleine's expression was unreadable. He reached in and unlocked his door.

"What was that? What did I just see?"

"Nothing important. Just passing on a few life lessons to today's youth."

"But they had knives. They wanted to kill you."

"Not really. They had no clue, no plan. And they certainly hadn't done their homework."

"What did you say to them? I only heard the last bit."

"I said the same thing before and after I dropped him. If you're bored, find a hobby, but stealing cars is no hobby."

"Is that all?"

"Pretty much. They just needed some convincing."

"Holy Mother, I'm still shaking."

"Hey, hey." He put his arm around her shoulder. "Look at me. You'll always be safe with me, Madeleine."

"Would you please just call me Maddie?"

"Sure. Maddie."

Neither of them seemed to know what to say as Bruno drove them back to her apartment. Maddie turned on the radio.

"That scene could have ended very differently."

"Maddie, you have nothing to worry about…"

He continued, but she was lost in her thoughts, wondering *who is this guy*? He did exactly what was necessary to neutralize the situation. No more, no less. And he took care to get me out of harm's way first. Papà taught me to be tough, but I never felt completely safe when I was away at school. You always hear about America being so dangerous. Then I come home, first date, and two kids try to kill the guy I just met.

She stared out the window, seeing nothing, trying to make sense of it. *A race day rescue, a couple of drinks, a crazy dinner, and I'm suddenly smitten. How did this happen? I just wanted to have some fun. Now I can't even remember who I was four hours ago.*

Outside her apartment, he parked half on the sidewalk and escorted her to her door. "Thank you for a most wonderful evening."

She looked down at his extended hand. "Really, Tipo? You'll have to do better than that." She threw her hands around his neck and melted him with her lips.

Bruno drew back and tried to refocus.

Maddie pulled him down again and pecked his cheek. "Goodnight, Bruno." Her smile seemed to be a mix of flirtation and awe. She backed into the apartment, holding eye contact until the front door latched.

Bruno floated back to his car. He anchored in, reached for the ignition, and stopped. He needed to memorize every detail of this night. *What just happened? She's smart, beautiful, and big trouble, but in the best of ways. Just the way Papà describes Mamma. I think I finally get what he means.*

Across town, ten minutes later, Bruno filled a payphone with a pocketful of change and dialed a number in Genoa. In a voice nothing like the one he used with Madeleine, he commanded, "Talk to me."

Chapter 6

It was midday. Milan's big city bustle had slowed for the lunch hour. A tall, well-dressed man with dark but graying hair stepped out of the bright sun. He paused just inside the antique mahogany door, letting his eyes adjust. He scanned the tables, smiled, and crossed the room. An elderly gentleman rose, greeted him with a strong embrace, then lowered himself back into a plush chair with a commanding view of the entire restaurant.

"Thank you for taking the time to meet today. How was your drive?"

Dante sat across from the older man. "Long, but it is always good to see you, sir. Thank you for the invitation."

"Of course! You have celebrated another birthday. Tell me, how does it feel to be closer to sixty than fifty?"

"You tell me sir, if you can remember that far back."

"Touché." Antonio chuckled. "And how's your dear sweet mother?"

"Managing well, thank you. It has been difficult for her since Rémy passed, but she is getting out more. She sends her regards."

"And of course, I must ask about my old friend Mario. I miss our visits together."

"He misses you as well. He has slowed a step since the heart attack, but he still keeps a sharp edge, and makes sure everyone knows it. If one did not know better, one would think he is a real restaurateur like yourself." He shook his head. "That restaurant is his pride and joy."

"I was there at the opening, not so long ago."

"Seems like a lifetime," Dante said.

"He and I, we took some time together afterward. It is a fine establishment. The food is outstanding, of course, but it is Mario's charm, this is what makes the difference. Everyone feels welcome."

"You know Mario still speaks about you, how you saved his life."

"Ah, that. It was war. What can you do, eh? He was wounded, he was my amico. It was nothing." Antonio studied his hands with a sad smile.

"He says you are a hero. You carried him out over your shoulder, blasting away at the Austros when they jumped your trench."

"Adrenaline and luck. Honestly, it is a faded picture now. Thank the Holy Mother that Mario ate less in those days." Dante laughed. "And you, Dante. How are you?"

"Fine, fine, thank you but the work is harder as the birthdays pass. I am adjusting to Mario's son shadowing me most days."

"Bruno."

"He's a natural businessman, like his father, but he has some growing up to do. Mario insisted Bruno learn the operation from the ground up. I know, when the time is right, he will step into his father's shoes."

"Certainly, that is Mario's plan. If someday, if Bruno is not a good leader… Well, as I remind you every year, a position waits for you in my little empire of dough. With the Porcelli's blessing, of course. Perhaps soon the timing will be right?"

"Family is always right."

"Yes, yes. That reminds me, Madeleine is just home from America! You know I have not seen her in four years. I love Syrina equally, but Maddie will always be my baby."

"Ah, that's why you're so cheerful, eh? Congratulations. When will you see her?"

"Soon, I hope. She is too independent these days, but I understand. She is twenty-one. I can be a little patient and allow her time to settle in Monaco before I demand a visit."

Chapter 7

"Buonasera. Welcome everyone! My name is Syrina Costanzo. Thank you for attending tonight's benefit for Lake Como Animal Rescue. Give yourself a round of applause!"

Syrina paused, imagining an overflow crowd, slightly drunk, raising their glasses and whooping their approval.

"I hope you are enjoying your dinner. Dessert will be served shortly. For tonight's entertainment, as you may know, Uri Geller was scheduled to perform for us. That's why we each have two spoons." She paused again, hoping for chuckles. "Speaking of psychics, don't you think it's amazing that all one hundred and fifty of us chose green salad and vegetarian lasagna for dinner tonight?"

She put down the script and resumed touching up her hair. "Silvan, did you hear? How's that sound?"

Her partner knew when to be coy. "Darling, I love you very much."

"That's not an answer. And this is all your fault. The only reason they asked me to speak is because I'm the girlfriend of Silvan Keller, the rich-as-shit king of integrated circuits."

"Very funny, and not true. They asked you because your father is Italy's rich-as-shit king of pizza pie." He hugged her from behind. "Seriously Syrina, just accept that it's because of all the hours you volunteer at the rescue center. How many nights have you spent feeding newbies with an eyedropper? What I have comes from the head. Yours comes from the heart."

"Good answer." She turned and pecked him on the cheek. "Zip me?"

They had left the dressing room door open, and their housekeeper tapped lightly. "Excuse me, Miss Syrina, there is a telephone call, it is from your sister."

"Thank you, Lenora, I'll pick it up here." She waited until the extension clicked. "So, how's my two and ten baby sister?" Syrina couldn't resist picking on her.

"Hey grandma. Got any gray hair yet?"

"You'll never know, dearie. How are you? No, where are you?"

"I'm on my terrace, overlooking Monaco."

"*Your* terrace? Nice! How long have you been back? Papà has been asking."

"Just a week. I needed to get settled first, catch my breath."

"When are you coming to visit? The lake misses you."

"That's why I called. I'm thinking about taking the train up next week. What's your schedule like?"

"I'm open. Except I still go down to Milan every Tuesday for lunch with Papà. We could meet there—"

"Tuesday? You don't have to go. Let me go alone, surprise him, have lunch, then I'll come up to the lake house on the evening train."

"Perfect, he'll love it. Lately, we've been doing Tuesdays at Tenjin Kushikatsu, near the corner of Corso Garibaldi and Via Anfiteatro. It's an easy walk from the Metro. Meet him at one o'clock."

"I'll find it. I can't wait to see everyone."

"Hold on, Sis. Silvan? Honey, do you have anything other than work next week?" She muffled the phone for a moment. "Okay, he'll be around for dinner. He can't wait to meet you. And bring your swimsuit. He wants you to meet Bridgette, too."

"Is that some sort of boat?"

"It's his pride and joy."

Silvan took the phone. "It's a 1959 Riva Super Florida, mint condition."

Syrina grabbed it back. "Yeah, it's some sort of boat. Ha. Oops, he's not laughing. See you Tuesday night. Wear a daisy in your hair so I'll know it's you."

"Ciao."

Silvan took the receiver and hung it up for her. "Am I reading you right? You seem a little hesitant about seeing your sister."

"It's been too long since I visited her in New York. She's a mystery these days."

"And you aren't?" He zipped her dress. "Does she even know we're getting married?"

"Well, not exactly. I mean, no. The time just hasn't been right."

"Mystery seems to swing both ways. Maybe it's genetic. The enigma sisters."

Chapter 8

For Madeleine, a long train ride was a touchstone to her mother. As the engine chugged out of the station now, she was flooded with memories; she could hear her voice. *A choice between plane and train is no choice.* The rides themselves had been the best part of their many journeys. Slow summer Saturdays, they would choose a random destination and buy tickets, just to watch the world reel by their window like a movie, or to sit across from a stranger and make a new friend. They were the adventurous ones in the family, while Syrina and Papà were homebodies.

From Milan to the Cote d'Azur, a favorite destination, they traveled POSH for the best views. Port Outbound, Starboard Home. Once past Genoa, the Mediterranean accompanied them most of the way south. Her father would tease her for applying nautical terms to trains. She didn't mind—she knew her mother was smiling down from heaven.

Madeleine would never say it, but after their mother passed, Syrina became her guidepost and protector. She closed her eyes. It had been two years since Syrina spent that long weekend with her in New York City. Museums, matinees, unreasonable amounts of food and drink. As much as her older sister could push her buttons, their relationship was solid. They disagreed on countless issues and, as adults, had little in common, except they each trusted the other without reserve.

Madeleine smiled when she recalled the boundaries they stretched growing up. Even when playing within the rules, they were scheming to bend them. To keep secrets from their overprotective father, they developed a code that assigned different meanings to certain words. They could carry on side-channel conversations around the family dinner table, at school, or hanging out with friends. Smiles, compliments, even simple statements could mean anything in their private reality.

Somewhere in those years, they adopted a line from an American rock song: up against the wall mother fucker. They weren't sure what it meant, but they knew rebellion when they heard it, and it became a catch phrase. Unspeakable at home, they shortened it to U-A-W-M-F or made their own phrases to fit the acronym. "Underwear Always Wrinkles, My Friend," "You Are Welcome, Maddie Faye," and countless combinations had the same secret meaning. It became a game. When spoken, the other had to immediately back into the nearest wall. They took turns, and with time the use became less frequent but more devious. Having the next turn was power. Imagine being on your knees in St. Mary's or in a kayak in the middle of Lake Como when the code was invoked.

It was a silly code, a silly game. It would, one day, be the difference between life and death.

Chapter 9

At one o'clock on Tuesday afternoon, Antonio Costanzo slid into his reserved booth near the rear of Tenjin Kushikatsu, his restaurant-of-choice for the past several weeks.

"Welcome back, Signore Costanzo," the owner bellowed, then poured from a chilled bottle of Pelligrino.

"Thank you, Botan. I trust you are well today?"

"Very well, thank you for asking. Will your daughter be joining you?"

"Yes, she should arrive shortly."

"May I bring you something while you wait?"

"Junmai Ginjo, please."

Botan nodded toward the bar and the warm sake arrived seconds later. "You need anything else, I will be nearby."

"Of course, Botan. Thank you."

The food here was prepared fresh in the Osaka tradition, and everything was excellent. Avocado salad, hibachi beef, kushikatsu deep-fried meat and veggies. He was never disappointed.

As Italy's undisputed king of pizza, lunch for Antonio had always meant a slice or two of his signature pepperoni pie. But his cardiologist, who had the nerve to call himself Italian, warned him there was only so much tomato sauce and pasta a man could eat in a lifetime. He scoffed, but with time the message resonated—he wanted to see his grandchildren born. Now, to vary his diet, each weekday found him in one or another of the city's finest international restaurants. On Tuesdays Syrina joined him whenever she could.

Antonio treasured the lunches with his older daughter. Time was scarce given her crowded schedule—charitable fund raising, working for an animal protection society, and building a life with Silvan. Antonio adored Syrina's boyfriend, but he would never adjust to them living together unwed.

The memories of the early years with his daughters were treasures, though sometimes painful. Syrina and Madeleine, sitting across the dinner table, talking about boys, fooling him with their wordplay. The bumps and bruises. The fatherly advice that seemed to fall on deaf ears. Children grow up and leave you empty, people you knew everything about who now reveal themselves in measured doses, leaving you with photographs and trinkets.

Antonio took a slow mouthful of sake and let it trickle under his tongue.

Seven years had passed since his precious Donice had been with them. She was a cherished prize, beautiful and brilliant, with a creative energy that brightened his life. Their age difference turned a few heads when they married. He thought the years would pass and the gap would close, but God had other plans. Just shy of her thirty-seventh birthday, Donice perished in a fiery instant along a narrow mountain road. Without her gentle guiding hand, Antonio and his daughters were left with more conflict than harmony. He had folded in on himself. His girls, his business, his relationships all suffered because he suffered.

"Papà."

A familiar voice jarred him from his reverie. He looked up, expecting

Syrina, and his eyes filled with tears as Madeleine floated through the busy room.

"My baby girl is home! It has been too long. Let me look at you." He held her at arm's length and spun her around. As the waiter filled her water glass, Antonio stared. Madeleine had grown into the image of her beautiful mother.

"It's good to see you too, Papà. I've missed you." She hugged him before kissing his cheek.

"How is your new place? When did you arrive?"

"About an hour ago. I grabbed a coffee at Centrale and walked. Oh, you mean to Italy? Last week. I found a perfect and reasonable one bedroom near Monaco, and I'm looking for work."

"Are you circulating your CV? I have many restaurant friends in Monaco. Let me make a few calls."

"That's sweet of you Papà. I may take you up on that, but for now I'm looking for something to make use of all the degrees I have, thanks to you."

"You did the work. I just gave you the pizza 'dough'."

She squeezed his hand. "Still so silly, Papà!" She picked up the menu.

"Is your sister joining us?"

"No, just me. We thought this would be a nice surprise."

"And you were right. Shall we order some starters?"

Antonio looked for Botan but didn't see him. "Tell me, what is on your agenda? Have you seen your sister yet?"

"No, in fact I'm taking the 4:30 to Lake Como. We're going to spend all week together, and I hope to meet Silvan. I hear he works all the time."

"He is not Italian, this boy. Nice, but…." Antonio's face darkened and he took a sip of wine.

"But not traditional?" Madeleine suggested. He looked at his hands. "Oh dear, Papà, you don't approve? I think they're pretty serious about each other."

"Serious is good. Not being married, this does not make me happy. Your mother would be crying. You talk to Syrina, she may listen to you."

"Not a chance. I mean, yes I will talk to her, but no chance she will listen to me about her living arrangements."

"Thank you, Madeleine. You are a good daughter."

Madeleine had to hide her smirk. Did that mean Syrina was not a good daughter? My, how the tables have shifted. This trip to Lake Como could prove to be interesting.

The food was excellent, from warm sake to cold dessert, but they barely noticed. It was good to see him healthy, to hear him laugh, to feel his embrace. It was good to be back. Father and daughter laughed and cried until Madeleine had to rush to catch her train.

Chapter 10

The trainline ended in Como. The last leg of the trip to her sister's villa in Lenno was via a standing-room-only local bus. It jostled and jerked its way along the west coast, making more stops than a star football goalkeeper. She was sandwiched between commuters like a Vienna sausage, but the glorious views made up for the bag of crusty ciabattas smushed against her back.

This was Madeleine's first visit to Syrina's new place, which was in fact Syrina's first real place. She had moved out at eighteen, migrating from her childhood room to the guesthouse behind the pool, in search of breathing space away from her papà and fifteen-year-old sister. Four years later she met Silvan. He was sketching integrated circuits on a napkin over a pizza and beer at her papà's flagship restaurant, Antonio's #1. She made a smart remark, he offered her a slice, and they'd been together since.

The bus pulled into a nearly deserted parking lot and Madeleine panicked. Was the bus late? Or early? Maybe she took the wrong line. Syrina was supposed to meet her, but all she could see were a couple of old men and a lone hippie-looking type.

When she stepped off the bus the long-haired guy in shorts, sandals, and a Dylan tee shirt approached her. Did he want her or just money? He smiled and wagged a yellow index card. 'Maddie' was written in her sister's unmistakable hand. So, this was Silvan.

"Greetings, Maddie. Syrina had a last-minute thing and knew you'd recognize her writing." He kissed her cheeks, left, right.

"So very nice to meet you. I've heard much, some good."

"Ha, Syrina told me to wear my armor." He grabbed her suitcase. "Car's over here. We don't have far."

Silvan pointed out the best and most interesting in the neighborhood, but Madeleine could barely hear him over the growl of his green 1968 Shelby Mustang. This guy is a walking contradiction, she thought. Computers, inventions, a classic muscle car, Haight-Ashbury couture. And a bazillion Swiss Francs.

Ten minutes later, he turned right and they disappeared through a sturdy but inconspicuous gate onto what was little more than a path cut through dense forest. He downshifted and hit the gas, showing off his private Grand Prix course. Bumped and tossed, she gripped the lap belt and prayed for a quick checkered flag.

When Madeleine dared to open her eyes, she was greeted by a classic ivy-covered, red-tiled villa that sprawled across the ridge overlooking Lake Como. Picturesque Bellagio decorated the far shore; beyond that, the white-capped Southern Alps completed the tableau.

Syrina opened the passenger door. "You didn't scare her, did you, Bello? Hey baby sis. Welcome to our little hideaway."

Madeleine opened her arms, closed her eyes, and held tight as years of absence drained away. Pulling back, she raised her eyebrows. "I was expecting something larger."

Syrina laughed. "You mean me or the house? Silvan, please take Maddie's bags to her room. We'll meet you—and the bubbly—on the veranda. Come on Mad's, it's grand tour time."

"This is the best, Syrina. Absolutely amazing. I thought my dream house was on a square mile of ocean front with waves crashing on the rocks. I'd trade that for this any day. Just needs a private rail stop to my favorite city."

"That's what the helicopter is for, silly."

"No!"

"Teasing, no chopper. It's less than an hour to Silvan's office in Lugano, though he rarely goes in, and an hour fifteen to Papà's in Milano by car.

"Not bad. So, what's up with Silvan?"

"What do you mean?"

"Damn, girl, the guy could pay cash for a large island nation. But when I saw him at the bus station? I thought he was a gypsy. Major paradox."

"Let's say money hasn't changed him. Mostly jeans and tees when it's warm, wool sweaters when it's not. I did lasso him into Huntsman's on Savile Row for a suit when we were in London last year. The tailor taking measurements said there might be an upcharge for the extra fabric he'd need in the crotch area." She cackled.

"Whoa, that's more than I needed to hear. So, I take it he's not compensating for something with the muscle car, and the Super Florida?"

"Ah, he was making payments on the Mustang when we met, before his first patent hit. The Riva? Between you and me, I think he has a big crush on Brigitte Bardot. Anyway, I take care of the finances. Doing the books for Papà at Antonio's was good training. This is a whole other level but I'm really good at it."

"I have no doubt. Sounds like a nice problem to have anyway."

"It's like play money at this level. We give and give and it still piles up. Silvan says computers are going to be everywhere and the trick is to stay at the front of the wave."

"With your head for numbers you should start a business."

"You know, I have been thinking about that. Something I'm passionate about. For you it's art, for me…?" She shrugged.

"Relax. It'll sneak up and find you someday."

"There he is. My Adonis with the Champagne." They climbed the back stairs to the veranda and joined Silvan on the wicker chaise lounges. "Bello, tomorrow morning Madds and I are going to take the Riva across the lake to Bellagio. Shop, eat, drink. Shop some more."

Silvan frowned. "Not tomorrow. One, we need to get you checked out on The Riva first, and two, she won't start."

Syrina looked at Madeleine and smirked. "She grew up on the lake, dummy. After she repairs the motor, she'll give *you* a lesson in piloting, all before you start work. Then she and I will head out to greener pastures. Capisci?"

The next morning, Madeleine was down at the dock. She had the carburetor apart and soaking in gasoline when she heard Silvan shout that breakfast was ready. He liked to cook, and had prepared a traditional Swiss spread. Bircher Müesli, bread, and preserves, all homemade, and Swiss cheese from the village where he grew up. Coffee, tea, hot chocolate.

"This is fantastic, Silvan. Where'd you find this guy, Syrina?" Her sister was in a daze, staring at the lake, a half-smile on her face. "Sis? What are you thinking?"

Syrina looked at her and squinted. "What? Hey, you have some grease or something on your cheek."

Madeleine rubbed her face with the white cloth napkin and checked it for stains. "No I don't. Where?"

Syrina tapped her own cheek with her left hand and then wiggled her fingers. Sunlight refracted in the enormous diamond ring on her third finger. Madeleine squealed.

"Oh my God, oh my God, oh my God!" She grabbed the hand for a closer look. "When did this happen? Congratulations Reenie!" She jumped up and kissed her sister. "Congratulations Silvan. I take it you had something to do with this. When's the wedding. Have you set a date? Am I invited?"

"September twenty-ninth. You are invited, and you are required to bring someone. Male, preferably rich and handsome."

"Are you kidding? That's barely three months. How long have you been planning this?"

Syrina glanced at Silvan. "Not long. I wanted to tell you in person."

Silvan grunted. "Okay. It's off to work I go. You ladies have much to talk about, I'm sure. Check to make sure you have enough gas to make it back from the far side. I can't remember when I last filled the tank. That's assuming you can get the motor started." He winked at Madeleine and kissed the top of Syrina's head. "See you this evening. I hope."

Madeleine grinned. "Wait a sec. September twenty-ninth? You'll have to reschedule. I have a root canal planned that day."

She laughed with them, then waved as Silvan headed back into the villa.

Syrina buttered a piece of toast and took a bite. "So, what time does the boat leave?"

****

Back from a full day of shopping, Madeleine couldn't wait to call Bruno, to fill him in on her sister's plans and make sure he blocked out the wedding date.

"Porcelli Industriale."

"Bruno, please. This is Madeleine Costanzo." She heard a muffled conversation like someone's hand was over the mouthpiece."

"Maddie! Great to hear from you."

"Just wanted to make sure you actually work there."

"Ha. So how are you?"

"Absolutely no complaints here. I'm visiting my sister outside of Lenno. You wouldn't believe her place. Right on the lake, amazing scenery, private beach, tennis court, and a boathouse cut into the rock under the villa. Even my bedroom has a view."

"Sounds fantastic."

"I could get used to it if I had to. Say, I really called to tell you we're meeting Saturday."

"You and me?"

"Unless you're on call again, making the port safe."

"Yeah, that'll be me patrolling the docks with my night stick and whistle."

"Don't forget your career advice and pearls of wisdom to the youth of today."

"There is that. So, why do you ask?"

"I change trains in Genoa on the way back home. I thought you'd like to meet me, take a drive down the coast, pick up some lunch. I know this place."

"Let me check my calendar…Saturday. Oh sorry, I have an outing with this beautiful woman from Monaco."

"Too bad. Another time then," she said.

"Hey, not so fast. I just had a cancellation. Where shall we meet?"

"There's a little café just next to platform seventeen. Let's say noon."

"I'll see you then."

"Bring Dino. I owe him an apology. Oh, and don't make any plans for September twenty-ninth. I'll explain later."

"Um, okay. Saturday at noon, platform seventeen."

"Ciao."

Chapter 11

The train was early, a miracle by modern Italian standards. She stowed her suitcase in a jumbo locker and then ordered a coffee. Perusing the magazine stand, waiting for Bruno, she contemplated the significance of this simple outing, what it could mean. It slowly hit her that, while Syrina hadn't said anything directly, it was clear that she was leery of Bruno Porcelli. She kept referring to him using his full name. Were Syrina's instincts right? Was she pushing things too fast? What did she really know about this guy, beyond his being tall and handsome, and tolerating her teases, and driving a fancy car? She knew he worked in his family's business. She knew she felt safe when she was with him.

And there he was, strolling across the platform, eyes smiling, head and shoulders above the crowd. She let out the breath she was holding.

"Right on time, Mr. Porcelli!" She rose and extended her hand. He kissed it.

"Ciao! So nice to see you, Miss Costanzo. Do you need anything before we hit the road?"

"I think I have what I need." She winked.

Bruno's cheeks flushed. "Shall we go? Your chariot awaits."

"Let us depart," she said in a royal British accent. Outside the terminal, double parked in a loading zone, sat the Dino with a stranger in the driver's seat. "Well, Mr. Porcelli, I see only one empty seat. How are you traveling today?"

"Very funny. Maddie, this is Paulo. He's just keeping an eye on the car."

"Hello Paulo, I'm pleased to meet you."

"The same. Enjoy your outing, ma'am. I'll take care of everything at the office, sir."

Once belted and buckled, Bruno turned and aped a Hollywood accent. "Where to my lady?"

"East to Eden, my Orsone. Water on my right. And that is the worst James

Dean imitation I've ever heard."

The car was a dream, and the drive along the coast was magnificent. Madeleine was in a fairytale, running on adrenaline. She pushed her head back against the black leather headrest, closed her eyes, let the sun wash over her face and the fresh breeze tousle her hair. They rode for several miles, soaking in the abandon, before she spoke.

"You're going to love lunch."

"Did you make a reservation?"

"No. Don't need one."

"What's the name of the restaurant?"

"There isn't one."

"You chose a restaurant with no name, like I did?"

"No, there's no restaurant."

"Excuse me?"

"Relax, Bruno. Trust your co-pilot." She studied the map before refolding it. "Follow this to Sestri Levante then head toward Tuscany. We're going on an excursion. A scampagnata in the countryside." Bruno smiled and turned up the music.

An hour later, somewhere in the Tuscan Apennines, they found a village market. Bruno purchased a basket and Madeleine filled it with ripe olives, Pecorino cheese, a tabouli salad, a panino con la frittata, and chilled strawberries dusted with raw sugar.

"We just need some wine," he said.

"I'm sure we'll find some along the way."

The road twisted along the Magra River as they continued through the lovely rural landscape. Madeleine studied a map sketched on notebook paper. At the bottom of a long hill, the Dino was flying. She shouted for Bruno to stop, back up and pointed to a handmade sign promising Chianti. They turned right onto a tiny dirt road and followed it up a steep incline, thick with trees. Where the copse opened, acres of grapevines heavy with fruit spread out before them.

An old man in faded overalls and a long gray beard waved. He slid down from a battered Porsche tractor and eyed the visitors. "Benvenuto amici. That's a funny looking car."

"It's a Ferrari, sir. New model."

"Never seen one like that. Bet it's fast."

"It can be."

Madeleine said, "We saw the signs for vino and wondered if we could picnic in the vineyard."

"Well now, that depends." He dragged the toe of a ragged brogan in the dirt.

Madeleine broke the awkward silence. "Of course, we'll need some of your best Chianti. Four fiascos, perhaps?"

"Um, in that case you can stay all afternoon. If you buy five bottles, I'll throw in the sunset for free."

She laughed and glanced at Bruno. "Now that is a very generous offer, sir. Mister…uh…"

"Russo. Vincenzo Russo."

"Pleased to meet you, Mr. Russo. I am Madeleine, this is Bruno. Is this your place?"

"Yep, my empire of dirt. Been in the family for a long time, but it ends with me. My wife passed, and I'm the last of the line."

"You ever hear the legend of the twelve sisters? It's supposed to be from around this area."

"Our family's been here for generations. Stories come and go in these hills."

"Some lost paintings of young prostitutes?"

She saw his eyes flicker, but he shrugged, non-committal.

Madeleine made a mental note of the location. They had just arrived, but she loved it—the vineyard, the views, the solitude. "I like the way you've made it all about the grapes," she said, putting a positive spin on the poor condition of the outbuildings and machinery.

"Keeps me busy. Drive on up to the barn and I'll show you what there is. May still have some fiascos of the '64. It's everyone's favorite."

****

Madeleine leaned back on her elbows and sighed. They were nestled in a shady, secluded nook atop a ridge, their luncheon spread on the grass. The slow, muddy river cut through the valley at the foot of the ridge, and rolling green hills slouched to the western horizon beyond.

They said little as the savory cheese and olives, the crunchy bread, and the smoky-rich wine opened their senses. Bruno uncorked a second bottle. "What was that about me blocking out a day in September?"

"Not *a* day. September twenty-ninth. Did you write it down?"

"I told my assistant, which is much better, believe me."

"I believe you. Anyway, my sister is getting married in Milan and I need a date. She insists that I arrive on someone's arm."

"You have a sister?"

"Yep, just the two of us and our dad," she said slowly. "Mamma passed away a few years ago. How about you?"

"Only child. Mamma is thirty years younger than Papà, and they are a perfect match, true love."

"Good to know that still exists," she said.

"Um. Why do you think it's so rare?"

She didn't hesitate. "Because it takes a lot of work and people are lazy." She met his eyes. "Are you lazy?"

"Actions speak louder than words." He squeezed her shoulder and let his fingers trickle down to her hand. She sat up and faced him. "My sister seems to be in love, but she and Silvan are so different I don't understand how it works. At least Papà will be happy. They're currently *living together in sin*."

"Don't laugh. The world is changing too fast." He sat up as well then. "Speaking of family, what was that you asked the farmer, about some sisters?"

She leaned back on her elbows again. "Want to hear a good story?"

"Sure. Something you made up?"

"No, and it may even be true. It's from an old handwritten document I discovered while working on my thesis, *Ex-Florentine Renaissance Art, Beyond the Medici.*

"What's it about?"

"Love, art, a brothel. A fugitive from justice. Mostly love."

"You had my attention when you said brothel."

"Ha! Figures. Tell me if you've heard this one." She slapped his knee, then turned serious. "During my research, I received permission to scour the closed stacks at the National Art Library, and, long story short, I found a crumbling parchment with old Florentine writing. My translation was rough, but it was basically a love story from around the end of the fifteenth century. Probably an oral history, preserved by the family generation after generation, until it was finally committed to paper in the seventeenth century."

Bruno absorbed every word as Madeleine shared the story of Giuseppe's long journey from fortune to poverty, from romance to heartbreak. Falling in love with Angelina, painting the portraits of her and the other prostitutes, running afoul of a mercenary as he defended Angelina's honor before finally dying at his hand. And then the interment of eleven portraits.

The sun was halfway to the horizon by the time she finished. "And from my research, it happened very close to where we are now, almost five hundred years ago."

"This is why you dragged me out into the middle of nowhere?"

"Well, yes. But also, this." She kissed him lightly on the lips. "Plus, I needed a ride."

"You are something, Maddie Costanzo. Don't know what yet, but I'll figure it out."

"Don't count on it, my Orsone." Her Big Bear.

Chapter 12

Madeleine woke with a start from a dark dream. Disoriented, with a stabbing pain in one elbow and her thoughts on the edge of a precipice, she found herself half under and half atop Bruno. They were entwined on a ragged packing quilt, the gnarled limbs of Sangiovese grapevines casting sinister shadows.

She counted breaths. As her pulse slowed, she could feel the cool hillside air through her light dress and the warmth radiating from Bruno's body. Her head was pressed to his heart.

At the moment, she couldn't recall a word she had said before they had fallen asleep. The wine had relaxed her tongue and she had felt complete trust, that she could tell him anything. Whatever she had said, it all seemed perfect now. Fresh country air, dapples of afternoon sun, nowhere to be, nothing to do.

She closed her eyes, willing the moment to last, but she could ignore her bladder for only so long. "Bruno?" she whispered.

"Hm?" He groaned and stretched. "Are you okay?"

"Yes. No, I have to pee. I didn't notice any toilet facilities down by the barn."

"You read my mind. There was a place back up the road a couple of miles."

"I can't hold it that long. How about I contribute to the terroir of a future vintage."

"As long as it's downhill."

"Ha! Sounds like the voice of experience."

When she returned from her outing through the vines, everything from the picnic had been packed away and the blanket had been moved to the edge of the cliff. They held hands as the western clouds turned to peach and strawberry gelato, a perfect sunset, all for the price of an extra bottle of wine.

"Do you need to get back?" he said.

"I told you, I have everything I need." She laughed. "Except maybe some supper."

"You can't be hungry again already."

"Make a note. Madeleine can always eat."

"We should probably clear out anyway," he said, "before it gets too dark."

"Before the farmer adds another bottle to our bill?"

He stood, still holding her hand, and pulled her up to face him. "If you can wait a bit to eat, there's a wonderful little place on the coast, in Portovenere. Maybe an hour?"

****

The wonderful little place in Portovenere was closed for renovations, and Madeleine decided a long walk was a better idea anyway. She could stand to miss a meal— three weeks back in Italy and her clothes were getting a bit snug.

They strolled hand in hand along the quay, passing a bottle back and forth. Just south of the small marina on the eastern shore of Portovenere's peninsula, the sandy beach ended. They continued south along the peninsula, clambering over boulders that plunged into the surf, lit by nothing but a few dim stars. They were both in great shape, but Bruno's long legs were a clear advantage for negotiating the big rocks. Near the tip of the peninsula, he stopped for Madeleine to catch up.

Looming high above them, she could just make out the silhouette of a Gothic-style church perched atop the rocky headland. "What is that?"

"Come take a look," he said, and sprinted up a set of ancient stone steps. When she caught up, he was leaning against a smooth block wall.

"The Church of Saint Peter."

"Is it open?"

"We'll have to come back tomorrow if you want to see inside. But come look down here."

She followed him down the western side of the outcropping along a series of steps and disheveled rocks that meandered back and forth, up and down, finally leading them to a long finger of land that extended west from the rocky headland. Where it met the water, tiers of flatter rocks, like long steps, slipped into the Gulf of Poets.

A waxing three-quarter moon had risen as they climbed down from the church, and in the distance, they could make out foamy waves crashing on steep cliffs.

"See the cave?" Bruno asked. "That's La Grotta di Lord Byron. He used to swim here and meditate in the cave. And above, on the clifftop, that fortress is Castello Doria. Thirteenth century."

 Madeleine squatted on a rock and pointed to the northwest. "And way up there along the coast. That would be Cinque Terre."

The string of villages—colorful villas packed together on the sheer rock face and decorating the night like Christmas tree ornaments—were indeed there, but hidden by the turns of the coastline. "Five fiercely independent towns, one for every fiasco of wine we bought." She waggled the bottle in her hand and held it up. "Empty."

"Is that the last one?" he asked.

"I think there's one or two still in the car."

Bruno took the bottle from her fingers and sent it flying in a high arc. It disappeared in the darkness before landing noiselessly in the near-distant water. They stood motionless as the next wave swept over their feet. It was beautiful, with the backlit church behind them and the specter of lacy waves breaking on moonlit crags to their right. They were alone with the night birds and the breeze and their thoughts. After hours together, sharing secrets and dreams and regrets, it seemed they had run out of words. Or that the next words to be spoken would be profound, and premature.

"Bruno, I don't think either of us is in any shape to drive back. Not that you would let me drive the Dino even sober."

"So, we should find a place to stay?"

"I think so, but I, um…. I left my suitcase in the train locker. I have nothing to wear." She grinned. "Problem?"

"The hotel has a boutique. Oh." He stopped. "You mean, is it a problem if…"

Maddie turned her back and released the shoulder straps of her sundress. She stepped out of it and splashed into the sea.

When she turned in the chin deep water and beckoned him with a crooked finger, Bruno finally blinked.

He flicked his now soaked handmade Italian loafers from his sockless feet and shuffled to the water, trying at the same time to wriggle out of his pants and pull his polo over his head. The sleeve caught on his Rolex. Wet up to his knees now, he tossed the shirt, then skidded on the rocks and face-planted into a half-meter of water—it was much colder than he had anticipated.

She scissors-kicked to him. "So good of you to join me. Now that you have me naked and alone in the starlight, what's the plan?" She slowly treaded backwards into deeper water. He followed her on tiptoes until the waves lapped his shoulders.

"The plan? This was your idea."

"So, my love, you mean getting close to me like this has never crossed your mind?"

"No, that's not, well…."

"No, it hasn't crossed your mind?"

"No. Yes! Every minute since the first time you kissed me. It's just…"

"Just what?"

"I, um…I don't know how to swim."

"You what?" She laughed. "A man who basically lives at the docks does not swim?"

He lowered his head and turned back toward the shore.

She swam to him and grabbed his arm. "You're serious. I am so sorry I laughed, Bruno. I honestly thought you were kidding."

She wrapped her legs around his waist, pulled him close, and whispered, "There's nothing between us now. Except water."

They should have gotten a room before their swim, or at least a couple of towels. The night air blew cold from the hills to the sea. They were shivering, and the fifteen-minute walk to the hotel across the disheveled rocks was an eternity.

The desk clerk managed a straight face when the two, hair still dripping, presented themselves for a room. "Mr. Porcelli, welcome back to the Grand Hotel. Always good to have you, sir."

"It's good to see you, Carlos. Do you have a room for tonight?"

Madeleine touched his arm and whispered, "Two rooms, please." She held a straight face for an instant before cackling.

The clerk ducked his head and glanced up at Bruno. "Will a seaside king suite be acceptable?"

"Perfect. Is the dining room still open?"

"Sorry, sir, it closed an hour ago, but our kitchen is always at your service. When you get settled, call down and we'll prepare whatever you like."

"Thank you, Carlos."

"Do you have baggage for tonight?"

"This is it." He held his hands wide.

"Very good sir. I'll just ring for the—"

"No need to bother. We'll find our way." Bruno slid the keys to the Dino, wrapped in a large bank note, across the counter and looked the clerk squarely in the eye. "And take care of my car for the night."

When they reached the staircase, Madeleine put an arm around his neck and leapt into his arms. "I'm awfully tired."

Bruno eyed at the stairs. "Is this a test?"

"The first of many," she said. "One question. Is there anyone in this country who doesn't know you?"

Chapter 13

After a leisurely breakfast on the balcony of their suite, Madeleine and Bruno dressed in the new clothing the hotel had provided. She brushed her teeth and walked back into the bedroom, happy she had no makeup to fuss with other than a lipstick in her purse. Bruno was standing on the balcony, blowing cigar smoke into the courtyard, clearly anxious to hit the road. She noticed the small trashcan by the door was stuffed with yesterday's clothing—his shirt, pants, and underwear, and her dress and panties.

"What's this?" She held up the can.

"Trash. Are you ready?"

"Are you crazy?"

"What? They're still wet. Salt water."

"I guess big strong men don't do laundry?" She put the clothes in a plastic laundry bag and handed it to him. "You carry it down and I'll take care of it."

The elevator ride to the lobby was uncomfortable, with three mirrored walls she had to ignore to avoid eye contact. The car was waiting outside the lobby. He threw the laundry bag in the trunk and opened her door. "Happy?"

"Yes, thank you. Don't we need to check out?"

"It's probably gratis. If not, they'll send a bill to the office. They know I don't like to fool with details."

"Wow. Okay. Drive on, chief. What is it, two hours to the train in Genoa?"

"Yeah, about that."

She settled back and studied the gorgeous coastline that rimmed the eastern edge of the city, imagining the motifs a painter would pick out to capture. He raced through the Dino's gears, taking curves borderline too fast. He certainly didn't seem compelled to talk. Is this what marriage feels like? You love someone, you have romantic interludes, but in between the fabulous times, life, personality, intervene?

"Are you preoccupied with something?" It sounded snippier than she intended.

"I guess so." He took a slow breath and glanced at her. "Sorry. Dante called while you were getting ready, and there's an issue I need to deal with. Nothing serious, but I'm a little pissed. That's why I threw away the clothes."

"Okay, but they were my clothes, too."

"You're right. I need to start thinking about someone other than myself." He forced an apologetic smile and patted her thigh. Then he closed himself off again.

I understand, she thought. A job can be grueling. What will I be like when my career is in full swing? Note to self: compartmentalize in order to thrive. This morning, he's in his work compartment. As long as we can communicate, sort through the issues as they arise, as long as we can have the occasional interlude like the last twenty-four hours. Whoa, here I am thinking like this is long term. We just met. But he had been so incredibly attentive, almost childlike, all afternoon and evening. And last night! Nothing childlike then. More like a lightning bolt that struck again and again followed by thunder that rolled in deep waves until it could roll no more.

She would remember every detail of that tiny shower room as the site of their first time. Hot, slightly salty water. Electric light shimmering dimly through the steam. Water splashed onto every inch of Mediterranean-blue floor and wall tile. Fluffy white robes hanging on the back of the door—

And finally, she had melted, exhausted, into the wrinkles of the cool, crisp sheets. She had awakened an hour later, the same as after their post-picnic nap at the vineyard, entangled in his arms and legs, and needing to pee.

Then waking with the sun. Opening the lidded basket on the food cart to find every toiletry item they could possibly need. Answering a knock at the door to find the box of new clothing, perfect in size and design. Opening her heart, her whole self, to find a man she knew little about beyond the fact that she was falling for him. The sunset in the vineyard, the night in Portovenere, discovering the next phase of her life—treasures all. The thought struck her that she could make a life out of those pieces.

Just then the car hit a sharp dip in the road.

No, no, no. She was too much of a realist to believe that fairytale. Life has to be more than dessert. She had a career to think about. Investors to court, money to raise for creating the kind of fine art gallery she envisioned. The mark she wanted to make on the art world—she had dreamed of little else for the past year. But last night, her dreams were in a different dimension; in them, she had a partner. It's just a matter of finding a way to make it all fit.

Bruno sighed and turned on the radio. What is wrong with me, he thought? Here I am, in the most beautiful country in the world, next to the most amazing girl I've ever met, and I'm thinking about work. That, and what Papà will say when I go in. But there is nothing I can do now about the skirmish in the south. He chocked the steering wheel with his leg for a moment and rubbed his face with both hands. Look at her! The word gorgeous does not begin to do her justice. She's funny, confident, clever. Definitely smarter than me, and yet somehow that seems like an attractive quality. And last night! She knows more positions than I do. Claims it's from a book. Maybe it is. Who cares? I just have to make sure she doesn't have the opportunity to, or the desire to, get any more outside experience. He squeezed her arm.

"Would you mind if we listen to something else?" she said. "Italian pop music leaves me sort of flat."

"Sure. Find anything you like, but there aren't many stations around here."

She fished a cassette from her purse. "It's a mixtape I made," she said. "American folk and pop music. I'm kind of addicted."

Bob Dylan crooned 'Lay lady, lay. Lay across my big brass bed'.

"What the hell is this?" Bruno turned it up. "What's he saying?" She shot him a glare with scissors, and a laugh burst from his belly. "I'm kidding. It sounds great, but, really, what is it?"

"Just listen. Then we'll talk."

They rode for ninety minutes with Dylan and Carole King, New Grass Revival and CSNY, Paul Simon and Carly Simon. The tape ran through twice. Bruno said he enjoyed it. She sighed. They both love wine and American music. Does a successful relationship need more than that?

As they neared the train station, she crossed her arms. "Question. You said you were into art. My girlfriends thought you were just trying to score points."

"You told your girlfriends I said that I was into art? Seriously?"

"Yes, this is important to me. How much do you love it?"

"Love art? On a scale of—"

"Could you live without it? Do you think about it at random times? Does your pulse race when you see a masterpiece in person?" She saw a hint of panic on his face, a cornered animal. What was she doing? This was not a deal breaker. "Maybe I'm being unfair. Forget it."

"No, it's okay," he said. "I understand it's important to you, but I'm not sure how to answer. You're an art expert, you have degrees. I like what I like without knowing anything about it. But you can teach me. I'd like to learn."

"Perfect answer."

He yanked the hand brake, double parked outside the train station—Genoa was his town after all. "So, tell me more about those paintings the prostitutes had to bury." As if they had all the time in the world.

She laughed. "Hold that thought. We can start your lessons there, absolutely, but next time. And yes, there will be a next time." She hopped out of the car and stood by the trunk. "I need to get the laundry bag."

"You don't want to carry that on the train. I'll be happy to take care of it."

"Perfecter and perfecter."

He walked her inside. She tiptoed to kiss his cheek and he lifted her, lips to lips, until she relaxed. "And perfecter," she whispered. He slowly lowered her to the platform. She held onto his forearms until the swoon cleared.

"See you, my Tesoro." He pecked her forehead and turned to go.

"See you, my Orsone."

She stood still, enjoying the foggy brain, half aware of the bustle on all sides, until her train rolled to a halt. She had one foot on the step before she remembered her luggage in the locker. She raced to retrieve it and made it back, stepping on board as her heart pounded and the train inched forward.

Chapter 14

In a city where Lamborghinis and Bentleys climbed winding concrete canyons, the afternoon shadows were beginning to creep down the hillside. Madeleine's taxi stopped in front of the hotel and she rubbed her eyes. The train ride from Genoa to Monaco was a blur. She had rehashed the past twenty-four hours, trying to sort what she felt and guess what Bruno felt. Could she fit a serious romance into her career plans? Had he really been quiet during the drive because of the phone call from work, or was he miffed with her about something? The wet clothes. Why had she made a big deal about the clothes? Had she drunk too much? Been too forward? And on and on. In fact, she didn't snap out of the mental fog until the driver said "eleven seventeen, Mademoiselle".

Merda! She had given him the address of the hotel she had moved out of more than a week ago. Mumbling sorry, change of plans, she fished in her purse for the address of her new apartment.

Home at last, she climbed the stairs to the third floor and drew a quick breath when the key turned in the lock. It was no surprise this didn't feel like home; she'd spent more time away than here since she'd moved. She unpacked, brewed a strong medicinal cup of black tea, and settled on her balcony. It was only three o'clock, but most of her hillside view was in shadow now except the sea, some nine hundred meters below. Clouds toyed with the sun and lit the water in moving zebra stripes. It was peacefully exquisite, and, with the tea, helped hone the dull edge she felt from too much Chianti and too little sleep. Yesterday seemed like a month ago.

She finished her tea, pushed the saucer away, and upended her purse onto the table. The label and cork, souvenirs from farmer Russo's sunset wine, tumbled out along with lipstick, keys, and hairbrush. She flipped the pages of her new, glossy-red day calendar. It was blank except for her new address and phone number, and Bruno's office number. She hadn't decided which parts of her past life should be copied over—school was behind her, old friends felt disconnected—this would be the guidebook of a fresh journey.

She knew the destination. All she had to do was work the plan. Tonight, she would do more research, add to the list of possible jobs, then hit the search again in the morning. Her no nonsense job-seeking outfit was clean, and she still had plenty of CV's printed on linen embossed paper.

Hang on. She hadn't checked the mail. She scooped up her keys and plodded barefoot down to the lobby. Three envelopes were waiting behind the little window in her mailbox. The first was something from the French Government, the second was a one-time money saving offer good only until yesterday. The last letter was from a gallery. A quick glance: it was from the owner saying her resume looks impeccable. Please stop by for a chat!

She skipped back to her apartment, reread the letter, and freshened her tea. Her first call was to her papà. He was happy and encouraging about her job prospects. She thanked him again for their lunch and promised to visit again soon. She told him about meeting Silvan and said she had a good feeling about the relationship. She didn't mention the wedding plans—that was Syrina's news to tell. She hung up feeling buoyed and poured herself a glass of cold Asti. But the next call, to Syrina, stuck a big needle in her shiny new balloon.

"That's wonderful news, Maddie. Good luck with the interviews but I know you don't need luck."

"I can't believe things are moving this fast. I'm a little, um…." She wasn't sure how to put it.

"You're worried how you're going to adjust to a new city and start a new job and build a career, *and* handle a long-distance relationship."

"Am I that obvious?"

"Well, you did tell me all about your sleep-over with what's his name before you mentioned the interviews. But was it really that great? I get the feeling you didn't tell me everything."

"Damn, I am obvious." She needed to get it out, if only to help her think it through. She sat down and told Syrina about the wet clothes and the silent treatment on the drive back and the fact that work is clearly his priority. "I wish I understood a little better what he does."

"Oh." Her voice dropped. "Promise not to hate me if I tell you something?"

"You will tell me, but I'm not promising anything," Madeleine said.

"Okay. Silvan did a little digging. The Porcelli's are the single largest importer and wholesaler of illegal drugs in the country. They run a low-key operation, but are ruthless when need be. And Bruno—"

"Stop! Why would you say that?" Madeleine felt the top of her head lift off. "Just because they're in shipping and importation doesn't mean—"

"Girl! Listen to yourself. This is not gossip, and you need to consider what it means. If you can live with it, that's your decision. Just don't go into anything with blinders on."

"Thanks for nothing. As usual." She slammed the receiver onto the cradle, got up and poured a glass full of the Asti, then dumped the glass and the bottle into the sink. The urge to throw something was nearly overwhelming. She picked up her keys, slammed the door, and stomped down the stairs with no destination in mind.

Lights had yet to come on and the street was nearly dark. "I'll show her," she mumbled through gritted teeth. She walked for an hour, pounding up and down the steep streets of her new city, and then had dinner out. Back at the apartment, out of breath from the stairs, she flicked on the lights and flopped on the sofa. She was relaxed from the power walk and the food, and she was no longer angry at Syrina. In fact, she wanted to talk to her, maybe thank her for sharing her concerns. Yeah, that felt right.

Chapter 15

Bruno had snuck away from Genoa without informing anyone. The plan was, after all, a simple lunch and an afternoon drive with Madeleine. An afternoon drive which turned into a lengthy picnic which turned into an overnight stay. And it was twenty-four hours that he would never forget—in part because of the life-changing bond that had been forged, in part because of the reprimand he received upon returning home.

Bruno had never shown the slightest deference to a girlfriend; they were there for the using. But after a few hours with Madeleine, everything felt different. He knew he should check in with the office but worried she would judge him for mixing work with pleasure. So, he waited until the next morning, when she was in the shower. He took the room phone onto the balcony, closed the door on the cord, and called Dante. There was a brief moment of joy when Dante understood that Bruno was alive, followed by five minutes of fuming.

While Bruno had been "out having fun", a squad of Sicilians had killed two soldiers of the Garofalo family, a small clan in Pisa under the protection of Del Coltello. It was retribution the Sicilians had promised the Garofalos if they did not leave The Collective and resume buying drugs from them.

Dante did not shout, which somehow made the message even more degrading to Bruno. "You're in Portovenere? That's halfway to Pisa. You screwed up, sir. You could have met me there and learned how to clean up a nasty situation like that. Instead, I had to tell your father his son was missing."

"He thinks I'm…" Bruno choked.

"I'm going to hang up, call him, tell him you're okay, and that you will be at his villa in two hours. It is in your best interest to be on time, no excuses."

No one had ever dared talk like that to him. Dante had crossed a line, and Bruno would not forget it. But that did not diminish what he was about to face. He had been involved in the family business since he was fifteen years old, and this was the first time he had been called on the carpet.

The drive from the train station to the villa was fifteen minutes that dragged on for hours. His thoughts were like someone flipping through TV channels. Family, freedom. Work, pleasure. Business, dreams. Money, love. Madeleine, Madeleine.

She'd gotten into his head. He had to maintain focus on what was most important. He would apologize and move on.

Villa Gazza, the Porcelli estate, was unnaturally quiet. No one greeted him when he parked or as he walked through the foyer, up the stairs, and down the hallway to his father's study. The door was open. Mario looked up from his desk.

"Papà, it will never happen again. I am sorry and I beg to be forgiven."

"Stop." The older man rose to his feet. Bruno winced to see the pain that caused him. "Save your words until you fully understand what you have done. Sit down and listen." Bruno sank into an unpadded chair across the room. "I try to teach you, and you refuse to use your head. I give you Dante to learn from. He is the best in the business, and you learn nothing. What in the name of all the Saints was so important that you disappear? *You were on call*. That means someone knows how to reach you. Period. What is so hard?"

"Yes, but…"

"Do not interrupt." Mario turned his back on his son and walked to the window. That gesture was a message, loud and clear, and Bruno held his breath.

"There are reasons why I saved your time with Dante until last. You think your world is easy because you have your sweet mother's looks? No, it is because of Del Coltello. *Of the knife*. It is the first priority of The Collective because it equals stability and prosperity to those inside of that bubble. For those on the outside, it means fear. Without Dante, there is no Del Coltello, no bubble, no Collective."

Mario paused, out of breath, and his voice softened. "Dante is like a flame. You see him, but when you reach for him, he is gone and still you get burned. Someone crossed a line yesterday. It was an ideal situation for you to see Del Coltello in action and you were absent. Do you understand what could have happened? In our business, one mistake can mean a war."

His fist struck the credenza. "You must be present to win, and you were not. Fortunately, the situation is contained. Our people are now safe and under watch, and there will be retribution, ten-fold. One by one the Sicilians will disappear. Today, next week, next year, it does not matter. The job will be done. The Frenchman will move in the shadows, cut deep in the night, and leave the mark of the knife. Then The Collective will fill the void these foolish souls leave behind. In the end, the message is always clear." Mario turned and gingerly lowered himself into his chair.

"Perhaps I have sheltered you too much. Few know the history of Del Coltello, how our family acquired that epithet. It is time you know the origin of the legend that protects us all." He snapped shut the agenda on his desk. "It began with a turf war...."

By the time Mario finished the story, Bruno was trembling. He had enjoyed the reputation of being tattooed with the image of the knife, but he had taken it for granted. Now, he fully grasped the importance, the depth and complexity of the power it wielded.

"You must remember what we are responsible for, what Dante is protecting. Think, if he fails to do his job, what will be lost. You consider him only as a hired hand for The Collective. But he *created* the image of Del Coltello. His job, by my design, is to protect and serve all families in The Collective, not only Porcelli. It is his sworn duty. And, God forbid, if the Porcelli family is ever on the wrong side of The Collective, even we would feel the hot breath of Dante. That will not happen on my watch. I pray it never happens on yours."

It had been years since Bruno felt his eyes well up. He fought now to keep the burning tears from spilling. "I understand. And again, I apologize for yesterday."

"Enough. You keep me waiting for my lunch and now I have no appetite." Bruno watched his father retrieve two cut-glass tumblers from the side drawer. He poured into each a full measure of grappa and handed one to his son. Another gesture with an unmistakable message.

"To my son, his health, his prosperity. May God grant a long life."

Chapter 16

Madeleine landed the job on the first interview. The owner of the gallery was planning for retirement. He wanted someone with fresh ideas and a lot of energy to learn the business and eventually take it over. She was perfect. She would start right away.

A lot needed doing quickly. Operations had been neglected for the past few years. Contract renewals were past due, fresh talent needed scouting, the decor was sorely out of date. She threw herself into it.

The more she worked the more there was to do, and she felt great satisfaction for doing a job well. But as she pulled the covers to her chin each night, alone, the thought came that another day had passed with no word from Bruno. Two weeks, three weeks, four….

And then there he was, sitting in the lobby as she returned from her lunch break, looking nervous and gorgeous. She had an instant hot flash followed by a moment of pique.

"Hello. How may I help you?" She stuck out her hand.

He shook it, tentatively. "Hi, Maddie. I was hoping we could talk."

"Um, sure. My office?" she said and strode toward the back room. How distant could she act when every nerve in her body was screaming to wrap her arms around his big chest?

She sat behind her desk. He shut the door and remained standing. She glared and crossed her arms.

"I've missed you. I mean really missed you—"

"Well, that explains the nice bouquet of roses that I received last week."

He looked confused, then embarrassed as he sank into a chair. "You're right. I could have sent flowers. I should have sent something—"

"Or called."

"Or called you. Made a date. Put you at the top of my priority list. The truth is—"

"Here we go."

"Seriously, the truth is, I got in a shitload of trouble for going AWOL during our day together—"

"Our day, our night…" she said.

He smiled. "Yes. Unfortunately, something serious happened that weekend, and they couldn't get in touch with me." His face clouded. "My father came down on me so hard. He thinks his time is limited, that he will soon have to appoint a successor. Let's just say I can't afford to disappoint him again." He locked eyes with her. "Not if I want to have the kind of future that I'm being groomed for."

Madeleine nodded. "I remember Papà telling me that one of his top people screwed up big time. He said it took ten positives to overcome one negative."

"That's why I have to be one hundred percent focused on business right now."

"It's like me in a way. I get the impression the honeymoon period with my boss is about over. I have to continue exceeding his expectations if I want to take over for him someday."

"Madeleine, it is so fantastic that you understand. Most girls would be whining about being neglected."

"Let's don't talk about most girls, okay? It's just you and me here. And I have to ask you a question about your business. You must, *must* promise to be straight with me."

"I will never not be straight with you. If I can't tell you something, I will at least tell you everything you should know, and need to know."

"Deal. So, I don't know how to say this except to say it. Is your family business street drugs?"

She could hear the wall clock ticking as Bruno took a slow breath. "Madeleine, Porcelli Industriale is a shipping company based out of Genoa. Fifteen million metric tons of goods will pass through our hands this year now that the Suez is open again. On the delivery side, Porcelli Spedizone operates in five European countries. We have almost seventy-five hundred independent contractors delivering thousands and thousands of items to homes and businesses—"

"I can learn that from a brochure. Do you know what's inside all those shipping containers?"

"Yes and no. We don't go around opening containers, but each one is labeled and we have the corresponding paperwork. If there is an issue, we can figure it out. Why are you asking all this?"

"People with enough resources to know have told me that some of what's in the containers is illegal."

He didn't blink. "I don't doubt that's true. We don't pack them, we just move them around. Inspections are the government's responsibility."

"That all sounds so rehearsed. I'm going to ask you a direct question."

"The others weren't direct?" he said, as if he could lighten the mood. "Fire away."

"Do you sell drugs?"

"Do I look like the kind of guy who stands on a street corner giving 'secret' handshakes?"

She crossed her arms. "That is not an answer."

"The streets in America are overrun with drug related violence. All you have to do is watch their news. Killings every night."

"I lived there for four years. Your point?"

"Well, when was the last time you heard of a drug related killing in Genoa or Milan?"

She shrugged. "I don't recall. It's been years."

"Exactly. And it has nothing to do with some government war on drugs program. People who want drugs will find them, and the harder they are to find, the more crime there is. Robbery, bloodshed, neighborhoods destroyed. Our family created a service that stabilizes the trade and takes the violence out of the equation. No surprises. Just peace. Any money we make is a small price to pay. The police are in our debt for doing what they could never have done."

Madeleine was not naïve, but it all sounded so logical, and she wanted to believe him, trust him. She got up and came around the desk to tower over him. "Explanation accepted, but I reserve the right to revisit the subject." She leaned back on the desk. "So, now I'll be honest. I thought you hadn't called because you were mad at me about something."

"Of course not. I thought about you a lot. All the time."

Sweet! It seemed the air had just gone from smoggy to crystal clear. "Do you still want to go to my sister's wedding in Milan, next month?"

"Yes! Absolutely. And I'm definitely not on call, I've had it blocked out since you invited me." He sat back and crossed his legs. "We need to, or rather, I need to make sure to always block out time for us."

"Agreed. We have September twenty-ninth planned. What about between now and then?"

"We could start with a coffee. Right now, I want to hear about your new job—"

"Right now, you can shut up." She bent down, grabbed a handful of his shirt, and kissed him hard. She then pulled away and picked up her purse. "Let's go."

She left her assistant in charge of the gallery. They walked arm in arm to a café. Sitting outside under the awning, the service was slow, which suited her fine. The feeling had come back, the natural ease of being with Bruno, as if they had seen each other yesterday, entirely content to chat about nothing, to laugh and tease. She started to think about the evening, wondering the best way to invite him up to her apartment, but he suddenly looked at the enormous diver's watch on his wrist.

"Merda. I have to go. There's a meeting tonight I cannot miss."

"I understand," she said. "Really. Thanks for driving down here. It's been lovely. Just give me a call when you can."

"I will. Thank you, Maddie. This has been great."

For three weeks, actually, twenty-three days, she did not get a call. Work kept her more than occupied, but her spirits began to sag. Day twenty-four was the worst: her birthday. She spent it working and feeling sorry for herself. An hour before closing time, an extravagant bouquet of fresh cut flowers arrived. There was a thoughtful handwritten card, wishing her a wonderful day, and signed "Talk to you soon, Bruno".

How did he know it was her birthday? She called him immediately. The tension lasted only seconds this time before they were chatting like high school chums. An hour later, he promised to call her soon. They did talk again, but not soon by her reckoning. It wasn't until two days before the wedding. He called to say he would be a few minutes late but would definitely meet her there. Duomo di Milano. He was looking forward to it.

Chapter 17

The dinner conversation had been light and cheery, with Madeleine and Syrina speaking in their old 'sister code', Antonio pretending to not understand. As the dessert plates were passed around, Antonio said he could hardly believe Syrina was to be married and that his baby girl was a college graduate. There was a quiet pause —as if the same thought had struck them all: how many years since they had been all together in this house? Antonio opened a second bottle and topped off his daughters' glasses. Neither girl moved to spoon out the salted caramel budino, their late mother's favorite. No one glanced at the empty place at the table where she should have been. No one spoke of the fact that, tomorrow, Syrina would wear the once-white wedding dress, now aged to a light sepia, that their mother had made and worn at her own wedding.

Madeleine used to think she had been cheated because Syrina had had two years and ten months more time with their mother. Antonio never allowed the girls to talk about her, but on this night, Madeleine suddenly needed to. She needed to ask questions and reminisce and cry with her father and her sister. And so, she said it. She said "I miss Mamma". Antonio took a sharp breath, but he did not rise from the table and walk away. Syrina nodded and said "she would have loved Silvan". Antonio wiped his cheek and raised his glass and made the most beautiful toast, ending with "to my wife who will be with us tomorrow, who will bless this marriage, who loves us all forever".

As soon as the dishes were cleared and good night kisses exchanged, all three retired to their rooms. Tomorrow would come early. It would be a long, joyous, and sad day.

The Lombardy sun rose the next morning with a soft, ochre glow to rival any sunrise in Tuscany. It arced through the cloudless blue sky, and by early afternoon, as the wedding party arrived, the western face of the Duomo di Milano was ablaze. Madeleine, maid of honor, was humbled and uncharacteristically quiet.

Music from the skyscraping pipe organ—largest in Italy and second largest in all of Europe—began promptly at 3:30. It echoed from the cathedral ceiling and transformed every molecule of air into a magical atmosphere, setting the ambiance for the ceremony. The crowd filtered in, a who's who of Italy's cultural and business elite. They filled the nave and overflowed into the transept.

Suddenly the music changed, and the festive energy of every soul in the cathedral—which had been focused on the grandeur of the soaring marble columns, arches, and domes—was redirected to a single point: the tableau struck by Madeleine's stunning sister as she gracefully walked down the aisle on the arm of their father. Madeleine wiped a tear and then another. She beamed as Antonio shook the hand of the groom, kissed Syrina's cheek, and left her standing with her soon to be husband.

The archbishop was jovial and at the same time serene. He welcomed the guests and set the mood for a heartwarming but reverential mass. As he opened the Bible, Madeleine's attention shifted from his voice to a movement in the back of the cathedral. Someone had entered. Her near-sighted eyes struggled to resolve the face, but the physique filling out that immaculate suit was unmistakable. Bruno was a few minutes late, just as he had anticipated. He made the sign of the cross and stole into a seat near the rear. Her heart pounded.

The Sacrament of Marriage and the full Catholic mass that followed all ran together for Madeleine. Even the impeccable rendition of Ave Maria by Franco Corelli after the nuptial blessing was wasted on her. She could concentrate on only one thing, the man who had walked in late, the man she wanted to talk to. With the archbishop's next words, "two individuals have become as forever one", the enormity of what her sister had just done struck her. Marriage is forever!

To the familiar strains of Mendelssohn, the bride and groom rushed from the Duomo through a throng of guests and a shower of rice and rose petals. They ducked into the waiting limo, a gleaming black Rolls Royce smothered in white lilies, to relax somewhere before the festivities. Madeleine took advantage of her break from maid of honor duties to search for Bruno. She entered the white reception tent set up outside the cathedral. The gigantic structure seemed to cover the entire Piazza del Duomo. It was so vast and packed with people drinking and munching that she almost panicked. But there he was in a far corner, hugging an attractive middle-aged woman. He stood out like a Mediterranean cypress among shrubs.

He was dressed in a black classic-cut suit, starched white shirt, French cuffs, silk tie, waistcoat, and handmade black oxford shoes. He could have been in the wedding party, she thought, except he would have sorely outshone the groom and groomsmen. As she closed the gap between them, eager to kiss his freshly shaved cheek and slip her arm through his, she spied her father across the room. He was standing alone and empty handed. Her natural joie de vivre changed to panic. She needed to tell him about Bruno before introducing them to each other. Duty first.

What should she say? She plucked two flutes from a passing tray and headed toward her father, but by the time she got close an elderly gentleman had approached him. She stopped at a discrete distance and half turned away.

She heard her father's voice rise over the din. "Hello, my old friend. So wonderful to see you."

The friend clapped him on both shoulders. "And you, Antonio. Congratulations on the marriage. And this reception—magnifico! With Italy's finest chefs preparing the food here, I can only wonder why I was not included!"

Antonio laughed. "What kind of host asks his guests to cook, eh?"

"It would have been my pleasure, but of course." He tapped his heart with his right palm. "Seriously, thank you for inviting us to celebrate this beautiful day with your family. We are honored to be here."

"And your lovely bride? Where is she?"

"Guen is where you would expect. She has cornered Bruno, as if she never sees him."

Madeleine almost dropped the flutes. *My father knows Bruno's parents?*

"Your son is here?" Antonio continued. "I have not seen this fine boy since your restaurant opening. How many years?"

Mario turned and with a grand wave shouted, "Bruno, come pay your respects to my dear friend!"

Looking over the crowd then, Antonio spied Madeleine. A simple flick of his eyebrow and she was summoned. She arrived at the same moment as Bruno and Guendalina.

Bruno shook Antonio's hand. "It is a pleasure to see you again, sir. Congratulations on the day."

"Wonderful that you join us, Bruno. All grown up. I did not expect to see you here."

Bruno glanced at Madeleine. Before he could reply, she said, "Papà, Bruno is my escort this evening."

"Our children know each other!" Antonio beamed at Mario. "So nice, the next generation carries on our friendship. My little girl has recently returned from America...."

Madeleine was vaguely aware that she was being discussed. She was searching for the urge she had felt a moment ago—to slip away somewhere for a quiet chat with Bruno. But the impulse was gone, eclipsed by the fact, the faux pas, that she had not told her father about Bruno.

She forced a dry swallow—she might be her papà's little girl, but she was also her own woman—and slipped her arm around Bruno's back. Other guests soon joined their little group and the conversation veered into safe territory. As soon a decorum allowed, with a slight pressure on Bruno's back she directed him to follow her outside the tent.

The breeze hit her face and her shoulders relaxed down. "Well, my Orsone. I see you kept to your schedule." He looked confused. She laughed. Would their conversations always start awkwardly? "You said you would be a few minutes late, and you were."

"Oh, right. A bit embarrassing, but at least I made it."

"And I'm glad you did. Can we sit? I feel like I've been on my feet all day."

"Are you telling me those four-inch heels are not your everyday shoes?"

At the edge of the piazza, she stopped. "Hardly. How about here?" On a concrete bench she sat at a quarter angle, removed her shoes, and got comfortable with one ankle tucked under the other thigh. He sat but left a space between them big enough for two people. What did that mean? She was calculating what to say when she heard her name called.

"Maddie! There's my Madds!" The Rolls had stopped and was purring behind them. Syrina jumped out. "Baby sis! Kisses. Hey, who's this big guy?" She was tipsy and on top of the world. "Introduce me!"

"Uh…." Madeleine's mouth hung open.

"Hello, Syrina. I'm Bruno Porcelli. It is so nice to finally meet you. You are a stunning bride, and the service was beautiful. Congratulations to you and your lucky husband." He kissed her cheek and then shook Silvan's hand.

Madeleine felt she'd been outmaneuvered again. "Okay. You ready, big sis? I'm going in and tell the emcee that the guests of honor are ready to make their grand entrance."

She scooted off without waiting for a reply.

Chapter 18

Considering the large number of guests, the waited dinner service was exceptional. The emcee kept things lively between courses. In other words, the event was perfectly executed, yet Madeleine felt hollow—abandoned, if she dared to admit it. She was at the bride's table instead of sitting with Bruno, who was assigned to sit with her high school chums. She kept tabs on him and grew less and less amused as the flirting escalated at his table. He was his natural charming self, keeping everyone's glasses filled, telling jokes, and fixing his full attention on anyone who spoke. The woman two seats down from her was no longer the girl she had grown up with; a few fairy-tale words, and poof, she was a wife, a partner for life with another person. She needed either to apologize to Syrina for every nasty thing she'd ever said to her, or to get sloppy drunk and have a good cry. Or both.

The large ensemble that played big band standards during dinner and between speeches finally ceded the stage to a pop group. While most of the guests were still waiting on their desert, the band opened with "Mama Mia". A well-lubricated mob rushed the wooden platform. Dancers were soon shoulder to shoulder. Even the older generation seemed to appreciate the music, although it was too loud. ABBA had just finished their first European tour following their victory at Eurovision 1974. Silvan predicted they were going to be huge.

Madeleine's friends, especially Rosa and Bella, continued to act like Bruno was fair game, flaunting themselves and flirting with him on the dance floor. It was close to seven p.m. when she decided it was time to intervene. *Enough is enough.* At the end of "Waterloo", she climbed on stage and grabbed a microphone.

"Okay, girls, it's that time! All single females get your butts down here in front. Mrs. Keller, my much older sister, will now pass on her good fortune to some lucky maiden!"

Madeleine watched as two dozen girls formed a frantic mini-mob with waving arms and shrieks and giggles. Syrina strode to the clearing in front of them. She stopped and gravely pointed to Madeleine on the stage.

"Someone haul that little girl down here where she belongs!"

Madeleine slowly backed away, hoping to disappear into the wall of amplifiers and stage gear, but Rosa and Bella managed to drag her down to join the ritual. Syrina turned her back and tossed the flowers. The bouquet toss is traditionally a high lob. This was a line drive. Rosa and Bella blocked the other girls who leapt to cut in front, and before she knew what had happened, Madeleine had the flowers in her hands.

When the laughter and screams died down, Syrina pulled Madeleine aside and planted a lingering kiss on her forehead. "I love you little sis. Sorry about the bouquet, I honestly did not do that on purpose. At least not consciously! You are going to make a beautiful bride someday though, and I pray you find someone at least half as wonderful as I have. Someone who will make all your dreams come true."

It was a rare moment, even if her sister was drunk. Madeleine quashed the wisecrack that popped into her head and gave her a long hug. "I love you, too, Reenie. You are one lucky girl."

Syrina pulled back. "And you. This is also your lucky day." She looked at her pointedly. "Up against the wall, Maddie Faye!"

"No!"

"Tent walls don't count!"

"You, shit! Are you sure it's even your turn?"

"Stop. No talking allowed until you've done it!"

Madeleine grinned and shook her finger at her sister. Plucking her dress up to her shins, she made a beeline out of the tent and across the square to the Duomo, praying that Bruno would see her and follow.

The Champagne was outstanding, and Bruno wished he were not on call—another half bottle would have suited him fine. As the music and dancing started back up, he looked for Madeleine. Someone said they saw her dash across the piazza toward the cathedral. Just as he got to the entrance of the house of worship, she was exiting.

"Is everything okay? Someone said you were running."

"It's no big deal, just a silly sisters' game. I was coming back to get you anyway. There's something I just remembered and thought you should see."

Back inside the Duomo, she took his hand and led him up a broad stone stairway, past intricate stained-glass windows to the dimly lit mezzanine. The walls were lined with life-sized statues of long forgotten saints. She slipped easily between two of them, and he managed to squeeze himself through, barely. Behind the statues, she pressed her palm on the face of a cherub in the wooden scrollwork. A door clicked open to reveal a narrow spiral staircase.

It was almost too dark to see, and she made her way up slowly. He followed with his hands on her hips. When she stopped, there was a scrape of metal and a slit of light as she pushed open a heavy door onto the roof. The slit of light became the sky. The temperature was cooler than down on the piazza, and a breeze swept up odors of dust, and rust, and wet moss.

The part of the roof they were on overlooked the piazza and the western horizon. Brilliant orange and red clouds, like orchids, backlit the city and colored the reception tent below.

Bruno took her hand and walked to the edge. "Holy Mother, the view! You can see the entire city."

"I thought you'd like it," she said.

"It's breathtaking."

"And another perfect sunset to enjoy with no one to interrupt us. Timing is—"

"—everything." He bent to kiss her, but she stepped back and spun around with arms out, taking in the entire scene.

"Don't you want to know how I know about this place?"

"That's not exactly what I was thinking."

"Lucia found it. Her Father was the contractor general for restoration and she had free rein. All us girls would sneak up when we needed to drink wine and talk about boys. We used to even sunbathe up here."

"Now that's something I would have appreciated seeing. Not that seeing you alone isn't enough."

With that, she kissed him.

Five minutes later, as Madeleine stopped to catch her breath, the brilliant sunset was largely gray. And the tension, the lust, from a moment ago was gone, replaced with an assurance that the path she and Bruno were on was as inevitable as it was correct. He seemed to be as euphoric as she felt, what her Psych 101 instructor would call a dissolution of ego boundaries. But she knew that, at this moment, he was still thinking short term, about making love on this sacred roof—which was out of the question—while she was thinking that everything in her life was on course and the inevitable conclusion would be something permanent. Why else had Syrina's bouquet sailed right at her face? And the archbishop's words, two individuals have become as forever one—why had they seemed channeled at her? She was not infatuated with Bruno. She was converted.

She felt a jolt back from the brink of paradise—Bruno had slithered his hand under her long dress to the inside of her thigh. "Um. Hey, not here." She kissed him quickly and put her hand on his chest. "I wish you could spend the night, but I'm at Papà's."

He groaned. "I can't anyway. I have to leave shortly. But I have a free weekend coming up, a long weekend."

"That's it. Block it out, have what's her name put it on your calendar. I want to get away, just the two of us."

"I would love to. Yes, let's do it! You decide where to go. I'll take you anywhere."

"You got a deal! I'll make all the arrangements."

Paris! she thought.

Chapter 19

You should be celebrating tonight, old man, Antonio thought. Your elder daughter is safely married. Your guests are more than satisfied. Instead, you feel guilty, ashamed that you asked Syrina prying questions on her wedding day. But they are the kind of questions that keep one awake until they can be answered. And when would you have another opportunity to speak with her?

So, he had asked. Has your sister talked to you about this Bruno Porcelli? She seems to be crazy about him, no? Does she know his family's business? He asked, and he received no satisfaction. If the girls had discussed this new boyfriend, Syrina respected her sister too much to betray the confidence.

The irony of his concern was not lost on Antonio—he was fretting over Maddie's involvement with the son of his most cherished friend, the friend whose life he had saved when they were so, so young.

And how hypocritical it was, when he had sent his own son, Dante, to work for this same friend. Yes, Dante's first job was in the legitimate shipping side of the business; but had he not swelled with pride when Mario gave Dante credit for inventing the concept of The Collective, dealing small doses of criminal activity to manage the greater good? Dante himself had likened it to his work in the French Resistance, dealing harm to criminals in order to save innocent lives.

Still, Dante had gone into the underbelly of Mario's world with open eyes. He imagined that Madeleine, on the other hand, was largely unaware of the life, the risk, she was exposing herself to.

He would speak to Mario. If there was to be a future between their children, Antonio would require some assurance.

Chapter 20

"Well, dear, we're here." Bruno stored their suitcases in the armoire as Madeleine swished open the drapes. "What would you like to do first?"

"You know exactly what I want to do first." She glanced toward the king size bed. It was almost midnight. The Eiffel Tower and Trocadero were still lit up like Christmas, as were the Arc de Triomphe and Champs-Élysées. "It's all so beautiful. But kidding aside, I can't focus on anything else until I get my fill of the Louvre. So, first thing tomorrow, we hit the museum."

"First thing? If I know you, the first thing tomorrow is breakfast."

She laughed. "I yam what I yam. But after that, the Louvre. All day, okay? Come look, you can see it from the balcony."

"How is it you've never been?"

"I've been, once. I was thirteen."

Madeleine's hazy childhood memory of visiting the Louvre with her mother was a treasure. She knew that, not only was it the finest art museum in the world, but that Italian Renaissance Art—the subject she had studied for four years—was the highlight of their collection.

Friday morning, she rushed through breakfast and they made it to the ticket line well before it opened. Once inside, they spent four hours before lunch, then four and a half hours after lunch. Security guards shooed them out at closing time or Madeleine would have skipped dinner and stayed.

They had a quiet dinner at the hotel. She tried to focus as he quizzed her about di Vinci and Michelangelo. Her expectations for the museum had been high—and they had been exceeded—but something else occupied her mind now. After spending another full day with Bruno, in Paris, the City of Love, she could confirm, *she had fallen in love*. Which made it time to obsess over how serious Bruno was about her. She began mining for clues, analyzing every nuance of all that he did or said. So much so that, before the dinner was over, he had asked twice if something was wrong.

"I feel like you're studying me," he said.

She laughed. "You got a problem with that? Get used to it. I like the way you look, my Orsone."

Saturday morning, they decided to take a guided tour of the Paris Catacombs and by eleven o'clock were queued to buy tickets. The line stretched for two blocks and was barely moving. Madeleine said she would kill for a coffee. Bruno said hold my place and disappeared around the corner. When he finally came back, he asked if she was game for a slightly different adventure. An unofficial guide had offered to take them to a secret entrance and give them a private tour.

She said, "I'm game. Where's my coffee?"

"Let's have lunch and I'll explain."

The plan was to meet the guy, Marcel, at four p.m. at an old entrance to

Paris's abandoned underground rail system, La Petite Ceinture, at a spot near where it connected to the catacombs. He had provided a short list of items they should bring with them. The tour would last ninety minutes. Less than one percent of the two-hundred-mile-long system is open to the public. Marcel promised they would see a lot more than the tourists did.

"We'll need to shower after the tour, and our dinner reservation is at nine."

"Plenty of time," Bruno said. "We'll be back at the hotel by six, easily."

They took their time shopping for the items on Marcel's list: flashlights, sweaters, waterproof shoes. Madeleine also managed to find two additional pairs of shoes that she just had to have. Bruno bought a Tag Heuer watch and a blue and white *pull marin*, the striped sailor's sweaters common in Brittany. They took their packages to the hotel, grabbed some pastries— Paris-Brest for her, Napoleon for him—and made it to the secret location on time.

When Bruno introduced Madeleine to Marcel, she had a quick revulsion to him. He spoke Italian with a put-on accent, like he was making fun of the language. And, the skinny little man stank! She imagined being jammed together in the confined spaces below. Would his stench be on her by the end of the tour?

They squeezed through an iron grate that had been jimmied open and followed him, single file, twenty-five meters down a creaky, winding staircase. At the bottom, they entered the catacombs. Marcel said, "Stay close. I've been in here at midnight when the walls begin to speak. The disembodied voices will convince you to venture deeper and deeper into the labyrinth, never to return!" He laughed. "But not to worry, we should be out of here long before that."

Marcel's knowledge of the incredible myths and legends surrounding the underground system was encyclopedic. He explained that as the city grew and parochial cemeteries filled to overflowing, abandoned limestone mine shafts and tunnels were repurposed as a repository for the bones. Over a period of thirty years, beginning in 1786, more than six million skeletons were relocated here.

His storytelling skills were well honed, mixing truth into the anecdotes and legends, making it all sound believable. They rounded corner after corner, left and right, stepping around puddles and over scattered debris. The three flashlights independently drifted through the passages. Madeleine shivered at the stacks of skulls and limb bones lining the walls from floor to ceiling, some bizarrely arranged in decorative patterns.

At the dead end of a long narrow tunnel that sloped steeply downward,

Marcel stopped. "On this spot in 1787, The Count of Artois killed his lover and hid the body among this rack of bones. Sometimes you can still hear the strangled cries she made as her life was swept into the next realm. Doubters believe it is only the gurgling sound of the aqueducts that channel water from natural springs into the city, but you be the judge. Turn off your lights for one full minute and listen."

When all three flashlights were out, Bruno gasped. "Merda! It is one hundred percent dark."

"Shh. Listen. I can hear the Count's lover," she said.

He was quiet for several seconds. "I hear it. But that's no woman gurgling."

"Pretty creepy, though." She laughed and turned on her light. "Where exactly is the aqueduct from here?" She spun in a full circle. "Marcel?"

He had disappeared. "Marcel! This is not funny!"

Bruno ran back up the tunnel to where it teed left and right. He picked his way back to Madeleine, washing his light into every alcove and passage along the slope. There was no sign of their guide. Madeleine's legs gave out and she plopped on the hard-packed earth. It was cold and damp. She couldn't speak around the short gasps of breath racking her lungs. Bruno took her flashlight and clicked it off.

"Let's save one, use the other to navigate," he said.

"Navigate? I have no…no idea how we got here. I can't think."

He sat and hugged her from behind until she relaxed enough to lean back against him. He checked his watch. "It's four thirty-three. Subtract the time we stood listening to him, and I'd say we're no more than fifteen minutes from the entrance."

"But there's a hundred tunnels going off in every direction between here and there. I have no idea—" She bent forward until her head was between her knees. "People die in this—"

"There's no need to panic." He wrapped his arms around her. "We'll find our way out. Just relax—"

"I'm claustrophobic! Pathologically. I feel like these stacks of bones are going to collapse and bury us."

The more she panicked, the softer he spoke. "Let's start back. I know we turned right to come down this passage. I remember turning left where he pointed out the twin pillars. You can help me remember as we go along.

Come on."

She turned to bury her face in his chest. "Don't leave me, don't leave me, please, don't." He whispered and kissed her hair and stroked her back until her breathing slowed. A deep, involuntary breath swept out and she shuddered. "Okay. Pull me up. Just don't ask me to look at the skeletons."

Holding hands, they walked to the top and turned left. The puddles, the musty humidity, the grimy bones that had all seemed part of the attraction were now repulsive. Moving helped. Her head began to clear as she listened to Bruno prattle about how to navigate a maze. To her, the shadows seemed entirely different now with one light instead of three playing along the floor and walls. Five minutes and three turns later, he stopped suddenly. She grabbed his arm.

"What? Are we lost?"

"Here. Left." He pointed. "I remember that cross of leg bones stuck between two skulls."

"You said look for tunnels that go up," she said. "That one goes down."

"They won't all go up."

After another ten minutes he stopped at the intersection of two tunnels. Ancient bone fragments crunched under their shoes where a wall had collapsed. "We should be close, but none of this looks familiar."

"Get me out of here!" she shouted. Echoes from the limestone felt like they were mocking her.

"We're going to be alright," he said. "I have an idea." He took a cigar from his pocket and lit it.

"God! How can you take a nicotine break? You want a cognac, too?"

"No. There's a small draft. Look at the smoke."

She rubbed her eyes and stared. The smoke rose to the ceiling before wafting toward one of the tunnels. "What does it mean?"

"That air has to be going somewhere, and it's probably toward an exit."

She grabbed him and kissed his mouth. "Brilliant!"

They stopped at every intersection then to check the flow of the smoke. Twenty minutes later, she stopped short. "No!" They were back at the cross of femurs stuck between two skulls. "We just went in a circle. We're going to die." She dropped to all-fours, too weak to continue, those last words reverberating in her head. *We're going to die we're going to die we going to....*

A quiet voice broke through the muddle and she heard: *no, not today, not today*.

"Not today." Bruno raked his fingers through the earth at his feet. "Guano," he said. He pointed to the ceiling. "Bats."

She covered her head. "I don't need any fricking bats! Get me out—"

"Think about it, Maddie. As soon as it gets dark outside, these guys are going to head for the nearest exit. We can follow them."

An hour later, the bats began to stir. It was six-thirty. New bats flew in from the darkness to join the colony of fifty or so above their heads. In a few minutes, individuals began to fly away. Madeleine's light was getting weak. They checked Bruno's. It was still strong. "We'll use yours as long as it lasts. You ready?" he asked.

The bats flew much faster than the humans could follow, but the stream of them was steady. Some took longer than others to get their engines in gear. The flow led through wider and wider tunnels that sloped gradually but consistently upwards.

The procession of bats finally stopped in a large, high-ceilinged chamber. The frantic little mammals flapped around the top of a decrepit steel ladder. They clung to the rails and rungs, waiting their turn to squeeze through a small opening in the center of a manhole cover.

Madeleine focused her light on the ladder as Bruno climbed. At the top, he shoved with his hands, his forearms, his head, but the thick, metal disk would not budge. He went up another step, put his shoulder against it, and heaved with his legs. The rung supporting his weight broke loose and he plunged to the rung below, which also broke. Madeleine screamed and instinctively threw her arms up to catch him. At the same instant, the flashlight she was holding died. When Bruno managed to click on the backup light, she saw him wrapped around a side rail, dangling halfway down the ladder. One handhold at a time, avoiding the unreliable rungs, he worked his way to the bottom. He cradled her in his arms, and she sank her fingers into his love handles.

She pushed him away then and grabbed the light. "No more stupid tricks! You could have died! My mind is going to explode if you— What's that noise? What the—!"

A chorus of squeaks and clicks rose from behind them as another colony of bats swarmed into the chamber and began landing on them. Madeleine shrieked and flailed her arms, and the backup light flew from her hand. It hit the rock wall with a sickening crack that broke the bulb. They were in complete darkness again.

She shook so violently, her attempts to speak were gibberish. She grabbed for his shirt as her legs gave out.

"Let's just think for a minute," he said. "Maybe someone can hear us. Remember what Marcel said?"

"Fuck Marcel! He should be flayed!"

"Some of the homes in this area, he said they have access to the tunnels from their sub-basements. If we yell—"

She didn't need prompting. They both screamed into the darkness until their vocal cords were raw and they stopped for breath. She heard him then, crawling through the rubble on the damp earth.

"Stop! You are not leaving me."

"Maddie, dear, I'm not leaving. If I can find the second flashlight, maybe I can use parts from each to make one that will—" He stopped moving. "Oh god. Oh god, thank you, Holy Mother. Look."

"You want me to look at the fricking black hole we're in?"

He felt his way back to her, took her head in his hands, and turned her face to the left. "There. I couldn't see it until my eyes adjusted to the darkness."

It was barely visible. A dim yellow glow in the distance, like a small patch of hope. "It must be coming from one of the side tunnels."

They crawled toward the glow, sloshing through a frigid puddle until the distant light suddenly disappeared. Standing, they could see it again. The glow was indeed coming from a side tunnel, and the entrance was partially obscured by a waist-high pile of bones.

She held her breath as he cleared a path through the pile. They crept along the wet floor with their fingers trailing the slimy walls for balance. At the end of the tunnel, they discovered the light was coming through cracks in a plank door. But a metal security grate, hinged to the rock wall, stood between them and that door. Bruno punched through the grate until the rotten wooden boards were demolished. A single low-watt light bulb that dangled from a wire lit the small room beyond. A corroded boiler and stacks of crates covered in spiderwebs filled the space. With a fresh surge of adrenaline, they heaved and pulled, kicked and cursed the grate, but the rusty bolts, hinges, chain, and padlock were solid, as immovable as the manhole cover Bruno had wrestled.

Her muscles burned from the exertion, and her emotions crashed from the high of thinking they had found their freedom. "We're never getting out of here!"

She crumpled to the ground like her bones had joined those littering the floor. She let herself remember that Bruno was strong and logical and fearless; but could he get her out of this? She was petrified.

"Hang on. I'll be right back."

She was too weak to protest. He sloshed back down the tunnel and raked through the pile of human remains. He returned with three leg bones. "This should work."

He crisscrossed the bones on a rocky section of the floor and cracked them with his heel. Taking a single sliver, he began twisting and turning it in the keyhole of the padlock. One piece after another broke off inside and had to be worked back out.

"It's too rusty and the bones are too fragile." He ran his hands through his damp hair. "What's in your purse?"

She dumped the contents on the floor. A small bottle of argan oil, like the answer to a prayer, rolled to his feet. He kissed the bottle and crossed himself. Holding the lock horizontally, he gently poured oil into the keyhole until it overflowed.

"It can't hurt," he said. "What else is there?"

She held up a nail file in triumph.

It was too large.

"There's got to be something," he said. "Here. Hold the lock this way."

She stood frozen as oil slowly dripped from the back of the padlock. Bruno dropped to the floor and reached as far as he could through the grate into the boiler room, groping beyond where he could see. A stack of crates tumbled as Bruno snatched something loose. He whooped and shouted. "This could work!"

He waved a length of electrical cable like a victory flag. With the nail file, he scraped and poked the rubber coating, finally extracting two strands of stiff copper wire. He probed the lock with them, and in seconds a tumbler clicked. Bruno yanked open the shackle.

As she looked up at his shadowed face her expression was one of pure reverence.

Chapter 21

In their hotel room, they showered but could still smell the caves. Another shower then before donning their eveningwear and making it to their nine o'clock reservation only a few minutes late. They were at the most expensive restaurant in the city, La Tour d'Argent. It opened in 1582 and was dubbed "The Tower of Silver" because the building literally sparkled in the sun due to the high mica content of the Champenoise stone used for construction. For years it had been the only restaurant with proximity to the Louvre, which at that time was the royal palace, guaranteeing frequent visits by the aristocracy. Bruno seemed to feel right at home.

Their table on the second floor overlooked the Seine River where Notre Dame Cathedral's reflection lit the water. She was quiet during the foie gras appetizer, her thoughts swirling around the way Bruno had handled himself in the tunnels. Calm. Resourceful. *Heroic*.

"How scared were you?"

He twirled his wine glass. "Risk is part of my life. At work, every day, death is in the background. I guess being smart is part of staying alive, but not panicking is just as important, so I simply don't."

"On the other hand," she said, "I went from panic about starving to death in an ossuary to panic about getting caught in someone's basement. I might have died of embarrassment if they'd been home."

"The owners are probably away during renovations."

She grinned. "I want to find the workman who left that light on in the basement and give him a big ole kiss."

She was beginning to feel separated from the day's near disaster thanks to a belly full of a 1953 Chateau Margaux and the house specialty, blood duck. The menu had noted that the recipe—duck crushed in a press, served with sauce made of its blood and bone marrow—dated back to the 1700's.

She sighed and leaned back. The day could have turned out so differently. She was lucky to be alive. "This is just what I needed to put that nightmare out of my mind."

"So, my dear, tomorrow's agenda. Another trip to the catacombs?"

"Ha. You would have to kill me first. Besides, I think you earned the right to choose an activity."

"I would not kill you, but…." He nodded toward the cathedral just across the river. "I would like to attend mass tomorrow."

"Of course—"

He rushed ahead. "And to make it up to you—"

"Nothing needs to be made up—"

"I was thinking Paris could be a regular part of our travel plans."

"Um—"

"Once a year? Twice a year? Would you like that?" Was he holding his breath?

"For a tough guy you sure know how to sweet talk a girl. I could probably stand to come back every year. I'll keep it in mind." She winked. "Right now, though, I could stand to walk off some of this dinner. What do you say?"

"One of your better ideas, I'd say." He stood, tucked a five hundred franc note under his plate, and pulled out her chair.

It was midnight or a little past. The air was warm for October and the sky was clear. They walked a few blocks past Trocadero and climbed the steps up to Pont Bir-Hakeim. Near the middle of the bridge, they had a picturesque view of the Eiffel Tower. Just below them on the northeastern tip of Swan Island, a light flashed again and again. Someone's camera was in overdrive. Madeleine peeked over the railing. A small wedding was in progress. The marriage vows had apparently been completed; the party of five posed with the tower behind them. As the photographer paused to change film, Champagne corks popped like a five-gun salute and the revelers lightened their bottles.

Bruno started laughing and called down to them. "Who the hell gets married at midnight on a Saturday?" Then he whispered to Madeleine, "And where are all the guests? This is crazy."

"I think I love it." She slipped her arm around him.

"You don't want a big blowout, like your sister's?"

"Nothing against what she did. It was great, and so completely Syrina, but it's not me." She pointed below. "*This* appeals to me. Quiet, personal, discrete. I'd be happy to get married with no guests there."

"Like, elope?"

She thought about what a traditional wedding would entail, all the preparation, months of stress, a gazillion decisions, a bazillion lire. And, what she really dreaded, dealing with a sister and a father who would likely grouse about her choice of a mate until the deal was done.

"Yeah. I could elope, with the right guy, of course."

As if that were a queue, he dropped to one knee and reached for her hand. He missed as her hands flew to her mouth.

"Oh, Dio!"

"Madeleine Fayecesca Costanzo. Would you do me the honor of becoming my wife?"

She didn't think. She didn't blink. She said yes!

Later, she did think. *How did he know my middle name*? It was a combination of her grandmothers' names, Fayelnn and Francesca, and she hated it.

At eight a.m., after a good five hours of sleep, Maddie was still in dreamland in the king size bed of their hotel suite. Bruno prayed she would sleep for another couple of hours—he had something to take care of. He dressed and stole downstairs to hail a taxi. A few blocks from the catacombs ticket office, he paid the driver, checked his surroundings, and stole around a corner. He walked, head down, until he spotted the underground guide, Marcel, who appeared to be negotiating with his next mark. Exchanging a handful of bills for a hand-drawn map, the tourist wandered away. Before Marcel could pocket the money, iron fingers bore into his shoulder and a voice whispered: *one sound and we end this right here. Start walking.*

Two kilometers away, they turned into a quiet street that ended at the front steps of the home Bruno and Madeleine had used to escape from the tunnels yesterday. Marcel made a pathetic attempt to break away as he shoved him through the rear door. Inside, Bruno twisted his arm behind his back and he screamed, but there was no one to hear. The two of them disappeared down the stairs; fifteen minutes later, only one of them emerged.

Madeleine was just beginning to stir under the covers when Bruno opened the hotel room door. He sat a small white paper bag on the nightstand and kissed her awake. She stretched, smiled, and took a deep breath.

"Whoa, what is that smell?"

"Coffee and croissants, for my fiancée!" He beamed.

"No, I think the catacombs are still lingering." She rubbed her nose in his shirt. "Definitely. How about another shower before breakfast?"

"Excellent idea. I might need someone to soap my back."

"Call the concierge and see what they offer."

He laughed and scooped her from the bed.

They showered, engaged in twenty minutes of vigorous aerobic activity, then showered again before devouring the flakey croissants. Finally dressed and ready to head out for a walking tour, the sound of distant church bells wafted through the window. Bruno remembered it was Sunday. He checked his watch.

"Let's go," he said. "Mass is about to start."

"I'm not dressed for—"

"No one cares."

"I care. Five minutes." The issue was not open for discussion.

Taxis were waiting outside the hotel. The trip to Notre Dame Cathedral took five minutes thanks to Sunday morning traffic and to the tip Bruno promised the driver. Worshipers were still streaming in when they arrived. At the entrance to the nave, Bruno hesitated before dipping his fingers in the stoup. His eyes squeezed tight against the image that appeared—his right hand crushing a man's throat. A man, but a scoundrel, whose last words were a choking admission of hatred for all Italians because of their alliance with Germany during the war. Madeleine touched Bruno's arm and gave a questioning look. She would never know what he had done for her. He realized he would always protect her, no matter the cost. He dipped his fingers then in the holy water, made the sign, and proudly guided his fiancée down the center aisle.

They returned to their room after the mass. Madeleine pulled out the city map, on which she had drawn possible routes for their walking tour, and then coaxed him up to the hotel rooftop.

"From here you can see almost everything on the list," she said and pointed to the northeast. "The only question is whether to visit the Sacre Coeur first or last. It's really out of the way, so I think first, while we have the most energy. Then Les Invalides, the tower and Trocadero, Place de la Concorde, Place de l'Opera, Galeries Lafayette, L'Arc de Triomphe, and back here. Or save Sacre Coeur till last and take a taxi if we're too tired at that point."

She would be married in a few days or weeks, and was bristling with more energy than she could contain. The world looked different to her, and there was so much to see! She turned to him expectantly. He looked troubled.

"What's wrong?"

"Before we start, I need an hour on the phone." Her expression fell and he rushed ahead. "Or maybe less. I need to contact a couple of people to set some things in motion for tomorrow."

"What's tomorrow?"

"October sixth."

"I mean, I thought we would be here all day and then fly back late to Genoa."

He smiled. "I always wanted to get married on October sixth. It's Feast Day of Saint Bruno."

Her eyes flashed yes, yes, yes! If she had any doubts about marrying this man—and she didn't think she did—they were swept away now.

Back in their room, he called his pilot and gave instructions. Then she listened to him schmooze the mayor of Crocefieschi, the village outside Genoa where Porcelli Industriale kept their plane. The King Air 350i would land at the tiny airfield there at five p.m. The mayor would do his best to accommodate all of Bruno's requests, and if everything worked out, a helicopter would shuttle them to a nearby castle. The civil service would begin at fifteen minutes before sunset, at the base of the castle, on an escarpment overlooking a quilt of tiled roofs comprising the village below. Tomorrow.

Bruno didn't accept that the mayor's promised "best" would be good enough. He called Dante, swore him to secrecy, and told him he was getting married tomorrow. He did not say to whom, and Dante did not ask. Bruno said he needed him in Crocefieschi early tomorrow, to make sure the mayor did not screw up. Dante balked. The request was clearly beyond his duties. Bruno swallowed his pride and asked him to do it as a personal favor. Being indebted to Dante was loathsome.

When Bruno was satisfied that everything would be taken care of, they walked all the way to Sacre Coeur. They drank espresso in Montmartre, although Madeleine insisted the French don't know how to make it.

"We'll be back in Italy tomorrow. You can have all the espresso you want," he said.

"Tomorrow! What am I going to wear?"

"We're eloping." He laughed. "It doesn't matter what you wear."

"The hell it doesn't!"

And to hell with the rest of their walking tour. At her insistence, they hailed a taxi. Bruno opened the door and said, "The Galeries Lafayette, please."

The driver turned slowly and shook his head. Stupid Italians. They had stopped him for nothing. It was Sunday, and every retail store in the entire city was closed. Of course. Bruno slammed the door.

"What was I thinking!" she said. "I wasn't thinking. Damn it! Bruno, what am I going to do?"

"Let me make a phone call. I know a guy."

An hour later, they slipped into the Galeries through a freight entrance where a private assistant was waiting. She found everything they needed, including rings. The bill would be paid later, on a less holy day.

Chapter 22

Antonio Costanzo stood at his office window and took in the rooftops across Milan's business district. But in his mind's eye was the picture of what his workdays had been like years ago: trips to the all-night wholesale market, early morning baking, smiles and laughter from loyal customers. Now, all that had endeared him to the restaurant business as a young man was stripped away. These days he was the face of the business. Public appearances, serving on boards, supporting charities. And the two thumbs up he waved during surprise visits all across northern Italy were what kept his employees on their toes.

How many more years did he have left to enjoy this life? He knew why he was pensive. His baby girl had skated away, into the arms of a man whose business he did not condone. He picked up the phone and dialed.

"Mario Porcelli here."

"Antonio Costanzo here."

"Caporale Costanzo!"

"Ah, Caporale Porcelli." He laughed with joy. "So good to hear your voice, Mario. How are you?"

"I am a lucky man, my friend. Business is booming, health is good, three square meals a day."

"From what I hear, it is more often four squares."

"Very funny. You have spies in my camp?"

"Just an educated guest from one restaurateur to another," Antonio said. "I myself have had to make changes. The doctors warn me every visit."

"It's the curse of old age. Guendalina has put the chef at Mario's on notice."

"Count your blessings, Mario. How is your beautiful bride?"

"She is well, thank you. But there is a new woman in my life." He let the silence hang for a moment. "Antonio, are you there?"

"A new woman?"

"Yes. Young, beautiful, intelligent. And she is in love." He laughed. "With her husband. My son!"

"You old goat. I was thinking you have lost your mind to betray Guendalina."

"So tell me what you think of all this? We really like her. She's the daughter we always wished for."

"I am happy for them, but I am concerned they moved too fast. They are so young," Antonio said.

"I understand. But when Guen and I saw them together, after they eloped? No more concerns. I have never seen Bruno so happy. No more all-night parties or chasing tail. Like me when I met Guendalina."

"I know the feeling so well, my friend. First with Maria and then Donice. I miss them both still. I can see Maddie is in love, but Mario, she's my youngest, and she is the image of her mother. It was hard enough with Syrina. With all due respect, no man will ever be good enough for my baby, not even the Archangel Gabriel. But I am an old man. Who am I to stand in the way of love?"

"Antonio, I understand. I'm sure I would feel the same way."

"This may sound hypocritical since I sent Dante to work for you, but I am concerned about Maddie being in the life."

"That concern is only natural, my friend; especially, no offense, from a civilian. But thanks to Dante, our business model has eliminated the old risks. As long as I live, Madeleine will be protected. You have my personal guarantee. She's family now." He lowered his voice. "Plus, I still owe you."

"Grazie mille, Mario, but you know we were just lucky that day."

 "Perhaps, but it is never forgotten."

"Let's have lunch one day soon."

"I would like that, Caporale Costanzo. Ciao"

Chapter 23   TWO YEARS LATER

Madeleine looked up from the stack of papers on her desk. She had been married for two years, and life was becoming routine. She closed her eyes and covered her ears against the noise from the showroom. Moments like this made the walls of her office creep in around her, and she longed for the view from her old apartment in Monaco. As she shut out thoughts of this toxic work environment, she had to admit that living in Genoa had its upsides, that her reasons for moving here were worth it. The proximity to Bruno's parents was a godsend. Mario and Guen adored her and, after surviving the shock of the elopement, welcomed her into the family. And her new friends could be so much fun, just not overly classy. Oh, and shopping was less expensive. But none of it made up for the fact that her sister rarely visited. Syrina had never warmed to Bruno. She avoided family gatherings and was, at best, civil when she had to be around him. Madeleine had to content herself with solo trips to visit her in Lenno. At least Syrina held her tongue when Madeleine gushed about her amazing husband.

But the gallery! The racket erupted again, loud and angry. She shut the door to her office, resisting the urge to slam it, and instead slapped the top of her desk. Her boss, Luigi, who had promised to retire last year, was still there. The man had no control over his temper, and his disrespect for the artists he represented was an embarrassment. In truth, he respected no one—clients, employees—and least of all, her. Fortunately, Madeleine got a pass from the verbal abuse because Luigi feared Bruno. And the business experience and the contacts she made were valuable. Still, she couldn't rationalize the fact that she continued to work for this man after a year and a half.

What had driven her to take the job was six months of daily boredom at home. Bruno worked, and she was not housewife material. What kept her sane now—now that her days were overseen by an egotistical schmuck—was everything outside the job. She was married, and her husband was a dream. Yes, his hours were long, he came home drained, but he made time for her as promised. The lazy weekends on the boat, the regular trips to Paris, the bedroom. They were so much better together than apart, like The Beatles, she thought.

Still, something had to give. Luigi ran the business as if he owned everyone he had a professional relationship with. Her degree in art meant nothing to him. She imagined he called her Barbie behind her back. Her ideas for improving the business were pooh-poohed, but they continued to flow, changes that could take the retail market for top-end artwork to the next level, potentially transforming the face of the modern gallery. Her ideas had value; she knew it in her soul.

She stopped sharing her ideas with Luigi and began to keep a notebook—she dreamed it would be the blueprint for her own gallery someday. Now, instead of grumbling when Bruno asked about her day, she was energized and laid out her new concepts.

"So why don't you take the plunge and start your own gallery?" he asked.

"Because I haven't saved enough," she said. "I'm not going to ask Papà to finance me. I want to do it on my own."

"And how long will that take?"

They were in the kitchen. She'd given the staff the night off and prepared dinner herself. Bruno was overstuffed on tomato feta salad and lasagna. She turned to the sink and let a stack of plates slosh into the dishwater. "While you're fully supporting us, I'm saving every penny I earn."

"How long?"

She sighed. "I don't even know. Three or four years maybe, if I'm lucky."

"What you need is an investor. Hey, I know just the guy." Even with her back turned she could see his boyish grin. "Terms would be outrageous, but nothing he's not already getting for free."

She laughed but couldn't speak. She dried her hands and gazed at him for a moment before running and leaping. Her legs cinched around his waist.

She nuzzled his shoulder and whispered, "Ready for dessert?"

"Lord, not now. I'm too full of—" Light bulb moment. "Oh, you mean *dessert* dessert."

****

Bruno waited patiently for Madeleine to come up with a business plan and a realistic appraisal of what it would take to start a gallery from scratch. He knew she was shocked by her first estimate and was struggling to bring that number down. Then like manna from heaven, a certified letter arrived for her.

"Is someone suing you?" he asked. "You've got something here from a high-end attorney in Monaco."

"It's probably just the guy renting my apartment there. He keeps bitching about the noise from the courtyard and I keep explaining that that is not my issue to resolve." She tore open the envelope, ready to do battle, but sat down and read the letter slowly. The deep breath she was holding came out in a woosh.

She handed him the paper. The first paragraph said that Alessandro Oscar— owner of Gallery Oscar in Monaco where she had worked before moving to Genoa—was dead at sixty-eight. Bruno knew that she had adored him and that he had felt the same about her. But that did not explain the strange expression on her face now. He read to the bottom of the cover letter. Oscar had no heirs and had left the gallery to Madeleine. The details that followed were stunning. She would gain immediate ownership simply by assuming all debts and liabilities. The sum of debts listed in the addendum were a small fraction of what a greenfield operation would cost to start up. Quick calculation, her savings would cover at least half. Bruno could contribute the balance as an investor.

When he looked up from the papers, she was shaking. "You need a drink," he said. She tried to stand but her legs were weak. "Sit still. I'll get it."

"My renter's lease is up at the end of next month." She was staring into space. "I can live in my apartment."

"Wait. You want to move back to Monaco? I can't work from there."

"Once the gallery is running my way, I won't have to be there all the time. In six months, I can train someone to manage the day-to-day. Then I can open a branch here in Genoa! The name recognition is worth a fortune." Her mind was racing. "We can alternate weekends here and there, take your new yacht back and forth. You like Monaco well enough. Hell, I'll be the boss." Her focus returned from the hazy distance. "I can take off as much time as I want, as much time as you need. Babe, I have to do this."

His new yacht. He had named it *The Madeleine*, and she knew he was always looking for excuses to sail.

But her sell job was unnecessary. Bruno was almost as thrilled with the prospect of her taking over the gallery as she was. "If this will make you happy, we'll make the long-distance thing work." His thoughts switched to the annual revenue—how much, what percentage was in cash? Money laundering was a basic component of his operations, and new channels were hard to come by. He could, would, think that through, someday soon.

Chapter 24

"Coffee toast! Everyone, make yourself a shot. Someone make one for me, please. I have a story for you."

Madeleine's team headed for the espresso machine, listening to their new boss with whom they had fallen in love. For the past five weeks, with the gallery closed to the public, her staff of six experienced individuals had remodeled and redecorated and then rehung the studio to include the new paintings Madeleine brought in. The team planned the opening night gala, sent hand-written invitations, dealt with the caterers, ordered Champagne. Finally, they covered the windows with *"Oscar-Porcelli Gallery: Grand Opening"*. Tonight was the payoff. Caffeine was required to keep the exhaustion at bay.

When everyone was seated, Madeleine stood and raised her tiny cup. "To our benefactor, Alessandro Oscar, founder of Gallery Oscar, may he rest in peace. And," she raised her voice, "to the new Oscar-Porcelli Gallery!" She dabbed her eyes at the applause and acknowledged each employee in turn with a tight smile and nod.

"Here's the story I want to share. I have dreamed of opening my own gallery since I was thirteen, which is a tribute to my mother, the woman who instilled in me a love for fine art. On my birthday that year, she surprised me with a trip to Paris, just the two of us. Papà stayed home with my sister, Syrina, who never let me forget that she was two years and ten months older. I often felt she was two light years ahead of me in many ways. But this trip to Paris, so momentous, gave me a precious new perspective on my position in our family.

"Mother and I took the overnight train from Milan and arrived as Paris opened her sleepy eyes to the rising sun. That first day, we walked and climbed through landmark after landmark, ending at sunset atop the tower, watching the City of Lights refresh below us.

"I remember our hotel fronted the Rue de Lille in the Saint-Germain-des-Prés quarter. It was a stone's throw from The Rodin, L'Orangerie, The Louvre, plus more private galleries than I could believe existed. She let me spend the entirety of the next day in The Louvre, on my own, with just a map and a fifty franc note.

"Our final day there, we visited private galleries until I was ready to drop. Near closing time, we rang one last doorbell and were admitted to a large arcade with walls covered in contemporary art. The room was warm with the sleepy aroma of linseed oil, but I remember feeling electrified by the paintings. Two men were talking and gesturing toward the artwork. The older of the two, who turned out to be the gallery owner, raised himself from the column he was leaning against and welcomed us. He said our timing was lucky, as we could meet the artist whose work he had just hung. Long story short, Mamma bought one of his pieces. As we left, I saw the men shake hands, and I saw overwhelming gratitude in the young artist's eyes. That painting hung in our living room for years and now hangs behind my desk here. Every time I look at it, I'm reminded that since the day we walked out of that gallery, I have dreamed of being a gallery owner. Thank you all for helping me make my dream come true. Salute!"

"Santé!"

"Cin cin!"

"Will your mother be at the opening tonight?"

"In spirit only, I'm afraid. She passed before I turned fourteen. I feel that tonight is as much for her as it is for me. She wisely pointed me toward the light then left me to find my life. That's why I am where I am today, here with all of you.

"To Madeleine's mother!"

The team raised their cups again and Madeleine turned toward the espresso machine, hiding her tears.

"Now," she held up her hand, "convince me we haven't forgotten anything. The opening is in a few hours. Max, tell us about the RSVP list."

"On the press side of things, every invited newspaper will be represented, including Reuters. Television from Milan, Genoa, Nice, Paris, and Turin have committed, plus a number of freelance photographers."

"Thanks Max, great job. Stella, how about our tastemakers."

"We're expecting most of the Rosemont Society, our regular high rollers of note, and I'm thrilled to say I finally got through to the Royal Family's security detail. At least one of the family will be in attendance."

"Excellent! If that happens, well, free Champagne for everyone for a week." She laughed.

"Will Bruno be with us tonight?" Stella asked.

"Absolutely. He's almost as excited as I am and wouldn't miss it. Paula, update us on catering."

"Everything looks good, all the earlier issues are resolved. Setup begins three hours before. Non-stop food and drink from open to close."

"Make sure we have leftovers. I'll be too nervous to eat during the event. Thanks for a great job dealing with all that, Paula, I know it wasn't easy. And finally, Simone, I trust all five of the featured artists are excited about 'their' evening. Do you think everything is under control, as much as it can be?"

"Fingers crossed. I insisted on name tags and had to quell a rebellion. They've agreed to circulate in shifts, spend just enough time with each guest and move on before the awkward silences take over."

She nodded. "How about Jean-François? Make sure you don't let him out of your sight for a second."

"Got it. I think he and I have an understanding."

"That's about the best we can hope for with him. Remember, everyone, any issues at all during the night, find me and whisper in my ear. Okay, see you all back here two hours before opening, dressed and ready to go."

Chapter 25

After a day of details, last minute phone calls, and a vital twenty-minute nap, Madeleine arrived back at the gallery for a professional makeover. She had reviewed the night's checklist until she could recite it, but no matter how many boxes were ticked, she still heard, "Something will go wrong, you just don't know what it is yet." Her father's words calmed her.

The staff was early—a good sign.

"Hello everyone. I'll be in my office putting on the final touches. Wish me luck. Anthony and an assistant will be here soon. Please point them in my direction."

Madeleine felt the presence of Oscar, her benefactor, in the large office she now occupied. She had redecorated but kept his oversized desk as well as the leather chairs and matching sofa along the wall opposite the window. Fifty years ago, that window would have had a great view of the harbor. Today, the view was mostly concrete, glass, and steel with an occasional ray of sunlight peeking through it all.

There was a quick knock and the heavy wooden door swung wide. "Hello, hello! If it isn't the lady of the hour!"

"Tony, how's my favorite stylist? I'm nervous as hell and I need lots of help."

"Who are you fooling, Miss Maddie? God shined a special light on you. Everyone says. Right, Pearle?'

"I imagine her parents had a bit to do with it, Tony."

"Hello Pearle, Tony said he was bringing reinforcements. To be clear, there's no special light. It's all down to clean living and having a good man in your life."

"I hear that Miss M." Tony said, then blushed.

"Let's move to the powder room." Madeleine rose and led them through a side door.

"This is a great space. Really makes it easy on us. So, what are we doing this evening?"

"Pearl, show Tony the dress if you would please. It's hanging behind the door. Tony, I ripped a photo from Vogue last month. Are my features soft enough for this off-the-face style?"

"Love it. It's a wonderful look for you. Classic. Won't take any time at all."

"I hope I'm not overdoing it. But you know, there can only be one grand opening for the Oscar-Porcelli Gallery. And this *is* Monaco."

"I'm with you. You have to do it up right for something this special."

"What are we looking at, Tony?"

"Thirty minutes, forty tops."

"Pearle, we'll use this rose magenta nail polish, same as the new company logo."

"You can't go wrong with red and black." Pearl held up the dress and brushed her hand down the side.

There was a quick rap as Simone appeared at the door. "I'm so sorry, Madeleine, there's a phone call. It's Bruno. He says it's urgent."

Her face fell. "Okay, transfer it back here."

"I did." Simone set the speaker extension from Madeleine's desk on the makeup table. The others backed out of the room.

She shouted toward the box. "Bruno, what's wrong? Are you hurt?"

"I'm fine. It's nothing like that."

"Are you at the apartment? I put your cufflinks on the bureau."

"Hold on Maddie. I have some bad news."

Her breath caught in her throat. "Just tell me you will be here tonight."

He hesitated a moment, and she knew.

"Something big has come up. My Father called a last-minute meeting with the heads of The Collective. It's serious. There hasn't been an emergency meeting like this in years."

"Can't you get out of it? You're his son."

"If you could have heard the tone in his voice." He softened. "Listen, Papà knows how important tonight is, to both of us. This is critical or he wouldn't have insisted. I have no idea how long it will last, but I've got a charter standing by. Maybe I can be there before you close. Worst case, I'll kiss you when you wake up tomorrow."

"Bruno, my Orsone. You have helped me so much getting to this point, it kills me you can't enjoy the opening. But I understand. Your family business requires loyalty without question, and I respect you for your commitment. The important thing is that you are there when your father needs you. Please call me when you know your timing. I love you."

"Madeleine, you are so precious to me, and I will make this up to you. Thank you for understanding."

"I love you."

"I love you too, my Tesoro. Ciao."

Chapter 26

The back of Bruno's shirt was soaked with sweat despite the air conditioning. Weapons had been collected in the outer room; otherwise, Bruno knew, there would have been blood on the floor.

Under the table, his hands trembled as he listened to The Collective's six family heads shout their complaints against his father. Each member seemed emboldened by the previous speaker until their demands were tantamount to open threats. Mario sat quietly and expressionless. The members sensed a lamb, and the teeth and claws came out. Murmurs and grumbling turned into curses. Allegations of betrayal and corruption flew. Mario was skimming off the top. Mario needed to open the books. Fists pounded the table. Finally, someone said it. Mario must be replaced as Chairman, one way or another.

With hearts still pounding, the men fell silent. As Mario seemed to anticipate, they had run out of steam. He slowly rose from his position at the head of the table. Starting from his left, he looked each member in the eye, softly spoke their name, and compared the state of their business today to when they joined The Collective many years ago. He reminded them of the times that costly wars were avoided because of his better business solutions. "Power is useless without profit. Profit is impossible without peace. Concern yourself with only one thing. Not my profit, not my methods. *Your* family's profit."

And then he said something that made no sense. Just six words. Bruno thought he must have misunderstood. The temperature of the room dropped from inferno to summer breeze. Now, instead of shooting stilettos, each face around the olive wood table was humbled. When Mario asked for additional comments, no one spoke.

With a glance from his father, Bruno hurried to the credenza and returned with four bottles of whisky. Mario opened each one and passed it to his left. The members were soon milling around the room, laughing at old stories, embracing one another, shaking hands.

Mario alone remained seated at the table. Bruno joined him and whispered, "What the hell just happened?"

Mario hooked his finger in his son's shirt collar and tugged him down, ear to mouth. "Your mother and I are meeting for a late supper at Mario's. Join us. I will explain what just took place."

****

Bruno gripped the wheel of the Dino. No matter how he looked at it, the flow of the meeting made no sense. Like going from night to day with no dawn. How had the current changed so swiftly? A hidden card had been played, something not on the table, and which his father could not explain to him with members still in the room.

Bruno had planned to update Madeleine during the crosstown drive, but first he needed to level his head—he didn't want to ruin her evening for a second time. He lowered the windows and sped through the downhill twists. 'Born To Run' blasting from his two-hundred-watt stereo cassette system did the trick. He parked outside his father's restaurant and called his wife.

"801 this is 742. 801 this is 742."

"Go ahead 742."

"801, call The Oscar-Porcelli Gallery in Monaco. It should be on my quick list. Over."

"Hold on… You are connected 742. Over."

"Thank you 801."

"The Oscar-Porcelli Gallery."

"Simone? Bruno again. Over."

"Oh, hi Bruno. I recognized your walkie-talkie phone. Uh, over?"

"Nice to know I can still leave an impression. Sounds like you're having a good night. Over."

"It has been fantastic! But I'll leave the details to your lovely wife, who incidentally is the belle of the ball. She is simply stunning. I'll find her for you. Over."

"Thanks." As he waited, Bruno could hear snippets of conversation from the room. *Game changer… Only twenty-three years old… I'd like to get in her—*

"Bruno, it's you! Sorry for the noise. We are over capacity. Had to send for more food. It's a huge success! Over."

"I had no doubts, Maddie. Congratulations! Over."

"You will never guess in a million years. Princess Grace was here! I couldn't believe it. She is so beautiful. And so charming and gracious. Every time a camera flashed it reminded me of *Rear Window*. I'm still pinching myself. Over."

"Don't rub it in. I really wanted to be there. I'm so happy for you. Did you sell anything? Over."

"No, not one thing…. We sold everything! Every piece. Remember that abstract I told you about, like a fish skeleton and butter patties floating in a toilet. Sold. Over."

"No kidding. But hey, what do I know about art. Over."

"Come on, you're learning. You don't mix up Picasso and Rembrandt anymore. You'll get there. Over."

"Did you cover your expenses? Over."

"Bruno, darling. We cleared enough to pay rent and staff for at least a year! So yes, we covered expenses. Over."

"How much of that was cash? Over."

"You are so silly. How was your meeting, or can you even say? Over."

"Maddie, I was floored. It was much more serious than I anticipated, but Papà worked it out. I'll tell you everything I can when I see you later tonight. Over."

"Oh, you're coming! I can't wait for you to undress me and whisper all those supply and demand economic tips in my ear. Over."

"Ha, now who's being silly? But save those thoughts and I'll meet you at the apartment in about four hours. Over."

"I can't wait. Wait! Four hours? Over."

"Papà asked me to Mario's for a late supper. He wants to explain something about the meeting. Another teaching moment. It can't be that serious; Mamma will be there, too. Sharing her recipes with the chef, no doubt. I'll make it as quick as possible. See you soon. I love you. Over."

"Okay, if you must. I'll be waiting for you, my love. Ciao."

Chapter 27

The doors were locked, lights in the main gallery were dimmed, and only the staff and a few special friends were left to finish off the last of the food— caviar tartlets topped with crème fraîche, flatbread with fava beans, cucumber sticks, burrata—and of course the Champagne. Halfway into the third bottle, the sing-alongs began. Instrumental tracks to "Tonight's The Night", "Dancing Queen", and "Les Champs-Elysées", blazing from overhead speakers, were drowned out by the karaoke chorus below.

It was a celebration and a news-watch party in one. Channel 10 and Channel 35 had both been there in the early minutes and captured The Princess making her entrance. The publicity would be priceless.

Madeleine, swaying with emotion and the celebration Champagne on her empty stomach, held up her flute and tapped it with a cocktail fork. "Everyone, I just want to…."

"Shh."

"I just want to say thank me for being with us today. We couldn't have done this without us and I'm proud to begin to say we are beginning to start a wonderful gallery for very long. Salute."

The crowd, too tired to notice their boss was a bit tipsy, responded as one, "Salute." Someone started chanting: "Maddie, Maddie, Maddie…."

"Open another bottle," she shouted. "There shall be no glass without the bubbles full."

"Hey, look. We're on! We're on!"

Max and Stella had rolled in the television and warmed it up. The late news opened with a shot of Princess Grace entering the lobby, the large "Oscar-Porcelli Grand Opening" sign in full view behind her. There was a short clip of Madeleine with a couple of big-name locals; a shot of all the employees taking a bow on the sidewalk out front. The announcer read a list of the featured artists and commented that sales were brisk. When the segment ended, attention returned to the food and drink. Max was about to roll the set back to the conference room when he stopped and turned the volume back up.

"Hey, everyone, listen a second. There's a breaking news story. Something about Genoa."

"What are they saying?"

"Quiet!"

"Turn it up more."

"I repeat, this just in. A tremendous explosion ripped through a section of downtown Genoa about forty-five minutes ago. Early reports indicate the blast originated inside Mario's, one of the city's finest dinner clubs. Stay tuned for details, we'll update you as new information becomes available. Back to you, Andrea."

Max hit the mute button. Silence rang through the room like a sonic blast. Madeleine's frozen face broke and she screamed. Max caught her as she buckled and lowered her onto a chair. Simone ran into the office and snatched the phone. Paula filled a glass with water. Stella turned the volume back up and scanned channels for more news. Others stood rooted to the floor, shell shocked.

Madeleine's screams ended as abruptly as they began. Her eyes were now glazed and blank. She took a sip of water and glanced up as Simone returned.

"I called Bruno's mobile. The radio operator couldn't get a connection, but she promised to give him a message when he checks in."

"I just realized he's probably waiting for me at the apartment. I'll call him."

"No, you sit down Maddie. I'll call."

"Thank you, Simone. He's probably planning one of his surprises. He hated missing tonight."

"Should we try your place in Genoa?"

"Yes, of course. No, wait, I'm not thinking straight. I'll call his father's house. The housekeeper, Gina, she's always there. She'll know what's going on."

"Stay there, Madeleine, I think the phone will reach."

The color was not returning to her face. Paula suggested getting her feet up and head down, covering her with something warm.

Simone yelled from the office. "There's still no answer at the apartment."

"Keep trying Simone." She took the extension from Stella. "God! What is Mario's number?"

Her hands trembled and it took three tries to dial correctly. "It's busy! Porca puttane!"

"Let me try." Max took the phone. "Operator I have an emergency call. It's urgent. Please break in." Madeleine recited the number.

"Hush, there's more news." Stella turned up the volume.

"Updating the explosion in downtown Genoa, we've learned that at least three are dead at the scene. The injured, sixteen at last count, have been transported to Ospedali Galliera. The cause of the explosion is under investigation. Police advise all to avoid old town until further notice. Stay tuned to Channel 35 for updates." Stella hit the mute button.

"Thank you, operator." Max handed the phone to Madeleine.

"Gina! Is Bruno okay? Have you heard anything?' She squeezed her eyes shut. "Oh, thank God! Are you sure? Where?" She listened, her fingers blanched white on the handset. "I'm on the way. Grazie mille, Gina."

"He's alive," she whispered, then looked up. "Bruno is alive!" A mission seemed to be written on her face. "I need my bag. My keys. I've got a long drive ahead of me."

A half dozen people spoke at once. "Madeleine, you are in no condition to drive." "I'll call my brother." "I'll take you." "It's two and a half hours to Genoa." "I'm parked just outside...."

One voice, with the ring of authority, rose above the chatter. "Is anyone here sober enough to drive?" At that, the group fell silent. "Madeleine, I'm Franco, Stella's friend. I have an idea. Give me two minutes."

"Maddie, what did you find out from Gina?"

"They don't know much yet. It could have been a gas leak or...something intentional. There's no official information yet. Gina only knows about Bruno because her brother works at the hospital. The restaurant, Mario's, she said it's...." Her voice broke. "It's gone. Like it wasn't there. Just a pile of stone and timbers. Mario will be devastated. That restaurant was like a member of the family to him."

Franco interrupted. "I think we have a solution. I called a football friend who owes me a favor. He works for a private transportation company down by the docks. He'll meet you at this address in ten minutes. Ask for Cristoforo."

"I'll find you a taxi, Maddie."

"I'm right behind you, Simone."

"Take my jacket to cover up the chill."

"Thank you all. I'd still be sitting here paralyzed without your help. I'll call when I know something." Madeleine pushed through the front door into the cool night.

Simone held the taxi door. "He knows the address and has been tipped handsomely for disregarding the traffic laws. Godspeed, Maddie."

A few fuzzy moments later, Madeleine was out of the cab and rotors were beating overhead. She turned to the pilot. "I've never been in a helicopter before."

"Well, strap in and hang on, madame. This may be the bumpiest twenty minutes of your life."

Chapter 28

Madeleine fell asleep the moment the lights of Monaco faded into the distance. The short flight to Genoa may have been bumpy, but rather than keep her alert, the turbulence combined with exhaustion and alcohol created a violent dream of drowning. She watched from safety as someone she loved thrashed in vivid, storm-fueled waves, just beyond her reach. A mix of emotions quickened her breath, but her hands were oddly calm as she reached into the blackness for the one she loved, and hated, and feared. A faceless man she wanted to both rescue and condemn.

She gasped at a sudden drop in the pitch of the background roar.

"We have arrived in Genoa madame."

"Thank you, ah . . ."

"Cristoforo."

"Yes, of course. I'm sorry. Do you know Ospedali Galliera?"

"Yes madame, it's on this side of the city. Shall I radio for a taxi for you?"

"That would be— Wait, someone is here for me." She pointed across the street. "Thank you again. How much?"

"It's taken care of. I pray for the best for you and your family."

Stepping out under the chopper blades, Madeleine kept her head low and ran toward the black Mercedes. Gina was crying openly, gripping the car door.

"Sweet Gina. How did you know?"

"The gallery called us back. We just got here."

On the short drive to the hospital she gave Madeleine what little news she had. Her brother said Bruno was in emergency, the authorities continue to search the scene, some are believed to have died.

As the car rolled to a stop, Madeleine grabbed her purse, took two steps, and broke a heel. Shoes in hand, she ran on stockinged feet into the overflowing emergency room. Minutes, hours, a lifetime later she found an E.R. nurse with some answers.

"Yes Mrs. Porcelli, your husband is alive. He has a head injury, multiple fractures, and possible internal damage. We've stabilized him for immediate surgery. Follow me, please."

Madeleine speed-walked through multiple corridors until the nurse stopped at a gurney waiting for an elevator. She wailed through the hand clamped over her mouth. Like a burn victim, the man was naked except for a towel over his groin and a scattering of small bandages. Swelling had closed both of his eyes. Every inch of exposed skin was covered in cuts large and small; his face was unrecognizable, seared as if he had run a gauntlet of sandblasters. His blood oozed from the Betadine-soaked gauze.

She whispered in his ear, "I'm here, my love. Be strong for me. I will see you soon."

She detected, or imagined, a dim smile before the elevator closed, separating them.

The nurse touched her arm. "Mrs. Porcelli, the doctor will speak with you once your husband is out of surgery. You can rest in the third floor waiting room. Considering the number of injuries, I expect at least four hours. You'll have time to freshen up, get a bite to eat. In the meantime, if there is anything I can do, I'm Nurse Amato. I'm on duty till seven a.m."

"Thank you, nurse. I think I'm alright."

As she walked away, Madeleine caught a distorted glimpse of herself in the metal elevator door. An hour ago, she was fashion magazine ready. Now she looked like a punk rocker on a bad night, squeezed into a skinny, slinky black dress, layered under a man's herringbone sports jacket that reached her knees. To top it off, her high heels had disappeared from her fingers somewhere along one of the corridors and one painted-red toenail was poking through her left stocking.

She stopped in the Ladies to discard her stockings and restore order to chaos, emerging minutes later feeling a little less the sideshow attraction. Someone at the nurses' station had her shoes. She snapped off the other heel and slipped them on. As the elevator jerked and banged its way to the third floor, she sagged under the weight of what was happening, in no way prepared for the next few hours.

In the nearly empty waiting room, a mother and two children tossed and turned under thin blankets. Across the room, a muted television dangled from the wall. As she approached the set, she recognized Gina and Cosmo sitting with their heads bowed.

"Do you have room for one more?"

Gina leapt to her side. "Oh, Mrs. Madeleine, how is Mr. Bruno? What do you know?"

Cosmo stood and clutched his chauffer's cap. He spoke to the floor. "We have been very worried, Mrs. Madeleine."

"I met the nurse who was on duty when they brought him in. He has a lot of broken bones, some internal damage they think, and a head injury. I saw him briefly. He gave me a little smile, but oh, Gina! He looked so bad. They've taken him to surgery…." She stifled a sob. "Four hours at least, the nurse thought." She realized her face was wet with tears that she didn't know were flowing.

Ignoring an unwritten taboo, Gina threw her arms around Madeleine and sobbed. Cosmo instinctively stepped back, giving distance to their awkward embrace.

Madeleine sat and fought to regain her composure. "Thank you, Gina. Thank you both. I've been on autopilot this entire night, even before I heard about Bruno. It's so strange. I feel like I'm watching myself live this. I'm so thankful you are here with me."

"You are so kind, Mrs. Madeleine," Gina said.

She tried to smile. "One of these days I'm going to steal you away from Mario and Guendalina."

Gina suddenly looked stricken. Cosmo ducked his head.

"What is it? Oh God! Gina, what's happened?"

She had to lean in close to hear the housekeeper. "It was an unofficial report, but they said that…Mario and Guendalina…" She burst into tears again. "Oh, Mrs. Madeleine. We just heard it on the television."

"No, no, no, no! That can't be. Bruno made it out alive. How can they even be sure they were both at the restaurant?"

Cosmo turned half away. "They were there, Mrs. Madeleine. I dropped them at the front door just thirty minutes before the…" He whimpered, "It's my fault."

"God no! You can't think like that Cosmo. Both of you, look at me please. We can't tell Bruno. He cannot know his parents are gone while he's still fighting to survive."

Madeleine glimpsed then something beyond the sadness on their faces: it was raw fear. Of course. Gina and Cosmo had been attached to the Porcelli family since before Bruno was born. Not only did they lose Mario and Guendalina, they were no longer employed, and were getting on in years. If Bruno, no, *when* Bruno gets through this, she thought, he'll be consumed with running the family business. *Managing the household will fall solely on my shoulders.*

"Gina. Cosmo. Please forgive me for thinking of this tragedy only from my perspective. You are as much a part of this family as I am. Your relationship with Mamma and Papà was so very important to them. They loved you, and as long as I have anything to do with it, you will have a job, you will remain a part of our family. Bruno and I need you."

Madeleine threw open her arms, pulling them both in.

Gina seemed to gather strength from the embrace. As she dried her face with a scarf, she said, "I brought you a change of clothes. Come with me to the rest room. Cosmo, save our seats."

A quick laugh burst through their grief, a bright gift at the threshold of a new era.

Chapter 29

When Madeleine and Gina returned to the waiting room, Cosmo confirmed there was nothing new. The reports contained the same information, the same aerial clips of the explosion site and emergency workers sifting through rubble. The announcers kept repeating that the authorities had not ruled out the possibility of a bomb, when in fact the chief investigator stated simply that the cause of the explosion had not been determined.

"But you did have a call, Mrs. Madeleine. I wrote down the message."

"Thank you, Cosmo." She took the paper and squeezed his hand. "And please, both of you, call me Maddie. I'm not one for formality. Do you know where there's a phone?"

Gina's face lit. "Yes, I saw pay phones." She jumped up to show her.

The message was from Enzo, Mario's long-time friend. Madeleine returned the call. He had heard the news and was devastated. *Mario was like a brother*. He thanked God that Bruno was still alive and pledged his support to the family. She promised to update him after the surgery.

She made other calls and answered those that were incoming until she felt the conversations were scripted. Her father wept. Syrina promised to be there with her tomorrow. Simone from the gallery assured her they would keep things running and said not to worry. By the early hours of the morning, the phones had gone silent. It had been four hours with no word from the doctors. Gina and Cosmo snored softly beneath the blue glow of the television.

As Madeleine began to fade, she noticed a man in a suit and overcoat, standing in a dim corner, watching the room. He certainly didn't have the body language of hospital staff. She tried to ignore him, but he caught her eye and moved forward.

Her stomach tightened as he approached. He smiled gently, and she saw that the right side of his face was paralyzed. "Madeleine, I'm Dante. I was at your wedding."

"Dante. Yes, of course. Please forgive me. My eyes are bleary. You were with us at the world's smallest Italian wedding. We never really got a chance to talk." He smiled again, bashfully. She remembered she liked this man, and that he had seemed awkward or uncomfortable around her.

"I am sorry for your loss. It seems impossible that Mario and Guendalina are gone. We go back many years. He gave me my start in the business. There is nothing I wouldn't do for them."

"I am sorry for your loss as well, Dante. I've heard Mario and Bruno both say how much your trust means to them."

"Have you heard anything other than what the police are saying to the press?"

"No, I haven't thought of much beyond the hospital."

"With your permission, I'll reach out to some of my contacts on the investigation team to see what they can tell me."

"Thank you. I wouldn't know where to start."

"Ma'am, could I speak to you more privately?" She steeled herself as he led her away from Gina and Cosmo. "Forgive me, but I have to be blunt. How much do you know about the family business?"

She blinked. "I know it's one of the largest import-export, shipping, and delivery companies in Italy. Mario built it from nothing. I've been to the container port at the harbor. I see their trucks everywhere."

"Do you know what they import?" he said softly.

"Oh. I'll just say I understand some of the goods may not be suitable for inspection, if that's what you mean."

"Then what I'm about to say will make sense. Mario had a lot of rainy-day friends in high places, but just as many enemies. He kept everything in balance using favors and information. Now that he's gone, there's a vacuum." He looked at her pointedly. "Those friends and enemies alike are already plotting to fill that void."

"That is serious. Should I be concerned personally?"

"No question." She recoiled. "I am sorry Madeleine, but as long as Bruno is disabled, you are in charge. We have to assume both of your lives are in danger. The explosion may not have been an accident."

"Dante, you're scaring me. I have no idea what to do."

"The simplest answer, and the only thing that matters short term is, stay alive."

She tried to swallow.

"I've put the word on the street that Bruno has a few minor injuries and he'll be up and around in a few days. Meantime, it's business as usual. We'll keep that story going as long as we can. It's easy enough to believe. His strength is legendary, both physical and mental, and he's respected at all levels. Here is the number of Vincenzo Moretti, the family lawyer."

"I've heard his name."

"He will be back in the country this morning and will come here directly from the airport. He can help with funeral arrangements. You can trust Vincenzo. He knows all of Mario's personal and business wishes. Meanwhile, I will station a few men here to keep watch on both you and Bruno. They'll stay out of your way but will always be nearby. If one should approach you, he will say Dante sent me then touch his right ear. Anything you would say to me, you can say to them. Page me if you need anything. Use a pay phone. Enter your number then add 555 so I'll know it's you."

Her fingers trembled as she took the card with his number.

"Dante, my head is spinning. What about the press?"

"Vincenzo will be the spokesman for the family and the business. All inquiries go through him. He'll ask for privacy as Bruno grieves the loss of his beloved parents. You, stay off camera as much as possible, cover up when you're on the move. You're in mourning, people will understand. Remember, the story is that Bruno will be just fine. You must lie to everyone, including family and friends."

"I'm not sure I can do this."

"Yes, you can and will. You have no choice. This is all hitting you at once, but I know you better than you think, and I have complete confidence in your abilities. I'm going now. Update me with anything new on Bruno. And keep this in mind. You are now the most powerful woman in Northern Italy."

Chapter 30

"Gina, did you see the man I was just speaking with? I know he works for Bruno and Mario. Do you know him?"

"Yes, everyone knows Dante."

"What can you tell me?"

"He's a quiet one. I've never heard him speak in anger. Always the gentleman. We don't interact much, but I can tell he is looking out for us. Not just Mario and Guendalina, but everyone in the family."

"Well, he and I just had a very frank conversation. He acted like he was in charge. Seemed strange."

"I can tell you he was with Mario before Cosmo and I were hired. They were so close I thought they were father and son at first. Cosmo has been around him more than me."

Cosmo stared down at the floor.

"Tell Mrs. Madeleine what you know."

"I can tell you Dante was important to Mario and the business. He's a good man. I've spent more than twenty-five years driving them. They speak about business, but I never repeat what I hear."

"Cosmo, you listen to Mrs…er, to Maddie! Mario is gone and Maddie is his family. Anything you tell her may help find who killed Mario and Guendalina."

 Cosmo's face reddened as he took a steadying breath. "Of course, Gina, of course. Dante is French. It's rumored he was in the Resistance and that's where he learned his skills. How he ended up in Genoa I've never heard."

Cosmo scanned the nearly empty room to see if anyone might overhear. He whispered, "This I can tell you; it is common knowledge. Their world is all about reputation and street cred. But where people respect Mario, everyone fears Dante! When Mario made his move to clean up the streets, Dante was the ram, the tip of the knife that parted the waters. He did something so shocking, so brazen, that afterwards, he became a legend on the street. To the extent that if you ask today, Del Coltello *is* Dante!"

Madeleine said, "But what exactly is Del Coltello?"

Gina sat then, suddenly deflated. Madeleine followed, and Cosmo took the seat between them.

"After the second war, Mario saw the opportunity to advance his small shipping interest into something much more lucrative. He could supply, let's say 'hard to get' products, at wholesale rates, but he had no stomach for the retail side. His business plan was revolutionary. It was based on trust and cooperation, things unheard of in that world. But presenting a plan so radical was dangerous, so he recruited Dante from the docks to watch his back, and to develop the independent enforcement part of the plan. Together they laid the groundwork for The Collective."

Gina rose and asked who wanted coffee. It seemed she knew the rest of story and had no desire to hear it repeated.

"At a pre-Collective sit-down some thirty years ago now, Mario finally convinced most of the rival families that the potential profit numbers were real. His proposed cut was significant, but with the Porcelli family not involved at the street level, everyone stood to earn more. The key was an independent enforcement arm to prevent turf wars, and Dante would head that up, would be accountable only to The Collective, and would report daily to Mario. No negotiation on that. Any grievances were brought to The Collective and the decisions enforced by Dante."

Gina returned but remained standing, sipping from a paper cup.

"Less than a year after the system began, one family insisted Porcelli was taking too much profit. They tried to undermine The Collective and expand outside their boundaries. Within weeks, the don, capos, soldiers, associates…they had all disappeared, save for one. The don's son was found hanging upside down with the words 'Del Coltello' carved deep into the flesh of his chest."

Madeleine was silent for a long time. "I have seen the tattoo on Bruno's left inner wrist."

"Dante is the only person in The Collective without that ink. Some say it's because he can never be a made man since he's not Italian. Most say 'Dante non indossa il coltello, lo regala!'"

Madeleine closed her eyes and repeated. "Dante does not wear the knife, he gives it away."

Chapter 31

She heard her name and twisted in the chair. She had fallen asleep around three and now was instantly, rudely awake, with a stabbing pain in her shoulder from the seatback. Through the third-floor windows she could see the dawn sky. Cosmo stood in front of her, proudly holding a tray with four large cappuccinos and a box full of cornetti.

"Cosmo, you are a Godsend." She needed to eat before the phones started ringing. "Why the extra cups? Am I that hung over?"

He glanced through his lashes and tilted his head toward a sturdy man sitting with his back to the wall. When she met the stranger's gaze, he pulled his right ear lobe and bobbed his head slightly.

Half a cup of hot coffee later, her thoughts clicked into place. It had been six hours since she had seen Bruno on the gurney, six hours with no news. But regardless of his actual condition, her message to the world would be the same.

She took the first phone call. "Bruno is a lucky man. A couple of minor fractures and a few cuts and bruises. He deeply appreciates your love and support. Right now, he's dealing with the loss of his parents but looks forward to talking with you soon." The statement would be tailored to each caller, but the ruse would not change. The hardest call was to Syrina, reporting the "good news" and insisting that she not come to visit.

Just after the hospital's seven o'clock shift change, Gina took over the phones and Madeleine marched to the nurses' station. She should have heard something by now. "Yes, that's correct. Porcelli." She spelled the name.

"Just checking ma'am. I remember he was transferred last night from emergency to surgery on this floor...."

"This much I know. Where is he now, please?"

"Well.... Hmm, this is strange."

"What do you mean, strange?"

"His file is not in the system."

"I don't care about his file. Where is my husband? Is there another place to check? Where is Nurse Amato?"

"Hold on. Let me call admissions."

"Thanks." Madeleine finished her coffee and looked around. She reached over the counter and tossed the cup into a wastebasket next to the file cabinet.

"Okay, admissions say Bruno Porcelli was discharged about an hour ago. Signed out by his wife."

"That's not...." Madeleine heard a subtle cough and turned. Just behind her, a gentleman smiled and nodded. He was tall and slender, with the skin of someone who enjoyed the outdoors. He politely folded his hands in front of his expensive suit.

"Oh, sorry," she said to the nurse. "I must have just missed them. Thank you for your help."

"Madeleine, my name is Vincenzo Moretti. I'm the Porcelli family attorney. I am *your* attorney." He formally extended his right hand, placed his left hand on her shoulder, and led her toward the elevators. She noticed Dante then, unobtrusive at the far end of the corridor.

"I'm pleased to meet you, Mr. Moretti."

"Please call me Vincenzo. First, I apologize for what just happened. Bruno is safe. He's on the second floor under the name Adrian Rossi. As far as the world is concerned, Bruno has been discharged."

"I thought maybe something like that. I hope I didn't compromise security."

"No, the system will work in our favor, Mrs. *Rossi.*"

"Right, I understand."

"I'll be speaking with the press in about twenty minutes, confirming the deaths of Mario and Guendalina and basically repeat what you've been telling people all morning about Bruno. I will add that the family would like privacy during this difficult time. Meanwhile we are making arrangements for Adrian Rossi to be moved to a private hospital out of the area."

"Is Bruno healthy enough to be moved?"

"Adrian's doctors are not in full agreement on the timing, but we have a specially equipped air ambulance on standby. At any rate, they believe it will be less traumatic if he is moved before he regains consciousness."

"May I see him first?"

"Of course. We're headed there now."

Madeleine had been fooling herself. She froze at the doorway, unprepared for the sight of her husband lying unconscious, swollen, and bruised. His left arm was poised in the air like an artist's wooden mannequin, his only movement a rhythmic rise and fall as the ventilator filled and emptied his lungs. So many tubes and wires, so many machines, doing God knows what.

Dead or alive, she couldn't tell. That's what the system was for. The sounds were as disturbing as the images. Drag…step, step. Drag…step, step. Beep, beep, beep, everything eerily out of sync, like the indeterminacy of an avant-garde musical score. Somewhere, someone watched and listened. This one is alive, this one needs help, wheel this one to the basement. The whole thing reminded her of riding a horse for the first time—the animal in charge, her life tethered to him for the duration.

She felt the eyes of the private nurse follow her as she crossed the room. She wrapped her fingers around Bruno's swollen hand and pressed gently. The skin was cool and limp and unresponsive. She realized he had seemed more alive last night on the gurney. Tears flooded her eyes.

The nurse saw her distress and came to her side. "He's okay, Mrs. Rossi. It looks worse than it really is. His vitals are strong. He is sedated to assist in his recovery, allowing the body to focus on healing. Give it some time. It has been less than twelve hours."

"Thank you. I knew that on some level. It's just, I've never seen him as anything less than Superman."

"I sensed that. I can tell he's important to many people."

"You have no idea."

Madeleine chose the closest chair and allowed herself a few minutes to sit and process the situation. What scared her most was the strange knowledge that she was in charge but had no sense of where to go, much less how to get there. Task one, keeping everyone alive, was in progress, thank God and Dante.

Vincenzo had sketched the logic driving their short-term plan: the defensive advantage of this particular recovery room, the placement of Dante's men, the name change. The key was Bruno's forged discharge and the as-yet unspecified destination of Adrian Rossi. Until they uncovered the who and the why of the explosion, she understood they had no choice but assume the worst and unofficially disappear. Someone out there was putting just as much effort into this takeover as the family was into preventing it. How long had these vultures been watching? Was it someone they knew?

Before today, she had merely glimpsed the shoreline of Bruno's world. Now, she was in over her head.

Chapter 32

At Genoa Harbor, dozens of warehouses crowded beneath the imposing eye of the Genoa Lantern lighthouse. Inside one of the warehouses belonging to Porcelli Industriale, dozens of shipping containers were neatly stacked three high in row after row. Near the center of the building, inside one travel-worn forty-foot shipping container, Dante sat across from Vincenzo at a narrow conference table in Mario's old office.

The special container was well-appointed from front to back. In addition to the office, it had a lounge, kitchenette, toilet, conference room, bedroom, and emergency exit. With food, utilities, and communications, it was designed to be self-sufficient for sixty days—enough time and provisions for two people to be shipped to anywhere in the world.

Vincenzo scratched through a sentence on the notepad in front of him. "Outside of the usual "trust, loyalty, and prayers during this difficult time", is there anything you want to add to Bruno's letter?"

Dante shook his head. "This is your area. Maybe something about business as usual, keep your eyes and ears open?"

"I have that. What else?"

"Bruno is in control. People are watching so act natural."

"Got it. It'll go out first thing in the morning, appearing to come from Bruno. Speaking of, I got an update from his team at the hospital about an hour ago."

Dante leaned forward to rest on his elbows. "What's the latest?"

"The sugarless truth is that Bruno is not out of the woods. It could still go either way. The more time he spends unconscious the worse his chances. And if he comes through, there's no guarantee he'll be the Bruno we know."

"So be prepared for anything."

"Exactly."

"Have you run the scenarios?"

"It's my job." Vincenzo shot him a look. "Have you?"

"Of course. If Bruno can't take hold of the reins within a reasonable timeframe, we have some hard decisions to make. But the options are all down in black and white."

"What's your take on Madeleine?"

Dante said, "I told her she's the most powerful woman in Northern Italy. She's smart, but she's young and inexperienced. And I don't know how much she knows."

Vincenzo shrugged. "I doubt Bruno told her much of anything that's sensitive. But I agree she's smart. Maybe smarter than any of us. No doubt she could do harm if she were inclined."

"For now, we're making sure she's untouchable and unconnected to anything critical. But what if Bruno is out of the picture? What are the legal ramifications?"

"I drew their wills just after the wedding," Vincenzo said. "As his wife, Madeleine inherits all his personal assets, currently just short of nine thousand million lire. That doesn't include what Bruno inherits from Mario's fortune. If there were children, their share would be held in trust until they turn twenty-five. If she died before the children reached twenty-five, her will adds her assets to the children's trust."

"So, as it stands now, Madeleine is set."

"The family business is another thing entirely. It's a complex series of SpA's and SrL's with a few strategically placed LLC's to cloud the corporate veil. To be honest, it's so complicated it confuses me and I'm the one who set it up. With Mario and Guen gone, once we know Bruno's fate I'll review the structure and make changes. Not something I look forward to." He folded his arms. "Enough of that. What about the explosion?"

"That's the main reason I wanted to meet," Dante said. "What we know so far is that this was no simple gas leak. The energy, fuel, and oxidizer were consumed almost instantaneously, suggesting a high explosive device. The blast pattern indicates placement in the women's restroom utility closet, just behind Mario's booth. It appears to have been deliberate and professional, designed to kill as many people as possible. If Mario and Bruno were the targets, who the hell could have known they would be there together at that time? Madeleine said Bruno was planning to drive to Monaco directly after The Collective meeting. His stop at Mario's was a last-minute request from his father."

"The meeting with The Collective, I understand turned out positive after a rough start."

Dante said, "That's what I gather. I've spoken with almost everyone in attendance and the stories all line up. I know these guys. They're telling the truth. Most of them owe their fortunes to Mario and are sincerely grieving."

"Maybe the plan was set in motion earlier, by one of the members who expected a negative outcome from the meeting?"

Dante nodded. "Take it a step further. Say it was someone outside The Collective who heard the meeting was going to be a showdown, wanted to use the chaos to gain control of Mario's holdings."

"It would be the perfect deflection."

"Knowing we would suspect those in the meeting who sided against Mario." Dante clinched his fists.

"This widens the search a great deal. Could be anyone. A friend of a friend of a girlfriend, or something equally remote."

"Let's sleep on this, Vincenzo. I'll have a plan of action by tomorrow midday."

"Whatever it takes. Keep me posted. I'll keep you in the loop on Bruno."

"Mary Mother of Jesus, he has to recover. I'm too old to go through a bunch of power-ego crap."

"Watch your back, Dante."

"Always. By the way, I have a man on you."

"Thanks. I noticed, but ever so slightly." Vincenzo extended his hand.

Chapter 33

Much had happened in the days since the explosion. Adrian Rossi and his wife had been airlifted to an ultra-secure private hospital somewhere in the mountains. Madeleine's best guess was Switzerland, but no one would confirm or deny. Officially, the family was in mourning, waiting for the bodies of Mario and Guendalina to be released. Funeral arrangements were pending.

Madeleine had freedom to roam the interior perimeter of the large octagon-shaped structure with white walls, patterned carpet, and burgundy-colored pots sprouting palms and rubber plants. A full-service hospital occupied the center of the building. This core was ringed with private ICU units; a corresponding guest suite joined each ICU. The suites had a full kitchen, two bedrooms with ensuite baths, and a comfortable gathering room. She had a direct entrance to Bruno's room through an airlock. An eight-foot atrium brought the outside into the patient's room. Meals were room service only from a twenty-four-hour gourmet kitchen. One of Dante's men used the second bedroom as a base to provide around-the-clock protection for Mr. and Mrs. Rossi.

The hospital core, off limits to the guests, was cutting edge. The top-tier general staff was augmented by a team of specialists specific to their patient's needs. A member of the medical team was in Bruno's room at all times, and Madeleine's suite had a direct phone line to the room as well as the central ICU station. Bruno's attending physician checked his status hourly and was available for questions upon request.

Vincenzo said this hospital was among the world's best, and she had no doubt that was true. It redefined the term private care facility. She had access to unlimited in room movies, a recreation center, and spa. She could not imagine the cost; it was cash only and no records existed. Vincenzo let it slip (if attorneys ever let anything just slip) that Mario had been one of the hospital's founders, so Bruno had a preferred rate.

The compound itself was surrounded by two sections of unscalable fence topped with razor wire, which was patrolled by armed guards and monitored by cameras day and night. Access was limited to a helipad out of earshot to the north and two roads, east and west, gated and secured on each end. Visitors had to be approved in advance and confirmed visually via closed circuit camera from the numbered suite at the time of arrival. Every visitor's car was detained inside a concrete and chain link enclosure for the duration of the visit. They were then scanned and strip-searched before being escorted to the suite. Vincenzo didn't visit often, preferring to give and receive updates on a secure line.

The security was comforting, the high level of care was encouraging, but Madeleine's anxiety never subsided—after nearly two weeks, Bruno had regained consciousness only three times. And each time, her explanations frightened and confused him, as if his mind were a blank slate.

"Bruno, you're in hospital. There was an accident. Everything will be alright. You have the best doctors in the entire world." In a few seconds he would be back asleep.

"You'll be as good as new, very, very soon." *From my lips to God's ears.*

Madeleine was halfway through her nine o'clock swim in the rec center when she was summoned to Bruno's room: a calm voice from the metal wall speakers announced *number eight, code blue.*

The pool and the air were both warm, but she continued to shiver even after toweling off. The page, designed to have no inflection, could mean Bruno was holding bedside court, or that he was dead, or anything in between.

An escort met her at the door with a thick cotton bathing robe and hurried her through a shortcut to her suite. She pulled the hood over her wet hair before stepping through the airlock into Bruno's air-conditioned room. Seconds later, she burst into tears. Bruno was wide-awake and sitting halfway up in his hospital bed. He radiated the smile that he reserved for her alone and mouthed her name. Through a tangle of hoses and wires, she wrapped herself around as much of him as she could and then gently kissed his forehead. "I've missed you so much, my Orsone."

Bruno tried to speak but it was impossible with a tube snaking from his lips to his lungs. Anger flared across his face.

"We'll take care of that right away, Mr. Rossi. Nurse, remove his ET and then let's give them time alone."

Bruno looked at Madeleine with a confused look. "Rossi?" he mouthed.

She pressed an index finger to her lips.

The nurse inched out the tube. "You may experience a bit of discomfort at first."

Bruno gagged and coughed. "Water." His voice was unrecognizable.

"Here are some ice chips for now. We'll be in the next room should you need anything more."

"Thank you, nurse."

"Maddie, what the hell?"

"Shh. I'll explain everything in a moment." Or not everything, she thought.

When they were finally alone, he said, "Where the fuck am I? Why won't anyone tell me what happened?" Trying to shout but getting no more than as raspy whisper increased his fury.

"We are in a secluded, ultra-secure private hospital somewhere in the mountains. Switzerland, if I had to guess. You had an accident."

"The last thing I remember is blasting out Springsteen, pulling g's coming down the hill. Oh my god, is the Dino okay? How much damage is there?"

"The Dino will be fine. Just a few dents."

"You may have to tell me this all over again. My brain feels like mud."

"I'm not surprised. You could well have died."

Bruno seemed to notice his body for the first time. He surveyed his left arm, then squinted at his legs as if they belonged to someone else. "I'm injured."

"Yes, sweetheart. You have a couple of fractures, a few internal issues. You have a bad concussion. But it's all going to heal. You're really very lucky."

"Not the kind of luck I like. Why did they call me Rossi?"

"That's Vincenzo's doing. In here, you are Adrian Rossi. He's concerned for your safety."

"I don't understand. Why am I at risk because of a traffic accident? Did I run over the sovereign prince of Monaco or something?"

"Bruno, it wasn't a traffic accident. It was…" She couldn't form the words.

"Help me out here," he snapped. "There was no crash, but the Dino has a couple of dents, and I've got more tubes and wires than a space capsule, in a private ICU in nowhere Switzerland…. How long have I been here?"

"Oh, only a few days." Not exactly a lie.

His expression went from angry to resigned. "Okay, from the beginning and don't hold anything back."

She took a deep breath and started with the newscast at the gallery after party. She told him everything, the simple truth as she knew it.

He asked her to repeat sections, shaking his head, saying it sounded like a bad Hollywood movie. She watched the curtain of this new reality slowly eclipse his courage. He closed his eyes. Tears rolled down his face as he drifted into a motionless sleep.

She dropped her Superwoman act, buried her face in the blanket, and sobbed.

Chapter 34

Madeleine thrashed against a heaviness that dragged her into cold and bottomless black water. Like quicksand, the more she struggled the faster she sank. Bubbles from her silent screams formed faces that swirled and laughed around her.

"Signora Rossi, Signora Rossi?"

She gasped for air as the dream parted. "What is it? Is he…"

"He is fine. You were having a nightmare." The nurse handed her a cup of coffee.

"Oh, I was. Thank you."

The night had been long and exhausting. She had tossed and dozed under a wool blanket in the leather recliner next to his hospital bed for what seemed like the hundredth day. Bruno, still fully dosed, had scarcely moved all night.

His support team planned to begin assessment tests today. She would not be allowed to observe; accuracy of the results depended on them having his total attention.

"Signora. We're about to get him started. If you want a few minutes to visit, now would be a good time."

"May I wake him? I like to be the first thing he sees in the morning."

"Certainly. We'll be back soon."

"Bruno. She whispered in his ear. "Bruno…it's time to wake up, my Orsone."

Bruno smiled like he was returning to wonderland. He focused his eyes and said, "Who are you?"

Madeleine's face slumped. "I'm your—"

"You're Maddie, my lady. I got ya."

His sense of humor! Madeleine was thrilled and punched him lightly. "You asshole. I'm this close to falling apart. I've been so worried about you."

"I'm sorry, sweetheart. Where am I? What happened? I feel like I've been hit by a bull."

She held his gaze long enough to realize he wasn't joking. "You're in hospital. There was an accident but you're going to be okay. We can talk about the details later. Right now, they need to run some tests and figure out your best treatment options. It'll take a few hours. We can eat when you're done."

He glanced around. "Something I can chew, please."

"What are you hungry for? A steak, medium rare? Lobster? Lasagna?"

"Mm, I'm thinking a nice salad with finely chopped lettuce and fresh veggies, extra virgin olive oil and red wine vinegar on the side. Lots of parmesan."

She waited another beat; again, he wasn't joking. "Oh, okay. Sure. I'll check with the dietitian." Madeleine had never seen Bruno turn down a steak, much less actually request a salad. Was his stomach telling him something?

The door to the central core swished open. "Good morning. How is everyone today?"

"Not so good, Doc. Feeling the pain this morning."

"Well, believe it or not, that's a positive sign. Mrs. Rossi, we should have today's tests completed by early afternoon. Then we'll share our thoughts and answer your questions."

"Of course, doctor." She squeezed Bruno's hand and kissed his forehead. "I'll see you soon, my love."

Chapter 35

The evaluation took much longer than expected. At precisely seventeen-hundred hours UTC, Madeleine was paged and then escorted to the Post Evaluation Patient Debriefing Room, or PEP-DR. Located beyond the recreation center, in the hospital's "no-man zone", the room was state of the art and reserved for evaluations and consultations only.

As she followed the quiet escort, the powerful images that had been imprinted for the past two weeks filled her thoughts: the broken, bruised, and swollen body of her husband, the tubes and machines, and the ceaseless, repetitious sounds as his body was sustained by a ventilator. Thirteen breaths to the minute. She wasn't superstitious, but why not twelve? Why not fourteen? She prayed the "PEP" talk would be as positive as it sounded.

Just outside the door, Madeleine imagined stepping into an uncomfortable parent/teacher conference, Bruno's artwork pinned to the corkboard, his behavior being discussed. Instead, she found herself at ease the moment the doors opened. The room was graced with soothing Fibonacci-based artwork, and tasteful elements of feng shui design cloaked the impersonal machines. The X-ray and CAT scan viewers, overhead projectors and Advent Videobeam were in balance with an offset King Arthur conference table. The acoustics of the room and the sound of the modest waterfall harmonized with soft lines, indirect lighting, and muted colors.

Bruno's full medical team, dressed in white lab coats and black slacks, stood until she settled into the only empty chair. Pen and paper, water, and a box of tissues were within her reach. The team leader, Dr. Hulsey, remained standing and wasted no time. "Mrs. Rossi, thank you for meeting with us. We apologize for the delay as we waited on a few key test results. The information we'll share is up to the minute."

"I understand, thank you. Your team, the systems here, they're all impeccable."

"Thank you. We prefer for the patient to be included in this discussion, but it would likely cause him confusion at this point, until his short-term memory improves. So, let's start with the big picture. Your husband is very lucky to be alive. He is in excellent physical condition, and apparently was in the best possible location in a nearly impossible situation. Two steps in either direction and we wouldn't be here today. The bottom line, we expect him to lead a long and reasonably healthy life."

Madeleine burst into tears and expelled the breath she'd been holding since Hulsey said "the big picture". "Grazie Dio. When can I take him home?"

"We'll get to that. Why don't you take a moment?"

She snatched three tissues and made good use of them. After a sip of water, she said, "Thank you. Please continue."

"Now that you know how the story ends, let's start at the beginning and talk about what you can expect."

"Good." She sniffed loudly and forced a smile.

Hulsey said, "And please feel free to interrupt at any time. Dr. Mezzetta will lead us off."

A mid-fifties woman with short black hair and bold-framed glasses stood. "Percussive injuries can—"

"Explosions?" Madeleine asked.

"Yes, explosions can injure the human body in four ways. Primary injury is caused by the pressure wave moving through the body. In Mr. Rossi's case the eardrums and left testicle were ruptured. He was concussed and we found lesions on the frontal lobe. Also fractures to the vertebrae from T-12 through L3, a compound fracture to the left tibia, a shattered left patella, broken left ulna and most of the bones in his left wrist."

"The secondary injuries result from debris being driven by the blast wind. From what your investigator shared with us, Mr. Rossi was standing by a fortified walk-in freezer on the opposite side of the explosion. His secondary injuries were limited to the soft tissue: one deep laceration and many superficial cuts where the skin was exposed. There were corneal abrasions to both eyes as well."

"Tertiary blast injuries are caused when a structure collapses on the person or the person is propelled and impacts an object. Both occurred, but other than three broken ribs on the right it seems only to have exacerbated the primary injuries. That said, the structural collapse delayed rescue and exposed him to smoke, fumes and dust that caused quaternary injuries to his lungs and eyes."

"Just a moment, I'm a bit overwhelmed." Madeleine rubbed her face and eyes with her palms.

"Take your time, Mrs. Rossi," Hulsey said. "We think it's important that you understand his condition before we talk about what to expect going forward."

"You mean before you lower my expectations?"

"Not necessarily, just a realistic picture of what's possible."

"Fair enough. Give it to me straight."

"Okay then. Your husband's bones will heal. His kneecap has been replaced and he has a metal plate in his wrist that may cause some discomfort from time to time. We removed one testicle and are monitoring the other which was damaged and still swollen."

"Does that mean we can't have children?"

"At this point, we can't say. The human body can be quite resilient, so with time—"

"Is that all? Please tell me that's all."

"I'm afraid there's more. Dr. Micca, with your permission I'll summarize. The back is a concern. He has extensive disc damage in addition to the fracture. We've done everything possible but again, only time will tell. Back injuries are different for everyone. He could be pain free and out on the golf course by the end of the year or he could have chronic pain the rest of his life."

"So, wait and see."

"Yes, wait and see. I know this is a lot to take in. But there is one more issue. Dr. Klein." He nodded to a no-nonsense woman who looked no more than twenty-five. She clicked a remote and pointed to the overhead screen.

"The head trauma is the most concerning issue we face, and the prognosis is the most difficult to predict. The concussion is clearing nicely, but the frontal lobe lesions he sustained could result in a number of complications. As we've seen, short-term memory loss is presenting. It's improving and that's good news. But this part of the brain is responsible for far more than memory. It also controls intelligence, concentration, temperament, and personality. Plus, voluntary movement, language, and behavioral and intellectual functions. Although we are seeing no evidence of change in those areas now, that sometimes progresses over time. Problems may come and go or may never appear."

Madeleine cleared her throat. "This morning, I asked if he wanted a steak for dinner, he said he'd like a chopped salad. Bru—, um, my husband would never say that." Her eyes brimmed.

"Thank you for reporting that. It could be an indicator. Please continue to update us on your observations. You know him better than anyone."

All eyes turned to Dr. Hulsey. "That's all we have at this time. We'd like to hear your questions, concerns, thoughts…"

"So, worst case, we can't have children, the man I love will have constant back pain, and my carnivore of a husband will become a vegetarian?" She tried to laugh, but there was no humor.

"Or he could be back to his old self in six months. As far as when might you take him home, it depends on the rudimentary physical therapy we'll begin here, how he responds to that, and how his injuries continue to mend. But my best guess is seven to ten days."

"Thank you. Thank you all for putting my husband back together."

"You are most welcome. Thank you for the opportunity to work with you. Anyone have more to add? If not, we have the room for another thirty minutes, Mrs. Rossi, if you wish to relax or just collect your thoughts. Refreshments are in the cabinet behind you."

The team stood and made their way toward the door. Madeleine picked up the pen and paper, already lost in thought.

Chapter 36

Dante rose from the conference table and extended his hand. "Vincenzo. Thanks for meeting me on such short notice."

"Not a problem. A lot's changed in two weeks."

The Porcelli family lawyer had only one client, so his priorities were seldom complicated.

"Join me?" Dante held up his coffee cup.

"It's a bit late in the day for me."

"My days and nights are all running together lately." He added two mounds of sugar to the cup and stirred. "You said you have an update on Bruno?"

"Yes. The good news from Madeleine is that he will be released in a week or so. He's alert, in reasonably good spirits."

Dante raised an eyebrow. "I assume there is a 'but'?"

"His head injury. He has memory problems, keeps asking the same questions over and over."

"What kind of questions? Did she say?"

Vincenzo pushed back from the table. "Like why he's in hospital. He thinks it was a car crash. The worst part? He keeps asking about his mom and dad."

"Scat. What have they told him?"

"The truth. But then he forgets or blocks it. Seeing him react to the news of their death, time after time, it's really getting to her."

Dante squeezed the chair arms. "I hate that, for both of them. What do the doctors recommend?"

"Basically, it's kick that ball down the pitch and hope his short-term memory improves."

"This could be a nightmare."

"No shit." Vincenzo took a deep breath. "Okay, anything new on the investigation?"

Dante's eyes brightened. "Yes, I have more on the blast itself. I brought in an old buddy from the resistance. He's a munitions expert, so good we called him Master Blaster. After the war, he continued in The Fire Arts, as he calls them, working both sides of the shadows. Then retired to the Côte d'Azur a few years back."

Vincenzo shook his head. "Well deserved, I'd say. That line of work is a whole other mindset."

"It is. And survival with your mind and other parts intact is tantamount to several advanced degrees."

"Was he allowed to walk the site?"

"Yeah, he spent the better part of an afternoon there collecting samples, taking measurements and photographs."

"He agrees with what the authorities concluded?"

"Only in part. His unique skills took him on a deeper dive. He agrees it was high explosives, but he found traces that are consistent with military grade munitions, World War II vintage. That means it was either from a random unexploded ordnance, or something sold on the black market."

Vincenzo looked confused. "The blast came from the utility closet area. If it had been there since the war, someone would have noticed it."

Dante refilled his cup. "That's what I thought, but the original building plans show there was a coal furnace just under that closet. The furnace was removed at some point and the space converted to a storage cellar. During the war, they might have laid a false floor over the hatch."

"To hide resistance fighters or Jews?"

"Correct. When Mario renovated for the restaurant, I guess they never knew the space was there."

"Does this shed any light on how and why Mario's exploded?"

"My buddy thinks there are two possibilities. One, someone knew of the hidden root cellar, planted the vintage explosive, and detonated it remotely. Or two, the unexploded ordnance sat deteriorating in the root cellar since the 1940's. Above it in the utility closet was a gas-fired water heater. What if a slow gas leak filled the closet until the pilot flame ignited it? The gas explosion in the closet detonates the ordnance in the cellar below. Based on the physical evidence, he's leaning toward that second scenario."

"Jesus, Dante! That seems almost impossible odds."

"It's easier to believe it was a professional hit job, I agree. So, who would do this and how? I even dug through the rubble again, hoping we'd missed something that would indicate a hit."

"Surely at least one of the staff would have been in on it," Vincenzo reasoned. "It was a weekend, all hands on deck."

"Except everyone on the payroll was killed or severely injured. They were a loyal bunch. No turnovers in the last eighteen months. They loved Mario. But the other possibility—"

"Outside services?" Vincenzo guessed.

"Like a plumber servicing the water heater."

"Or the gas company. An electrician. Food delivery."

"Could be, but if it were me," Dante said, "I'd come in the kitchen door during the peak, when everyone was focused on food prep, shout 'Building Inspector, just routine', flash some credentials."

"But how would you walk the explosives past them unnoticed?"

"I wouldn't. I'd go in—"

"Through the old coal chute!" Vincenzo said.

"It is possible. The opening was cut into the foundation and still had the original metal cover. You squeeze through the chute, place the ordnance, and then create a gas leak."

"Why go to the trouble with the gas?"

"To make it look like an accident, and to increase the explosive yield."

"Bottom line, it could have been a hit," Vincenzo reasoned.

"Yes, but the thing is, I've looked under stones all across Europe and found nothing. Not a hint, not a whisper. Trust me, no one's that good. It's just not the way things go in this business. There's always a trail, and if I can't find one, there's only one conclusion. It was an accident." Dante leaned back. "Now the only question is, if we know it was an accident while everyone believes it was intentional, how do we work it to our advantage?"

"I understand now why you wanted to talk."

"We give vague or ambiguous answers. As long as you and I are in sync, we let The Collective and Bruno believe what they will."

Chapter 37

Three weeks ago, a devastating explosion changed the lives of everyone associated with the Porcelli family. Today, Bruno would be discharged from the hospital. Once out of the coma, he had rebounded quickly. His appetite slowly returned, although his tastes were different now; Madeleine could never predict his next craving.

The physical therapist had told her that Mr. Rossi was limited in what he could attempt, but he was still wearing her out. She'd noticed it as well, a side of Bruno she had never seen. He was single-mindedly obsessed with getting his physical abilities back, fighting through the pain, driving himself to accomplish each goal until exhaustion overwhelmed him. He despised the wheelchair; he cursed the plaster casts and other restrictions. If he was awake, he was in pain and therefore angry. They deemed him ready for release sooner than anyone had expected.

His discharge from the private hospital occurred near midnight. Dr. Hulsey himself wheeled Bruno to the elevator. On the helipad, they boarded a custom air ambulance. The vehicle was equipped like a small emergency room, and Hulsey monitored his vitals, insisting that his responsibility continued until his patient safely returned to the ground.

Dante and his team were waiting at the Crocefieschi airfield northeast of Genoa. On radio signal, infrared lights outlined the covert landing zone and the pilot brought the three-ton machine to a feather-soft landing. Once clear, Bruno shook his doctor's hand and yelled a thank you over the noise. It was a quick goodbye. The rotors never stopped turning and once the sound dissolved into the distance, Dante whispered in Bruno's ear. He nodded slightly before being wheeled into the nondescript black van waiting between two escort cars.

The caravan pulled into the drive at Villa Gazza, Mario and Guen's former home, Bruno and Madeleine's new home. Gina and Cosmo had overseen the transition, preparing everything in anticipation of Bruno's release and his need for a more accommodating space. Villa Gazza had better wheelchair access, better views, more room.

Bruno's sense was that he had survived the worst of it, but the real ordeal, the test of his emotional strength, would come two days later at his parents' funeral.

****

La cattedrale di san Lorenzo—Genoa's Metropolitan Cathedral of Saint Lawrence—was situated a few blocks from the Port of Genoa, painfully close to the rubble that was once Mario's restaurant. The original medieval construction, first consecrated in 1118, now revealed centuries of modifications with interwoven Romanesque, Gothic, and Renaissance architectural influences.

Inside its walls, the remains of Mario and his wife, Guendalina, rested side by side in matching hand-carved burl walnut caskets beneath the cathedral's massive dome. Horribly disrupted by the blast, only fragments of their bones, teeth, scalp, and skin had been recovered. The mortuary staff knew that the permanently sealed coffins held additional weight to augment the lack of identifiable remains. The delay in conducting the Porcelli funeral, well beyond the customary five-to-ten-day window, had been explained as necessary due to the recovery effort and the ongoing investigation. Dante, Vincenzo, and Madeleine knew the timing had been dictated by Bruno's discharge from the hospital.

The doors of the cathedral remained closed until fifteen minutes before the scheduled three o'clock service. Family and close friends were cued to enter first, followed by the hoi polloi who were there simply for the spectacle, knowing the deceased by reputation only. As the doors opened, the chaotic inrush of the capacity crowd, as anticipated, kept attention away from the man dressed in black and seated in the front row.

The Porcelli's had been respected members of both their church and their community. Mario was recognized by the archbishop as the man who quietly shared his wealth in the name of San Lorenzo, patron saint of the cathedral, patron saint of cooks. To the public, he was known as the man behind the famous restaurant and whose name was emblazoned on an impressive fleet of delivery vehicles. He was respected as the community leader who generously underwrote local causes. His philanthropic reputation extended well beyond Genoa, throughout Northern Italy, and generally wherever his business interests required expansion or goodwill.

Before his father's death, few had given much thought to Bruno beyond the simple fact that he was Mario's son. Now he was under a microscope, his health uppermost in the minds of many in attendance. In the reserved sections near the front of the nave, politicians and business leaders sat with the uncomfortable knowledge that Mario's money lined their pockets, just as they had been, comfortably or not, nestled in his. Each contemplated who knew of their corrupt involvement with the family and worried whether the relationship would continue.

Chief among the business leaders, and most concerned with the future, were the heads of each family in The Collective. Necks craned to catch a glimpse of, to evaluate the fitness of, the new head of the Porcelli family. Few dared to betray their thoughts. Those who did spoke in hushed tones behind cupped hands, none of which went undetected: above them all, in the rear balcony, Dante watched from the shadows.

In the minutes before all were settled in their seats, a few mourners ventured to the front row to pay their respects to the son. They saw little more than Bruno's lowered head and dark glasses. His hands were folded under the prayer shawl covering his lap. Madeleine, sitting to his right, economically deflected their questions and accepted their words of condolence.

The solemn service began quietly. The list of eulogizers included only two family members and one friend. All spoke briefly, but from the heart, about their love of the deceased. When Madeleine's father, Antonio, spoke, his were the only words she would remember. She had never known that he fought alongside Mario on the front lines in Northern Italy.

"The year was nineteen-eighteen. We were both little more than boys, together at the second battle of the Marne. We were among the few who made it out of the trenches alive. Mario was injured but fought his way back to health. So many of our friends did not see the end of the war, and we vowed to never take life for granted. Although we disagreed on many topics, there was no one I would rather have beside me in a battle than Mario. I will miss you. You were my friend, my brother in spirit."

Throughout the cathedral, a flurry of tissues dabbed at eyes and cheeks as the archbishop took his place in the pulpit. He continued the somber tone set by the eulogizers, and at the family's request conducted the mass with unusual efficiency. Bruno would remember nothing of the service, unable to focus beyond the timing of his next prescription opiate dose. When the final benediction began, a large man rose from the end of the front row and wheeled Bruno down the left transept and outside. Only a few noticed; they were the few with unbowed heads and undisclosed intentions.

Chapter 38

Dante could hear raised voices in the next room.

"He will never be the leader his father was."

"If distribution slips for even a week, we suffer unrecoverable losses."

"He's a playboy with only one thing on his mind."

"They've been ripping us off ever since—"

"Gentlemen!" Don Pillarella, the second most powerful member of The Collective, interrupted. "Let's keep this professional. Is there a motion for debate on new distribution management—"

Dante opened the door. Pillarella stopped, and the chin of every attendee tucked like a turtle retracting into its shell. Suddenly an extra seat was available at the table. The bulge under Dante's jacket, a violation of the no-weapons policy, was not ignored but neither was it mentioned.

"Don't let me interrupt. I believe Don Pillarella was about to tell you why his family should take over distribution. Please continue."

He let a full minute pass as grown men acted like they'd been caught playing with themselves. No one made eye contact.

"Gentlemen, did you think I wouldn't hear about your meeting?"

This time he waited only a few seconds.

"First let me remind you, we speak here with impunity. Nothing leaves this room, and nothing you say during a meeting of The Collective will be used against you. Agreed?"

Dante waited until every member had met his gaze and nodded. "The agreement each of you swore an oath to clearly states that the Porcelli family shall control wholesale and distribution and will not be involved with retail in any way. My singular role is to protect and defend The Collective from enemies both outside and inside the circle. To that end, I worked closely with Mario, but I do not work for the Porcelli family.

"And despite the recent devastating events, they continue to honor their obligations. Does anyone have issues with allotment? Is quality good? Deliveries on time? Are you making a profit? Speak up."

One brave soul found his voice. "Bruno is too new to be managing wholesale."

"In other words, you have no issues other than your own fear. Fear of the unknown."

"There is simply too much at stake," he said.

"So, again. Fear. Bruno is not Mario. But he was born into Del Coltello. Mario did not hide from his own mortality, which is why Bruno has spent years working toward this transition. Under his father's tutelage, he has worked every job from dock to distribution. He understands the business as a whole and can make informed decisions. He even worked with me and passed every test I threw at him. But training and holding the reins are different things. You must give him time."

"We need a leader who is visible."

"The man was at ground zero in an explosion that killed thirty people. He has shown strength and determination in fighting his way back. He's still fighting. Give him a chance."

One by one, the members shifted the weight off their forearms and leaned back.

"Gentlemen, the bottom line is this," Dante said. "Until you can present evidence that the Porcelli family is not honoring their agreement, I strongly suggest you refrain from any takeover attempts. If there are documented issues with the way the business is being handled, then this is the forum to discuss them. If that day comes, I'll protect The Collective and deal with issues accordingly. Is there anything more I can add?"

"Do you know who's responsible for killing Mario?"

Dante relaxed a bit. "Police inquiries are ongoing, but our own investigation is complete. We are taking aggressive action to make sure something like this never happens again. Keep your eye on the news during the next few weeks and read between the lines. That's all I have to say."

The atmosphere, while not light, was lifting. Dante rose and thanked the leadership for considering his words, wished them a profitable week, and strode out the door.

Chapter 39

Had it been two months since the funeral, or three? She'd lost track of time, but in the grand scheme a few weeks meant nothing. And she had to admit that her self-imposed exile in the villa had been rewarding—responding to Bruno's every whim, offering moral support as he forced himself through the twice daily therapy sessions. She had been needed, if not always appreciated.

She watched as Bruno pushed himself relentlessly, obsessed with achieving a quick recovery. He repeated the exercises on his own when the therapist left. His rate of improvement exceeded all expectations, but the cost was high; every step toward better strength and balance resulted in more pain. His prescribed opiates were insufficient, but the physician warned that a higher dosage would be toxic. His moods were erratic, his patience was non-existent. He was hurtful to the staff, reducing many to tears, while others took long walks to cool off, praying he would soon be back to his old self. Worst of all, he either ignored or barked at Madeleine. Every encounter felt like Russian roulette with only one empty chamber.

She had been by his side twenty-four hours a day, every day, responding to every request, remaining stoic during the ill moods. She ached to confide in Syrina, her only trusted confidant, but hesitated to give her sister the satisfaction of admitting any fault with Bruno. With the tension and anxiety locked inside, she developed self-doubts. Could all this somehow be her fault?

When Bruno napped, Madeleine's daydreams replayed the wonderful times they had spent together. So many of those moments had been on their yacht, she thought perhaps his mood, both of their moods, would improve with a change of scene. She proposed a long afternoon on the water, just the two of them, and he agreed.

They started with lunch at the harbor, which was his first trip outside of the villa. He managed the fifty meters from the parking lot to the trattoria with the aid of his walker. He didn't complain as they took their seats facing the picturesque harbor, but she ached in sympathy seeing the suppressed pain on his face. After a lunch of oysters and one glass of pilsner each, they walked to *The Madeleine's* berth. Two hundred meters.

He didn't argue when she suggested piloting the yacht herself. But once they were beyond the breakwater, he insisted on taking the helm. Within minutes she saw that he could not tolerate standing and balancing against the yaw and pitch of the boat. He cursed as he surrendered the wheel and said he was done for the day. By the time they docked, he was screaming at her, at the weather, at the dock boy. She understood and sympathized; the outbursts were solely the product of pain and frustration. His expectations were simply too high.

Chapter 40

He despised himself for the way he treated Madeleine on the yacht that afternoon. She was a saint. Patient, supportive, never responding in anger to his outbursts. She said his apologies were unnecessary. That fact made him love her more than ever and curse himself for not showing it. But how do you act like a gentleman when every physical movement—twist, bend, sit, stand—is a potential blasting cap in your lumbar igniting a volcanic eruption in your brain?

It was not all bad. After each dose of the prescription painkillers, a one-hour window opened through which he was lucid enough to focus on work. He could spend time each morning and each afternoon on the phone reinforcing Dante's message that everything was under control, that Bruno was in charge but still grieving. He talked with his legitimate business contacts as well as members of The Collective, instilling confidence in his leadership. It was a start, but an hour or two per day behind closed doors would only go so far. He had to get back out there, be seen, shake hands, buy drinks, none of which was possible until he was back to normal. It was a goal that seemed further away each morning when he opened his eyes.

He could see the price Madeleine paid as well. He encouraged her to return to the gallery for a few days. She needed the break, and her business no doubt needed her presence. When she consented to go, the realization that she would be gone forced him to face reality. Could he cope without her moral support?

Yes, he had to stop relying on others for assistance. He would test himself.

The day before she was to leave for Monaco, he wheeled into his office and locked the door. In the middle of the room, he could hear the therapist's mantra in his head. Right foot back, left foot forward, squeeze armrests, bend at waist, then rise slowly. Yes! He was standing, alone, stable. He shoved the wheelchair away. No choice now but to walk. Step one. His reconstructed left leg accepted his weight but began to shake. A burn notice shot down his spine as he brought his right foot off the floor. The left knee buckled, and he crumpled in agony. He refused to cry out and instead dragged himself to the antique mahogany desk. Pulling out the side drawers for support, he managed to work his way into the desk chair.

By doing everything the experts prescribed, he had regained the physical strength to navigate the world, but what use was strength when debilitating pain hijacked every effort?

That night, obsessed with this ruthless reality, sleep refused to come. He would never be what he once had been. Pain was a permanent part of him now, and it was stronger than he was. For the first time in his life, he admitted defeat. He was weak, worthless, less than the man Madeleine needed him to be. Worst of all, he would never live up to his dead father's expectations. Without full recovery, could he go on living? A wall of black depression, part and parcel of personal loss, crushed him.

He suffered through the night, through one short spurt of fitful sleep after another. Nightmares soaked through the sheets and left him exhausted.

As Madeleine kissed him goodbye the next morning, he opened his eyes but did not respond. She was leaving for Monaco, the gallery, she loved him, she would call him tonight.

He fell back asleep. The dream that visited him then was brief, but it would change everything.

She appeared as a heavenly spirit. Cool, luminous white, and airy. Her fingers like a butterfly touched his heart. He awoke slowly and found he was at peace, but suddenly sat up. The spirit had told him something. She had let him understand a solution existed, something just beyond his recollection. He closed his eyes and listened to his breath flow in and out. Finally relaxed, the answer appeared and his eyes flashed open: the solution was in his liquor cabinet in the den.

The experts had warned him that alcohol and opiates could not be mixed, but the mere thought that a solution might exist was enough to lift his mood. He rose and took his pain meds, then showered, shaved, and ate breakfast, his first customary morning routine in days. But by late afternoon, when the pain inevitably returned, he cursed the experts.

A divine spirit's counsel was worth at least a shot. A shot! He laughed.

In fact, it only took a single shot on top of two prescription pills to almost eliminate the pain. One more, and he felt normal. He marveled at the clarity of his mind and the simple pleasure of not feeling angry! He swallowed a third shot. As those blessed molecules swept through his veins, Madeleine phoned.

She reported that her first day back in the gallery had been fine, but she was worried about him. He told her there was nothing to worry about! He had learned how to cope with his pain. He felt like a different person. No, he felt like himself, only better. He missed her terribly but understood she needed the time for herself. She should stay in Monaco as planned. She agreed to call him a bit earlier tomorrow.

As he hung up and surveyed his den, a wave of isolation, the hollow of Madeleine's absence, swept over him. He reached for his shot glass and saw himself as if from above. The illusion of being back to normal crumbled. He had gone from being a man with everything to a weakling who couldn't function without mixing pills and booze. He swept the glass and the bottle from the desk and fell asleep in the chair.

When he awoke it was after midnight. As he tried to stand, the pain from the awkward position he'd slept in seemed to penetrate his entire being. He buried his head in his arms on the desk and wept. The risk—the price he would have to pay to be pain free—was worth it. Give the devil his due, or as the wise men say, enlightenment is a destructive process. He hadn't asked for his injuries.

Minutes later, after two pills and a simple jigger of vodka, he again felt so, so good, capable of anything.

So be it.

****

Madeleine's mood soared when she saw Simone waiting for her at the train station in Monaco and talked non-stop on the drive to the gallery. The team had strung a 'welcome back' banner across the entrance. Every face lit with joy as she walked through the doors. After hugs and tears all around, a big cup of coffee appeared in her hand, and she made her way to her private office. Fresh cut flowers adorned her desk and she thought: *home*! Then just as suddenly she felt guilty and questioned whether she belonged there at all.

She quietly closed the door, plopped into the executive chair, and raked her fingers down the leather arm rests. The last time she had left this gallery, *her* gallery, it was for an emergency helicopter flight to Genoa. Now she was back in Monaco, her favorite place in the world, but something had changed inside of her. Almost losing her husband had plowed a jagged trench through the center of her world. A new middle ground bridging the old life and the new would be required.

She turned her back to the door. Tears erupted. The ocean she had held in check for weeks emptied and continued to flow until her thoughts seemed to rinse clear. Look at all she had to be thankful for, treasures she had come so close to losing in a flash. Madeleine Costanzo Porcelli was not cut out for self-pity.

She dragged the large box of correspondence across the desk and upended it. Artists interested in representation, laminated reviews of the gallery's opening night, invitations to charity events, notes of condolence. It would take the better part of today and tomorrow to dispatch. She plopped her sensible pumps on the desk, leaned back, and ripped open the first envelope.

The staff hung around until late. She finally told them to go home, there was no need to try to impress the boss. To clear her head, she skipped the taxi and made the long walk back to her old apartment. Someone, probably Simone, had aired it out and left a pile of mail on the counter. There were cut flowers on the credenza and a bottle of rosé in the fridge, both of which she took to the terrace along with the extension phone. She had prepared a little speech for Bruno, to apologize for abandoning him, to tell him she would cut her trip short. He answered on the first ring, and he was like a different man. His tone was sweet and playful, as if his recent trauma never happened. He asked about her work, they chatted about the future, the past, food, friends. He asked her to call earlier tomorrow.

Where was the man she had left sulking in bed that morning? Perhaps they had simply spent too much time together, Bruno pushing himself like an Olympic marathon trainee, both of them anxious to get back to work. She called him daily for the next two weeks. Every conversation was a gift, so natural and relaxed. Had she imagined the tension between them? Gradually, her longing to see him, to touch him again, grew too strong to ignore.

Chapter 41

For rookie Agent Carlo Esposito, it had been a routine night in Genoa so far. A few domestic disturbances, a single bar fight. But when it's your first week on the job, nothing is routine. The graveyard shift was a given for a newbie, but with his seasoned partner on administrative leave, Esposito was driving solo in his new city. Still reading maps, trying to figure out where he was and where he was going. He'd get it, but for now north was the mountains and south was the sea.

Hoping to get a jump on the night's paperwork, he pulled off the main road on the high side of town. Lights of container ships winked far out on the black water to his left. To his right the lights of streets and houses petered out up into the hills. The reports were boring, and his eyes closed for a moment. The scream of tires on asphalt and the squall of a powerful engine snapped him awake. In the distance, he saw headlights weaving and sliding from lane to lane down the switchback into the city. How could this car still be on the road?

There was no traffic. He reasoned, correctly, that rushing in with lights and siren would only add to the risk. In thirty seconds, he was going to meet the driver anyway, one way or the other, unless the driver met St. Peter first.

At the bottom of the hill, still a good three hundred meters away, the red car's tires grabbed and fishtailed onto the straightaway. Esposito hit the lights and siren and inched his government-issue Alfa Romeo into the center of the street. The driver had plenty of time to see him and slow to a safe stop.

Five seconds later, a wake of wind rocked his Alfa. The Ferrari had other plans than chatting with a police officer. He wheeled in pursuit, knowing his car, while fast, would be no match. But the chase was over before it began. One kilometer into the city the street made a hard left. The sports car did not. It jumped the curb, grazing park benches and shrubs before spinning out mid-field on the soccer pitch. The car mired in fresh mud courtesy of the sprinkler system.

Esposito left his engine running and swaggered to the Ferrari. It was still revving, throwing sod and mud, digging an escape route to nowhere. The two-seater was occupied by a lone male, brown hair, mid to late twenties, large muscular frame. He was slumped over the wheel. Esposito carefully opened the driver's door, reached across, turned off the engine, and pocketed the keys.

A basic triage found a strong pulse and no apparent injuries. He smelled alcohol and saw a pair of crutches wedged in on the passenger side.

"Sir, can you hear me? You've been in an accident. Sir?" There was no response.

Esposito jogged back to his car and radioed in. He requested an ambulance and backup—the driver was enormous and powerfully built. Returning to the scene he found the man coming round.

"Sir, I'm Agent Esposito. You've been in a car crash. Are you all right?"

"Oh yeah. What time is it?"

"Sir, you've been in an accident. Are you injured?"

"I've got it here somewhere."

"Have you been drinking?"

"Drinking? If you only knew."

"What's your name, sir?"

"My name is Sue. How do you do? And who are you?"

"I'm Agent Esposito. Can you tell me how many fingers I'm holding up?"

The man didn't look. "Um, I see five on each hand. No, no eight fingers, two thumbs, and one asshole."

"Sir, I called for help. An ambulance will be here soon. Do you recall driving here?"

"Oh yeah, that was some ride. Can you give me a hand with the car?"

"Sir, I'm afraid you are not going anywhere. You may be injured, and your car is buried in mud up to the axle. Help is on the way."

"I'm not hurt. Just get me out of here. I have to be somewhere."

"Sir, I need to see your papers."

"Do you know who I am?"

"No sir, I do not. That's why I need your papers."

"You're new, but that's no excuse. Should be part of your basic training. I'm Bruno Porcelli."

"And?"

Bruno turned for the first time and glared at him.

"Sir, you've broken several laws here tonight. Reckless driving, speeding, driving under the influence—"

"Did anyone get hurt?"

"That remains to be determined."

"I'm fine!"

"But you did cause major damage to a public park."

"I'll write a check. Hell, I probably paid for the whole frigging park to begin with. What the hell are those sirens for?"

"The medics will check you out. Then, sir, you are either going to hospital or back to the station with me."

"What's your name again Mr. Policeman? You are making a big, big mistake. I won't forget."

"I'm sure you won't, sir."

"Does Del Coltello mean anything to you?"

"Should it?"

Bruno felt the first twinge in his back then. The alcohol was wearing off.

"Esposito! Having fun yet? I hear you've got one in the car."

"Hey Sarge. Yeah, some rich guy who thinks he's above the law. He had to be doing over two hundred coming off the mountain. Reckless driving, speeding, drunk behind the wheel, resisting arrest, destruction of public property. I can probably think of a few more. Says he's not hurt but that could be the alcohol talking. He needs to get checked out."

"How does it feel? Your first solo arrest?"

That stopped him. "Well, like the perp said, it'll be one to remember."

"You start the write up and I'll take it from here. Save us some time. I wanna get home before the sun comes up for a change."

"Thanks, Sarge."

Esposito led the big man into the booking room. The night sergeant glanced at him and blanched. He jumped up and pulled a chair over to his desk.

"Please, have a seat Mr. Porcelli. We'll get you some coffee. Can I call someone for you? Or we can drop you somewhere after I get a few details."

Esposito shook his head and huffed out the door.

Bruno sat alone in the Vice Commissioner's private office waiting for Vincenzo to drive him home. The sergeant had told him, as pleasantly as possible, that he had hit the curve at Campomorone at over one hundred fifty kph. The sobering realization of what he had done, of what could have happened, overshadowed the fire returning to his back and leg. Had he misunderstood the spirit? If being pain free meant being out of control, he had to come up with a better plan. Evading the grim reaper twice was lucky; no sane man would tempt fate a third time. So he thought.

Chapter 42

Madeleine recognized the voice that called to her from across the platform as she stepped off the train. It was Cosmo, Mario's former chauffeur, her chauffeur now; would she ever get used to that? Her two weeks in Monaco had flown by, but she was so happy to see him. They stopped at a local market. He carried the basket as she chose items to prepare dinner.

When Cosmo parked the Mercedes on the circular drive in front of Villa Gazza, the Dino was nowhere in sight. In fact, the villa was empty; Gina had the night off. She was disappointed that Bruno was not there to greet her, but on the positive side, it meant he was well enough to be at work. They had spoken last night and made plans to have an early dinner at home, just the two of them. Had it skipped his mind that she was arriving back this afternoon; was that possible? Of course it was. His bouts of absent-mindedness had become a running joke between them.

At six p.m., she uncorked a bottle of Barolo to let it breathe. At seven, she lit the candles. At seven thirty, she blew out the candles, took the lasagna out of the oven to cool, and prepared the antipasto. At eight, she called his mobile phone and left a message with the answering service. At nine, the bottle of red was empty, and she called Dante. He had no information but promised to find him. At ten she threw the lasagna in the garbage bin, casserole dish and all, and opened another bottle—the most expensive one in the cabinet. She fell asleep on the sofa around midnight.

Some hours later, the sound of an angry, one-sided conversation woke her. She opened the front door and folded her arms, glaring down as he stumbled and cursed with each step up, half stooped, one hand pressed on a thigh, the other pressed on his lower spine.

"Where's the Dino?"

He looked up. "What the hell are you doing here?"

She didn't blink. "It's nice to see you, too." She stepped back and left him supporting himself against the doorjamb.

"Madeleine. My god, you could have told me you were…" He lowered his head. "Oh. Oh, no."

The pitiful look on his face! She could have cried if she'd been less angry.

"Precious, I am so sorry. We had a crisis at work—"

"Stop it! Just stop. What have you been doing? You can barely stand. And answer my question. Where is the Dino?"

"Dante brought me home. Let me explain, please."

She followed him into the living room, unsure whether his twisted features were from physical pain or guilt. They sat and he reached to embrace her. She smelled his breath.

"You've been drinking! That means you stopped the pain meds, yes?" From his expression, the answer was clear.

"You don't understand." He grabbed her arm as she tried to stand. "Maddie, listen. Someone suggested I try alcohol for the pain."

"Who?"

"It's…whatever. It only took a little and it was, it is, a miracle. The pain disappears and for a while I feel like myself—"

"That's why you've been so pleasant on the phone."

"I suppose. You can't imagine the difference!"

"Bruno. Love. You cannot, can *not* mix the two." Fear, dread, raised her pitch a fraction. "You can't do that."

His cheeks flushed red. "You don't understand!" One second a heavy brass ashtray was on the coffee table and the next it was sailing toward the plate glass window across the room. As a hundred shards peppered the terrazzo tiles, he wailed, "My back!" The sofa broke his fall. He pulled his knees to his chest. "Get my meds!" Madeleine was already in the foyer. She strode to the bedroom and slammed the door.

He must have slept on the sofa. The next morning, she found him on the veranda, his wheelchair pulled up to the round granite pedestal table. Gina had just placed a maritozzi and a cappuccino next to him. Madeleine caught her eye, nodded, and Gina followed her to the kitchen.

"How is he this morning, Gina? My apologies. First, how are you this morning?"

"I am fine. You have been missed but we have managed. This morning, he is quiet. Something troubling him other than his pain, I think. Maybe he will talk with you."

"I'm certainly going to try. Please bring me an espresso and juice."

Bruno had rolled himself to the rail and was staring at the sea. Madeleine sat at the table across from his untouched breakfast.

"Bruno, can we talk?" She saw him take a deep breath and hold it. When he spun the chair around, his eyes were lowered.

"Sure. What's on your mind?"

"Don't be coy. We're not going to get anywhere until we hash out this thing with you mixing pills and booze. There is simply—"

"Stop. Baby, I love you. Please listen." He sounded sincere and calm. "I had an epiphany, a message from above that I cannot ignore."

"A message. From above."

"Yes. Don't mock me. The message was from a higher authority. The doctors' warnings hold no weight now."

"What message?"

"That alcohol was the answer to my pain. And it is. It works, and the only word for it is miracle."

"Was it a miracle that you could barely walk up the steps last night. That you destroyed the window and then collapsed in anguish?"

"Of course not. I just overdid it. As soon as I get a handle on how much to use, how to pace it, you'll never even know. I'll be just like I used to be."

"You are seriously deluding yourself. It's dangerous, not something you can play with."

"I'll say it again. I love you, and I'm doing this for you as much as for myself. I am a grown man, and I'm going to manage it. You have no reason to concern yourself. End of discussion."

She fought to gather her wits as he rolled himself toward the sunroom. He was at the doorway before she could speak without yelling.

"In that case, I'm leaving again."

He stopped short but did not turn back. "What do you mean?"

"Take it for what you will. But I am scheduled to speak on a panel discussion in London on Thursday. I was going to cancel, but..." She hesitated. It meant abandoning him again, leaving him to find his own way through this dilemma of pain management. "But if you won't listen to me, nor the doctors, I'm not going to stay here and watch you destroy yourself. You get it sorted out, then we'll talk." Tough love.

He continued into the villa. She reached for the extension phone.

Chapter 43

The New Contemporaries Exhibition and Conference in London ran for six days, billed as the perfect time to see what was on the horizon in the fine art world. Individuals and companies from every facet of the industry were represented. Visitors came and went, but many planned their time around Thursday's panel discussion: *Galleries, friend or foe? How to get your work shown without selling your soul.* Madeleine's invitation to join the panel boosted her ego, almost as much as the remarkable response to her gala opening three months ago. Her name clearly meant something.

The biggest draw of the entire event was the meet-and-greet that followed the panel discussion. It was a rare opportunity for students and newbies to present their portfolios and talk one-on-one with industry leaders. Madeleine took it as an opportunity to comb the masses for new talent. "You never know when you'll stumble upon the next Picasso," she had told Simone.

She was exhausted after ninety minutes of smiling and telling mediocre students to keep up the good work. A mid-thirties gentleman with a ponytail and sandals, who had stood patiently at the end of the line, smiled as he reached her table.

"I enjoyed your contribution to the discussion very much."

"Thank you."

"The point you made about new artists remaining true to themselves really hit home. I wish someone had spelled it out so clearly when I was standing at that crossroads."

"Thanks. Are you one of the professors here?"

"No, I'm here to support a friend."

"Didn't think you were a student."

"But aren't we all students?"

"Or should be. I'm Madeleine Porcelli." He shook her extended hand.

"Yes, The Oscar-Porcelli Gallery. I'm hearing good things. My name is Fabron Leclerc."

"You're not…" She blinked. "You can't be serious. *The Reclining Nude in Blue?* That Fabron Leclerc?"

"Yes, that's mine. In fact, it was my first commercial sale. How do you know this work?"

"I own it!"

"No, you may be confused. There are countless 'reclining nudes' out there. I sold that piece to a beautiful woman in—"

"In Paris, ten or eleven years ago. The beautiful woman was my mother. I was with her. I met you."

"Oh, my God." He leaned against the table. "That moment changed my life. I was down to my last centime, no place to live, selling everything I owned that wasn't paint or canvas. I was ready to give up on my crazy dream, but this angel sent from heaven bought my art. I think the gallery owner was acquainted with your mother. For some reason, he waved his commission, and I never looked back."

Madeleine rubbed her arms. "I'm getting goosebumps. That moment impacted me as well. It was my first step along the path I'm still on, my first glimpse at how much art can mean, for so many different reasons." She shook her head in wonder. "The look on your face when you realized that someone had purchased your work, and the smile in my mother's eyes knowing she was responsible."

"This is simply incredible," he said. "Where is it now?"

"The nude? It's in my office, across from my desk. It reminds me why I do what I do. And how much I still love my mother."

"Your mother…"

"She passed less than a year after she bought that painting."

"Oh, I'm sorry."

"Thank you. It was sudden, an accident. She was gone in a second but never forgotten."

"Nor by me. And running into you, that old black and white memory is once again in full color." Words failed them both for a moment as they waded out of deep emotions. "Madeleine, I must say goodbye for now. I'm due at a dinner on the other side of town, then I'm off to New York first thing in the morning. I'm so glad we met."

e stood quickly. "Please promise you'll visit the gallery soon. We'll get some lunch and spend time with your painting. Drink some wine, who knows, talk some business. Make a day of it. I'd love to hear about what you are working on. Here's my card. Call anytime. The staff can always find me."

"I will do that. I can think of nothing I'd enjoy more. Have a good rest of the conference."

She watched him walk away in his tight jeans. He had a nice butt. Whoa. Where was her head? Ha! With the atmosphere of the conference and all the students, she felt for a moment like she was back in school. Unattached. Unencumbered.

Unfricking believable. Fabron Leclerc.

The next morning, she made her way to the library at The Tate. He was listed in the International Who's Who in Art and Antiques 1972. He was currently represented by Dransberg in New York and Argento in Milan. No representation in France that she could find. She closed the books and thought about getting herself back to Monaco. She couldn't stop thinking about him.

Chapter 44

The ten days seemed like a month. Bruno worked from home, afraid to risk the additional pain that going to the office guaranteed. He spent a lot of time in his den with the door closed. Every hour he charted the amount of alcohol he took and then rated his pain from one to ten and made notes on his mood. One shot of eighty-proof vodka per hour was about right, unless he was active, in which case he needed two. When the twice-a-day pain pills inevitably wore off two hours before his next scheduled dose, three shots kept the pain at bay but triggered angry spells. He vowed to suffer through those hours with only two shots.

He called her in London each day, eager to tell her he had it worked out. She never took those calls. Instead, Madeleine called Gina every evening for a report.

Gina didn't know about the chart, but she knew Mr. Bruno was far from being back to normal. He left the villa every evening around eight, returned in the wee hours, and slept until noon. He acted less angry around her, but more forgetful and quite confused. He complained about things she did or did not do, he said she was stupid, he called her things she would not repeat, when in each case she had simply followed his instructions. Why wasn't the window replaced? (He had told her to leave it as is.) Why did she serve pepper steak when he had never liked it? (It was what he had requested.) She was in knots from the verbal abuse.

Madeleine knew Gina's loyalty to the family would stretch only so far. She had to return to Genoa now, to make certain Gina did not quit. Once she was back home, the same ill-treatment Gina had reported was directed now at her, interspersed with short spells of the charming and considerate husband she loved. He never remembered the bouts of abuse; his memory was in shambles, from losing his toothbrush to forgetting to use antiperspirant. He had headaches, slept pitifully, ate little. One night, after he passed out, she searched his den and found the alcohol dosage chart.

In a moment of desperation, she called Dr. Hulsey and told him everything. Pills, booze, memory lapse, temper, changes in taste. The drugs and alcohol could explain some of it, but he surmised that Bruno's brain injuries were not resolving, and in fact might be worsening. He recommended a full evaluation by a specialist in Milan who was known to work miracles, but the sooner they intervened the better. With a glimmer of hope, she took a sheet of her new powder blue stationary from the desk and wrote down the specialist's contact information.

That evening, she sat down with Bruno, shared what Hulsey had said, and handed him the paper. He crumpled it without looking. "It's just some more tests," she said. "What could it hurt?" She was ready to beg, but the mere suggestion of more doctors sent him into a rage. He disappeared into his den and came out an hour later, stormed through the front doors, and peeled away in the Dino. That was Friday. He was gone all weekend. Monday morning, with still no word from him, Madeleine left again for Monaco.

From the villa, Bruno, half drunk, had driven to the harbor and parked. He stomped into the main Porcelli warehouse, unlocked the office, called Dante, and demanded an update on The Collective's activities. Dante said he would be there in a few minutes, he wanted to talk in person. When he arrived, Bruno was leaning back with his feet on the desk.

"I'm glad you called. You've been out of touch for a while now."

"I'm a busy man, Dante. Just cut to the chase. What's going on with The Collective? What are the issues?"

Dante poured a cup of coffee for each of them and then sat across the desk from Bruno. "There's only one issue that concerns me. Your late-night activities are sounding alarm bells with several members. Wives are telling their husbands—"

"Wives! Don't give me that bull—"

"You need to shut up and listen Bruno. The Collective wives may be gossip mongers, but they hit the truth sometimes. When you blatantly disregard the rules of acceptable behavior, flaunt these hookers in plain sight, your stupidity means the Dons have to lie and walk on eggshells about their own discrete activities. The whispers are coming out into the open. If you're making these poor decisions with your personal life, your business decisions are now suspect. Keep it in your pants or at least somewhere private, or changes *will* be made."

"Screw 'em! And screw you. If that's the only issue, I'd say things are in excellent shape. Lock up when you leave."

He stood and a pain shot up his leg. Doing his best to hide the limp, he walked out, fell into the Dino, and pulled a bottle from the glove box. *They don't want to see me in the nightclubs? No problem.*

Chapter 45

It had been slow for a Saturday. Only two customers and the night was almost half over. No one on the block was doing much better. Crystal knew there was no way she was going to meet quota and that sucked. But it was just too hot for June in Genoa. The past few days had been sweltering. Even at the waterfront with the sun long set, the air still hung close and sticky.

"Damn these high heel boots!" she muttered. "There's not enough moleskin in the world to keep my feet from blistering. And now the tops are sticking to my knees." Screw it, she thought. I've got a full bowl in my handbag.

Ten minutes later her luck changed. A red sports car turned the corner and moved slowly up the street. A curb-crawler, looking for entertainment.

Leaving little to the imagination, Crystal moved into her "I'm your woman" pose. The car stopped. Resting both forearms on the bottom of the window, she leaned in on full display.

"Hey baby. I like your car. You see anything you like?"

"Maybe. Whatcha got in mind?

"You got the cash, anything goes."

"Not an issue. Got a friend to join us?"

"Sure, baby doll." She stood up and whistled through two fingers. "Hey Tiff!"

A blonde in fishnet stockings and little else strolled up. Crystal nodded to the car. "Wanna go out with me and Signor Giusto for a sandwich?"

Tiffany nodded. "Nothing else going on."

Crystal opened the door. "Hey, where's she gonna sit? We ain't getting in no trunk."

"Relax. What's your name?"

"Crystal."

"Crystal, we're not going far, and I'd like to see the two of you scrunched up real close together. You ever do it out on the water?"

"Now you're talking. Tiff, you're on my lap."

"Good girls. Short ride, then we'll see what we can get up to. Either of you young ladies ever spend the night on a yacht?"

Tiffany squealed. Crystal said, "No offense mister, but we ain't getting in no car unless we got details. We gotta check in during the night, too."

"How about half a million lire now and another half in the morning? Each. And I'll talk with your 'handler' at our first stop."

Her eyes lit up. "Tiffany, whatcha think?"

"I think shut up and get in."

Chapter 46

Bruno woke when a rush of cold water swept over him. Sand-laden waves had half-buried his legs. Grit and drool caked his face. He ran his tongue around his teeth and spit sand. There were no stars, no moon, no glow of a distant town, so black that everything looked the same whether his eyes were open or shut. The only sounds were the crash of waves and the fizz of disintegrating sea foam.

The pain of rolling up onto all-fours woke him sufficiently to realize he had no clue where he was or how he got there. On thing was clear, he'd been unconscious so long the meds and booze had worn off; along with the pain from his injuries, he was hungover, his head pounded, and his tongue felt like a dirty sock. A coughing fit brought up salt water and acid that burned his throat.

Out of the pure dark, a spot of intense light appeared up the slope to his right, illuminating a line of small dunes. And a pair of legs.

"Hey, a little help here!" The night was suddenly black again as the blaze of light stabbed his eyes. "Hey, point that down! I can't see anything!" He squatted back onto his haunches. The dress shirt he had on, soaked heavy with water, dragged the beach, as did some stringy thing that was wrapped around his neck. A chill prickled his skin as he realized he was naked from the waist down.

"Excusez-moi, monsieur. Vous pouvez pas coucher la."

"I don't speak French. Hey, I said get that light out of my eyes."

"There is no sleeping on the beach, sir."

"Does it look like I'm fricking sleeping, you snot ball? I just woke up in the sand here."

"One must sleep before one can wake. Don't you agree, sir?"

"Yeah smartass, I get it. What do you want?"

"To remove you from this beach. But I must first thank you for the entertainment. It is not often we have a guest passed out in the sand, wearing only a shirt and an ascot of fishnet stockings. Judging from the lipstick, it must have been quite the party."

"You don't get out much, do you."

"Time to go, sir. My beach does not open until the sunrise."

"How is this your fucking beach?"

"If I could just take a look at your Italian carte national, please. I take it you are not French."

"You dumbfuck. Do I look like I've got my national I.D. on me?"

"If you would come with me sir, a few hours in the jail and your perspective may improve."

"No, I'll just be on my way. Can you, uh, tell me where we are?"

"France, generally. Obviously. The island of Levant to be precise. You are fortunate it is a naturalists' beach or you would be facing additional charges for your immodesty." He lowered the light beam to Bruno's groin area.

His eyes quickly adjusted and he saw handcuffs and a truncheon hanging from the man's belt.

"The problem is, I don't know how I got here."

The man swept his light out over the water. "Perhaps you recognize this vessel? It will be impounded at first light."

The Madeleine was the only boat in the cove, anchored about fifty meters out. "Yeah, that's mine." He straightened himself to a kneeling position. "Help me up, then I'll just be on my way."

"No, you will not be on your way." The man put one hand on his truncheon, bent over, and with the other hand clutched Bruno's shirt collar. He tried to heave the much larger man to his feet. Instead, two handfuls of moist sand spattered him in the eyes. He howled and tried to step back, but Bruno snatched his ankles and tipped him over. Bruno grabbed the flashlight, a metal cylinder containing five heavy D-cell batteries. Bone cracked as the first blow smashed just below the man's left ear. The next strike, this one to the groin, drew no response, but he followed with two blows to the man's forehead for good measure.

He needed time to catch his breath but feared backup might arrive. In the near distance, something gleamed, like a stack of brightly colored crayons. Kayaks, chained to the side of a small cabin. He limped to the rental shop.

With a metal oar he twisted the security chain until it broke. Six personal watercrafts tumbled to the ground. He dragged the red one to the water.

The yacht was deserted. The dinghy was gone. The soundtrack to Jesus Christ Superstar wailed on repeat from the eight-track tape player. Party residue scattered the decks—spilled ashtrays, overturned chairs, and dozens of empty bottles, one broken. He could find no evidence of who had been on board or where they might be. Not his problem. He could find zero booze—no wonder his guests had disappeared—but plenty of pills in his cabin safe. He crushed two and snorted them. Okay, one more.

He checked the date on the LORAN display…what the Holy Pope in Rome! Three days since his last memory. A quick calculation told him the little island where he was anchored was just south of St. Tropez. Based on the fuel gauge, he had enough to get back to Genoa without refilling. Maybe.

An odd sound in the distance made him stop the anchor hoist. He could hear the dinghy's motor then, and two young voices. "Hey, mister! Wait! Don't leave us!"

Maybe this party was not over.

Chapter 47

Back in Monaco, Madeleine tried to forget that no one had heard from Bruno for four days now. She called Simone into her office for a status report. It was all good. Sales were steady, the staff was happy, and there were no operational issues. She thanked her for the update and asked her to close the door on her way out. Sales were fine, but fine was not good enough. They clearly needed new talent, a mix of the unknown and the famous. She opened her Rolodex and called every name with a star by it, gratified by the ease with which doors opened at the mere mention of her name. Between calls, her phone rang.

"Oscar-Porcelli, Madeleine speaking."

"Well, welcome back."

The voice, that accent. "Fabron?"

"The one and only. I've been trying to reach you."

"I didn't get your message."

"I didn't leave one. I was about to give up on your invitation for lunch, et cetera." He laughed. "Seriously, I'll be in your area first thing next week. Would that work for you? I have a new series no one has seen, I thought you might like to preview it."

Her heart leapt. He wanted her to represent him? She couldn't speak for a moment.

"You want to check your calendar?"

"Uh, no. Yes. Next Monday is wide open." She had no idea if that was true, but it was now. "And I would love to see your new portfolio. We can compare and contrast it with me Reclining Nude, sorry, with *my* Reclining Nude. Or you Reclin—, *your* Reclining Nude." *Crap, what is wrong with me?*

"Mid-morning then?"

"Perfect."

She spent the rest of the day in the clouds, imagining a solo exhibit with Fabron's new series plus as many older pieces as she could beg, borrow, or steal. Ha! Steal a painting. How did some people have the guts to do something like that? She was so buoyed with the ideas coursing through her veins that Bruno's decline seemed a distant concern. She would be able to spend time with Fabron planning and executing the show. It would be the biggest event at the gallery since the grand opening.

She wound herself down that evening, alone in her apartment. She had ignored the blinking light on the answering machine until bedtime. It was Bruno's sloppy voice. Was he drunk, stoned, brain damaged, all of the above? She was suddenly back to reality. The thoughts she had entertained about Fabron, intrusive thoughts not solely along professional lines, had no place in her life. First priority was to get Bruno the help he needed. She would return to Genoa at the end of the week and do whatever it took to turn things around.

Before work on Wednesday, she called to let Gina know she would be home again this weekend, but no one answered at the main villa or at Gina and Cosmos separate lodgings. When she got to her office at the gallery, the phone was ringing. It was Gina, hysterical. She and Cosmo had been fired.

Between sobs and gasps for air, she relayed the incident. Bruno had not been back since he left on Friday. This morning, while putting clean towels in the master suite, she saw three empty pill bottles in the trash. It seemed strange because all the labels looked the same, so she read them. Each one was for the pain medication that Bruno takes, each for a one-month supply, all for this month, and each from a different doctor. She turned to drop the bottles back in the trash, and Bruno was in the doorway.

"Mr. Bruno was a crazy man, Miss Madeleine. His eyes were not right. He said he should kill me for spying on him. He smashed a big glass of liquor and ice on the floor. He said Cosmo and I are fired."

The words stabbed her heart. "Oh, no, Gina. I am so sorry. Please, just stay out of his way until I get there. He may not even remember tomorrow."

"He said we had to leave the property immediately. I told him we have nowhere to go, and he said it is not his problem. I thought he was going to hit me, but he threw a big roll of lire at me and said stay in a hotel. I was afraid to touch the money."

"Where are you now?"

"With a friend, but we cannot stay here."

"Give me the number you're calling from, Gina. I'll find you a place to stay for the next few days, but you are not fired. You understand? You and Cosmo are still employed. The two of you enjoy some time off until I get this sorted."

Triple dosing. And alcohol. She was angry beyond words but not beyond reason. She had a mission. One way or another, Bruno was going to get the help he needed.

****

The taxi stopped at the top of the circular drive. Lights were on throughout the villa. Madeleine dropped her suitcase in the foyer. The place was a wreck, cushions littered the floor, dirty dishes and empty bottles, pictures hung crooked on the walls.

She heard a noise and followed it to the long hallway. There were muffled voices coming from the far end. A woman screeched. She ran to the half-opened door of the master bedroom.

The scene playing out on her marriage bed was so bizarre that it failed to register for a moment. She must have gasped because the blonde girl looked up, then she shook the brunette's tattoo covered arm until she stopped what she was doing. They scrabbled off the bed, snatched clothes and shoes from the floor, and ran past Madeleine. Her skin turned to ice. She heard the distant front door slam at the same moment a bewildered Bruno groaned and rolled onto his back.

"Hey, bitches. What the hell? We're not finished here."

The words were slurred almost beyond comprehension. His eyes, mere slits, slowly opened as he scanned the room. Recognition spread across his face. *Hey, what are you doing here, you come to help, why'd you scare everyone off?* Or maybe he said something completely different, or nothing at all— her memory of those first moments was sketchy. But she would remember her own screams, calling him filthy names, then being thrown to the floor. She struggled against a crushing weight with her knees, fists, and teeth until she was overpowered. Her wrists pinned above her head. The sound of fabric ripping. Finally, the crunch of her cheekbone just below her left eye. That was the last fragment she recalled, mercifully, because when she awoke with morning sun on her face, she was caked with dried blood from the buttocks down.

She found herself curled in a ball on the terrazzo in the far corner of the balcony. Dazed and in shock, she crawled back inside the master suite, tiptoed silently past Bruno's snores and walked naked down the hallway to the guest bathroom. When the shower water ran cold, she stepped out and left it running. Wrapped in a towel, she walked barefoot back to the master suite. The bed was now empty. She stuffed a single change of clothes and a bottle of aspirin into a tote, what else did she need? No idea. Wearing her largest sunglasses and floppiest hat, she walked to the foyer. Her suitcase was right where she had dropped it last night.

Bruno's voice echoed through the passageway. "Gina? Where have you been? The place is a mess." He was in the breakfast nook. Madeleine stopped under the arch. Her heart hammered. He looked up from the newspaper. "Hey! I thought I heard someone. How was your trip? You must have gotten an early start."

A blank glare was the only response she could muster.

"What's with the movie star sunglasses? It's going to rain all day." He stood and took a step. She flinched and stepped back. "Are you limping? Maddie? What's going on?"

She took off the glasses and attempted to meet his eyes. Her hands shook so violently the glasses dropped and she stooped to pick them up. He reached for her hand and she screamed.

"My God, baby, what happened? Who did this to you?"

"Someone who used to love me."

"What the… Who? Sit down, talk to me."

Sit? Sit and talk? The haze behind her eyes evaporated in a flame of anger. "Last night! You expect me to believe you remember nothing? Two puttane in *our* bed? You pinned me to the floor, ripped my clothes off, forced— You bastard!" Tears burned her eyes and she saw a dangerous world of rage flare in his.

"What are you talking about? There was no one here last night. I'm going to kill whoever did this to you. Kill him! Trying to protect him is not going to change that!"

"You need help, before you kill someone!"

He took a step toward her. She turned, grabbed her suitcase and ran.

He limped to the front door and saw her step into the waiting taxi. She did not look back. She did not see the confused, helpless look on his face framed in the doorway.

Her last words echoed in his head. *You need help*. He had all the help he needed. In his den, he lifted a full bottle of vodka from the liquor cabinet. A sheet of crumpled blue paper was stuck to the bottom. Madeleine had put it there. On it was the name and number of some fancy-dancy specialist who could cure all his ills. He cracked the seal on the vodka and pulled the stopper. The stopper as well as the re-crumpled blue paper he tossed in the wastebasket. Didn't need either of them. He poured the first tumbler full and stared off into the muddy distance.

Chapter 48

Less than twenty-four hours after the attack, she was in tiny Campione d'Italia, an enclave near Lake Lugano that was sovereign Italian land but completely surrounded by, and guarded by, Switzerland. No one knew she was there.

She had expected to feel safe—but the irrational thoughts from clinical anxiety knew no geographical bounds.

Bright red welts on her face and neck had darkened, and by the next morning all the angry colors of bruising encircled her left eye. Her vision was blurry. Her body throbbed, and her mind ached for human contact. Syrina and Silvan's villa in Lenno had been her first idea of a refuge; even if Bruno found her there, they could shield her. But she was too ashamed to show her face. Nor could she tell her father; that would end in a confrontation with Bruno and likely an early grave for Antonio. More than anything, she wanted to curl up in her mother's arms. Campione d'Italia would have to do for now.

She rented the apartment with cash, under an assumed name. The kind manager arranged for her meals to be delivered. Food was tasteless, and the wine she had ordered had no appeal. The simplest tasks required uncommon effort—opening the blinds, making the bed, preparing tea. Every act of daily life seemed to come from an actor outside her body. Reading, even listening to the radio, impossible. No focus. On the third day, she saw the sun rise. Her thoughts strayed to the gallery in Monaco, how extraordinary it was that she owned it, how lucky that her team could manage so well without her. Her spirit began to return. She would call Simone, pretend all was right with the world, first thing Monday. Was that tomorrow? Today? She'd lost track of time and called the manager.

It was Monday. Monday! She had an appointment with Fabron, and no way to reschedule; his card was in her office. Simone answered on the first ring. No, Fabron had not arrived yet. When he showed, the story would be that a family emergency had pulled Madeleine away and she would call him as soon as possible. How long should she say she would be out? How long did it take bruises to disappear? The scrape on her cheek from Bruno's ring looked infected. What if her face healed, but she never regained the courage to look a man in the eye? Self-doubts were foreign to her. Which would heal first, her flesh or her spirit?

Goddamn Bruno! Her sympathy for him had been stretched before. Now it was at the point of no return. It was his decision to abuse the alcohol and pills, his choice to ignore the doctors and refuse to see the specialist.

Still, she was condemning a man who had found himself in an impossible situation. How much of his behavior was pain response and how much was brain damage? What had Dr. Hulsey said? The damage could get worse instead of better. She wiped away a tear and closed the blinds.

***

Two weeks passed and proved ever again that time creates miracles. The only physical remnants of the attack—the rape, as she had come to think of it—was a slight droop in her left eye. Ironically, it was noticeable only when she smiled too broadly.

During the recovery, she'd had no contact with anyone Porcelli related. The internal drive to regain her independence, to return to work and initiate some of her business ideas slowly tamed the recent nightmare. Throwing herself into the job was the right thing to do. Her chipper personality emerged naturally as soon as she entered the gallery. She loved the staff, the art, her office. If Monaco had seemed a bit like home before, now it was a haven.

She resumed contact with artists interested in representation, designed a media campaign that would start in the fall, set Paula and Max to work on planning the second annual gala for the spring. Fabron was on tour in the States now, but they kept in touch; and perhaps best of all, he was holding his new series under wraps until they could meet.

Despite her immersion in the work she loved, the next month passed slowly. The days were full, but every passing night seemed longer than the previous one. The staff repeatedly asked her to join them for drinks after work, but she wasn't ready to socialize, and alcohol seemed repugnant. A reaction to Bruno's abuse, she reasoned. The fact that she'd not reached out for news about him, not once in six weeks, fed her imagination. What was he up to? The possibilities were limited, and none of them were likely to be good.

Following a particularly spicy dinner of Thai takeout, she had a vivid dream. In it, Bruno was miraculously healed, but he had moved on to someone new. He was on an island, she stood on the deck of her namesake yacht. He did not turn when she called to him. Standing in a cold rain, shivering, she prayed to be off the unsteady deck. A wave of nausea swept her entire body, and she awoke drenched in sweat. The nausea was real. She stumbled from bed and ran to the toilet.

After losing her breakfast for three consecutive mornings, she made an appointment to see a doctor. The test was positive.

Chapter 49

Something tragic had happened to Madeleine, no denying that, but Bruno refused to accept that he was responsible. The episode on the French island, those three days missing from his memory? That was no proof that he had brought the prostitutes home and then attacked his own beloved wife. He loved her too much. And bringing prostitutes to Villa Gazza, the estate his father had built, was a line he would never cross, even drunk. Madeleine's ridiculous account was a cover for something.

He could continue to obsess about it, but the truth was he missed her terribly;

the need to have her back was unbearable. It was time to forgive and move on. He could honestly tell her that he had reformed. For six weeks he'd done nothing but eat, sleep, and work. By sticking to the prescribed dose of pain meds, he was learning to stay on task, and the task was to function responsibly despite constant, poorly controlled physical pain. It was a battle in a war he had to win.

He prepared a speech. He had reformed, he missed her, he loved her, without her his life was flat. Meaningless.

If she would only answer his calls.

When the phone rang, he was on the veranda watching the sun set, brooding, wanting a drink but denying himself, again.

She spoke before he said hello. "We need to talk."

"Maddie! Love! Where are you? When are you coming home?"

"I don't know when I am coming back, Bruno. I had thought maybe never, but now…"

"Never? Please come home. I miss you, and I'm better, completely sober, I swear. We'll work it out."

She breathed into the phone. "Right. We *have* to work it out now, now that…" Her next words were less than a whisper.

"What?" He couldn't have heard correctly.

She found her voice. In fact, she shouted. "I'm pregnant!"

"You…what? You're going to have a…" His heart was in his throat. "You're saying…"

"Yes, *you* are going to be a father."

"Holy Mother. That's wonderful! When is it due?" Silence. "Hello?" She said nothing as their recent history—the days, weeks, months—tumbled into their slots. Once he added it up, the realization jolted him. And when it did, his voice ignited. "We have not had sex in six months! Six. Months!"

"Are you out of your mind? You raped me! Six weeks ago!"

He had to control his temper, but it teetered on a precipice. "That was bullshit the first time you said it and it's still bullshit. Besides, you're too smart to get pregnant. What kind of game is this?"

"No games Bruno. It's a fact. You are the father. We are having a child."

He was beyond hearing her now. "If you're pregnant, then who's the father?"

She let the question hang.

He stopped. It had to be the guy who beat her up. "I'm not raising another man's child!" Suddenly he could barely catch his breath. "Say something. Where are you now? Who is the father!"

The habitual back and leg pain he was learning to live with flamed through his entire body. He dropped the phone, choking, rasping. His throat constricted and he couldn't breathe. In some part of his awareness Madeleine screamed over the phone.

"I'm calling an ambulance!"

Precious minutes passed before the long-distance operator made the connection in Genoa.

"Emergency Services. What is the nature and location of your emergency?"

Her chin began to quiver.

"Hello. Emergency Services. Are you in danger?"

What a question.

"Hello—"

She gently put the receiver back in the cradle and closed her eyes.

Chapter 50

Dante received a phone call before daybreak. Bruno, strangely polite, asked to meet him at the private container-office as soon as possible. When he arrived, Bruno was taking a fresh pot of coffee from the machine, but there was a full cup steaming on his desk. It seemed he had already finished one pot himself.

"Good afternoon! Come in, come in."

"It's six-thirty, Bruno."

"Hey, learn to take a joke, old man. Early bird and all that."

"What are you doing here at this hour?"

Bruno was disheveled and seriously wired. Wild eyes, rapid speech, jittery. He looked like he hadn't slept at all. The caffeine might explain it, but Dante noticed a dusting of white powder on one nostril. He cringed to see that the combination safe was open. Bruno kept product samples for The Collective in there now, something Mario would never have allowed.

Bruno's hand trembled as he filled Dante's cup. "I'm worried about Maddie. She was acting strange for a while, always preoccupied. I thought she was having an affair. But then she said someone was following her. I tried to calm her down, told her it was probably just an admirer, she's so beautiful."

"Maddie's smart enough to know the difference between a fan and a threat. Tell me what you know."

"She kept seeing some guy outside her apartment in Monaco, outside the gallery, even tailing her around the city. Driving a yellow Fiat."

"There's a million of those."

"Well, I think I saw it."

"Here? In Genoa?"

"She came home this weekend. They apparently followed her, because when I went out yesterday, I saw a yellow Fiat 128 with the front fender rusted out. Near the villa. She confirmed it's the same car. I saw it again today."

"A car with damage like that's too easy to spot. The guy can't be very smart. I'll track it down."

"Maddie's an easy target if someone is trying to get to me. You put a tail on her, starting today. I want a full report daily. Surveillance photos of everyone she meets with, even talks to. You can use the tap on our house phone, she doesn't have a mobile yet. Get taps on her phones in Monaco, too. Apartment and office. I want a full report daily. You got it?"

"Sure. You want a full daily report. I got it." He sat down across from Bruno and folded his hands. Something didn't add up. Maddie says she is being stalked and he wants to know who she meets with, who she talks to? "Sounds like there's more to this. I need to know what you know."

"I don't know anything! Yellow car. I have a lot of enemies. Maybe that southern family who hit the restaurant. It's been going on for a week or two."

"A week or two?" No wonder Bruno was a wreck. "How long exactly, and why didn't you come to me earlier?"

His face reddened. He swiveled one-eighty in his chair and shouted to the wall. "I told you! Because I thought she was having an affair. Capisci? But now, the same car's tracking me." He spun back around. "You find out who. Someone in a yellow car, that's all I can tell you."

"I'm on it." He stood and left without another word.

Dante's investigation into the explosion that killed Mario had convinced him that it had been an accident. Bruno's southern family theory was based on zero evidence. Dante and Vincenzo had deliberately allowed those misconceptions to fester. But if someone was in fact targeting Bruno now, he would find out and deal with it. Just part of the job. But if they were plotting to use Madeleine to get to Bruno? Different story. That would be a blood debt, to be repaid in full.

Bruno dumped the coffee in the sink, snatched the phone, and called his secretary. It wasn't yet seven o'clock. He left a message. "Marta, soon as you get this, send a bouquet to Maddie's office, the most expensive one they make, have it there before she arrives for work today." He hung up, called her Monaco apartment, and got the machine. "Maddie, my treasure, I love you. Call me as soon as you get this. I can't believe I was so stupid. A baby. Our baby! It's a reason to live. It's beyond words. I would never intentionally hurt you. It'll never happen again. I realize I have memory lapses, but listen, I've stopped drinking. I'm going to get help from that specialist. I love you and I will make it all up to you. I love you. Call me!"

He leaned back and stared at the ceiling for a second. Then he jerked open the lap drawer on the desk. His first ever taste of a street drug had been two hours earlier. He knew he had to come down sometime, but not just yet. He did another line of coke and then called his secretary again. "Marta. One more thing. Send a teddy bear to her apartment. The biggest one they have."

His thoughts were flying, but there was no focus, no way to do any real work. This white powder must take some getting used to. He poured a tumbler full of vodka and gulped it like water. From the front of the office he paced to the bedroom and back to the desk. He called Villa Gazza and listened to it ring. "Pick up the fricking phone Gina!" Then he remembered. He had fired Gina. Six weeks ago. He laid his forehead on the desk and laced his fingers behind his neck. *A baby. Another man's baby. Holy Mother Mary in heaven, what in hell's name am I supposed to do now?*

Chapter 51

She deleted the message on her machine as soon as she had heard enough of Bruno's voice to know he was not dead. The giant vase of tropical flowers on her desk she put in the gallery's lobby for everyone to enjoy. She gave the teddy bear to a woman in her apartment building, a single mother with two young daughters, which was poignant—the possibility of becoming a single mother was among her limited options, and she gave herself a two-week deadline to decide. To keep from going crazy, she focused on work. If divorce turned out to be the best course, she would be supporting herself, managing a career in an industry that glittered in her mind's eye. Not a terrible option, and one too many women could not claim.

She redoubled her efforts to expand the gallery's scope of offerings. Week one of her two-week countdown, she touched base with Fabron and scheduled a meeting for the following month. She arranged meetings with another half-dozen artists, as well as two local museums and four serious collectors. She met face to face with a potential investment partner. The opportunities seemed unlimited.

But the second week, something odd began to happen. One after another, artists and clients stopped returning her phone calls. Meetings were cancelled with no explanation. Her plans ground to a halt. Other than wandering through the gallery, tweaking displays and encouraging the staff, she was idle, left to wonder what was happening—until she returned to her apartment at the end of another frustrating day. A plain envelope had been slipped under her door. *Call me from a payphone at the following number around seven pm your time, any day this week.* It was signed "The artist your mother saved".

Her fingers trembled as she dropped the coins into the slot. He answered on the first ring.

Fabron said, "I hope my letter didn't frighten you too badly."

"I have so many things going on right now, a little more bad news probably won't hurt. I assume it's bad news."

"Well, it's not a fair-weather report. You want to talk first about what's got you down?"

"It's a long list of things, but the most recent is that suddenly no one wants to work with Oscar-Porcelli Gallery."

"Ah, well then, I'm glad I reached out, although it was against my instincts for self-preservation."

"That sounds a bit ominous," she said.

"Which is how it feels. I received a call not long after we talked last week. Let's just say someone does not want me associating with you. The language was not threatening exactly, but not to be taken lightly either, I would say."

"Well that certainly explains a lot. If I think for half a second, I know who's behind it."

"Listen, I don't like bullies. And I like you a lot. So, if there is anything I can do to help…"

"I appreciate that," she said, "but now that I understand what's going on, I can deal with it. Meanwhile, let's delay our meeting until I straighten this out. I don't imagine you're in any real danger, but better safe than sorry."

"I understand. And now I'm even more intrigued about working with you. I would love to have you represent my new series, if you're still interested."

"I can't wait to see it. And thank you again, for everything."

"My pleasure, Madeleine."

"I'll call again when I know it's safe."

She plopped on the sofa. At least now she knew why progress on her business plans had stopped. Bruno threatened her contacts, imagining she'd had an affair with one of them. *But who at the gallery sold me out, who gave Bruno's goons a list of my associates?*

How best to reassure those who had been threatened and then get the projects restarted? How to confront Bruno about his attack on her business; ha, would he even remember doing it? And what about the baby, and her marriage? Her fourteen-day deadline to make a decision on that expired in three days. This latest twist—Bruno mucking around in her career—was a new factor in that equation. She felt like pulling her hair out. Continuing to spend ten hours a day at work, butting her head against his interference, would solve nothing. She needed some air to breathe, some room to disconnect and think. Pack a bag. Rent a car. Drive north to the lake region.

At noon the next day, she arrived unannounced at Syrina and Silvan's estate in Lenno. Standing in the foyer, she melted into a bear hug from her sister. In the middle of the hug, she broke down and sobbed. Suddenly there was no reason to hide her recent history, at least the part she could bring herself to speak aloud. She sat in a wicker rocker across from Syrina as the raw grief spilled out. Bruno's decline, his mixing of alcohol and pills, the duplicate prescriptions. His pain, temper, wild mood swings, memory lapses. The living hell of it all. Syrina reacted as only a sister could; she told her how important her love was to her. Madeleine broke down again. After crying and snuffling and even a little laughter, after they reminisced about their mother and the good old days, they settled into twin hammocks on the veranda, holding hands, rocking in sync. The lake breeze picked up, then died down, and finally the hammocks stopped swaying.

"Maddie? Are you asleep?"

"I think I was. I haven't been this relaxed in months."

"You don't have to answer. But what happened to your eye?"

Her throat tightened first, then every muscle in her body. She wasn't going to lie, but neither could she tell the rest of the story.

"He hit you, didn't he?"

Madeleine didn't respond.

"Sis, you know my imagination is probably worse than reality. You might as well tell me."

Madeleine sighed. "Maybe someday. Not now."

When she awoke, it was dark. She padded barefoot into the villa. Syrina and Silvan were whispering in the kitchen. With a micro-glance between the sisters, Syrina knew Maddie did not want her story repeated, and Maddie knew Syrina had said nothing. As Silvan prepared dinner, he brought a pitcher of mojitos out to the ladies. Madeleine said she was off alcohol for a while and requested sparkling water. Her hosts were too polite to ask any questions.

The menu was veal piccata with wild mushrooms and an arugula salad, the greens and herbs fresh from their planter on the veranda. Over dinner, Madeleine downplayed the issues she was having at the gallery. She confessed it was a dream job with problems she loved solving. Silvan's stories of rooting out corporate ignorance and winning fights with patent office bozos soon had them laughing. When he noticed and asked about the droop in Madeleine's left eye, the story of a freak accident was easy to spin. She had no qualms about lying to her brother-in-law.

"I wanted to show I'm a hands-on-team-player kind of boss, you know, so I was helping unload a new shipment, a huge wooden crate. It shifted and I couldn't get out of the way fast enough, thanks to non-sensible shoes. My face took the brunt of it."

"Oh, my god," he said. "That's terrible!"

"It could have been worse. I could have ruined a perfectly good pair of outrageously expensive spiked heels."

He laughed. "Well, I'm glad you're okay. Tragedy can be funny once it's over."

"Right," she said, moving food around on her plate. "Thank goodness everything's okay now."

The evening with her sister and brother-in-law was lovely, but with the lights out she was haunted again by those few hours of terror, the nightmare she had bottled up with a cork that leaked at random. The incident at Villa Gazza had melted her down and cast her in a new mold, into a shape she struggled to recognize. The hookers in her bed. The attack. A man who was no longer the man she married. Now, the baby. It felt like being impaled at the center of a crossroad. She had decisions that were hers alone to make. Limited options, none of them appealing.

She had come to think of the baby as a girl, and she could not imagine giving her up—but if it somehow came to that, no one could know.

Bruno. Baby. Motherhood. Career. She slept fitfully for a while before coming fully awake. The bedroom was lit with an unusual glow from the window. She rose and walked to the veranda. The moonlight was bright enough to cast her shadow on the tiles. Low in the sky, it was a half moon, waning. In a few days it will be a dark moon, she thought. And then, as certain as death and crooked politicians, it will be full again. Suddenly, as clear as the moonlight, she knew exactly what she was going to do. As soon as she had spent a few more quality days with her sister. As soon as she gathered her courage.

Chapter 52

Dante had assigned Giacomo, his top man, to tail Madeleine. The most recent reports indicated that her male business associates were keeping their distance; Dante now understood why Bruno had made his specific requests.

When she left Monaco, Giacomo tracked her to her sister's estate in Lenno. He and two others set up a surveillance perimeter, including a post across the lake with a clear view of the terrace, lawn, and boat dock. For four days, the report stated that she had not moved beyond the grounds. She spent most of her time reading or swimming. A tap on the house phone revealed no incoming calls to her. Then yesterday, Dante got a different report—Madeleine had called Bruno. She told him they had to talk. He begged her to come home to talk face to face. She reluctantly agreed, but the meeting had to be in a public location. He pushed for it to be on their yacht at Genoa Marina. That would work, she said, but only if Dante was also present. The meeting was set for Monday.

Bruno had requested surveillance on Madeleine only, not on himself. That fact was so odd that Dante secretly put two men on Bruno as well. They were instructed to identify but not engage with anyone tailing him. Day after day, the reports were the same. The men never saw the rusted yellow Fiat. They were one hundred percent certain no one was on him. He went to the office sporadically but ate lunch at the same restaurant near the marina every day, picked up girls every night, and returned to his villa between one and two a.m., intoxicated.

The only change in Bruno's routine came the day after Madeleine called him. It started with a shopping trip after lunch. He went into two stores, both in the wholesale food district, and came out minutes later with a couple of small but heavy boxes. He put them into the trunk of his car. After dark, he drove to the marina and loaded the boxes onto his yacht. He spent an hour on board and then drove home, no party time that night. Dante investigated the two wholesale stores. Both sold a variety of foods and beverages, but both were also black-market fronts selling anything a customer could afford.

As instructed, Dante had provided Bruno with daily reports on Madeleine's activities. Now with the wiretap in Lenno, he was in the awkward position of revealing that he knew the content of Bruno's conversation with Madeleine, that they were to meet on the yacht in two days, and that he himself would be present as well. When Dante reported what the covert recording revealed, Bruno didn't blink. He laughed and said see you Monday evening, old man.

Why would Bruno buy provisions at a food store and load them on the boat himself, rather than delegate that to a minion? And if it was food, why would he stock the boat now, unless he was planning to spend a lot more time than the meeting with Madeleine was likely to require? Was he crazy enough to kidnap her?

Chapter 53

Her taxi arrived at the marina thirty minutes early. The dock sounded like an amplified marimba as the wheels of her suitcase drummed on the wooden slats. She might not have noticed the sound on a weekend night, but Mondays were quiet. After a hundred joyful trips across these boards, this was her first with a gut cramped from nerves.

Up ahead, calmly waiting in the outer slip, she saw *The Madeleine,* lights blazing across the water. Bruno and Dante were already there. So much for having a few minutes to get the lay of the land.

She stepped into the salon. Dante stood near the door. Bruno was leaned back in the sofa corner like it was a throne. His arms were outstretched along the cushion backs, and a clear iced beverage sweated on the table in front of him.

"Good evening, gentlemen." She looked at Dante, and pointedly not at Bruno. "I thought I was early."

"Ciao, Madeleine. I didn't beat you by much. Bruno was waiting when I arrived."

Madeleine kissed Dante on both cheeks, then offered her hand to Bruno and met his eyes briefly. She sat on the port settee across the room from him.

"I'll be just outside should either of you need anything." Dante closed the glass door behind him.

"Thank you for coming, Maddie. It's been far too long. I've missed you."

She turned toward him and crossed her arms. "What do you expect me to say?"

"Nothing. I'm here to apologize."

"I'm listening." She lowered her gaze, confused by the tiny window that opened in her heart. This man was the father of her unborn child.

"I've been out of line for a long while now. Out of control. In denial. I'm so ashamed of the pain I caused you, physical and emotional pain. It's not who I am. The doctors warned me, you warned me, pain meds and alcohol can't be mixed, but I didn't realize I might lose control, blackout, forget whole chunks of time. Instead of learning to deal with the pain in a safe way, I took the easy route. And there's no excuse. I'm here to beg you, *beg* you Maddie, to forgive me."

"And you expect me to believe you've changed?"

"You have to. I'm working hard to reshape my life. I want to start over and put this behind us and make it all up to you. I want to hold our child in my arms." He chuckled. "I want to see him win the Grand Prix Monaco in a red Ferrari."

"*Him*?" Like the word itself was distasteful. "Of course. Someone you can bring up into a life of crime. Make your dreams come true."

"Why are you being like this?"

"Why? You want to talk why? Why did you fracture my cheekbone with your fist? Why did you rip off my clothes and dangle me over the balcony before…" She forced her shout into a harsh whisper. "Before violating me in front of God in heaven. And then call me a liar when I said I'm carrying your child. You have no right to ask anything of me."

Bruno's muscles all seemed to solidify at once. He wasn't getting what he wanted. "But I don't remember any of that!"

"Yeah, that's convenient, but you saw the results. Did you think I just ran into a door three times?"

"How could I have known it wasn't someone else who did it?"

"You could have believed me!" This was going nowhere.

He clenched his hair with both hands and rocked his head. "I don't know what more I can do to—"

He stopped when Dante's radio telephone chimed on the aft deck. They could hear him through the open windows.

"This is 743. Go ahead 801. This is Dante…. His mobile is off, for a reason. Anything you can say to him you can say to me…. What? Are you sure about that?"

The door slid open. "Bruno, sorry to interrupt but I think you have to take this."

"I told those idiots not to interrupt me tonight. Who is it? Hand me the damn phone." He looked at Madeleine. "Give me a second to get rid of this arsewipe." The door clicked shut behind him.

How much of what she'd just said to Bruno had he overheard? "Dante, things are about to change, and if I don't get the chance again, I just want to tell you how much your kindness and counsel have meant to me. Being able to rely on you….” She stanched a tear. “I trust you like family.”

“You are welcome, Maddie Faye.”

You. *U.* Her jaw went slack. “*U.A.W.M.F!*” she whispered.

He gave her a shallow nod.

Her mind reeled. Syrina was the only person on earth who knew that code. Why Dante, why here, why now?

Bruno reopened the door. “Maddie, I’m afraid I have to leave. I apologize, but, well, it’s something I couldn’t have imagined. I have to take care of it tonight.”

She was in another world but managed to mumble, “Sure. I get it.”

“Are you comfortable staying here tonight? The kitchen is stocked, the beds have fresh linens. We can resume in the morning. Say nine, ten?”

“Whenever. After breakfast.”

Bruno strode toward the gangway without saying goodbye. “Let’s go, Dante.”

“I’m right behind you, Bruno.”

“Good night, Dante.” She whispered, “Can we talk later?”

“Goodbye, Madeleine.” He turned to leave without looking at her.

Her head spun. “Goodbye?”

He hesitated for a half-step before continuing out the door.

“Dante?”

Bruno took a lungful of the salty air. The dock bounced with each step, like a handshake from an old friend. Madeleine was alone on the boat; the evening was going exactly as he’d hoped. He mumbled, “She didn’t want to accept my apology, now she’ll find out what she really means to me.”

Dante caught up with him. “Sorry, what was that?”

“Nothing. Just talking to myself.”

Halfway to the cars, Dante stopped abruptly and dug through his pockets. “I’ll catch up with you. I must have left my keys on one of the deck chairs.”

"I'm going on then. Meet me at the office, old man."

"I'll be right behind you."

Bruno stopped. "On second thought, I don't feel like driving after all that. I'll pick up my car in the morning. If this business with Maddie doesn't give me a heart attack first."

"Sure. I'll make it quick." He jogged back to the yacht.

Bruno limped on to Dante's unlocked car. He adjusted the passenger seat, taking the pressure off his spine. When Dante got in and started the engine, Bruno snapped, "What took you so long?" It had been all of four minutes.

"Sorry, the keys were hiding under one of the cushions."

Chapter 54

Dante left Bruno at the container-office, where he slept well after turning off the phone ringer; it was not a night he wanted to be disturbed. But his sleep was disturbed anyway, by his thoughts. The following morning, as he got into Dante's car, he was visibly anxious. By the time they parked at the marina, his shirt was drenched in sweat.

"Are you okay, Bruno? Worried about the meeting with Madeleine?"

"I don't know. Something's wrong." He whispered, "All morning, I had this feeling, I should have left a guard here last night. I should have—"

Dante held up his hand. "Let's just go and see how she is, okay? No use worrying about what may be nothing."

And it was nothing, in a way. Halfway down the dock, they could see that the last slip, where *The Madeleine* always berthed, was empty. "What the…" Seconds passed as Bruno tried to make it make sense; gears were spinning, but nothing meshed. He looked at Dante. "What are you smiling about, old man?"

"Just thinking, maybe she got a better offer than brunch with you."

"But, there's nothing left. There's no…nothing."

"What's that supposed to mean?" Dante was enjoying this.

"Um, well, she could have…left a note. I mean, she could have waited for me. Where—"

A siren burped and the police commissioner's car squealed to a stop at the top of the pier.

Holding his oversized belly, Commissioner Franco Fierro jogged toward the men. "Mr. Porcelli. I've had people trying to find you all morning. You're here, so I guess you got the news."

"What news? No one called me. I'm here to spend the day with my wife. She slept on the yacht last night."

"Maybe we should sit down in the—"

"What news, Fierro! What the fuck is going on?" He took a step towards the commissioner.

"Take it easy, sir. Around midnight, a troller about twenty kilometers south of here saw an explosion in the distance. Their effort to get close was hampered by pieces of wreckage. At first light, the Guardia Costiera sent divers down. Another crew began examining the floating debris. It was the remains of a large vessel." He hesitated. "We have strong evidence that it was your yacht."

"No. Impossible. Maddie would never have taken it out in the dark. She wouldn't have taken it out at all. We planned to have brunch and then sail this afternoon."

Dante bit his tongue.

"Someone clearly took it out. It's not here."

Bruno glared at him. "My boat did not explode!"

"I'll just cut to the chase, Mr. Porcelli." Fierro gently gripped Bruno's forearm. "We're here to secure this area as a potential crime scene. The search crew seined the water and netted a waterproof case. It contained your wife's passport and driver's license. They've also recovered a rolling suitcase—"

"Stop! This is bullshit." He fought to catch his breath. "There has to be another explanation. Dante, you don't believe this do you? Tell him. Tell him this is not possible." Another gasp. "This can't be happening."

"I am so sorry, Bruno. Coming on the heels of your recent loss—" Fierro tried to put his arm around his shoulder.

Bruno collapsed. Dante caught him. Godspeed Maddie, he thought.

****

Antonio had been thrown back into the day-to-day operations because his purchasing manager was out on medical leave. A meeting with their flour supplier had not gone well; prices were rising faster than he could pass along. He would have to eat the loss, so to speak. When everyone had left for the day, he leaned back in his chair, loosened his tie, and sighed. He'd been at it since six a.m.

The phone rang. The last thing he wanted was another call, another problem to deal with. He let it ring eight times before snatching the handset.

"Antonio."

"Sir, this is Bruno."

"Bruno." His skin prickled. In over two years, his son-in-law had never called him. "Is Madeleine all right?"

"Did you hear the news about the offshore boat explosion?"

"I overheard the staff talking about it." Suddenly he was standing. "Why?"

"The authorities say it was our boat."

"Where is Madeleine. Tell me she's all right!"

"The Guardia Costiera still have divers out searching. They're convinced she was on board."

"Oh, God. Oh, God, no! This is a mistake. We talked just a few days ago. We made plans to have lunch, just next, um…" Fog suddenly mired his thoughts.

"I'm not sure I believe it either, sir. It makes no sense."

"Tell me what you know."

"Yesterday, she returned from a buying trip. We had dinner on the boat, planning to take it out this morning. You know how she loves the water. Around eight o'clock last night, I received an emergency call and had to leave. She wanted to stay on board. I went back to the marina this morning, and the boat was gone. No one's heard from her."

"You're right, it makes no sense. She's a first-rate sailor. But to go out alone, in the middle of the night, and without telling anyone? She was still there when you left?"

"Absolutely. She had her luggage with her."

"Why do they think it was her? Someone else could have taken it out, and…" He stopped. *Someone else could have taken it out and killed her.* His daughter could have paid the ultimate price for marrying a mobster.

"Antonio, sir." His voice softened. "They recovered a floating pouch with her passport inside."

He slumped into his chair. "But she's an excellent swimmer. She's alive. She has to be."

"If she were safe, she would have contacted one of us."

"Oh, sweet Mother. Who have you called? Syrina? The gallery?" A part of him understood Bruno would have been her first contact. Unless he was hiding something, a problem in their relationship.

"We've contacted everyone. I had to make sure before calling you. No one has heard from her."

"How could this happen?" Antonio choked back his tears. "She's my little girl!"

"The only explanation is that the explosion was meant for me. The bastards who murdered my parents are still trying to take over Porcelli Industriale."

Antonio spit on the floor. "You mean take over your drug business." The words felt like dung in his mouth. "Mario, *your father*, he promised me that Madeleine would always be safe. And she was, so long as he was alive."

"You better think again if you're trying to pin her death on me…!" He almost called him old man. "Sir, I would never do anything to put her in harm's way. She was my life. I can barely breathe knowing she's gone. This I can tell you: we will find those bastards and make them suffer!"

Antonio couldn't respond. No matter who did this, it happened on Bruno's watch. *And now, already he speaks of her in the past tense.* He was finished with Bruno. Finito! He had his own connections. They would deal with whoever murdered his daughter. His baby. He said, "thank you for calling" and hung up before Bruno could respond. He had some phone calls to make.

Chapter 55

It had been another routine day at la Questura, police headquarters in Palermo. Inspector Luca Rizzo had finished his shift. The only thing keeping him from dinner with his girlfriend was the paperwork he'd promised the Capo. Rizzo didn't cut corners; he took his police work to heart. It was a family tradition, and his Sicilian father and grandfather before him had set high standards.

After ten years on the force, his salary still didn't pay the bills. To make ends meet, he took any job that came his way. The ones that made a difference in his lifestyle were few and far between. The typical jobs meant working double shifts or standing in uniform at some museum or bank pretending to be vigilant while thinking about all the ways his mistress made him happy. Which was where his mind was now.

The desk sergeant interrupted his thoughts. "Hey Rizzo, call on line two. Something about a cat in a tree."

"You take it. I'm on unpaid overtime as it is."

"Yeah, but then you'd owe me, and we know how you hate that. Anyway, he asked for you by name."

"Merda!" He snatched the receiver. "Ispettore Rizzo. How can I help you?"

The expression on Rizzo's face did a one-eighty as he listened. "Thank you for your call, sir, but this line is for police business only. I'll be free in an hour. Let me give you my private number."

The desk sergeant couldn't miss the smile on his face.

"Wha'd I miss Rizzo?"

"Oh, some grand opening event next month. Blisters and just enough cash to cover a cheap dinner for two. You know the gig."

"Better you than me my friend."

An hour later, the pay phone rang in the piazza near Rizzo's casa. "Who is this and how the fuck did you get my number?"

Inspector Luca Rizzo, off duty, listened to the unfamiliar voice with a northern Italian accent. Rizzo had been highly recommended by a satisfied customer, and his services were urgently needed. He could do without the flattery, but the man had his attention: the deal was cash, and twice his usual rate. It would be paid all in advance, which was good, except it meant the client was powerful enough to make him seriously regret any screwups.

He was a bit nervous about a job of this magnitude without having a previous work relationship with the client, or at least an initial face-to-face, but he was a pro. Another five minutes and all the boxes were ticked. His target was a public figure in the North. The cash, photos, and other details would be delivered at a specified place and time. Once the job was done, Rizzo would call a pager and enter a two-digit code. Simple and lucrative. In other words, irresistible.

Chapter 56

Every chair at the round table inside the warehouse on pier three was occupied. The heads of all the families sat silently, avoiding eye contact, and waiting for Bruno to speak. Behind them, their number twos studied their hands. For once, there was no whisky, and no one had complained about leaving their weapons at the door.

Bruno cleared his throat. "Thank you for coming today my friends. It is appreciated. We all have businesses to run, so I'll be brief."

"Don Porcelli, if I may interrupt."

Bruno braced for a verbal attack. "Yes?"

The head of the largest family in The Collective stood. "Thank you. I will also be brief. I speak for everyone here when I say that Madeleine's death is a tragedy. She was forever the light in the room, and she is missed. Tell us what we can do to bring these killers to you."

"Thank you, Don Calderaio, for those heartfelt words. The support and kindness from this organization bring me comfort. You wish to know what you can do. I ask simply for your patience. Our unique system of protection and enforcement is the envy of the world, and the attack that killed Madeleine was an obvious attempt to take me out. To destabilize The Collective. We believe it is tied to the death of my mother and father two years ago. The trail will, no doubt, lead to one of the larger families in the south who would benefit from a takeover." Bruno paused to survey the room.

"All available resources are engaged in the hunt. Dante and his crew are on the streets, asking questions. Let your people know their cooperation is critical. And make it clear, no one in The Collective is suspect. We simply need to follow every rumor, every possible lead. Report anything out of the ordinary. An attack on one of us is an attack on every member of The

Collective."

"What about the police investigation?" Don Pillarella asked.

"Don't worry about the police. The commissioner and I have an understanding. He knows Del Coltello is leading the real investigation and that our methods tend to get better results faster. He'll keep the politicians and public happy and pass on anything he finds. We'll leave a few of the bastards for him to arrest when we're finished. We have one objective: find out who did this and remove the cancer."

Murmurs of approval broke into shouts of support.

Bruno held up his hand. "Lastly, if I may. Someone has been following me for a few days now. Dante is on it, and I am in no danger. We could have taken him out on day one, but he may be more useful alive. We've increased my perimeter security, but close up it's business as usual. Again, report anything suspicious, but do not engage. Our confidence is high." He stood and it was clear the time for questions was over. "Thank you for coming and again I appreciate your support."

From the back corner, Dante had listened to every word. And he knew it was all rubbish. No one following Bruno, no southern family, no takeover attempt. Everything was in Bruno's head. Since getting out of the hospital, his alternate reality had expanded with every dose of pain meds, shot of vodka, and line of coke. He apparently believed these fictions, which was why he was so convincing.

It was beautiful. It played perfectly into Dante's plan.

Chapter 57

A week had passed, but Bruno couldn't get it out of his mind. The memorial service. He had sat alongside Antonio, Syrina, and Silvan—Madeleine's only family. The eulogy was nice; she'd apparently been a saint. And the service was well attended. She had endless friends and business acquaintances. Plus, every politician and half of The Collective contingent made a point of being seen. It made for an interesting mix of government and mob, like a basket full of magnets with only negative poles.

The official police investigation was ongoing, and Bruno repeated his token response when asked. "Deep water and strong current limited the diver's efforts, but they've found enough of Madeleine's effects to determine that she was onboard at the time of the explosion. Sadly, that's all we know." And to a select few guests, sotto voce, he repeated the other mantra. "The southern family trying to take over our enterprise will be sorry they raised their ugly head in our territory."

The fact that she was now gone seemed almost like fantasy. They had been together for over two years. His dreams, bordering on nightmares, came every night, and they replayed as daydreams when he tried to work. Starting with their first night together in Portovenere, eating, drinking, making love, then suddenly they're arguing aboard *The Madeleine*. Then she's naked in the dark water, teasing him to follow. She laughs, knowing he can't swim. He's pushed from behind. He sinks and his last breath rises in bubbles to the surface where she's floating face down with eyes fixed in a cold stare—

Sergio, Bruno's current assistant, interrupted the daydream. "Excuse me sir."

He was back in a dim room at a desk strewn with papers, but his heart was pounding. "What is it?"

"Police Commissioner Fierro is at the garden entrance. He says he has news. Should I—"

"Yes, yes. Show him to the library and offer refreshment."

The commissioner had no business coming around here. They had an understanding. Bruno let him wait long enough to be annoying.

"Fierro. To what do I owe this surprise visit?"

"My apologies Bruno. We have a situation or I wouldn't be here. And with your recent loss, again I'm sorry."

"What's so important then?"

"We've been getting pressure from your late wife's father to dig deeper into the circumstances of her death."

"Antonio wants answers. No surprise. But you and I agreed that I'm better equipped to handle this in-house. We have every resource dedicated to finding those responsible. All you have to do is make a show, give the press the information we share with you."

"Normally that works, but this isn't just local. Antonio Costanzo is the frigging king of pizza, and he apparently knows everyone. We're getting calls from the President, the Prime Minister, hell someone even called from the Vatican. If my office doesn't show progress in ten days, they'll form a special investigation and I'll be, we'll be, out of the loop."

"Holy Mother, help us." He crossed to the window. "You were right to let me know. Leave Antonio to me. And we'll get those bastards who did this. Nothing is more important to me right now."

"What shall I say in the meantime?"

"Announce that you have evidence it's mob related. Say you have sources on the inside. You can't reveal details without jeopardizing the investigation and the lives of your undercover agents."

"I just hope that buys us some breathing room. Remember my office is at your disposal should you need assistance."

"I appreciate that, Franco. I'll let Dante know about Antonio's interference. He'll contact you at the appropriate time. Sergio!" Bruno shook the policeman's hand. "Sergio, please, see the commissioner out."

"Thank you, Don Porcelli."

Damn Antonio. Bruno mentally rearranged his priorities.

Chapter 58

Inspector Luca Rizzo took the ferry from Sicily to Villa San Giovanni, where he boarded an overnight train to his destination in the north. He enjoyed a meal in the dining car and took the remainder of the bottle of red back to his sleeper, planning to finish it as well as his prep-work. Once under the light wool blanket, the vibrations of the rails, the wine, and full stomach made it impossible to work. He thought of his wife and son, of all that he would be able to do for them with the money from this project. He was asleep in seconds, and he rested reasonably well considering the frequent announcements for every blasted stop.

When the kitchen opened, he was already seated at a sunlit table in the dining car. His schedule might not allow much time for meals, so he loaded up for the day with the large breakfast frittata, brioche with grape jam. And too much coffee, his one vice according to his wife. She thought this trip was undercover police work. His superiors pretended that he was on vacation; fortunately, they moonlighted as much as he did and never questioned such absences. Once the job was complete, he would scurry back to his family and his real job.

Stepping off the train, the brisk morning breeze greeted him, a nice change from the scorching sirocco wind in the south. Here, the bora that blunted the heat of late summer also kept the chill off in the winter. Maybe after this job he could afford a summer home up here.

First things first. He spent the morning getting the lay of the land. Without good options for a quick exit, the risk-reward was not in his favor. Once satisfied the departure would be no problem, he spent the next two days studying the target. What he observed was a pattern of movement like a regular citizen, so lax that Rizzo thought it might be a trap. The man was out in the open, taking meetings, going to lunch alone, talking to those who approached him on the street. Never more than two or three people around him at a time. Always different faces. That worried him. A typical professional detail would rotate a select few in and out, keeping a tight perimeter with their heads on a pivot, tracking who's inside the circle. He knew what to look for as well as the best, and he hadn't seen anyone who looked like security. These guys were good. He'd have to earn his money.

Chapter 59

"What are you doing here?" Bruno's eyes were bloodshot and his shirt looked like it had been slept in. "You didn't make any coffee?"

"I don't need it. What I need, Bruno, is for you to stop this southern conspiracy bullshit."

They were in the container-office. Dante had waited all morning for him to show up. What he had to say required complete privacy.

"How is it bullshit? I got it from you, asshole." His eyes were dilated. "You said the Sicilians were taken care of."

"That is not what I said. You heard what you wanted to hear."

Bruno sat at his desk and withdrew a flask from the file drawer. "I heard every word you announced."

"I don't make public statements. Listen carefully. The word on the street was that *it* was taken care of."

"The Sicilians. It. Same difference."

"No, it is not. Remember telling me to keep my nose out of your shipping business? Well the same goes for you and my business. Micro-managing is dangerous in your position. All you need to know is that a problem has gone away. Call it magic, call it an act of God, or be like your dad and just trust me to do the right thing.”

Bruno bristled. “I’m not my dad.” He was fed up with the comparisons.

“From the beginning, Mario and I had complete faith in each other. If we stayed within The Collective guidelines, results were all that mattered. And it always worked. But since that hasn’t sunk in yet for you, this one time I’m going to spell it out.”

“Don’t do me any favors.”

“Believe me, I’m not. I’m keeping you from getting yourself killed.” Dante waited until he locked eyes with him. “After the police investigated the explosion at Mario’s, I called in a friend from the resistance, an expert. He sifted through the debris and took samples. Based on his years of wartime and homemade explosive knowledge, he said it had very likely been an accident. The combination of a gas leak and an unexploded ordnance from World War II.”

“You can’t be serious. Does this guy know our business?”

“What do you think Bruno?” Dante could see sweat start to bead around his eyes. “I was aching, *aching* to punish someone for killing your parents. I sent my people all over the continent, running down leads. All they found were dead ends. You know as well as I do that is not how things go down in this business. People can’t keep their mouth shut. They brag. Couple of drinks and out it slips.”

Bruno clenched his jaw. “You can’t expect me to believe it was some old war accident.”

“Goddammit, listen to me. Have you seen anything to indicate a takeover attempt? Has supply or shipping been disrupted? Any issues on the street, other than stupidity?” He leaned across the desk. “It. Was. Handled!”

Bruno balled his fists and started to stand. Dante pointed a finger at his face.

“From now on, any issues with my results, complain to The Collective. Vote me out if you want, but you will never question my methods again.” Bruno’s jaw dropped. “Tell me you fully understand!”

Like a bear, Bruno’s answer was a powerful right hand thrown from the hip. In one motion Dante sidestepped the blow, swept Bruno’s fragile legs out from under him, and placed the edge of his knife, *the* knife, against Bruno’s jugular. “I said, do you understand?”

Embarrassed, in pain, and bested by an old man. He closed his eyes.

"Look, I know the explosion took a toll. It wrecked you. But hell, most men would not have even survived it." He withdrew the knife. "Just get some help. Listen to your doctors. No one wants to see you in pain."

When Bruno opened his eyes again, they were twin seas of boiling rage. They followed Dante out the door.

Chapter 60

After four tiring days in the city, Luca Rizzo was anxious for this project to be over. He missed his family, his girlfriend, and his Sicilian lifestyle; something about the north disagreed with him. There was one last detail to work out before he did the deed: make sure he could reach the target from inside the secure perimeter rather than risk passing through it. The skill of the target's protection team was surreal. Rizzo understood why the client was willing to pay so well for his services.

On the other hand, the target himself made it easy. He was a creature of habit during the workday, especially at lunch. Sometimes eating solo, sometimes talking business, but you could set your watch with his timing. Rizzo's plan was to arrive at the restaurant early, order food, and wait. The only problem, he looked like the third-generation cop that he was. That helped in his official job, but today blending in was critical. Fortunately, the weather forecast called for drizzle and cooler than normal temps. Stealth would be a bit easier.

Rizzo arrived before the lunch rush. He selected a table and sat with his back against the wall. It had a view of the main entrance but was near the kitchen in case an unexpected exit became necessary. He ordered appetizers and coffee, black. He paid the check in advance, then laid a large tip on the tray. The waiter kept the coffee coming.

Rizzo was not a religious man. This was as close as he ever got to God: he knew when this guy's life would end. And he knew the tension was inevitable, the pressure that builds as you prepare to kill. No matter how often you do it, it never gets easier. Just different. A stiletto through the heart, a garrote from the backseat of a moving car, or a plastic bag and a roll of tape. Rizzo's preference? A double tap to the forehead with a .38. Indoors, the sound is like a cannon and sends the innocents to the floor or out the door. No one looks at your face.

The target was due any minute, but the endless coffee refills suddenly had his full attention. As much as he wanted to witness the arrival, he had to hit the head. He casually made his way to the facilities. He was gone two minutes, but the target and another gentleman were just being seated when he returned.

The guy accompanying the target was a new face. A big man, like the mark, but in better shape. And judging by the way his jacket hung, he was carrying. Security was throwing curveballs. Why the obvious guardia del corpo now? No way he'd been spotted. What had changed?

In a few minutes, he thought he understood the muscle's presence. A much younger man, awkwardly uncomfortable and inappropriately dressed, entered and approached the table. The bodyguard snapped to high alert. As his hand moved to his weapon, the target stood and greeted the newcomer warmly. The guard relaxed. It had the look of a business meeting.

The booth where the target always sat was less than optimum. When it came time to make his move, the front door and most of the guests would be at his back. His assessment of the staff and patrons indicated a low threat level, but the bodyguard was bound to have well-honed counter moves for every possible scenario. Pulling the trigger would be easy, no way for anyone to stop that from happening. It was what came after that concerned him now. He considered waiting a day, but since his face had likely been registered by the target and the guard, it had to be today. This moment.

As he prepared to move, the mood at the other table turned contentious. It had the signs of a deal going bad. Voices were raised. All eyes turned to the younger guy, the late arrival. He abruptly pushed back from the table and hurried around the corner toward the toilets. Rizzo considered his options. Normally a target plus one was a slice of pie, but with the younger man out of sight, he decided to hold steady.

Ten minutes and counting. The kid had been gone too long. Something was up. If Rizzo hadn't cased the place the night before, he would have thought the defeated pup had bolted. But the corridor he'd disappeared into was a dead end.

Seconds later, the kid returned from his intermission with a spring in his step. He must have used a phone back there, because when he rejoined the others the conversation at the table lightened. Like they'd won the lottery. Champagne was ordered, backs were slapped. The kid had somehow pulled the business deal out of the toilet.

The celebration changed things for Rizzo, too. The clock was now his friend.

The more alcohol they consumed, the slower their reaction times. Let them drink and be merry, for tomorrow will never come. Or something like that, he thought.

Thirty minutes later, the target and his companions showed no signs of slowing down. The wine was taking hold.

For the second time, Rizzo decided the moment had come. He could hear his heart thrum over the buzz of conversation and the scrape of silver on china. His adrenaline pumped. Time slowed. He folded his newspaper and placed it on the corner of the table. In one motion he stood, turned his back to the target and with his left hand picked up his raincoat from the chair to his right. Simultaneously, he pulled his snub nose revolver from its speed draw holster and draped the coat over his right forearm and hand, covering the weapon.

Turning to his left, Rizzo kept his head down and averted his gaze, visualizing the next five seconds over and over. "Walk along the wall toward the kitchen. Turn right and cross. Make a quick ninety-degree pivot, face the table, push the muzzle clear of the coat, engage the bodyguard first, then the target, then the kid. Walk with purpose out the front door. Head down, no eye contact. Disappear."

Rizzo crossed near the front of the target's table. As soon as he turned, the bodyguard's instincts clicked in. Their eyes locked. Time stopped. A flash of surprise on the bodyguard's face, then confusion, and finally acceptance, knowing that today he was too slow. Still, he reached for his piece and cried out, but the warning had barely left his lips before Rizzo's .38 FBI load exploded lead at over three hundred meters per second, penetrating the bodyguard's right temple, spraying human debris into the air and onto the target's face.

One half second later, before the sound of the first round faded, Rizzo followed his aim into the stare of his target. No threat there, only terror. Arms crossed over his face were his only protection. The money shot formed a perfect triangle with the eyes, as if flesh had been sucked into a dark red hole that Rizzo had willed into existence. The target's head snapped back, spewing a trail to the ceiling and on the starched white tablecloth.

Suddenly, the screams. Movement in the room. If there was to be resistance, it would come now. It didn't.

The kid knew he was next. Rizzo could see him calculate his odds, but he was multiplying by zero. His gut said fight, but he closed his eyes and ducked his head. The last round bit into his skull and bounced around inside like a magic bullet. It exited the fleshy void just under his Adam's apple and pushed him forward and facedown onto the table now filling with blood.

Except for the intense ringing in his ears, the room was eerily silent. Rizzo turned to see chaos; tables upturned, people running, people hiding, food everywhere. Without another thought, he moved deliberately toward the exit. He stepped over chairs, people pretending to be dead, and random shoes. Why were there always shoes? No one confronted him and no one dared catch his eye.

Once on the street he wiped his face and hands with his handkerchief. He pulled on his raincoat and walked briskly toward the city center. Minutes later he stepped into the central railway station, inserted a coin into a pay phone, dialed a pager, and entered a prearranged two-digit number. One-five. Confirmation that the project was complete.

Inspector Luca Rizzo was never there.

Chapter 61

All Syrina had was a passport, an American Express Gold Card, and the clothes she'd been wearing when she opened the mail three hours earlier. Milan's Linate Airport was packed with late morning vacationers. Every non-stop flight to every New York City area airport was fully booked—it was Labor Day weekend there. She got on stand-by with three airlines and began searching for one-stop and layover solutions. Arriving tomorrow might be too late.

Ten minutes before a United departure for Newark, a seat in first class opened up. Ridiculously expensive. She grabbed it.

Syrina thanked God for Amex Gold. And Silvan's wealth. And first-class service. Who had come up with the hot towel idea? Brilliant. The Michelin starred meal. The first run movie. She needed the pampering.

Somewhere over France, after her second glass of Champagne, she pulled the postcard from her purse and stared at the words she'd circled. Reality began to creep in. Was this a goose chase, someone's sick joke? Maybe it had been sent by one of Maddie's college friends and she had only imagined the sister code; grief could play tricks, make you believe your fantasies. But game or reality, she had to continue the pursuit; her message to Silvan had dragged him and her father into the loop for Christ's sake. With a third flute full of bubbly, a blindfold, and a fleece blanket, Syrina fell asleep with the postcard still in her hand.

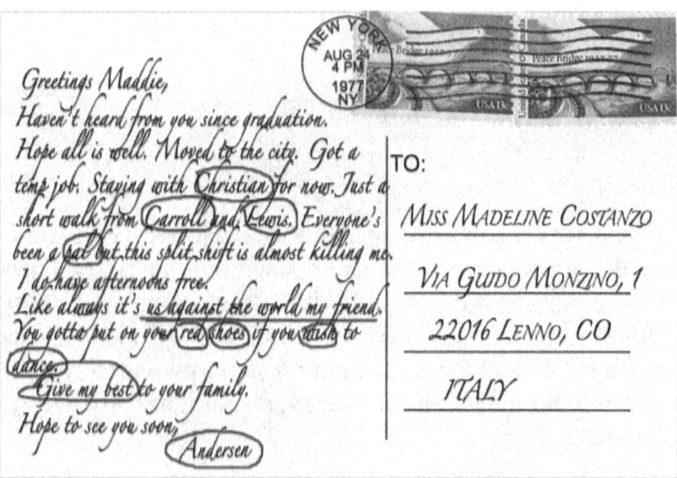

The flight was uneventful and she was first off the plane. Customs was a breeze—she had no luggage—although the agent did mumble it was too bad he couldn't rummage through her underwear. Pervert. Traffic in the Lincoln Tunnel moved and Hell's Kitchen was clear. The cab dropped her in front of the Dakota. She walked East into Central Park, caught her bearings at the Mall, then cut across Pilgrim Hill. She was practically running by now. When she reached the boat pond, she stopped short. It was packed with children and parents and radio-controlled boats. A perfect place to hide on a holiday afternoon, she thought.

She circled the Hans Christian Andersen statue, then turned north along the path to Wonderland. Nothing. It was just after three p.m. The postcard implied two to four p.m.

She retraced her steps, moving slowly, taking time to examine every face.

Back at the statue she plopped on the bench, rested an elbow on the top hat, and closed her eyes for a second. Hunger. Stress. Fatigue.

Some twenty minutes later a voice in her dream yelled *get off the bench, you're spoiling the photo.* Her eyelids fluttered and she heard it again, "Hey lady, move your fat ass, I wanna take a picture with my kid."

Jeeze, she thought. Why do all New Yorkers sound like they're from my neighborhood?

"Okay, okay. Sorry." She shuffled to her feet, then like a blast of wind had struck her, she sat back down hard. "Maddie!"

The silent embrace squeezed the breath out of them both, like that moment years ago when they learned their mother had been killed. But this time the emotion was elation. Death cheated, life restored, family reunited. They would never take such things for granted.

Madeleine pulled back first. "Does Papà know I'm alive?"

"He should know by now. I left a message on Silvan's machine. We were all supposed to have lunch, probably eight hours ago now. Tell me what happened."

She shook her head. "It's good news as well as bad, and it's almost beyond belief. But it's a long story and I'm starving."

"That's my Maddie. Isn't the Boathouse around here?"

"Good memory. We can walk."

Syrina said, "Are you too hungry to at least tell me the good news?"

"Sure. We have an older brother." Just like that.

Syrina's face flashed from confusion to disbelief. "That's not possible. Mother never said anything."

"She didn't know. It was before her time with Papà, when he was in the great war."

"A half-brother? What's his name? And how do you know this?"

"I'll save his identity for the end. How I know is, twenty years ago, Papà wrote us a letter. And our brother gave it to me."

"Are you fricking making this up?"

"Nope. Let me back up. There's too much to tell."

****

Service was incredibly slow. By the time they received menus and glasses of ice water, Maddie had covered what she knew about their brother's history. Syrina was tired of waiting to understand why her little sister was secretly back in America.

"Look, we may never get our food. Tell me the bad news."

"Sure. From the start. You knew Bruno and I were having issues?"

"If by issues you mean he was abusing you, of course I knew."

"Oh. Well, he wanted to meet, to clear the air. Said he was controlling his meds and had stopped drinking. Said he loved me and wanted us to be like we used to. He wanted to be a good father to his child."

"What?" Half the water that she was about to swallow spewed out. "Are you pregnant?"

She tried not to smile. "You're the first person after my doctor and Bruno to know. I was planning to tell you, that week when I last visited."

"That's why you were on the yacht, to tell him."

"Oh, he already knew I was pregnant. I met with him to discuss the future."

"But meeting him in private? Not your most brilliant move, little sis."

"Twenty-twenty. But I did have back up. Remember Dante?"

"Yeah, I've talked with him on occasion. Good guy."

"Hold that thought. When I arrived, Dante stepped out while Bruno and I talked. More like he rambled. I could see he wasn't about to change and I called him on it. He puffed up and things got tense, but then he got an urgent phone call and had to leave."

"Why didn't you leave as well?"

"I would have. My plan was to head up to your place at the lake. Until…" Madeleine gazed off into the distance.

"Until what?"

"While Bruno was on the call, Dante and I were alone. I realized I might never see him again. I told him how much I appreciated his help and kindness over the years. And he said, "You are welcome, Maddie Faye.""

"What the—? How could he, how could anyone know that?"

"Exactly. So, Bruno came back in and said something about me sleeping on the boat and us talking again after breakfast. Mentally, I was already at your place. Except, they left, and about two minutes later Dante rushed back on board. He handed me a small watertight pouch and said, "Maddie, I'm your half-brother, my mother and our father were in love in France at the end of the war. Trust me. Your life is in danger. Bruno plans to blow up the boat with you on it. It's important that he thinks you're dead or he'll keep trying. In this pouch is a letter from our father to you and Syrina. Also, there are instructions from me on how to survive this night. Follow them exactly." He gave me a quick hug and was gone.

"So, what he said was all true."

"Dante always seemed to just be there, and I always trusted him. Now I understand why."

"What did you do?"

"What do you think? I followed the instructions. I'm here aren't I?" She passed Syrina a handwritten note from her purse.

> Wait 15min. Then set a Waypoint to
> 44°20'18.0"N 9°09'14.7"E
> When you clear the harbor, pilot the boat full speed for 36 minutes. You'll find a buoy 80 meters offshore.
> Once there, set a new Waypoint to
> 44°16'30.8"N 8°54'14.3"E
>
> Engage the auto pilot at 3 knots and leave the boat. Regardless of what else may happen, be off the boat before midnight! Swim ashore. Take NOTHING. Leave all your clothes on the boat.
>
> Twenty paces up the cut in the hillside you will find a rock that looks out of place. Under it is a backpack with a fake passport, new clothes, and money. More instructions are inside. Disappear. Don't look back. Have a good life Maddie Faye.
>
> Dante

Syrina slapped the table. "Oh, that son of a bitch!" Half the restaurant turned to look. She whispered, "Bruno's acted like he was in mourning this whole time. Spreading lies, saying that the explosion was meant for him. He's blaming people and killing them because of it."

"Until this, I had held out hope. But he's not the man I loved. He's completely out of control. Papà and Silvan can't let on that I'm alive or he'll come after all of us."

"We'll call them and explain."

"No! If I could call, I would have the first day. Dante wrote that Bruno has been so paranoid he's been listening in on phone calls, opening mail, and having people followed. Me mostly."

"That's why the postcard to yourself."

"I prayed it would make it to you without raising suspicion."

"How did Dante know Bruno planted explosives? Oh my god. Dante, our brother."

"No idea. I just know he's very good at his job."

"What's next? Do you have any ideas?"

"Nothing solid. Why do you think I reached out to my two-and-ten big sister?"

"Ha. You're the smart one, Maddie Faye. We'll finish dinner if it ever comes, get a bottle of red to go, and come up with a plan. Where are you staying?"

Chapter 62

Maddie was staying in a cheap flop in mid-town. The anonymity was good, and she only had so much money left to live on, but Syrina cringed knowing her sister was stuck in this dump. She would take a cash advance on her card and make sure Maddie didn't have to worry about money going forward.

After they had finished the bottle and nearly talked themselves dry, Maddie remembered the letter Dante had passed along.

"Papà wrote this when we were little and gave it to Dante for safe keeping." She handed it to Syrina and watched her face change as she read.

December 1, 1960

Dearest Syrina and Madeleine,

I hope this finds you happy and well. If you are reading this, there has been a life-changing event in our family or I am unable to speak with you in person.

First of all please know that I love you both with all that I am. I have enjoyed every moment of our time together. You are gifts from God.

I was past my middle years when your wonderful mother and I met, and with her joyous nature she taught me how to love again. We were so very happy together.

What I tell you now comes without shame or disrespect to your mother. You have an older brother. His name is Dante Arsenault. He currently lives and works in Genoa. He knows about you and depending on when you read this you may be acquainted. He is a good and resourceful man whom I trust completely.

Let me tell you the story.

I enlisted in the Italian Army just before I turned 18. I saw more than my share of combat at the front. War is brutal. I experienced so much of which I can never speak. I was stationed in France for two years. After weeks of fighting, we would be given days of leave to rest and recuperate from the trauma. In one quiet village I met a refugee from northern France. Her name was Marie. We were the same age. We met because we shared the same birthday.

She was kind and beautiful and just as inexperienced in life as I was. From that day on we were together; we talked, drank wine, went for long walks in the countryside. We fell in love.

We made the best of our short time. When I prepared to return to the front, I promised Marie I would come back for her, and she promised to wait for me.

I wrote her every day never knowing if my words found her eyes. I waited in vain to hear my name at mail call. When the war ended, I returned to the village only to find someone else in Marie's room. She had gone. I was devastated. The kind old woman there placed a letter in my hand. I tore it open realizing the letter could spell out a reality I didn't want to hear. She had returned to her home to try to locate her family. I searched for months but never found her again. Years later, she found me.

She visited sometimes at the downtown pizzeria. The woman with the tiny music box that you played with, that was her. She sometimes brought her son with her. Our son. Your brother. You might remember.

Syrina looked up from the letter. Madeleine had fallen asleep. She had the most peaceful look on her face.

Chapter 63   SOME TWELVE HOURS EARLIER

Dante was on his way to Milan for lunch with his father, Syrina, and Silvan. Antonio had promised to reveal that Dante was his son. Dante planned to use the time before Syrina arrived to explain to his father what had happened to Madeleine, and how he hoped she might still be alive.

The key to it all had been the report Dante's man had given about Bruno carrying some unusual purchases aboard *The Madeleine*. Hours after hearing that, Dante had searched the yacht and found explosives in the engine room. They were set to detonate at midnight. The instant he realized that disabling the device was not a long-term solution, a plan, fully formed, appeared in his mind.

After the explosion, he had reduced the plan to a checklist and updated it daily.

- Keep Madeleine alive —Done, to be verified

- Bruno must think Madeleine died in the explosion —Done

- Let Bruno reinforce rumors of a southern family takeover attempt —On going

- Hire out-of-town talent to gun down Bruno in a public place —In progress

- After the hit, eliminate the 'southern shooter'. Use the knife. The Collective will be satisfied —Pending

- Madeleine returns with a story of being kidnapped, days after the shooter is eliminated —Pending

- Retire, move to Milan, make pizza —This year, God willing

Now, it was a beautiful morning. The whole of northern Italy was cast in sunshine and mild temperatures. During the two-hour drive to Milan, he thought of what he would and would not say to his father. First, he would explain why he had withheld the dark facts about Bruno—it had been to keep Antonio safe. Then he would describe the situation. Bruno had planted the explosives and spread rumors of a takeover to eliminate suspicion. And according to where the boat fragments were found, Madeleine had followed his instructions; she may have escaped unharmed. He would promise that, very soon, Bruno would never threaten or harm anyone again. Finally, if Antonio would still have him, he would ask to join the family business in Milan.

He rolled up the car windows as he neared the city. The sky had grayed as a chill wind picked up, but he beamed, proud to realize that Madeleine had shown complete trust in him prior to her learning that they had the same father.

He had so much to tell the family when the opportunity presented itself. Following Mario's death, and out of deep respect for the man, Dante had been cleaning up Bruno's missteps one after another. The Collective's charter had given Dante the latitude to remove anyone, even Bruno, who put their operation in jeopardy. His plan had been to wait for the right time and quietly remove Bruno from power, then let Maddie head up the shipping business and slowly transfer the bloody underbelly to someone else in The Collective. Bruno's unconscionable plot to kill Madeleine had not changed Dante's ultimate objectives, only the timing.

Dante's preferred method would have been to reintroduce Bruno to the knife, but sometimes a free kick needs to be from your off foot. Firearms were required. Anyone worth their salt could pull it off, but experience—a veteran respectful of the unwritten rules—was worth paying extra for. A disguise, a room full of civilians, a quick tap to the head. Walk away, disappear. Better odds than a sniper shot, and less difficult than the dangerous tasks he himself had completed behind enemy lines.

Antonio stood outside the door to Santiago's. Many of Milan's popular downtown restaurants were closed on Mondays, but Santiago's was always open, another reason it was Antonio's current favorite. It was a small, family run establishment serving authentic Mexican food from the Baja region. Each mid-day it was filled with locals who hoped to keep the secret to themselves.

Over lunch today, Antonio would introduce Dante to the rest of the family— Syrina and Silvan. It was overdue. He should have done it soon after the passing of Donice, the girls' mother. The time had never seemed right. Now, he thought, Maddie would never know she had had a brother.

The last days had been like a fog. The explosion, the investigation, the memorial service. He hadn't allowed himself to think of his daughter as dead. In his mind she was back at school. He would receive a call. She would be home for the holidays.

He took a deep breath as he touched the brass doorknob to the restaurant. Dante was waiting just inside, assessing the room. He forced a smile. "Dante, you beat me this time. It's good to see you."

"And you sir. I arrived just this minute. Let me take your umbrella."

Antonio smiled warmly. "Are you ready for today? You seem a little anxious."

"I've been looking forward to this for as long as I can remember. I suppose I am a bit tense." It was the acme of understatements. Dante was indeed nervous about Syrina and her husband learning that he was family. But he was also on edge because Bruno was a rich, unpredictable, and delusional narcissist with a well-developed sense of entitlement, who was angry that Antonio had pressured God and half the country to expand the investigation. He was like a runaway train capable of going off the rails at any moment. And if that wasn't enough, minutes after Antonio introduced him to Syrina and Silvan as part of their family, he would tell them that Bruno had been responsible for blowing up the yacht with Maddie on board. It was a trifecta of stresses.

"Welcome Signore Costanzo. It's always an honor to serve you."

"Thank you, Santiago. It's the magic of your recipes that keeps me coming back."

Santiago bowed his head slightly. "Right this way gentlemen. We have your booth ready as always. Are you expecting other guests?"

"There will be four of us today Santiago."

"Sangria to start?"

"Yes. All around please."

Antonio slid across the cool, dark leather to the booth's center while Dante sat at the curve on his right side. Antonio smiled as Dante rescanned the room for anything out of place. Old habits. A table of tourist practiced their Italian, a large group of co-workers celebrated someone's birthday, and an older well-dressed businessman studied the financial pages. Nothing out of the ordinary. Suddenly, chill air swept the room as the door to the sidewalk burst opened. A disheveled man rushed past the maître d' and hurried forward with his eyes fixed on Antonio. Dante reached under his suit coat and touched the steel grip in its holster. A split second later, he relaxed as Antonio spoke and stood to greet the man.

"Silvan, so good to see you. This is Dante Arsenault. Dante, this is Syrina's husband, Silvan Keller."

"I believe I saw you at the memorial, but we didn't get a chance to meet. It's a pleasure, sir."

"It's a pleasure to meet you as well, Silvan."

Antonio boomed, "Sit, sit. And where is that daughter of mine?"

"I thought she would be here by now," Silvan said. "The last thing she said this morning was, 'See you at noon. Don't be late.' It's probably traffic."

"The city is growing too fast," Antonio said.

"That's why Syrina and I love it so much at the lake. Dante, how do you know Antonio?"

"We go back many years." It was not his story to tell. "Antonio has mentioned your computer business is very successful. They say it's the future."

"Not much to tell really." Silvan liked nothing better than talking about his business. "I came up with a way to consolidate multiple miniature transistors into a single board. Of course, that original design is obsolete. On average we shrink and double the transistor count every eighteen months. I was just lucky to be there in the beginning. You work in Bruno's shipping business?"

"Yes, I've been with the business for many years. I started with Bruno's father, Mario. Let me ask you. As our shipping containers travel around the world, is there a way to keep track of them real-time?"

"Nothing that I know of, but that would be a game changer. I do know the United States is still sending navigation satellites into orbit. It has to be some sort of triangulation system, but it's all military. Top secret stuff as yet."

Antonio interrupted. "Silvan, I'm a little concerned, would you mind calling Syrina? Maybe she forgot."

Silvan looked at his watch. "Fudge. Two thousand dollars for this thing and I think it's stopped."

The others checked theirs. After a warm debate over whether it was twelve-fourteen or twelve-seventeen, Silvan said, "Anyway, I'll be right back."

Father and son shared another glass of sangria, talked about the sudden change in the weather, the subtle quality of Santiago's homemade chips and salsa fresco, the latest football match. Antonio glanced at the door where Silvan had disappeared a few minutes earlier. "Dante, I know you're ready for me to make this right. I should have done it years ago. I hope you will forgive me."

"I understand, sir. It can't be easy. And not all doughnuts come out with a hole."

"I believe you may have a second career as a poet, my son."

"Interesting you mention second careers. I would like to talk to you later about an idea I have."

But Antonio was distracted and looked at his watch again. "He is taking too long to track down Syrina. Would you check what's going on?"

Dante started to rise just as Silvan rushed back into the room. He was saying something.

"She's alive! Antonio, she's alive!"

"What? What's happened? Is she hurt?"

"Syrina's fine. It's Maddie. She's alive!"

"Maddie!" The blood rushed to his head. "Are you sure? How can you know?"

Dante said a prayer of thanks. He had known it in his gut, but the confirmation was ambrosia. And later, it would make his revelations about Bruno easier for them to hear.

Silvan was bubbling over, laughing, wiping away tears. "I called everywhere I could think. I checked with her friends. It was on my machine. She left two long messages on my answering machine at the office. She said that this morning she received a postcard, mailed from New York City, addressed to Madeleine Costanzo at our villa in Lenno."

"If it was *to* Maddie, not from her, I don't understand."

"To her, but Syrina is positive it was also from her. Something about a 'sister code'? Syrina was at the airport, about to board, when she left the messages. She got lucky with the flights and will land in New York at two p.m. their time."

Antonio checked his watch. "They're six hours behind us. So, about seven hours from now."

"Yes, sir. She said she will call you at home as soon as they connect."

"I cannot believe this. I knew in my bones Maddie was alive. This calls for a celebration. Santiago, your best bottle of Franciacorta, my friend!"

Now, the story Antonio came to share with Syrina need not wait. As Santiago opened a second bottle, he told Silvan, in loving detail, how he met and fell in love with a beautiful French girl during the last year of the war.

"I returned from the front, eager to see my love. The only thing waiting for me was a letter." He still had it memorized. "It said, 'Dearest Antonio, I waited as long as I could but I must return home to search for my family. Please find me. I love you always, Marie.' At the bottom, she had printed in clear block letters her family's address in the north of France."

He folded his hands in his lap and stared into the distance.

"As soon as the war ended, I made my way from Paris to the northeast. Her village had been destroyed and was now within the Zone Rouge. Signs there said 'Impossible to clean. Human life impossible.' I searched for her in increasing circles all around the zone. I scoured Paris and other cities and villages. I never gave up hope, even when my money was gone and there were no more leads. I wrote letters every month to her last address, waiting to search again when time and money aligned.

"A few years after the war, I opened my first restaurant. Antonio's Pizzeria in Milan. Short staffed on a busy Tuesday, I handed menus to a family at table number six, by the window. A man, a woman, and their young son. The woman, still looking at the menu, said, 'We'll each have the special, a carafe of white, and one water.' There was something about her voice. She looked up and our eyes locked. It was Marie. I could not move."

Antonio paused. His eyes filled with tears as he looked at Dante.

"In that instant I could see that she knew. She knew I still loved her and would keep her secret. She asked whether we had a toilet and I led her down the stairs. At the bottom, I stopped and faced her with no idea what to do. But Marie knew. She tiptoed up and kissed me, as if time no longer separated us, just the way I still dreamed. 'I am so happy to see you,' she said. 'Let me look at you. You've filled out a bit. Eating your own cooking I see.' I explained how I had searched for years, all the letters I had written. She touched her finger to my lips. 'I never doubted for a moment that you would try to find me. I left every trail I could and wrote to the Army repeatedly. Last year I was contacted by the Zone Rouge Resettlement Relief Program that reconnects displaced families. They said they had a stack of letters addressed to me. They were all from you, more than one hundred. I cried over each one as I read about where you were searching. Antonio, so many times we had been in the same village, just blocks from each other.' We had been that close."

He put his hand on Dante's. "So close, I told her, but you are married now.

You have a handsome young son. She told me about her husband, Rémy Arsenault. 'He works for the French Government. We have been married for seven years. Dante is eight.' She stopped as the news dawned on me. Dante was my son. 'He's a good child,' she said. 'He got all your best parts. Please forgive me for moving on. I had to think about Dante's future. Rémy is a good man. He has accepted Dante as his own.'

"She answered my question before I could ask. 'Rémy knows everything. He has come to understand that my heart has room to love more than one person. In fact, it was his idea to visit you. He thinks it's the first step in preparing Dante for the truth.'

"I can't put a name on what I was feeling in that moment," Antonio explained to Dante and Silvan. "My heart was so light but empty as well. Marie was alive. I had a son. I was shocked, happy, sad, and I had no idea what was yet to come. Marie led me back to the table and introduced me to Dante as a close friend from the war. I gave Dante a tour of the kitchen, showed him how to toss a pie and let him slide one out of the wood fired oven with the long-handled paddle. Later, I spoke with Rémy separately and thanked him for allowing me to be a part of Dante's life. Those two unexpected hours changed my life forever."

Dante had never heard the full story before, and he had never seen Antonio so happy. But the brief history of how he had found Marie had a twisted parallel—Antonio would soon realize that, in order for Madeleine to live, she would have to remain hidden, by all appearances, dead. Bruno would not fail if he had a second opportunity. The moment Silvan left the table, Dante would assure his father that Bruno would soon be neutralized.

Antonio's voice interrupted his thoughts. "Another toast gentlemen. Here's to our family!"

As the crystal ping touched his eardrum, Dante saw a metallic flash from the corner of his eye. He flung his glass at the man's face and yelled "Get down!". As he moved to cover Antonio, he simultaneously reached under his suit coat for his SIG Sauer. Before the pistol had cleared his shoulder holster, his head snapped back and exploded onto the leather upholstery. Silvan closed his eyes and ducked. Antonio crossed his forearms in front of his face. Two more shots erupted from the gun. As his last breath seeped out, Antonio slid slowly into Dante's outstretched arm. Silvan crumpled facedown onto his plate.

Chaos burst beneath tables and behind doors. Sulphur and screams pierced the air as blood dripped and mixed with sangria on the floor. It happened between heartbeats; no one would recall anything more than an older well-dressed businessman with a raincoat casually walking out the front door.

Chapter 64

Somewhere buried in the back of a desk drawer the muffled beeping of a pager sounded. Moving with effort from his leather recliner, a large man with a knife tattooed on his inner wrist reached to silence it. He poured another deep glass of clear liquid before flipping the display upside down turning '15' into 'Si'. Yes.

Bruno took a long drink and squeezed a shallow smile.

PIZZA KING DEAD

AP, MILAN

Antonio Costanzo, prominent Italian restaurateur, was gunned down today while dining at Santiago's in Milan. His son-in-law, SK Transistor founder Silvan Keller, was also killed, along with an unidentified private security guard. Police have not released the identity of a fourth man fitting the description of the assailant who was found dead just hours later less than four blocks away, the victim of strangulation. The investigation is ongoing.

Part III The Angel

2018

Chapter 1

A shiver ran down Alice's spine when Russell walked in and worked his way through the crowd. Someone near the front stood and gave him their seat. She had but a few minutes to decide whether to approach him after the auction—the final lot was up, and bidding would start any second.

"Ladies and gentlemen, we conclude this afternoon's activities with The Angel, a late fifteenth early sixteenth century treasure, believed to be by Giuseppe da San Russo. Roberta, if you please."

The auctioneer motioned and the curtains behind him parted to reveal an easel supporting a small portrait. The work was of a young, barely clad, hauntingly beautiful lady of the night, draped across a quattrocento sofa.

"If you've read the catalogue description, you know this piece has been recently authenticated to be from the high renaissance period, and is likely the only surviving work among the twelve paintings described in the so-called San Russo Legend, also from the high renaissance. Written on the back is *Il bellissimo angelo,* The Beautiful Angel, and it is signed Giuseppe. Oil on walnut board, minor crazing on the upper left background, otherwise impeccably preserved, the colors fresh as the day they were applied. We begin the bidding at the reserve of six hundred thousand euros. Do we have, yes, six hundred, thank you Mr. Modica. Seven hundred? Seven hundred on my left, number ten thirty-one."

By the time the bidding reached one-point-two million, seven of the nine bidders had dropped out. The two still in the hunt were both middle-aged men on their cell phones. Word of the escalating price had spread beyond the doors of the auction room, and gallery employees of all stripes were slipping in to witness what seemed a historic moment. The room was silent except for the whispers of the two bidders into their phones and the auctioneer's few words to each of them in turn. When the hammer came down, The Angel sold for one-point-seven million euros. The crowd erupted. Someone popped a Champagne bottle and the cork hit the ceiling.

Alice hadn't seen Russell in over a year. She remained in the back of the room as he shook hands and laughed with one patron after another. As the backslaps and high fives and noise faded and the crowd moved back into the gallery, she made her way toward the front where he was now seated at a table, about to sign a document.

She forced a dry swallow. "Don't let me interrupt."

"She said, interrupting." Russell shook his head and glanced up with a full-toothed grin. "Well, you just never know who you'll run into at one of these things." He patted the seat beside him. Alice was impeccably dressed and made up like an Italian movie star, but she suddenly felt plain. He winked and gave her an admiring glance up and down. She let out a breath. "Give me a sec," he said.

"That's all I've got. I just wanted to say hello. Any chance you'll still be around tomorrow?"

"No, not likely." Russell signed the last page of the document and handed it to a young man. "Grazie mille, giovanotto. E ringrazio la signora Areni," he said. The gallery owner's assistant nodded and hurried away.

"You know her? Mrs. Areni?" Alice's eyebrow arched as she thought of the elderly but notoriously reclusive proprietor of Areni Arte Gallery and Auction House. "What am I saying? Of course you know her."

Russell looked down and coughed. Alice thought she saw him blush. "The gallery recommended the family work with me to lead the authentication of The Angel—"

"You actually know the Florence Family? The sellers? Like, literally *nobody's* been able to figure out who they are. And you authenticated their masterpiece? Tell me!"

'The Florence Family' was how the media had come to refer to the owners of The Angel, the most talked about painting for the past six months.

Alice locked eyes with Russell. Yes, he was connected to almost everyone of significance in the world of fine art—and on a first name basis with many—but this was unbelievable. He held her gaze until she looked away.

The sellers' identity would remain secret.

"No, I organized the team but wasn't available to join the authentication. Once they decided it was indeed late fifteenth century, I came over and did the appraisal. That's when I met the family. They were convinced, or at least pretended to be, that their painting was tied to the San Russo village legend—"

"Which had just been made public?" she guessed.

"Yes, someone, probably the family, leaked it, which certainly complicated my job. If the legend is true, the value of the painting skyrockets. Obviously, today's bidders believe it's true."

"I heard the family tried to auction it once before," she said.

"A few years ago, but it didn't come close to their reserve price. Sixty thousand euros at that time, can you imagine? Once the authentication came back late 1400's, well, you see what just happened."

She nodded. "I can tell you the gallery did one fine job spreading the rumor that The Angel was likely one of the Twelve Sisters from the legend. And now, the way it sold? Everyone's going to believe it."

"You don't buy it?"

"Not sure. Anyway, it got a lot of people's attention," she said.

"You looked like you were about ready to join the bidding yourself."

"Wha— You noticed me back there?"

"Are you kidding? Prettiest woman in the room? Everyone noticed you, despite the naked lady on the easel." Alice tucked a strand of thick curly blonde hair behind one ear. "So, are you just here networking or were you bidding on something earlier?" he asked.

Alice was an artist's rep, forever pushing her clients' works while on the lookout for new talent. The idea that she would be bidding on fine art at this level was a joke. Russell knew that. His question was a dig.

"The gallery contacted me out of the blue, said they wanted to include two works that I represent. They sold earlier, before you came in. Alexandra Coleman?"

"Oh. Nice work. I saw them in the catalogue. Companion pieces." Russell seemed genuinely impressed. "So, you're still repping?"

Another dig? Well, he was right; she was not where she wanted to be at age thirty-five, after ten years of trying to break into the big leagues. She sighed and sat down beside him.

He must have read her face because he touched her arm and his tone softened. "Look, you know this business as well as anyone, and you've got the personality. You'd make an excellent art dealer, or even an art consultant. Or both. Let me hook you up with this guy who has a gallery in Monaco. I heard he's looking for the kind of skills you could offer."

He grinned and held her gaze a moment too long, but she let the innuendo pass. "I don't know, Russell."

"Listen, the only downside would be spending a lot of time in Italy, but I'll help any way I can. Why don't we have dinner and discuss it?"

Those few words. Her head was exploding. She could see the future. "You sure you're not around tomorrow? I have some things to do tonight."

"I'm not going to have time tomorrow. It's complicated. Plus, I have to be in New York on Thursday."

"You know what?" She thought for a moment. "To hell with it. I've done enough work today for a whole week. What about right now? You have time for a drink?"

Russell pushed his chair back and stood up. "Absolutely."

She noticed he let out a breath and his shoulders relaxed. A good sign. Her confidence came roaring back. "Where are you staying?" She stood up and latched onto his coat sleeve.

The temperature outside had dropped as the sun had set. Truly, the Brera district in Milan, the high fashion bohemian quarter, was gorgeous any time of day. But when the sky blackened and the glow of soft artificial light bounced off the sandstone walls of shops and cathedrals, arches and apartment buildings that were packed along the curvy alleys, well, it stole Alice's breath. She hooked her arm through Russell's and pulled him close as they maneuvered through the crowd outside the gallery.

Alice liked Russell, a lot. Actually, too much, she thought. He was not indecently wealthy, criteria numbers one, two, and three of what she thought she wanted. He had something else though, something less tangible.

The first time they met, a few years ago now, she had shamelessly flirted with him based simply on his looks and charm, before learning how valuable he might be for her career. He was a fixture in the world of fine art, and he had proven to be a great professional resource for Alice. Since then, they had run into each other a half-dozen times at various conferences, galas, and opening nights. The sex was invariably better than good, the kind that lasted an hour and left them both sweat-slick and exhausted. But the last time she had seen him, a year ago at the Masterworks Sale in New York, something unfamiliar had settled over her mind, a feeling for him beyond simple attraction.

This new feeling terrified her—Russell was simply not rich enough to be part of her personal long-range plan. It scared her to the point that some self-preservation mechanism lured her into acting like a bitch. It would either drive him away, or, God forbid, show he cared enough to forgive what she had done. She had had her answer—he had been on mute, impossible to reach, ever since the incident. She hated herself then, certain she had blown, professionally speaking, whatever "in" she had had with him, forfeited any chance of using him as a steppingstone into the exclusive, filthy rich and famous sandbox she was determined to play in.

Approaching his table after the auction this afternoon, hoping to make amends, she had trembled with what was at stake. And although he had acted the consummate gentleman, like nothing had happened last year, she was not naïve enough to think he had forgotten.

Chapter 2

"Nice place." She scooted closer to him on the bench seat and swept a mass of hair from her forehead. "Why's the bar so empty?"

"It'll be full in a couple of hours."

"Well, this is nice. Almost secluded, unlike New York."

"New York." He turned his head away. "Don't remind me."

"Hey, I was speaking in general." She squeezed his hand. "I'm hoping you've put our last *meeting* behind us."

"No doubt you are. When was that? March?"

"I wasn't sure I was ever going to see you again," she said.

"Me either. What would you like to drink?"

"Don't they have room service in this place?"

He stood up. Her heart skipped.

Alice joined Russell on the edge of the bed, refilled their glasses, and set the now empty bottle of Quarzo Bianco sparkling wine on the nightstand. Old times seemed poised to rush back in, to grease any friction left from the last time they were together, but her instincts said to play it cool. Let him initiate whatever he was up for.

"Mr. Williams, sir. You are one of the most respected fine art appraisers and restorers in the entire frickin' world." Words were starting to slur but she didn't care. "Can I ask you one question? I've known you for like seven years and I still don't understand how you got to where you are. And why do you still wear those cowboy boots, and Western-cut suits? And talk with that drawl when you're tipsy?"

She knew he had grown up in Texas and remembered he'd worked for the Guggenheim early on, or maybe that was an internship, anyway she couldn't figure out how all the pieces fit together to get him to where he was now. Which was pretty impressive for someone his age. Late thirties, she guessed. He was on a first-name basis with more billionaires than most people even knew existed. Major museums—names like Louvre, Prado, Hermitage— called him on a regular basis. Restorations, appraisals, authentications, keynote speaker for fundraisers. Recommendations and advice, gratis if he wasn't personally available. He was not a kingpin, more of a pinsetter. And she wanted to take advantage of whatever pins he could set up for her to knock down.

He drained his glass. "You want the short version? I grew up with art. My mother was crazy about it and, I guess you could say, pushed me into loving it, too. I spent too many years studying at UT Austin. You know, like Texas, where I grew up?" He playfully pinched her arm. "Then graduate work at Columbia, then Delaware. But the real education started with my apprenticeship in the MOMA conservation department, which led to contacts at every other major gallery in the world. The bottom line? I worked my ass off on the technical stuff, and at the same time learned how to rub elbows in a room full of money. The other side of it, just as important, was blending in with the lower echelon of the art world, the shady side of the business. I guess that part came naturally. All those years on ranches and in small towns, hustling for money—"

"But why do you still wear cowboy boots? We're in goddam Italy!"

He laughed and gently pushed her back on the bed. "Want me to take 'em off, darlin'?"

Alice sighed. It all felt so good. She turned toward him and trickled her fingers down his jawline. "Seriously, thanks for offering to help me connect with the guy in Monaco." she said.

"Was I right? You're burned out on repping artists?"

"I'm not burned out. Okay maybe, but mainly I'm not making the big bucks I expected. Or the contacts. And artists are so…weird. Too much hand holding. I never liked babysitting brats."

"I'm not surprised. You're too good to be an agent. I always imagined you as an art consultant or an art dealer, taking advantage of the rich and famous. This gallery gig would be just what you need."

"But Monaco?"

"Why not start at the top?"

Alice touched his thigh. "I don't mean to sound ungrateful—"

"Hey, all I'm going to do is make the introductions. The rest is up to you."

"I know. I just hope I'm not biting off too much." Why was she fighting this? It's exactly what she wanted. Needed. "You have more confidence in me than I do. But you know all that, and probably a lot more, huh? No?" She pushed his chest. "Russell?" He winked and seemed to stifle a grin. Maybe he'd had enough of business talk. "What's the problem, mister? Cat got your—"

His lips, brushing hers, took her breath, and when his hand cupped her neck the kiss deepened. He pulled back slowly and gazed at her still-closed eyes. "Still worried about that cat?"

She grinned and opened them, but only for a moment.

Russell groaned when his cell phone rang. Nat King Cole singing "Mona Lisa".

"That's the Areni Gallery. I'd better take it."

Alice watched as he put on a happy face and answered the call. "Signora Areni. Buona sera!" As he listened his smile slowly faded until his jaw dropped. "How is that—how is that even possible?" He sank to the bed. "Understood. What can I do?" He shook his head again and again. "I'll see what I can find out."

He almost dropped the phone trying to disconnect, then grabbed the bottle from the nightstand. It was empty. He headed for the minibar.

"Hey, get back over here. What could be so bad?"

He blew out a breath. "Not bad for me, but bad. The Angel was just stolen from the gallery's secure area. They want me to ask around."

"Oh my god. They called you? What about the police?"

"They're going to keep it quiet for now and want me to see what I can pick up from the grapevine."

"You can't get involved!"

"Nothing dangerous. She said they'll bring in a private investigator, and that someone will probably contact me. Same goes for you I would guess."

"Me? I don't know anything!"

"You were at the gallery. At the auction."

Alice picked up the room phone. "Can I order another bottle of Quarzo Bianco?"

Russell ran his hand through his hair. "I wish I'd been paying more attention to the crowd during the auction. Did you see anything odd?"

"Um, no. Not really. There was one woman who looked totally out of place. But not sinister, more like milquetoast. Back of the room near me, taking in everything but interacting with no one. Drab gray pantsuit, if you can believe that. You didn't notice her?"

"No." Russell thought a moment. "What did she look like?"

"Well, nondescript. I'm not even sure I would recognize her again. Kind of medium everything. Height, weight, hair. No makeup! That's what I noticed. Totally out of place. You sure you don't remember her?"

"I didn't come in until the final lot, and then I was pretty much focused on the painting. I'll have them check the security feeds, try to find out who she was. Anything else?"

"Well, any chance we can rewind back to before your phone rang?"

"I need to start making calls to the States before it gets too late over there."

****

Alice spent the night in Russell's room and woke up with the sun. Like a lot of good mid-western American girls, not only was she an early riser, she enjoyed a big breakfast. By the time Russell first stirred, room service had delivered eggs benedict with smoked salmon, fried tomatoes, an assortment of pastries, and the morning edition of Libero Quotidiano.

"How can you sleep when there's fresh espresso perfume in the air?" She pinched his cheeks and kissed the tip of his nose.

"Good morning to you, too," he said. "What did I miss?"

"Not much. Just eggs and a front-page story in the paper about The Angel."

"Not surprising. It's not every day an unknown artist's work sells for one-point-seven million."

"It's not about the sale." She tossed the paper in his lap. "Take a look at the headline."

THE ANGEL STOLEN AFTER AUCTION

Areni Gallery Avoids Police

"So much for keeping it quiet," she said. "CNN online is running a story as well."

"Oh my god!" Russell grabbed his phone. "I better make sure Madame Areni doesn't think I leaked the story."

Chapter 3

Alice stepped onto the wobbly gangplank, suddenly conscious of her gold, ankle-strap high heels. What was she thinking? She had no idea what constituted proper footwear for an evening on a superyacht, but this couldn't be it. It had taken six days of concentrated effort to get an appointment with the owner of the Oscar-Porcelli Gallery; then she came within two minutes of missing the only train that would get her to Genoa on time; and now she was at risk of breaking an ankle before ever meeting the man.

At the end of the ramp, the chief steward graciously offered a box for her shoes and without asking what size, handed her a pair of elegant, flat rubber-soled sandals that looked stylish and fit perfectly.

Her host had said the meeting was business casual, but what did that mean anymore? She'd chosen a cream angora plunge sweater that crossed well below where her bra would have been, and a Césarée choker with pendant that covered most of her exposed chest. Her black designer skinny jeans were distressed—exactly how she felt at the moment.

The first officer led her up to the second deck which was busy with people, all of whom she realized were employees. She accepted a glass of Champagne and stood awkwardly in the middle of the deck, forearms on a cocktail table, trying to look like she belonged. She waited. And drank. She studied the workers. She tried to remember why she had shaken her head when the server offered her a second drink.

Alice thought about The Angel, the fact that she had actually seen it, had been there when it sold for a price that stunned the world. News reports indicated that the painting had simply disappeared from the gallery's safe room overnight, and that investigators who had eventually been brought in had no clues. Every art blog was speculating about the high bidder's identity and the painting's potential value now with all the notoriety. Some guessed the price would double if the piece was ever recovered.

Ten minutes later, her thoughts were interrupted as a lone man ascended the staircase. He strode toward her, a king in his castle. Her stomach rose up and her knees almost buckled. *It's showtime!* She wanted to check her outfit, primp her hair, but there was no time. *Come on girl, you got this.* She stuck out her hand and radiated a smile she hoped was equal parts professional and seductive.

"It is a pleasure to finally—"

"Ms. Stevens. Welcome to my little home away from home. I trust my first officer has made you feel welcome."

Why had she tried to speak first? This was a man in control of everything, every second, every day. Sixtyish, swarthy, square jaw, clear and bottomless black eyes. Stylish hair and five o'clock shadow showing no signs of gray. His well-toned muscles were obvious beneath a tight knit shirt. She fought the swoon that was about to blossom across her face.

"Yes, everyone's been—"

"But your glass is empty! Another Cristal?" He raised his hand and caught the eye of a stewardess. "Or something stronger, perhaps? What do you prefer?"

"Actually." Did she dare? Yes, show she was someone with her own tastes. "You may not have it. I enjoy Quarzo Bianco."

"A glass of QB for Ms. Stevens."

His accent! She loved the way he pronounced her name. A gorgeous redhead glided noiselessly toward the bar and returned promptly with a new glass full of golden fizz.

"So, you know Russell Williams?" he said.

"Yes, fairly well. We met about seven years ago now, and seem to run in the same circles. It's a relatively—"

"Well, you come highly recommended. We can work out the details over dinner. First let me show you around my little home away from home.

"The *Madeleine Too*," she said. "That name must—"

"Beautiful, isn't she? She's a sixty-three meter, three deck Benetti. Not the biggest in Port Hercule, but the best, no question."

"Beautiful, yes. I was just wondering, was there a—?"

"A *Madeleine One*?" He looked to the horizon. "Madeleine was my wife, Ms. Stevens, many years ago. She was killed in a most unfortunate accident."

"Oh, I am so, so sorry. Sorry to bring up—"

"Please, not at all. Memories of the years we shared are the best of my life. Simpler times back then." He drained his glass and seemed to study her face. "You remind me of her."

Oh my god. If that wasn't a come on…. He probably just did that out of habit. She thought, no way he's hitting on me, then kicked herself for letting her confidence slip. It sounded like she already had the job and it was just a matter of, what had he said? Working out the details? *Relax. He said I remind him of his dead wife.*

"Tell me about her."

"Madeleine? She was dazzlingly beautiful. In every way." He held her eyes, then took her elbow. "This way, Ms. Stevens."

"Please call me Alice."

"Alice. Call me Bruno," he said, and headed for the stairs to the flybridge.

Dinner was simple, but extravagant. Bruno announced they would have a 2010 Chenin blanc from the Loire for the crab cake appetizers which he'd had flown in from Maryland. "It's the best vintage since '97."

"The nose is superb," Alice said. She knew nothing about wine, and everything tasted about the same to her except the QB she drank whenever given the choice. But she had learned a few safe phrases to throw out when expected to comment.

As the appetizer plates were being cleared, there was a small lag in the conversation, and she had a sudden urge to promote herself. "I notice the gallery does not have much of a web presence. I was thinking—"

He raised a finger and she stopped. A stewardess appeared carrying a pedestal and placed it between them.

"I trust, growing up in Green Bay, you enjoy Wisconsin cheese. I took the opportunity to educate myself on that subject." As a tray displaying a dozen cheeses was placed on the pedestal between them, Bruno pointed to a particular orange wedge. "Hook's cheddar, aged twenty years. More expensive than Kobe beef."

"I've rarely been back to Wisconsin since high school, and you don't run across these everywhere, so I appreciate your thoughtfulness." She took a breath, happy to have gotten in an entire sentence. "Have you spent much time—"

"In the States? Very little. My business keeps me tied to this corner of the world. You would think at my age I could loosen the reins a bit, but when I delegate, my stress level never comes down. It makes for painful holidays."

"I understand."

"And you, Alice. Do you travel? Much time in Europe? Other parts of the world? What brought you to Italy this time?"

She would have to learn which questions he actually wanted answered, and how to keep her answers brief. He liked to talk, and his mind raced ahead of her measured responses.

"I was here primarily for last week's auction at Areni's in Milan. A couple of paintings by an artist I represent were included and—"

"So, you saw this famous Angel painting that was stolen. It must have been insured for a lot less than the final hammer—no one expected it to go that high. What happens if it is not recovered? Does the insurance payout go to the seller? The gallery? The high bidder?"

Alice's head buzzed. He must already know the answers, being a gallery owner. "All good questions. Ownership depends on when the theft occurred versus completion of the paperwork. An insurance policy might have been written to cover the reserve price. Possibly even to cover the unknown sale price, but I doubt it. The premium would have been exorbitant—"

"Ah, insurance to cover the final hammer. Then the seller runs up the price at auction, steals the painting before ownership is transferred, destroys it, and collects a grand pezzo of cash. Nice."

He was watching her reaction as she considered the scenario. Another test? Like, how did she feel about a scam of those proportions?

"Interesting possibility," she said. "A lot goes on in this industry that is less than kosher, but I've never heard of that. It would take someone with a lot of nerve, a lot of creativity. And not too much conscience." She raised an eyebrow. "You could only do it once."

"It is a fascinating industry." He poured more wine. "So, did you get a good look at The Angel? Tell me about it. Why all this sudden interest? Do you believe this legend of its origin?"

"I think the legend is part of the reason, but it's also the painting itself. There's some mystique, something almost magical about the piece. It should have sold the first time it was offered. The work is absolutely exquisite. It draws you into its surface, makes you feel like you know the subject, this Angel. You feel her emotions, a mix of pain and pleasure, or loneliness and joy…I don't know. My first thought? That it was painted by someone deeply in love. Impossible to describe adequately…" For once he was letting her talk, and she was bungling it.

She looked up and he held her eyes again. "I think there is more to you than you want to reveal, young lady. I must thank Mr. Williams for sending you my way."

Alice hid her trembling fingers under the table. She was being included, accepted, at a level beyond the gallery position she was apparently being offered. She took a deep breath. "You asked about the legend, whether I think it's true. What matters is whether the public believes it's true, that somewhere there are eleven more paintings—"

"My thought exactly. Use your connections. Find out for me if anyone is searching for the eleven…"

He stared at the sky and she let his request, or rather his command, hang in the air for a moment. "I can certainly do that. I'll dig up whatever research has been done on the legend document to pin down where the others were likely buried."

"Perfect. Find out where that is. And if no one is looking, create a rumor that they are, that there is a frenzy of effort to find the spot. People digging up their gardens, breaking into private properties to search."

"You want to create a mystique around the eleven? To increase the value of the one, The Angel."

"To increase the fame of The Angel. I want it to resurface, and then I am going to own it. Imagine the prestige for my gallery."

He got that dreamy look again and she detected a hint of vulnerability. She could listen to his accent all night long, if it turned out he was up for it.

Chapter 4

Three days later, Russell answered his cell.

"Hey Tex." She knew he liked the nickname. "Where are you?"

"Amsterdam, quick project for the Rijks. What's up?"

"I got the job! With the Oscar-Porcelli Gallery. What the hell did you tell him? He didn't even interview me, just asked what kind of terms I was accustomed to and said fine, fine, fine. I should have asked for more. He's excited about me bringing on some of the artists I'm already repping, and branching out—"

"Alice. Take a breath. I only have a few minutes. Are you back in Milan?"

"No. That's the other thing. I'm hoping I can impose on your good graces again. It's just, I can't go back to the States while I'm setting up all this new business in Europe, and I'm a bit stretched at the moment. So, I was wondering, you know, whether you're going to be using your place in—"

He laughed from the belly. "Not only do I get you a job, you want to take over my get-away place? You are too much!" He laughed again. "I'm kidding. You can flop there anytime."

She was thrilled, and Russell's laugh was contagious. "Are you sure? Absolutely sure?"

"Hey, I'm never there, and when I am it'll be good to have someone to keep the fridge stocked."

"I can do that. And a lot more, as you may remember."

"Vaguely," he said. "Tell me, not to change the subject, but anything in the

Italian news about The Angel? I've been buried in work and haven't heard a thing."

"There's not much in the news, just rumors about how much more it's going to be worth if it's recovered. The other thing, though, someone did call, like you predicted, asking questions about the theft. Did anyone try to call you?"

"Yes. But you first. Who'd you talk to?"

"Some woman. Her English was as bad as my Italian. I got that she's working on the recent theft from the Areni Gallery and she knew I had been at the auction. Wanted to know if I had seen anything unusual. I just told her about that strange woman that I mentioned to you, the one with no makeup. She asked what time I left the gallery and where I went. Made me write down a number to call in case I remembered anything or learned anything new. I said who do I ask for, and she said 'it's a private number, I'll answer'. Never told me her name, but it's not a voice I would ever forget. Kind of strange."

"That has to be the same woman who called me," he said. "Had a weird voice. I insisted on a name before I would talk. She said she was Inspector Savante with the Guardia di Finanza. That's basically the Italian financial police. Money laundering, counterfeiting, any nonviolent Mafia activity."

"I thought the gallery wasn't involving the police yet."

"They haven't, as far as I know," he said. "She was probably lying."

"But why would—"

He wasn't listening. "Well, this is interesting. I'm just scanning my messages. Madame Areni has offered a quarter million-euro reward for the return of The Angel, no questions asked."

Chapter 5

"Alice, come in. How's my miracle worker?" Bruno was spending a few hours at the gallery each week now that Alice had come on board.

She sat across the desk from him and crossed her legs.

Bruno loved the idea of his gallery hosting online auctions. As soon as Alice had suggested it, the advantages were clear. She would purchase works from unknown artists at bargain prices. Once it was going, he planned to have someone set up thirty or forty fake accounts on the auction site. The accounts would bid against each other, run up the price. The money to pay for the pieces would come in dirty and get washed clean as a clear spring day.

Of course, he mentioned none of this to Alice. She was a nice girl, and the less she knew the better, for both their sakes. She'd been working non-stop since they'd consummated their deal. Her momentum was as impressive as it had been that night on the yacht, and he felt energized for the first time in years. She had a raft of young American artists eager to sell their best works outright to a prestigious European gallery. He had given her carte blanche to set up the auction website. The project was nearly complete, and the publicity she'd orchestrated had created tremendous interest in the…what had she called it? The First Day of Trading Sale. Discounts, loyalty rewards, members-only mini-galleries. She was going to make him a fortune in clean money without ever suspecting a thing.

She sat smiling, waiting for him to speak. He liked that.

"So, things are moving fast. Is there anything I can do to help? Remove any obstacles, buy you dinner?" He grinned. They had had that conversation and she always turned him down. He liked that, too, for some reason.

She uncrossed her legs and leaned forward. "You could speak to Simone. Maybe she's jealous of me, or feels threatened, or just doesn't like me. I don't care, I just don't need anyone spreading rumors about me among the staff."

"She's been managing the gallery since the beginning. I wouldn't worry about it too much. She'll be retiring in a few months, one way or the other."

"Great. Well, I'll let you get back to work. Oh, I almost forgot. The Legend. I got the word out to a few bloggers and it's gone viral. People are going crazy digging up the countryside looking for the eleven."

"Excellent. Keep me in the loop." He nodded toward the door and then watched her sashay out of his office.

Chapter 6

From his writing desk, in the study of his estate's main villa at Castello di Quarzo Vineyard, Federico Ricasoli looked out over the lush grapevines that flooded the rolling hills and valleys. The villa was a sprawling edifice dating to the early eighteenth century, its peach-colored stucco complimenting the darker terracotta roof tiles. The estate included a vineyard once known as Villa Svizzera, occupying forty hectares of hills that kissed the border of the Magra river in west-central Italy.

The annoying local reporter sitting across the desk from Federico brought him back to reality. "Signore Federico, can you share with our readers who will be attending? Any Hollywood names, business tycoons, politicians? Only four days until this year's Festa dell'apprezzamento, and the guest list has not been announced."

His appreciation festival. Always the same questions. Always the same evasive answers. Although he was a loner at heart, Federico did love the annual event. He just hated the requisite interviews. If they weren't so good for business, he would never agree to another one. But his publicity manager had it all down to numbers, each type of interview was worth a certain number of cases sold.

After the agreed-upon twenty minutes, Federico showed the reporter to the front entrance and returned to his writing desk. He stared at the document open on his laptop. He was editing the chapter of his memoir which addressed a much-debated topic in the wine world—the secret of how his now-famous sparkling wine had come to be. The fact that this written account would not be completely honest bothered him. Federico would prefer to give credit where credit was due.

The memoir would state that Federico had assembled a team of seven scientists, that over a period of two years the team had worked secretly on the project, that they had conducted exhaustive chemical analysis of soils, vines, mature grapes, finished products, everything related to the finest French Champagnes. Then with a regression analysis—comparing that information to their massive data base of every compound in every grape that could feasibly be grown in the Quarzo area—they created a formula and a process to duplicate the French benchmarks. The key was ripping out the old vines and planting three grape varieties—one never before grown in Italy—on a particular section of Federico's property, specifically the ten or so hectares called *Dorsale all'alba*. Sunrise Ridge. The eastern side of that highest hill had the most advantageous sun, elevation (above twelve hundred meters), precipitation, and drainage. Combining that with a complicated and costly cocktail of organic and mineral soil additives completed the terroir.

All of those details would be included in the memoir, to become public for the first time. It was a good story, and it was true—except there had never been a team of scientists. Instead, a single member of Federico's extended family had clandestinely obtained the samples of competitive soils and grapes, analyzed them, and crunched the data with complex statistical tools. He was an unassuming young man with an agricultural background and an IQ around one hundred ninety who held multiple advanced degrees, including biostatistics and analytical chemistry, from prestigious American universities. In his spare time, while not working on his degrees, he single-handedly created the formula and process for Federico's Italian sparkling wine. The product clearly surpassed some of the most respected French Champagnes. It was a feat many thought impossible, from a vineyard situated over six hundred kilometers south of the Champagne region.

The young genius was his first cousin. But no one could know about this relative's involvement. Not now, and maybe never.

On a clear day, that is to say most days, and from the top of *Dorsale all'alba*, one could glimpse the borders of three official Italian wine regions— Liguria, Tuscany, and Emilia Romagna. The entire vineyard was classified Vino da Tavola, generic wines without restriction as to geography, grape variety, or quality. This catch-all designation belied the extraordinary taste and high price of its flagship product, Quarzo Bianco. Given the many restrictions in the secret process, yields were low on the ten hectares dedicated to QB, limiting annual production to one hundred thousand bottles. That was two-thirds less wine than their biggest rival, Cristal Champagne, produced. But at fifty euros net profit per bottle, Federico considered it a nice hobby, worthy of his spare time.

Although he was a recluse, Federico preferred action, and, he realized, writing tired him. He closed the laptop and walked through the open French doors into the golden air.

Behind the wheel of his '63 Giulia Sprint, he drove away from the villa, past fields bright with green grape leaves, and turned right, up through a shady wooded hillside. He wanted to check on his latest construction project. Years ago, he had converted a centuries-old Italian farmhouse into a four-bedroom guesthouse. Now, he was in the process of transforming that into a visitors' center. A cozy spot where wine tours could begin and end. The number of visitors to the vineyard was increasing every year, people crazy to see the place where Quarzo sparkling wines were made and to potentially glimpse the reclusive, eccentric billionaire owner.

He parked under an arbor of ancient olive trees that bordered the house and ricked the handbrake. By now, he thought, the workers should have finished removing the tiles and subfloor from the interior courtyard. He was anxious to see the space underneath.

The roll of blueprints under his arm detailed three areas of the visitors' center which would be constructed underground, with access via modest granite steps leading down from the small interior courtyard. Plans included a museum for artifacts from the property's three hundred years as a working vineyard, a generous space for wine tasting and retail business, and a small cave to store cases of each vintage. The mystique behind Castello di Quarzo Vineyard was legendary, and the older vintages were now commanding prices well beyond the reach of most tourists. The gift shop would include memorabilia for those with smaller budgets and limited space in their luggage—bottle openers, tee shirts, crystal flutes and coupes—all with the Castello di Quarzo logo.

Federico killed the engine and stepped out of his car. A short muscular man rushed through the front door of the guesthouse, shouting and gesticulating. It was the crew foreman, Cristiano, spewing the local slang too fast to comprehend. Something about a cave-in. Federico imagined an injury, a common occurrence given the work habits of the locals. The foreman grabbed his arm, a gesture few would have dared, and pulled him into the interior courtyard. The tiles had indeed been removed, and a wooden ladder protruded from a gaping hole in the fragmented subfloor.

Federico took a flashlight from Cristiano and followed him down the ladder into a disarray of crumbling stone and timbers. As their eyes adjusted, Cristiano pointed to what resembled a rectangular vat made of stone. The lid had been pushed to one side. Federico leaned over the edge of the encasement and played his light along the surprisingly clean interior surfaces.

"What the Holy Mother—" He looked back, and Cristiano was grinning like a happy jack-o-lantern.

Chapter 7

Finding the key under the green flowerpot as promised was a comfort, a hint that this was a low-crime neighborhood. She slung her suitcase onto the bed and made a beeline for the toilet—she'd been holding it since getting off the train. It had taken the taxi driver an hour to find Russell's place in Seregno, twelve miles north of the train station in Milan. The toilet paper holder was empty. Typical bachelor's pad.

Once she could think again, Alice toured the house. The space charmed her, and that initial feeling of being an intruder fell away. His furniture was tasteful and comfortable, and in room after room the walls were covered in expensive looking paintings, styles ranging from classical to abstract. Why had Russell described his hideaway in less than glowing terms? She was going to love it here.

The fridge held exactly one bottle of hot sauce, three bottles of beer, and a tub of plain yogurt that had expired a month ago. She raised the blinds and sun filled the kitchen. The back door led to a courtyard surrounded with an eight-foot cinder block wall, stucco crumbling in places. The plants needed tending but Alice didn't dare; she had trouble keeping a plastic Ficus looking good in her Manhattan apartment.

In the left corner of the courtyard was a bungalow painted a soft pastel color, half-hidden by overgrown shrubs and climbing ivy. It was large enough to be a guest house. Would Russell expect her to sleep there if he returned? The door lock was an electronic keypad but it had a slot for a key as well. Through the side window she could make out little in the dim interior light, but as her eyes adjusted, they grew wide. She was looking at a studio, an artist's workplace filled with canvases in various stages of completion. She recognized one of the styles from a painting she had just admired in the main house. She searched under rocks and pots for a key to the door. No luck.

Back inside the main house she scanned every painting without finding a signature—until she took one from the wall. On the back, in thick black brush strokes, was the signature. R. R. Williams. Every painting was signed that way, with dates ranging from 2007 to the present. Eleven years. The more she looked at the paintings, the more she realized the quality was astonishingly good. Every style worthy of a wealthy collector's attention. Where was her cell phone?

"Russell, ciao! I made it. I love your place. Thank you so much." She was pacing in circles around the living room, trying to sound calm. She could make a fortune representing him. Her mind wandered. Maybe he was already semi-famous in the art world, using a pseudonym. He was asking her something.

"Oh. No, but the fridge needs restocking. Is there a market within walking distance?" She sat on the floor and leaned back against the front door. "I'll find it, no worries. Where are you anyway?"

He was still in Amsterdam, but said he had a couple of days free now and thought he might just crash in the hotel, unwind.

"Don't do that! Come down here and keep me company, show me the area. I can sleep in the guesthouse if you want."

She heard him laugh and say it was a great idea, but they'd have to discuss the part about the guesthouse. He would be there tomorrow afternoon and would prepare her a nice rack of ribs, coleslaw, Texas toast, and a mess of home fries. But she would have to do the shopping.

"Really? Where am I going to find all that?" She listened as he gave directions to the local market he preferred. "Okay. Wine or beer? Right. Dumb question."

The shopping list memorized, she hesitated to bring up his beautiful paintings, the thing foremost in her mind. She would wait until tomorrow.

"Did you hear?" she asked instead. "The entire text of the legend, about the twelve paintings by Giuseppe da San Russo? It's been published in some magazine, which immediately sold out. But it's online now. People are scouring it for details, trying to figure out where the works are buried, supposedly digging up their backyards and public spaces." Exactly what Bruno had asked her to engineer was suddenly happening on its own.

She told him most searchers were focusing in and around Villafranca, on the east bank of the Magra. She had also heard on CNBC that the reward for The Angel had been increased significantly. When she ran out of breath, Russell changed the subject. He needed to book a flight and wrap up some paperwork before hitting the hay. He would see her tomorrow around four or five.

She put her phone on the table and began to search inside the house for a key to the studio. The most likely place was in a kitchen drawer near the backdoor, no? How does a guy think? How does Russell think? She realized she didn't really know him at all. Leaning back against the counter, she poured one of the cold beers into a tall glass.

The key was staring her in the face, hanging on a hook by the kitchen door. It wasn't hidden at all really, so she felt unapologetic about opening up the studio, airing it out. It was bigger than she had thought, with a good-sized bedroom and a kitchenette in addition to the workspace.

Browsing through stacks of paintings leaned against one wall, she noticed a desktop computer, half-hidden by piles of file folders and books. It was next to a desk where the keyboard and screen were sitting. She booted it up and found the screen was password protected. The guilt she felt for going this far did not prevent her from searching for a list of passwords. She found it— taped to the bottom of the computer.

Once in, the desktop was covered with neat columns of small icons. Two were for his email accounts. The first was linked to his business website, RRWilliams@ArtisticSalvation.com, and the password was on the paper she'd found. She logged in and scanned the inbox. The list of senders read like a Who's Who of museum curators and gallery owners. The subject lines were boring and she logged out without reading any of the correspondence.

It was the second email account that piqued her interest, precisely because it wasn't included on the password list. It was on Gmail, and the user's name was remembered on the browser, rrwilliams.art. Could she guess the password without blocking the account with multiple tries? If it was something random, she was out of luck, but his other passwords were fairly simple. She thought about little else for the rest of the day.

****

The next afternoon, she was in the kitchen of the main house. The front door was locked, she was sure of that. When it creaked open and noise from the street swept in, her skin prickled, but not from fear of someone breaking in. Her sympathetic alert system wailed because the owner of the place had arrived, the man whose privacy she had invaded, the man who could ruin her career with a well-placed comment or two.

"Darlin', I'm home!" She listened to him laugh and waited until his suitcase dropped on the terra cotta foyer before peeking from the kitchen into the front room. In less than a blink his smile calmed her butterflies. She almost didn't recognize him. It wasn't his outfit, the Wrangler Bootcut jeans and a faded brown denim Levi's shirt, the top two studs unsnapped. It was that she'd never seen him completely relaxed, unguarded.

"You're not gonna believe what I saw at the airport. But first git me a cold one!" His Texas drawl was thick as day-old milk gravy. He must have taken advantage of the free booze in business class and was likely feeling no pain. He laughed again and guided her into the kitchen. "I'm just kidding. You don't need to wait on me. You want another one?"

"Sure Tex." He took the empty bottle from her hand and headed for the fridge. She herself had been on the tipsy side of sober by the time Russell opened the front door, self-medicating against the jitters of facing him after breaking into his email.

"Damn girl. Heineken? They make this export stuff with canal water. Was Callisto's outa Shiner Bock?" He wiggled his butt at her.

She could do little but watch the performance while her mind rearranged itself around what she was witnessing—a drunk Russell who had dropped all pretense and had apparently reverted to his roots. She read this to mean that he was comfortable around her, like, he completely trusted her. Swept up in the moment, in what this meant, she put her arms around him from the back. He bent forward, lifted her from the floor, and walked the two of them toward the bedroom, an open beer in each of his hands.

Chapter 8

"These charcoals are glowing like sunset on the Fourth of July. You got that meat rubbed down?"

"Yes, siree Bob, sir. Just like the doctor ordered. What's in this mix anyway."

"My own concoction. It's the only thing on the menu tonight with a nod to Italian cooking. Are you good at keeping secrets? Texas dry rub base minus half the brown sugar, plus some oregano, parsley, and rosemary. Olive oil to coat the meat first, as you saw. I call it my Tex-Wop."

She blinked. "That's racist."

"Probably."

Russell placed the two full racks of baby back ribs over the charcoals and pushed a button to start the mesquite chip feeder. "Not as good as smoking them slow for six hours, but seventy minutes and we'll have dinner." He sat beside her on the bench and rubbed her back. "Did you see everything you wanted to inside the studio yesterday, or would you like a proper tour?"

Gulp. She watched his grin fade. "Um." *Shit.* "How'd you know I went in? Did you put a secret piece of tape on the door or something?" Her mind flashed a picture of the piece of paper with his passwords that she'd taped back under the computer after making a copy. She slipped her hands between her knees to still them.

"Security camera with motion sensor. I get an alert anytime it trips."

"Sure, makes sense. What if you have a guest staying in there? Wouldn't that be illegal?"

"Nah. There's only one camera and it's on the outside. So, let me show you around."

"You need to set a timer for the meat?"

"I keep one running in my head all the time."

"Even when you're drunk?"

"Guess we'll find out. This way madame." The door clicked open when he punched a code into the lock. The main room, the studio she had explored yesterday, held two easels, shelves crammed with various supplies, and leaning against the wall were dozens of paintings on stretched canvas. Pencil drawings, charcoal sketches, and books on technical topics related to painting were scattered on a long workbench.

Alice picked up a volume on restoration of masterworks. "So, you do restoration here as well as originals," she said.

"Not so much. The occasional small job. Security's not good enough for me to have anything very pricy here."

"Tell me, what kind of originals do you like to paint? What fascinates you? You're really good at a lot of styles. Excellent, I would say. You ever sell anything?"

He snorted. "Never. But thanks. My opinions on fine art and the art market would bore you to death. Or scare you."

She sat in a metal folding chair not designed for comfort and thought about the meat outside, getting hot and smoky. She was hungry, craving some appetizers. Russell was running on beer carbs and seemed ready to talk. She wasn't going to interrupt. He opened a small fridge she hadn't noticed and took out two more beers. She waved no, but he opened both and sat the second one on his work bench.

"So, what do you want to know?"

"What do you do with all these beautiful originals. Besides hang them in your house here?"

"First of all, nothing's original. Everybody copies what they've seen."

"Come on," she frowned. "Jackson Pollock?"

"Ha." He sat his empty bottle on the bench and picked up the full one. "I hear a vandal broke into Pollock's studio and threw paint everywhere. Then Pollock made a fortune."

"Well, Picasso."

"You look at African art from the nineteenth century and tell me he didn't copy. What's the point of me trying to sell these?' He swept his arm around without looking. "The average artist makes less than ten percent of their income from their art. And those that make it big? It's because someone with influence said they were good, someone who has no idea what good is. Believe me, I know what good is. I look at Cy Twombly's stuff, bless his heart, and think kindergarten trash bin. I look at my stuff and I see everyone else's work I've ever seen. My brain just stirs up the images and something derivative comes out. It's all derivative. It's all bullshit."

"Music's all derivative, too, then. No?"

"Music is for the people, for sharing. A musician wants everyone to hear his work. Free, or at most for a small fee. But art!" He was getting angry. "The goddam buyer controls who can see it!"

Her idea of representing him—getting a commission on selling his work—seemed like a stretch now. "How about a portrait? Wouldn't that always be original?" Her hand stole up and undid the top button of her blouse.

"Only the subject is unique. Not the style. Composition. Mood. It's all been done."

"I mean, how about a portrait, of me, now?" She let her top slide off and turned three-quarters in the chair, looking over her shoulder at him. She heard a small gasp, and she felt a small victory.

"Yeah? Yeah, we could do that. You mean now? What about the grub?"

"Good food is good reheated." Her appetites had shifted.

He stood and looked at her for a full minute. And again from a different angle. He put a primed canvas on the easel and adjusted the studio lights. Then he squeezed an inch of acrylic paint, ultramarine blue, onto the pallet, and with a pallet knife mixed in a half-inch of burnt sienna. The resulting color was a rich black that he dipped a small filbert brush into.

"Don't hold your breath, but don't move."

"For how long, do you think?"

"Five minutes or so." He moved around the easel and stood behind her. She felt the cold tip of the paint-loaded brush move rapidly across her right shoulder blade.

"What are you doing?"

"Don't move!" He stepped back but remained behind her. "Another four minutes."

She felt trapped, and her skin itched under the drying paint.

"Trust me," he said.

"Is that a question?" She wanted to shout but it came out as a nervous laugh.

"Don't talk."

"Why not? This is creepy. You know?" She let out a deep breath. "I just got a déjà vu. Maybe it was a dream. First you tell me you've been spying on me with the security camera. Now you've got me afraid to move or even talk. And yesterday, on the train…" She didn't know whether to continue.

"What about the train?"

"It's stupid. I felt like someone was watching me. Nobody that I saw, I just had that feeling. But then when I went shopping for the ribs, I definitely saw a guy from the train, just standing in a doorway, looking at me like he was trying not to look at me. You know what I mean?"

"It either means you're beautiful and guys look at you, or it means you're paranoid. You got a guilty conscience about something?"

"Of course not." Of course yes. The market trip was after she broke into his computer.

"I guess I'm just nervous, new town, new job with a lot on the line."

He touched her back. "Okay, you can move now."

She started to redress and he said to hang on a minute. He took her hand and led her into the bedroom. He opened the mirrored bifold closet doors and stood her between the two so she could see what he had painted. RRWillams. The same brushstrokes he had used to sign the paintings in the house.

"What the hell does that mean?" She turned on him. "Are you trying to say you created me or something? You own me?"

His face blanched and he suddenly looked sober. "Oh god. I never meant to imply that. I just meant…." He sat on the bed. "I apologize. It just hit me that you are a work of art, but one that is forever unique, beyond capture, beyond anything I could do to improve." He looked at her again. "Wow. I should have thought that through."

"Forget about it. You were drunk. Are drunk. I kind of like you like this, with your shield down."

He smiled weakly and started to stand. "You can button up now."

"Not on your life," she said.

Chapter 9

"Who wants eggs?" She sat two cups of coffee on the kitchen table.

"Good lord, girl, I'm still full from dinner." He plopped into a chair, leaned back, and shot his legs out.

"You're full of something all right, but it's not dinner." She kind of liked the change in their relationship since he arrived yesterday. It just needed some getting used to.

"You know, I think I like having a housekeeper. You ought to move in here permanent."

"What the fuck?" She swallowed it. "You know, you let me start selling your paintings, and you'll be able to afford a housekeeper and a whole lot more."

"I can already afford a whole lot more. Life's not about money."

"But why not share your work with the world? You're good. Better than good."

"Look, I know exactly how good I am. And my paintings are going to belong to me until I die. Then they'll be auctioned off, one per year, until they're all gone. No one can buy more than one. No one can resell. And they have to be on public display somewhere for at least six months per year. That's the way it's gonna be. Unless I change my will between now and then."

"You're weird." She ruffled his hair and got up to rinse her cup.

A phone rang in the living room. Russell didn't move.

"You want me to get that?" Crap. She was starting to wait on him. Starting to want to.

"That would be great."

"It's the Areni Gallery," she shouted. "You want to take it?"

He grabbed the phone, waved her out of the room, and answered—in a different voice, the voice she was more used to. She watched him through the doorway.

"No, no problem. I've been up for hours. Business in Asia."

That wasn't true. He'd still been adrift in dreamland when she got up at seven.

"Excellent. That's excellent news. Do you know—" He frowned and listened. "No, of course not. But at least you've got it back. Does the buyer know yet?" He nodded thoughtfully. "I'm not surprised. The piece has appreciated at least.... Well, that's good for you. And the family.... Understood.... Yes, I'll check my email. Please use my private Gmail account." He listened for a moment, then thanked the caller.

Alice returned to the kitchen. Russell was staring into space.

"Was that Madame Areni?"

"What? Oh. Just some unfinished business." He wasn't looking at her. "So, what would you like to do today?"

"They found The Angel, didn't they?"

"Alice...." He thought for a second. "My clients tell me things in confidence, precisely because I don't betray that confidence. Something you need to consider."

"I know. Sorry."

"And even if you think you discerned what the conversation was about, you can't tell anyone. Just hold off until the news breaks in a day or two. A lot could be at stake depending on how the gallery and the owner decide to proceed."

"Of course not. I would never—"

"Listen." He snapped. "You're playing in a different league now. And you represent a competing gallery. There aren't enough ethics in this business as it is, and your best bet is to play it clean. Otherwise, you could get badly burned."

He was the old Russell again, and not the one she preferred. The advice was good, but the tone was frightening.

They spent the morning walking through Seregno's commercial district. He introduced her to shop keepers who smiled and spoke English but encouraged her to *pratica l'italiano*. At lunch, he helped her decipher the menu, practice pronunciation, and place their order.

He took a call during lunch and then announced he had to fly back to Amsterdam right away. She had to fake disappointment—as much as she liked the thought of another night with him, the craving to advance her career was stronger. She needed alone time to figure out the password to his Gmail account. To find out everything she could about the newly recovered painting. To score points with her boss. Bruno would kill to own The Angel, and she was going to make that happen. Without the killing part, she thought.

Russell didn't kiss her goodbye. She was okay with that. He was two different people, and at the moment professional-Russell was focused on his job in Amsterdam.

The password solution turned out to be simple. Working on her laptop, propped up in bed at 3 a.m. when she hoped he would not be online, she found an unsent email in the draft folder of Russell's business account.

Subject: PW

The note listed all of the sites on the paper under his desktop in the cottage, along with the confidential Gmail account, rrwilliams.art. Next to it was "Hint: State<area code". She looked up the area code for Austin.

She tried Texas<512. Incorrect password. Maybe the < symbol meant reverse order, so 512Texas. Nope. The < symbol could mean backwards. Texas215. saxeT215. How many tries before Gmail would lock his account? saxeT512. She was in!

Russell's Gmail had been humming since his phone call from Madame Areni that morning. Once Alice ran the texts through a translator, the notes between the two of them laid a bonanza of insider information in her lap. The euphoria made her light-headed.

ARENI - The Angel has been returned anonymously with a message that the painting is cursed and the reward money is refused.

Russell – Was the work damaged?

ARENI – It appears to be perfect. The high bidder from the auction now wants the gallery to sell it outright, the sooner the better. Probably worried the rumor will depress the price.

Russell – Understood. Has a new price been set?

ARENI – They want minimum 2.4 million euros net. We will take twenty percent of the gross. Sale announcement is being prepared for 3.2 to allow negotiation.

Russell – They get a 40% profit on what they paid three weeks ago from the auction, without ever actually taking possession. Nice.

Alice did a quick calculation. If the gallery took twenty percent, and she took her three percent, Bruno could buy it for three-point-one mil.

What did Areni mean, that the buyer—now the seller—is worried the rumor will depress the price? She researched "The Angel rumor" and found blogs about a hex on the painting; warnings that anyone daring to profit from it would be cursed. They listed a dozen various misfortunes within the family who owned it. The speculation went on and on, leading to more theories. Just reading it, goosebumps covered her arms.

She went back to Russell's private emails and read correspondence on various topics from names familiar and obscure, information that could be invaluable to her career. She snapped photos of various tidbits. An hour later she had to stop reading, to let the flood of adrenaline ebb. What had Russell said about clients telling him things in confidence? One mistake and he would destroy her reputation in the industry. Or, play it right, and she would be set for life.

To hell with it. If Russell was so persnickety about client information, he should have protected his email better. All's fair in love and business. How many times had she been kept down in her career by the simple fact that she was a woman?

She made sure all the emails were in the same read or unread state she had found them in, then closed her laptop and settled back into the pillows. She would call Bruno in the morning, let him know The Angel might be available for a cash offer. As his agent, she would take home over ninety thousand! Oh my god. She could make a down payment on a place in Milan. Or, better, Monaco. She switched off the light and ten seconds later switched it back on in panic.

Something had moved outside the window.

Chapter 10

Alice woke up at six a.m., if you could call what she did "sleeping" after the scare outside her window three hours earlier. It was a cat, and she chided herself for being so paranoid. Still, thoughts of the man from the train kept jumbling her mind, mixing into imagined conversations with Bruno about

The Angel. How was she going to convince him to let her negotiate the purchase for him?

But the sun was bright, and the coffee was excellent, and she was an independent consultant-slash-dealer with insider information that was potentially worth a fortune. What's the worst that could happen?

The call to Bruno couldn't have gone better. She reported The Angel had just been returned but the info was not yet public. The high bidder wanted to sell, and she could secure it for less than three and a quarter. He did not hesitate. She had his blessing up to three and a half. He was impressed and she was determined not to let him down. He laughed when she mentioned the crazed locals searching for the so-called Twelve Sisters, or more accurately, the remaining eleven.

She said, "The rumor now is that a part of the legend was not made public, that it actually includes a quote from Giuseppe himself, saying *Those who profit at my expense shall find evil in their midst.*"

He laughed. "Sounds serious. I'd better be careful."

"Someone reported discovering tales of strange illnesses and deaths on two occasions when the painting had been sold rather than being passed down through the family."

He loved it and thought publicity about the legend would be a goldmine for the gallery once they owned The Angel. It was the first significant Italian fifteenth century work to surface in decades, and it was cursed! If Alice could secure it for him, she would have a job with the gallery for life.

The high from that conversation was short-lived. How was she going to approach the Areni Gallery about buying The Angel—before they announced the sale?

****

The discussion with Bruno had been ridiculously easy; getting an appointment with Madame Areni at her gallery had been ridiculously difficult. The gatekeeper was a wiry little assistant manager with no hair and an imagined sense of self-importance. Alice was small potatoes and it was his job to make sure she knew it.

He pretended to have difficulty understanding her English. The fact that she had had a couple of paintings in a recent auction meant nothing to him. When she admitted she had a client interested in The Angel, he denied that the painting had been returned. When news of the recovery broke the next day, she went back in. He told her the work was not for sale. She threatened to sit in the lobby until Madame Areni walked through, and then tell her what an ass he had been. He grudgingly gave her an appointment for late the following week, but for only ten minutes, and insisted Alice bring an interpreter as the owner could not be bothered with trying to understand Alice's poor Italian. What?! In a fit of anger, she let it slip that she represented Bruno Porcelli. The little man blanched, blinked, and slowly picked up the phone. It sounded like he said simply "someone is here to see you", nothing more. He hung up and said please follow me.

Madame Areni could not have been more pleasant, nothing like the recluse she was rumored to be. Her English was impeccable. She remembered Alice from the last auction and inquired about other artists she represented. She seemed prepared to chitchat for hours about art, until Alice brought up the reason for her visit.

Her client, who wished to remain anonymous for the moment, was interested in The Angel. He would offer three-point-five million euros. She started at the top, not to maximize her fee, she simply was not willing to risk someone making a higher bid. Madame Areni confirmed the rumor that the work had been recovered. It would be her pleasure to present this bid to the new owner, and although a sale had not been announced, she admitted it was a solid offer. She felt optimistic.

Despite Madame Areni's confidence, Alice left with a prickly feeling. What had just happened? Why the warm reception and apparent trust in her from the gallery owner? The little man had not mentioned Bruno's name to Madame Areni on the phone or when he introduced Alice, and Alice had not mentioned him. Perhaps she knew of Alice's new position through the grapevine and had put two and two together. Now that news of The Angel's return was going public, could she dare to tell Russell what she was up to, ask him to explain the dynamics? Would that betray Bruno? His interest in The Angel needed to be kept confidential for now. Russell wouldn't try to undercut her, would he? Damn! What a business.

It was almost five o'clock. She deserved a drink before calling Bruno with an update. Leaving the gallery, she did a small double-take at a white-haired man standing across the street. Wearing a white collarless shirt, white linen pants, and white casual shoes, he looked so odd but somehow familiar.

She found a café with her GPS and followed the walking directions. All of the outdoor tables were taken, so she sat just inside with a view of the street. She ordered a glass of red wine in what sounded to her like perfect Italian. The waiter, kind of cute and about half her age, smiled and repeated what she had said. It sounded completely different. She took out her phone.

Twelve new emails, nothing pressing. She was on the verge of relaxing, thinking how one day she might actually feel comfortable in this foreign country, when the man dressed all in white took a seat outside at a table that had just been cleared, his profile to her. This close, he looked like the man from the train.

****

When Alice's phone alarm chimed, she had no idea where she was. It was pitch black except for the digital display in her hand. It read 2:30. And there were no Manhattan night-sounds seeping in from outside, nothing familiar to ground her—until the paranoia returned and she remembered the man who had followed her to the café. She was in Italy, in Russell's getaway place. If the man in white had followed her back, she hadn't seen him.

It had been midnight by the time she had talked to Bruno about the offer. Then she set the alarm in order to mine Russell's email again at an hour when he shouldn't be online.

She checked her own email first, but her brain wasn't grasping anything. She needed caffeine. No, she needed to stop worrying about being followed. It was stupid. No, it wasn't. The guy in white looked like the one from the train, but it probably wasn't him. But what if it was?

> *Hi Russell, having trouble sleeping. I think I saw that guy from the train again. He followed me ten blocks. Not my imagination. Hate to bother you, but what do you think is going on? Alice*

She used his business email, the only one she legitimately knew about, expecting to have a response from him in a few hours. Instead, she got a reply almost immediately. He was up. He was checking his mail. Damn. What if she had logged into his Gmail account at the same time he was on it? Would he have known? She had to learn more about that stuff if she was going to be a sleuth.

> *Alice, sorry you're having trouble sleeping. My guess is Bruno hired someone to keep an eye on you, just to make sure you're safe for a while. Wouldn't surprise me. Next time, just walk up to the guy and ask him who he works for. Night night, sleep tight. R*

Strangely, that did make some sense. Bruno wanted to make sure she was safe. She was valuable to him now. Why would anyone else be interested in what she was doing? She turned off the light. When would Russell definitely be offline, so she could check his email again? She was two inches away from falling asleep when it hit her. While he's in the air.

> *Hey. Me again. So, what are your plans? Would be great to have you "visit" again. How's this weekend look?*

His reply came while she sat in the morning sun, sipping a latte and planning her day. He couldn't be there this weekend. He was flying to Chicago, leaving tomorrow morning at 9:00. *Ta da.*

The next morning at 10:00, with the confidence of a tomcat, she browsed the inbox of Russell's private email. It was back and forth between Madame Areni and Russell. She had asked his advice about the three-point-five mil offer for The Angel. The offer Alice herself had made! He asked what the temperature of the market was, given the curse rumors. She said it's getting worse. He suggested she recommend the buyer to take any offer over three million gross.

Alice fist pumped the air and decided to have another fette biscottata with golden plum jam. And another latte. And after work, though she would be alone, this called for a glass or two, or three, of QB. She might have to eat peanut butter for the next week, but tonight she was going to treat herself.

Chapter 11

"What the Holy Mother—"

Federico took his head out of the stone tank and flashed his light into Cristiano's grinning face. "Who found this?"

"I find it Signore. The men are on lunch. No one knows but you and me and the church mouse. It is important, no?"

"Maybe, maybe not. I need to see what I can find out. For now, please tell no one. Not even your wife, okay?"

Cristiano laughed. "I never tell my wife nothing. You can believe me on the Holy Bible."

"Can you close it up?" He scratched his chin while Cristiano shoved the cover back in place. "By the way, we should stop work until the festival is over. Send the men home until Monday, I'll pay them for the rest of the week."

"Grazie molto, Signore."

Back in his study, Federico penciled a note in his agenda: eleven old paintings found, underground cistern. Contact appraisers. He searched on line, compiled a list of top appraisers, and emailed it to his assistant with a note. "Urgent. Invite R.R. Williams of Artistic Salvation to festival."

Chapter 12

"Guess what I'm doing. Drinking! Guess what I'm drinking." She giggled.

He guessed right away—it was the only drink she was not indifferent to. Russell had in fact introduced her to Quarzo Bianco years ago during their first ever dinner together. Trying to impress me, she'd thought. Two hundred dollars a bottle is ridiculous, she'd said, then apologized after tasting it. He told her a bit of the history then, like the fact that Federico Ricasoli had stunned the wine world when he introduced a knock-off for top-end French Champagne. The billionaire ran dozens of businesses solely by video conference, and was rarely seen in person except during his annual promotional event featuring celebrities of every stripe. Alice was smitten with the mystique of this billionaire recluse. She had photos of Federico saved to her phone. Despite his goatee—she generally hated facial hair— she fantasized about him.

"I'm going to go out on a limb here and say QB at 5 degrees C in a leaded crystal tulip glass that you found in the cabinet above the dishwasher."

"Now that's spooky. You don't have a spy camera inside the house, do you?" She couldn't stop giggling. The fact she had paid for this bottle herself was somehow liberating. Like maybe she was on her way to the big leagues she had dreamed about for years.

"You know they'll have all the QB you could want at the Castello di Quarzo Festival this weekend."

"Yeah, like I'm going to be there."

He switched to his Texas drawl. "Well, how much do you love me, little darlin'?"

She cocked her head and actually looked at the phone in her hand. "Uh, what?"

Back to his business-as-usual accent. "You'll have to go solo. It's day after tomorrow. Chicago's taking longer than I expected."

"How the—"

"I don't know. I got on somebody's A-list years ago, now I get these odd invitations from time to time. I only opened this one because I knew you were crazy about Quarzo Bianco. I'll email you the QR code they sent me, that's all you need."

"Would you do that? I would literally die to be there. Is it for both days? Do you know the dress code? I need to bring a gift for the host. Will he be mingling? Like I might actually meet him?"

"Everything you need to know will be in the email. Read it after you sober up. And promise not to embarrass me, or yourself."

"I promise." She closed her eyes. This is the life she had always imagined. Making a multimillion dollar offer on a painting and scoring a ticket to the hottest party of the year, all in the same week. "Thanks Tex. When are you back in Italy? I'd like to thank you personally."

"Wednesday morning. I'm on the overnight Chicago to Milan."

She refocused enough to make a mental note. *Next email check, Wednesday around 1 a.m.*

****

Alice rented a Fiat 500 in Milan at ten o'clock Saturday morning and arrived at the festival around two. It should have been a two-hour drive, and would have been if she had used the GPS on her phone instead of the one in the car. She arrived aggravated but got over it the moment the dazzle of actually being there struck. Soft music was playing everywhere, coming from nowhere. Food and wine bars were scattered across the grounds, some in tents, some under shade trees. The only downside was that photos were strictly forbidden—when the QR code was scanned at the entrance, a file was sent to her phone to disable the camera. It would be restored when she checked out. Crazy.

She was early, one of the first to arrive. After two quick glasses of QB she decided to pace herself, Russell's admonition, God bless him, ringing in her ears. She was about to muster the courage to join a group gathered around the Italian president when someone touched her shoulder. She turned and found herself nose-to-nose with Federico. He was her height, with smooth olive skin except sun-crinkled around the eyes. His smile was a bright invitation as he stuck out his hand.

"I don't believe I've had the pleasure. I'm the host of this little event."

"Oh, yes! Oh, I'm Alice Stevens—" She forced in a breath, her airway threatening to close down. "I, um, do you speak English? I only know a few words of Italian."

"Of course, it is not a problem," he said in a heart-melting Italian accent. "And what do you do, Mrs. Stevens?"

"Oh. I'm with the Oscar-Porcelli Gallery in Monaco, dealer and consultant." First time she had said that aloud. "But I'm here because of my friend Russell Williams, the art restorer? He couldn't make it."

"It is a pleasure to meet you. Yes, I remember the invitation for Mr. Williams. Your friend is highly respected in the business of fine art. I had hoped to meet him and possibly engage his services for an appraisal."

"Well, he's certainly one of the best. Appraiser *and* restorer. Is the artwork here? I would love to see it."

"I appreciate your interest, but I shall not trouble you with something that may be of no value."

"I understand. After the appraisal though, our gallery would be honored to work with you, should the need arise."

"I will keep that in mind, Mrs. Stevens."

He held her eyes a bit too long, and she rushed ahead to explain. "Actually, it's Ms. Stevens." Why had she not corrected him the first time? "But please, call me Alice."

"Indeed, Alice. May I show you around the grounds?"

Be still my heart.

The quick tour of the festival area turned into a grand tour of the main villa which led to a ride in his Alfa Romeo through the vineyards. They stopped at the guesthouse. He described his plans for the future welcome center and apologized for the reconstruction mess. She followed him inside, across the courtyard, and into the still-furnished bedroom which would become a manager's office. The conversation stopped. He seemed charmed by her, and she was genuinely taken with him as well. Her first time one-on-one with a billionaire, and she was pulling it off. Wealth and fame aside, he was a gentleman, clever and funny, *and* he had shaved his goatee! Kissing him would not be like— Oh, for heaven's sake, she thought. What are the chances of that?

As they left the bedroom, Alice broke the awkward silence. She apologized for taking so much of his time. Federico said he preferred showing her around to mingling with a crowd of gurms, but he should probably get back.

When they parted, back at the festival grounds, he shook the hand she extended. Then he kissed her cheek.

"I hope to see you again soon. If you would like to follow up on that artwork, you can reach me here." He handed her a card with his name printed on one side, and a handwritten email address on the other. Nothing else.

"This has been a dream come true. I should tell you, Quarzo Bianco has long been my favorite. Russell Williams in fact introduced me to it." Babbling to extend their time together. "Given the choice, I would drink nothing else!" How self-serving and insincere did that sound? "At any rate, thank you for the private tour. Ciao." She smiled and flipped a small wave as he walked away.

Everything else was anticlimactic. She wandered the grounds, talked to various people who looked like her—like they didn't belong—and listened in on conversations dominated by egotists. When the band started to play, close to midnight, she looked for Federico to say her goodbyes. But he was surrounded by a small mob, and she left without speaking with him again. A thank you email would have to do. She had his personal email address!

With no one on the road and Alice's buzz-heavy foot on the accelerator, the drive back to Russell's place took less than two hours. She slept like a tired puppy, and it was mid-afternoon by the time she strolled to the café for brunch. When she returned to Russell's house, a box covered in foil giftwrap sat blocking the front door. Inside were two bottles of Quarzo Bianco and a note. *Until next time. Ciao*

Chapter 13

One o'clock Wednesday morning. After making sure Russell's plane had left O'Hare as scheduled, she logged into his private Gmail. Her heart pounded when she saw a chain of notes between Federico and Russell, notes that started the previous Thursday, two days before the festival.

FEDERICO – Thank you for providing your private email address to continue our correspondence. The artwork I mentioned consists of eleven paintings on wood, apparently rather old. Each is of a young woman and has a woman's name on the back. Each is also signed on the back, "Giuseppe". None are dated. I am seeking advice on how to appraise the works. Your assistance would be appreciated. Warmly…

Russell – Thank you for the details. I am very interested in working with you. Unfortunately, my schedule is rather tight at the moment. I could recommend another appraiser, but I would very much appreciate the opportunity to evaluate these works personally. What are your needs in terms of timing? Best regards…

FEDERICO – I am delighted to hear of your interest in working with me and am happy to accommodate your timing as I have no deadline for completing the appraisal. This is little more than a curiosity for me. Please reach out when your schedule allows. The paintings are currently stored at Castello di Quarzo Vineyard near Filattiera.

Russell – Thank you in advance for your patience. I should be available to visit your estate within a few weeks. In the meantime, I recommend photographing each work front and back, and strictly limiting publicity about your discovery. Please secure the paintings with the thought that they could prove to be highly valuable.

FEDERICO – I understand and look forward to hearing back from you at your convenience.

It was two a.m. by the time Alice finished mining Russell's email. Lots of interesting morsels, but nothing more on the subject of the eleven paintings. Without even turning off the light, she knew sleep would be impossible. She was at the threshold of something huge—how to capitalize on it could keep her awake for days. She shuffled into the kitchen and opened the fridge. Two bottles of QB lying side by side stared back at her. A celebration was premature, but, why not?

Twelve hours later, Alice woke to the distant sound of bells ringing. Her head hurt and her mouth was dry. In five minutes, the bells sounded again. It was her phone. She groaned and managed to prop up on one elbow to answer. It was the voice of the little bald man from the Areni Gallery. Good news. The offer had been accepted. Madame Areni would see her at three o'clock. Alice squinted at the screen. It was already after two!

Plan. Coffee, shower, order a taxi, call Bruno. No, water and aspirin first. No, call Bruno first, make sure he was available for a conference call at three. It was a wise choice. Bruno was thrilled with the news but about to step on a plane. He would not be available for the teleconference. He would, however, have someone send her all the information necessary for the wire transfer. It would be on WhatsApp, fully encrypted. And an armored van would be there to collect the work.

Alice's jaw ached from clenching her teeth. She gulped three espressos and willed her cramping abs to relax. Welcome to the big leagues. A chant started in her head. Money money money! The taxi was waiting as she hurried out the front door. She was too stressed to wonder whether she was being watched.

She arrived at the gallery twenty minutes late. An armored van was parked outside and two armed guards stood outside the conference room. Inside were Madame Areni and her assistant, the young man Russell had spoken to after the auction. The transaction was clinical, strictly business, dozens of photographs were taken of the work, forms were signed. Alice lost count after seven. Finally, she read the wire transfer information from her phone as the assistant typed on a laptop. He made a phone call to Bruno's bank, then put Alice on the line to answer four questions that she was fairly sure she understood. The bank could not be responsible for any loss of funds due to incorrect information they had been given. The money would be sent to the routing number provided. She could not cancel. Did she understand? The room spun. She placed a hand on the desk for support. Did she understand? Yes, yes.

Espressos all around. Madame Areni made small talk while they waited. Alice was too wired to think. And then the laptop beeped and the assistant said congratulations. The shipping box was closed and the hot sealing wax was stamped. Alice signed another form. The van pulled away.

Madame Areni said she would like to discuss future opportunities with Alice but given the late hour asked if she could return tomorrow. They set a time to meet, shook hands, and Alice turned to thank the assistant. He was staring at his laptop in horror.

"Madame, there seems to be a problem. The seller has not received the funds."

Alice fainted. The back of her head hit the padded carpet.

Chapter 14

"Another perfect landing, Aldo."

"Grazie. When weather is good, landing is good, signore."

"Make sure it holds. We're taking off in less than an hour. Vinny, your first time making a drop with me. Don't say nothing, just look tough, capisci?

"Capisco."

"No talking, dummy!" He clapped his new soldier on the back and laughed.

Bruno had been making this trip once every three weeks for the past thirty-odd years, unwilling to trust anyone with a case full of cash. A lot had changed in that time, but a small bank in a small town was rarely a problem. And using this private airport was a pleasure, especially since 2008 when Switzerland joined the Schengen zone. He no longer had to enter the terminal—no immigration, no customs. The limo could pick him up directly on the tarmac.

The driver opened the rear door. Bruno climb in next to Vinny, unlocked the large briefcase from Vinny's wrist, and clicked the stainless-steel cuff to himself. He leaned back into the headrest and closed his eyes. The bank was eleven minutes by car. The deposit would take no more than twenty including small talk with the teller and the bank manager. Bruno respected the value of personal contact, making the little people feel important. Madeleine used to call it schmoozing, the term she had learned at her American university.

Madeleine. He still missed his Maddie. Her gallery in Monaco had been a cornerstone of his money laundering since its opening. Trusted members of the family business purchased non-existent artwork using dirty cash, which Bruno then deposited in Switzerland. The process morphed as technology changed. Insider members began to deposit cash in their bank accounts and pay for imaginary paintings with credit cards. Now most transactions were with debit cards. With the advent of security cameras on the streets and constant police surveillance, meticulous records began to be kept. Actual paintings, most nearly worthless, were shipped into the gallery, high priced sales were recorded, and paintings were carried or shipped out. Each member account would make no more than three purchases per year.

Once Alice had implemented her idea for on-line art auctions, Bruno instructed Aristotle, head of security, technology, and bribery, to automate the process. He set up multiple fake accounts. Then for each auction, two or three accounts would bid against each other until the winning bid was in the range of a few thousand euros. A debit card would be charged and a boxed painting shipped out. Paintings went in and out of a warehouse, never passing through the gallery. Alice knew nothing of the fake accounts. She simply purchased scads of paintings from minor artists—who were thrilled to move a piece for five hundred euros—and posted a photo of each to the auction site. They all watched as orders for more works continued to roll in.

Bruno's goal had been to increase the monthly wash three-fold. Once the site was fully operational, he achieved five-fold. He cleared his backlog, and began to offer safe, low-cost laundering to members of The Collective.

The limo slowed. Bruno smiled and opened his eyes as the driver pulled into a no-parking spot in front of the bank. Vinny opened Bruno's door, then stood on the sidewalk with arms folded as he strode through the smoked-glass doorway. The bank manager ran to greet him.

Bruno beamed. "My friend! Wonderful to see you as always. How is your son?" He stooped and kissed the slick-haired man's sagging cheeks.

"Ciao, Signore Porcelli. He is the same, unfortunately."

"If you need more help, just say the word."

"Thank you. You are too kind. But, a small moment to discuss your account, with your permission?"

"Of course, Benito. Of course." He followed the manager into a windowless office and squeezed around the furniture to take a seat, impatient to make the deposit and leave.

"Some activity just now I notice. I want to make sure you are aware. Just this hour, in fact…"

"Yes, Benito, there should have been three point five million sent." In his left hand was a yellow sticky-note with a password written in pencil. He waved it to shoo an insect he heard buzzing near his ear.

"Correct, but I find a second transfer after, strange. I do not recognize this type of number. I request a trace, it should be finished now…."

The manager entered a few strokes on his keyboard and stopped. The color drained from his face. He cursed, took a deep breath, and turned the monitor for his client to see. He snatched the handset of his desk phone and stabbed the keypad.

Bruno sat his readers on his nose and stared at a line of transactions that trailed down the screen. Forty minutes earlier, three point five million euros had gone to the number Bruno recognized. Twenty minutes after that, six million euros were withdrawn. Another six million went out ten minutes later, then another every sixty seconds thereafter. Each transfer was to a different numbered account. Bruno grabbed the monitor with both hands. He watched helplessly as his eyes trailed down to the last line on the screen, the final transfer. The account was overdrawn. Eighty million euros were gone.

The roar from Bruno's throat pierced his own ears. A black burst behind his eyes blinded him. Seconds later, when he could see again, blood was dripping from his wrist under the locked metallic cuff. The manager was cowered beneath his desk, the computer monitor was on the floor in two pieces, and the phone cord was ripped from the wall. But the chaos in the room barely registered. He grabbed his lower back and staggered under the agony, like a welding torch was focused on his lumbar. He fell, landing half on, half off the chair, crushed under a throbbing mass of pain centered on his old injury. He cried "my pills" before losing consciousness.

Light turbulence brought him round. He was in the air. It was dark outside. The familiar, hazy narcotic nothingness damped the flame still blazing in his back. Sounds that started as echoes from a dark chamber sharpened into voices he could understand: the pilot and Vinny were shouting over the engine noise. He struggled to speak.

"Vinny, get my phone. Text Alice Stevens. Where are you?"

"We don't have service yet."

"Now! It'll go when we descend. And don't you ever question me again!"

Chapter 15

Porcelli Investigation, Interim Report

> *He was so predictable. Like a pitcher showing his fingers on the laces. Like a card player with smiling eyes. Seventy-seven percent of each day was the same. Same places, same people, same route. On Saturday he either drove his classic red Ferrari into the hills to places he could wind her out, or he was solo sailing, 'braving' the waters of the Ligurian Sea.*

> *His security was a joke. Oh, he had a small army at his call 24/7, but electronically, where it really mattered these days, he was a child playing with matches. The warehouse and office at the shipyard, the villa, the gallery in Monaco, the Madeleine Too, all the same passcode.*

It wasn't 1234, but it wasn't rocket surgery either. Good thing the banking world had higher standards. Too high for him to know by heart it seems. But then he had no heart, right?

Predictable? Every third Wednesday, he and a soldier and a briefcase boarded a private plane at the local airfield and flew to a grass runway a few km's outside Giubiasco where a black Mercedes sat waiting. Every trip, same pilot, same driver. Then it was a short drive to a pre-war marble palace that held the small-town branch of his favorite Swiss bank, where he was greeted by the manager who had a disabled kid or something. A trip to the safe deposit box, then a sizable cash infusion into a numbered account, the password entered by the grace and convenience of a yellow post-it, a yellow sticky that was clearly readable via nano drone camera, the cute little bug the big man stared right at as it landed on the bookshelf.

With the password to that account in my hand, everything else was child's play.

Chapter 16

When Alice woke, she was stretched on a sofa with her shoes off and a cool cloth on her forehead. The lights were dim. The assistant was at the desk rubbing his face with both hands.

"What happened?"

"You fainted Ms. Stevens. Madame Areni had to leave and the gallery is closing in a few minutes."

"I know I fainted! What happened with the money!" She touched the back of her head and winced.

He told her they were looking into it but getting nowhere. He had personally spoken with both banks, twice each, and each time the story was different. They were dealing with numbered accounts, so he could understand the secrecy, but someone somewhere had to know what happened. The anonymous seller of The Angel was livid and threatening legal action. It could take a few days for an international transfer to actually appear in the recipient's account, but it should have hit the receiving bank immediately. The money was gone from the originating account with no record of the SWIFT system ever receiving it. He wanted to know what she could tell him about the buyer. A name? Anything that might help?

Help, she thought. Help indeed. She had to let Bruno know. She checked her phone. Thirteen messages from him.

> Where are you?

> Get your ass to Genoa now.

> Where are you?

> I'm sending a car to the Areni Gallery.

> Get here now!

Before she could respond, two men burst through the front entrance and shouted her name.

****

Some two hours later, the vehicle stopped abruptly. Carsick from riding blindfolded, she stumbled from the backseat onto the pavement. It was eerily quiet, the only sounds were from boats shifting, waves lapping their hollow hulls. A marina at night.

By the time the blindfold was removed, her hands and legs were zip-tied to a chair. The room, nearly dark, rocked side to side. Someone behind her said, "start talking".

"Bruno!" She whimpered. "Sir. I followed your instructions. The assistant entered the numbers that you sent, that someone sent. Everything was fine, I signed for the painting and those guys drove away with it. We celebrated. Then they told me the seller's bank did not receive the funds. That's all I know!"

"Who was there?"

"Madame Areni. Her assistant. Me. That's all."

"Who saw the numbers?"

"Only the assistant. I'm sure."

"I'm only going to say this once. What happened to all the money?"

"The gallery is trying to find out. Neither bank will tell them anything—"

Someone slapped her, hard. Her neck popped. She swallowed the hot liquid creeping up her throat.

"I'm talking about all of the money! Where is it? What did you do? Who are you working with?"

She opened her mouth but nothing came out.

"Find out what she knows. Don't touch her face again."

"What do you mean, all of the money? Bruno! Don't leave!"

The door slammed and she was blindfolded again. Something, the heel of a boot?, smashed her pinky. Excruciating pain shot through her arm and neck.

****

Bruno stood on the top deck and stared at the horizon until the long ash from his cigar fell onto his pant leg. The muffled sounds from below had stopped. He was losing patience, pacing now port to starboard. Never in his career had there been a problem with money, once it was in Switzerland. Automatic transfers to a private account in Panama happened when the Swiss balance hit twenty million. Thirty-five years of flawless history, starting before anything was computerized. But somehow the transfers had stopped and no one noticed. The balance had risen to over eighty. He was cursed with computers. The world moved like a Formula One car, technology changing faster than anyone could possibly keep up. He was practically helpless, ancient, dependent on people who understood how things work.

His phone sounded. His accountant. Speak of the devil. "Alonzo, anything?… Yes, what?… What do you mean unrelated? I don't believe in coincidence, and you just said he's the one who sold the painting…. You'd better be one hundred percent sure about that." He chomped his cigar as he listened. "All right, all right. I get it. Just go find my money and forget about Il Martello!"

But Bruno couldn't forget about him. Il Martello, The Hammer, was one of the few men Bruno feared, an assassin with a reputation of having unlimited skills, including invisibility. He took a final drag, spit the cigar into the water, and tramped down the stairs.

"Hold up. Untie her. Alice, sorry about that. We had to be sure. A lot of money went missing right after the wire transfer you initiated. We thought it had to be related. Seems you're clean. But we've got a big problem. Let's go up, get you some fresh air."

It was a different yacht, much smaller than the one they had first met on.

Bruno was acting again the same as he had during that initial meeting: soft, charming, and domineering. No apparent remorse for what he'd just done to her. It was business. He filled two glasses with cold grappa. Was this his way of apologizing, making everything all right again? She stared at her glass while he drained his and refilled it. He talked, more or less to himself, waxing philosophical. He switched to Italian she couldn't follow. She had to plan. First, get off this boat, then permanently extract herself from this nightmare. How? Play along, appear unruffled, bide her time. For the moment, relax. Ha. Good luck with that. She had a smashed right pinky finger and a crushed little toe on her left foot. Think. One thing was clear, this was not a ballpark she was prepared to play in. Just get the hell out of the game.

"What are you going to do with The Angel?" she asked. "The seller never got their money. They're going to sue."

He looked stunned at being interrupted. "You think I'm going to return it?" His laugh chilled her. "The money left my account. That painting hangs tomorrow in the gallery."

He threw his glass over the railing. She watched him wobble down the gangplank and across the pier to the parking lot. He waved his arm and the falcon-wing door of a sleek black SUV opened. Bruno wedged himself into the driver's seat and seconds later the vehicle was gone. She was stranded on the deck, not even sure where she was, but there was no way she was getting back in the car with those thugs.

She touched her pants pocket and squealed—her phone was there. Two bars. She almost cried when the taxi dispatcher responded in English to her broken Italian.

Chapter 17

Daylight was breaking when the taxi dropped her at Russell's house. An awareness of hunger pangs joined the throbs in her finger and toe. Using her left hand was a challenge, but she managed to fish for the key in her purse and unlock the door. She limped into the foyer. Someone shouted "Hey!".

She shrieked.

Russell stepped from the kitchen. His eyes popped. "What happened to you!"

"Goddammit, what are you doing here!" She ran at him with her arm cocked and a fist that sailed toward his face. "You son of a bitch!"

He ducked and grabbed her around the torso, pinning her upper arms. She flailed, thrashed his back, kicked his shins, screamed until her throat was raw.

"How could you! They wanted to kill me, those men. Bruno finally told them to stop and then he acted like it was nothing, what they did, what he let them do! I'll never trust you again as long as I live. I hate you!"

He let go and didn't stop her fists this time—the weak blows pummeled him, slowing until she gave up, exhausted. He scooped her in his arms.

She floated to the bedroom, took the pills and drank the water he brought, and fell asleep, vaguely aware he was sitting on the edge of the bed. In her fitful dreams, everything mixed and played and remixed and replayed. Dream Russell kept looking at her face and hands and feet, asking what did I do wrong? It was clear then why she blamed him—he was a soft target. The real evil was too frightening to confront, a black void that inched closer and closer as she ran past ship after ship down a never-ending pier. She leapt into the black water just as a scorching pain in her foot caused her to stumble. She jerked awake.

Russell was holding a tube of arnica, rubbing the cream on her toe. Afternoon light through the window had warmed the room and she felt like surrendering back into the sleep that dimmed her brain. Her left eye was swollen shut. When she touched it, the pain brought her fully alert.

"You can't use this around the eyes, but I've got a beefsteak half thawed we'll put on it. You'll be amazed."

"If you expect me to say thank you, you're going to have a long wait."

"Can you at least tell me what happened?"

"What do you think happened? Bruno's a lunatic. They kidnapped me out of Areni's gallery and drove me blindfolded to a marina somewhere and tied me to a chair. Bruno asked me where his money was and I said the wire transfer didn't go through and they were trying to trace it, but he was talking about a lot more money apparently, I don't know, some money just disappeared from the same account that we used to pay for The Angel. He kept saying where is it and then they broke my finger and toe. They were going to keep going but Bruno came in and stopped them."

"Bruno tried to buy The Angel? The owner decided to sell it outright?"

"That's what you're worried about? Christ! I negotiated it and Bruno bought it. Sort of. He's got possession. It's probably hanging in Monaco right now."

"Hey, you look like you could use something to eat. Can you make it to the kitchen?"

"What I could use is more of those pills."

"Expired Percocet, you took the last two. I've got some Tylenol 3."

"I'll take anything at this point."

"Tell me the rest of it."

"Yeah, well, it's a long story. You know the worst part? After letting them beat me, he acted like it was nothing, wanted to chat over shots of booze. The guy has ice water in his veins. How could you let me get involved with a maniac? How are you going to get me uninvolved?"

He helped her into a chair in the breakfast nook. "I did push you to work with him. I am so truly sorry this happened. I know he used to be volatile, but I thought all that craziness was in the past. He's got a lot of legitimate businesses. You understood he was a crime boss, though, right? No?" He cocked his head. "Oh, yeah. Big time."

"What does that mean?"

"It means, as long as he distrusts you, there's no getting away."

The sound from her throat was pitiful. "What do I do?"

"Make him think you're loyal. Then you could gradually sever business ties and skate away. First you need to ingratiate yourself to him. What does he want that you could deliver?"

"Besides his missing money? How the hell do I know? I only know about his gallery business." She sat her coffee mug on the table. Her back straightened. "So, maybe…"

"What are you thinking?"

She was suddenly energized. "Just remember, you owe me. Tell me about the art that Federico wants you to authenticate."

"How the hell do you know about that?"

"He told me, at the festival. Said he was hoping to meet you there. Surely he's reached out by now."

His eyes lit up. "I can't believe he told you. You guys got something going on? Never mind. You can't breathe a word of this yet. Federico found eleven paintings, buried in some sort of crypt or something. The photos he sent look to be consistent with The Angel. I'm pretty optimistic they're real, but who knows? The story's been around long enough for someone to have faked them."

"The public only heard the legend a couple months ago."

"True. But the family that sold The Angel has apparently known about it for years."

"I know Bruno would kill to own all twelve. Oh my god, that's a phrase I never want to repeat."

"It's not a bad idea, actually. You negotiate for him to buy them, and he's eternally grateful. You eventually extract yourself from his radar. You up for it? Yeah? Just don't say a word until I can authenticate them."

"What are they worth if they're real?"

"All twelve together? A hundred mill easy. I could make sure you get in early, ahead of the media hype. I don't think Federico is greedy, and I could give him a conservative estimate, assuming he wants to sell."

"Holy crap. Would you do that?"

"Absolutely. Just keep it quiet for now."

She stared into space, lost in another dream.

"Hey! I'm serious. Keep it quiet until I authenticate them."

Chapter 18

Bruno told his housekeeper, Beatriz, to leave for the night. He had little appetite and being alone seemed more important than supper. One bottle of Grey Goose VX remained at the wet bar. He cracked the seal.

This view from the balcony of his villa was immense and was once pure pleasure to him—graceful Mediterranean cypress trees that his mother had planted fifty years ago, red tiled rooftops far beyond the trees, and the ever-changing sunset colors on the sea beyond that.

Tonight he felt the years in his bones rather than the sea breeze on his skin. He had cut the opiate dose in half today so he could enjoy two or three drinks now without losing control, and he was going to savor it. He twirled the tumbler as dying sunrays fractured into rainbows in the crystal. The clear liquid inside was the only beauty that caught his eye.

From birth, anything that money could buy had been his. But the family business and the fight for constant growth had killed both of his parents, had destroyed his health, had robbed him of a wife and any prospect of leaving the only genuine legacy there was, a son. It had taken him years to appreciate what he had had with Madeleine and what he had lost by never loving again. He was left with nothing more than the problems of running a small empire. Compared to leaving an heir, it was meaningless.

He leaned his elbows on the bar and noticed what had been under his nose the whole time. It was a fat white envelope with a printed mailing label addressed to "Porcelli, Villa Gazza". Inside that was a tan envelope with "BRUNO" scrawled in block letters, as if a six-year-old had written it. He turned it up and a stack of high-res photos slid out, twenty or more, showing the interior of his estate. The grounds, garage, kitchen. His bath. Anger washed over him as he tried to understand what this meant. He yelled for the housekeeper who wasn't there. And then he looked at the final picture. His fury turned to icy fear. It showed his darkened bedroom with himself asleep on a jumbled mass of sheets. A message was written across the image in the same block letters.

You Have My Money And My Painting

But Your Life Is Mine!

He sat down hard on the edge of the olive wood bench. Pain shot from his tailbone to his teeth and erupted in a howl. Pigeons flew from their nests in the eaves. He hobbled to the desk where he'd left his cell phone.

"Vinny! Goddammit. Answer your goddam phone... Vinny, get the hell over here now. The villa."

He forgot about the painkillers still in his system, about needing to ration the vodka. In the twenty minutes it took Vinny to arrive, he had turned himself into the maniac everyone feared, everyone that is except Vinny, which is why Bruno kept him around. He was not the smartest guy on the payroll, but Vinny alone could step into the middle of a mad rage and remain undaunted. The effect was like Valium. It might take two minutes or twenty, but eventually Bruno would relax, listen to reason. How do you do it, he had asked Vinny once. I don't know, he said. I just imagine it's all a movie or something, I know you don't mean nothing by it.

Vinny looked at the photos and then tried to check the security feeds, but the computer was beyond him. He would talk to the staff tomorrow, see what anyone remembered. He suggested Bruno call Aristotle.

The head of security and bribery arrived in minutes. He was a fireplug with fat cheeks and a permanent five o'clock shadow, a former corrupt police chief who had been influential in the family's rise to the top. Bruno had never liked Aristotle, but he trusted him with his life and everything he owned. He was one of the most intelligent men he knew. Too smart to do anything but play it straight.

He listened to Bruno's story. Then from his personal laptop he logged into Villa Gazza's security system and discovered that all twenty-four camera feeds contained a forty second gap starting at eleven o'clock that morning. When the recording resumed, a camera on the main entrance showed an envelope on the concrete just inside the wrought iron gate. An hour later, the gardener discovered the envelope and took it to Beatriz, who placed it on the bar.

"I thought the photos might have been taken with a military-grade drone. But look at the one from inside your bedroom. You can see a shadow on the floor from the window light behind the photographer. That's no accident. Someone wants you to know he was here. I'll scan the video feeds going back day by day. There will be another gap telling us when these were taken."

"You assured me this system is the best money can buy."

"It all comes down to technology. Today's best system is tomorrow's old news."

Bruno looked at the empty tumbler in his hand and then toward the half-empty bottle of vodka across the room. Vinny picked up the tumbler and said he would take care of it.

Aristotle continued, "You could add another bodyguard for a while, but my guess? This guy just wants his money. Otherwise, you wouldn't be sitting here now."

Bruno could feel the pressure building behind his eyes. "Who buys a painting for millions, sells it, and also knows how to disable the security system—that you put in! Who can do that?" He was screaming.

Aristotle was unphased. "You're talking about three people. An art lover with loads of money, a high-end computer expert, and a contract killer with a camera."

"Il Martello!"

"Maybe. Whoever it is, you're lucky you didn't wake up when he was in your bedroom."

Vinny returned with a full tumbler. Bruno was too preoccupied to notice it was filled with Pellegrino. "I want to know who's behind this."

"The art lover? Your guess is better than mine. The computer geek, probably a small handful working domestically who could get around your system. The key is the contract killer willing to take on a job like this, a job inside Villa Gazza. It's a very short list of hit men. If it isn't Il Martello, odds are it's someone you've hired in the past."

Bruno closed his eyes and tried to create that list, but the adrenalin was gone and the need to sleep was crushing. "Both of you stay here tonight, stay awake so I can sleep."

Vinny said, "You got it boss. I'll be right outside your door. Ari, make some coffee."

The older man bristled but got up and headed for the kitchen. He stopped, turned, and snapped his fingers. "We'll take the entire villa security system off-line, permanently, operate it as a closed system. Inconvenient, but a small price to pay for peace of mind."

"You do what you have to."

Chapter 19

Alice and Russell talked until the kinks in the plan were unkinked. She would get back in the game as soon as possible, appear guileless, impress Bruno with her dedication, and, if the eleven were real, make him the owner of all twelve sisters.

Russell bought her a pair of crutches at the pharmacy, bandaged her toe, splinted her finger. By the next morning the bruise on her face was in full bloom. Her foundation was too shear to conceal it and she washed it off.

"I can't appear in public like this."

"Yes, you can," he said. "This is a good thing. My take on Bruno is, he's not heartless when he's sober and not in pain. Make him confront what he did. First thing, apologize to him. And make up a funny story for his staff, something that will be repeated. He needs to hear that you told them you tripped over your own feet."

It was late morning when she arrived at Oscar-Porcelli and hobbled into the lobby. A small crowd of employees gathered, asking about the bruise and crutches. Linda, the receptionist, helped translate. One wanted to take her to lunch. Another said she should go home. Linda was excited to show Alice the office they had set up for her. *Alice Stevens, Marketing Consultant* was stenciled outside the door. A flatscreen on the desk had a sticky note with a password scribbled on it. Alice said she had some ideas about tweaking the on-line auction site. When would Bruno be in? Linda said no one ever knew the answer to that and left for lunch. Alice logged on and reviewed the new site. Twenty minutes later, Bruno walked into her office.

"Alice. Great to see you. I didn't know when you would be in."

"A girl's got to make a living. The Areni Gallery is withholding my commission on The Angel." Not that she had discussed it with them, but it sounded good.

"I'll take care of that. Come look."

She had walked right past it. On the left-hand wall in the lobby hung The Angel, alone, glowing in a spotlight.

"Well, we did it." He squeezed her shoulder and laughed. "Not bad for a first project young lady. What's next? Linda said you had some ideas for the auction site. Let's go to my office."

She was two people, talking-to-him Alice and fearing-him Alice. He was half-listening to her ideas, too much detail for his attention span. Cocaine? He was definitely on something. She felt incapable of appearing natural, of hiding the terror of simply being in the same room with him.

"What about the rumors, the eleven sisters, are people still searching around Emilia Romagna?" he said.

"More to the north now. Villafranca. Digging in the backyards of strangers, yes." She faked a laugh.

"We need to play it up on the website, along with a photo of The Angel. Get some articles in the local papers. I want that lobby filled every day, people standing in line for a look. I'll put an armed guard on each side of her. Get on that—"

His phone rang. When he motioned, she stepped out and closed the door just as the shouting started. She heard everything and could translate a few words. "Money does not evaporate… account numbers… trace… someone's head… operating capital… today not tomorrow… I cannot continue… no, today!" It sounded like his phone bounced on the desk. "Alice! Get in here."

His eyes were dancing. "What if we announce that we found the eleven paintings? How much would that be worth?"

She stopped in the middle of sitting. She had had no thought of telling him, but he brought it up. *He asked me, remember that.*

"I don't understand."

"We put out a rumor, say we found them, but they're in bad shape, in for restoration. That will raise our profile, drive traffic. I am just thinking out loud. Or what if… Wait, hold on. There must be millions of old paintings of prostitutes, you just need to find some. This is brilliant!"

She had never seen him frenzied. Mood number three, after calm businessman and angry mobster.

"We display them behind a barrier, claim they are late fifteenth century. We never give access, no one can prove they're counterfeit. The publicity! You go out and find eleven. We put them in the temporary exhibits room, sell tickets. Mother of God, we must do this!"

He was manic, laying out an insane scheme, completely trusting her loyalty.

"Can I play the devil's advocate?" She waited for his eyes to refocus. "If I, we, come up with eleven and claim they are real, what if the real ones are later found? Our reputation would be ruined." Did her voice quiver?

"You make a joke? This will never happen." He stopped, cocked his head. *Never play poker with this guy.* "What do you know? Eh? Alice Stevens, my employees do not hide information from me!"

Employee?

She had zero time to think this through. "There is a chance…" *Jeeze Louise.* "Someone, uh…"

"Where? Who!"

"I didn't bring it up, because there are so many reports of old paintings being found. But…" *Screw Russell.* "Apparently someone has been commissioned to authenticate eleven very old paintings recently found buried in Tuscany, near Liguria, or vice versa. That's all I know."

He half rose from the desk and exploded. "When were you going to tell me!"

It was like being struck in the face again. Vomit filled the back of her throat, and she ran for the ladies' room. She leaned on the sink and counted breaths until her hands stopped shaking. She washed her face and crept back to his office. He was the soft-spoken businessman again, friend of the downtrodden. And he kept sniffing, pulling at his nose. He apologized for frightening her, confessed his frustration with the idiots searching for his stolen money. He had to inject some liquidity very soon, day-to-day operations were already suffering. If she had a lead on the eleven sisters, she had to drop everything else and secure them for him.

"You called me an employee. I thought I was independent."

"Figure of speech."

He thinks he owns me. "So, suppose these eleven are real? How do you make enough profit to mitigate your problem?"

She followed him to the lobby again. He stopped in front of The Angel, mumbling. "Are the twelve worth a lot more than the cost of one plus the cost of eleven?" He turned to her. "How much would all twelve together be worth to a collector?"

"Once the market has time to react? A conservative estimate is one hundred million…"

His gaze snapped back to The Angel. "I overpaid for this one, I understand that. Okay. Three million each for the other eleven. And a half-percent bonus for you above your three. When will the authentication be complete?"

Over one million dollars commission. I could disappear.

"Alice! Authentication, when?"

"I will find out."

****

She did not find out. Russell was gone when she got back to his place late that night. A note said he would be in London for three or four days. He answered on the sixth ring.

"I take it you met with Bruno. How'd it go?"

"It depends on your perspective. He acted like I was back in his good graces, but I don't trust him. He's too moody. I can tell you he's definitely interested in the eleven, up to thirty-three million euros."

"Three million each. That's reasonable, for him."

"I just need to know how long before you finish authentication."

"It's not a trivial process my dear, and I've barely started. We're talking weeks, maybe months. Not days."

"Months? He's really pressuring me."

"Do you realize there are at least eight steps for something with this high of a profile? We've done less than half the work—"

"How much longer!"

"I honestly don't know right now. You didn't tell him someone found—"

"Of course not." Dealing with Bruno had one benefit—it was now comparatively easy to lie to Russell. "I told him I hear lots of stories, people finding old paintings, and what would he do if the real ones are found."

"Stories have a life of their own. The fact is, I had a long conversation with a Japanese collector I've dealt with a few times. He contacted me about the rumors. Are you sitting? He suggested two hundred million for all twelve."

"You have got to be kidding!" She jumped up from the sofa.

"Suggesting a price and closing a deal are very different things, but no, I'm not kidding."

"Wow wow wow. Listen, the money that melted into thin air? Bruno is freaked. I overheard him yelling at someone about short-term working capital. I'm thinking, if he could buy these for thirty-three and sell them for two hundred—"

"Come on, if he's short on capital, how could he buy them?"

"Don't ask me. A loan? I just know he said he would pay three mill each if he could sell for a profit."

"His cash flow issue goes away, and you make a fortune."

"I can get out from under his thumb, is what I'm thinking." She hesitated. "I'm still being followed."

"Are you okay?"

"I'm almost getting used to it. That may be the scariest part."

"Just try to relax. We'll talk about it tomorrow. I've got to run."

She had tried to relax. The truth was, she was imagining spies at every turn. Her cell phone was acting funny. Tourists taking pictures were targeting her. The only place she had felt safe was here, in Russell's hideaway—until she remembered the security camera Russell had out back. What's to keep Bruno's spy from slipping his own cameras into Russell's house? Her head was going to explode if she didn't get out of this nightmare soon.

One bottle of QB and five hours of sleep later, she woke up with an epiphany. There just might be a way to speed things up.

****

"Bruno. Do you have a minute?"

"I answered your call, didn't I?"

"Sorry. I have information from a very reliable source that the eleven paintings are in the same style as The Angel. The owner is very wealthy, not into art, probably willing to sell."

"Nice work."

"Listen, the value of all twelve could be double what I suggested."

"Two hundred million!"

"It's possible." She took a deep breath. "I had a thought. What if I can lock them up for you, get the owner to sign a contract now, before the whole world finds out. I'll offer thirty-three, but make it contingent on authentication, of course."

"Assolutamente! Absolutely. But go as high as fifty if you have to. When will they be authenticated?"

"It's going to be at least a month."

"That's too long. Make it sooner."

He hung up. Her jaw dropped. Three and a half percent of fifty million….

Chapter 20

She drove the rental car back to Federico's estate, taking enough deserted backroads to feel confident no one was tailing her.

She had on the same cream-colored sweater she'd worn to meet Bruno on the *Madeleine Too*—but without the enormous necklace. Only sun-darkened freckles decorated her neck and chest where the sweater plunged bellybutton-ward. Her jeans were salmon-colored. Foundation hid the fading bruise on her face, and by enduring a bit of pain she could walk without limping. She'd even risked removing the splint on her pinky, hoping his greeting would be a kiss rather than a handshake.

He answered the door in a cream-colored polo shirt and salmon-colored slacks.

"I wonder what this means." He laughed and pointed to their matching outfits.

She said, "Something good, I hope. Thank you for fitting me into your schedule."

"My pleasure. In fact, your timing is impeccable." He kissed both cheeks and led her into his study. The sheers were open and mid-afternoon sunlight lit the sweeping vista of manicured lawn, topiary, and reflecting pool. "I believe a celebration is in order."

"Oh?"

"I just finished the first draft of my memoir. It needs to ferment before I start editing. Is it too early for a drink?"

"You know me."

"Not well enough, but I remember you enjoy Quarzo Bianco. I received your Thank You note by the way."

"That was such a nice surprise. Two bottles!"

"Well, I was sorry we didn't have more time to spend together during the festival—"

"Not at all. I completely understood. It was a treat to have a personal tour of your operations."

"You mentioned a proposal you would like to discuss?"

Crap. Right down to business. "Yes, I have a client who is very much interested in purchasing the legendary companion pieces to The Angel by

Giuseppe da San Russo, should they ever be found and authenticated."

"The so-called Eleven Sisters. And how might I help with that?"

"Okay, this is a stretch, but you mentioned authenticating some art, and I remember you were renovating that old guest house, digging a basement, and it just hit me. What if you discovered the Eleven Sisters?"

"Quite the sleuth, Alice Stevens." He laughed and opened a minifridge. "Have you tried our 2006 Quarzo Bianco? It's the only millésime we've ever produced. Twelve years old and just now reaching its peak."

"You really are in the mood for a celebration."

"Despite my reputation as a hermit, you can't imagine how nice it is to have someone as lovely as you to celebrate with." His voice indicated quotes around *celebrate*. "We could always discuss your proposal later."

"After…?"

"After dinner? After another bottle of 2006?"

"That sounds nice. Pleasure before business, so to speak." *Don't blush.*

"Yes. Life is short." He popped the cork with barely a sound and set two flutes on the glass-topped coffee table. "To your question, I have, in fact, uncovered eleven paintings. And I am told they appear to be consistent with the style of The Angel."

"That's incredible! I mean, not literally. Incredible means lacking credibility. I mean, you know." *Shut up Alice.* "Authentication is pending?"

"Authentication apparently calls for a lot of patience, when old paintings are the subject." He turned on the sofa until their knees slightly touched. "With some other treasures, however, I immediately recognize the real thing." They clinked glasses and paused to savor the wine. He held her gaze until she glanced away. "I'm just now wondering if you might prefer to discuss business after breakfast."

"Oh!" No use trying not to blush now. "Yes, I believe that's worth considering. Shall we see how dinner goes?"

****

The dinner, the evening, the night, the breakfast. All delicious and delightful, obtruded only by the lump in her stomach, the reminder that a multimillion-dollar negotiation was to come. Unfortunately, she would learn at the conclusion of their deal, her nerves would be worse, not better.

She had written the contract on-line, starting with a standard template, identifying Bruno only as "The Client", hoping she would not regret having bypassed a review by his lawyer. She explained the deal was for all eleven, and valid only if all were indeed late fifteenth century. They would pay a refundable deposit of one hundred thousand contingent on authentication. He agreed.

She said, "I will tell you in confidence that the companion piece, The Angel, eventually sold for three point five million. While these eleven may prove to be inferior due to their storage history, my client is prepared to offer forty million for the lot."

Dammit! She meant to start at thirty-three. When he countered with ninety-five, she panicked and jumped to fifty-five—five million euros above what she was authorized! The lump in her stomach was cemented.

He agreed to fifty-five immediately and happily, giving her the thought that it was a game and the money meant little to him. He carefully read the contract, signed it, and was ready to celebrate again. But a kind of buyer's remorse had struck her. She was queasy, almost dizzy, and in no mood to drink. She made her excuses before he could retrieve another bottle of QB from the fridge.

She drove back to Milan through haze, mindlessly responding to GPS commands that barely registered. How exactly had she acted when he suggested a celebratory drink? She appreciated the offer. It was a bit too early. She needed to get back on the road. She may have come across as dismissive once the contract was signed, but nothing was further from her heart. He had made her feel at home, like she belonged with him in that world. All the perks of the fabulously wealthy, none of the hype and pressure. Only the knowledge of—the fear of—what was at stake had paralyzed her natural instincts, kept her detached from his apparently genuine interest in her as a person.

The mob. Spies. Torture. Now, lust for playing in the world of high rollers had come up against another harsh reality—a contract with a billionaire had quashed her passion and replaced it with dread.

She threw her keys on the coffee table, flopped on the sofa, and took out her phone. No. It was almost one o'clock, his lunchtime. Wait until he's eaten. Less cranky. No. Get it over with. No. Drive there and tell him in person.

No. Safer to give him this kind of news on the phone. Would he even blink at an additional five million euros? Was it like five thousand to her? Fifty thousand? When the call went to voice mail, she hung up and closed her eyes.

Seconds, or maybe hours later, her phone roused her from a dreamless sleep. It was Bruno.

"You called. Tell me."

"I secured the right to buy, but he negotiated hard. I'm sorry, really sorry, but it was intense and there was no time to try to contact you for approval."

"What did you do?"

"I agreed to fifty-five million."

He thundered, and she felt a knife in the base of her neck. She could barely control her voice. "But, think, two hundred million for the twelve paintings together. Think about that."

"You think about it, Ms. Stevens. You think about getting your mystery buyer locked up with a contract for two hundred. At *least* two hundred! Then you and I can both start to breathe again. Understand?"

It was the second time in two days he had hung up on her. And this time it didn't feel good—despite the fact that, by contract, she would be owed three percent of the sale price. Six million. Even if he held back the five million she had overbid, she would still be rich enough to do whatever she wanted. One little detail. She had to get Russell to connect her with the guy who had offered two hundred million. Okay, two details. She had to then get him to sign a contract.

Chapter 21

One thing had become clear to Bruno. He couldn't afford to wait for authentication to be completed. In his heart he knew the eleven were real; he had to buy them, now. Once he had the twelve assembled, Alice would negotiate with the Asian buyer. She would start at three hundred million and hope for two hundred. No less than one hundred eighty. The notion that he might take it all and sail away to some South Sea island floated through his mind.

First step, transfer enough money to buy the eleven.

With his personal Swiss account compromised, he could see only three paths. The best choice was to borrow from Porcelli Industriale's working capital. Interest free, no oversight. A few invoice payments would be delayed until the funds were replaced. Minimal downsides really, nothing a little creative bookkeeping couldn't hide. All it would require was a quick call to his money man, Alonzo.

The second option was to use funds from his personal account in Panama. Given what happened with the Swiss bank, he was reluctant to touch that money.

Option three was to borrow from The Collective's funds. That would be only as a last resort. There would be too many questions. For Bruno, it was a non-starter.

He called Alonzo and told him what he needed. Fifty-five million in cash, from the business, as a short-term personal loan. No explanation was requested or offered.

Bruno liked Alonzo, a man with no apparent aspirations beyond counting the beans and making the numbers match at the end of each day. He'd never heard him sound tense, much less panicked. But late the next morning, Alonzo called him in a royal fit.

"There are no funds. Shipping and delivery accounts are all overdrawn. Creditors haven't been paid in weeks. Basically, Porcelli Industriale is under water."

Bruno bellowed. "What about Panama!?"

"I just checked your off-shore account as well. It was emptied out last night. No trace."

Bruno had answered the phone in a good mood, optimistic. Now the walls in his office were pressing in on him from all sides. His Swiss account being emptied had been a horror, but that seemed nothing more than a silly movie compared to the reality of his company being ruined along with his personal fortune disappearing. The edges of his vision slowly dimmed until he could see nothing but the unopened bottle on his desk.

Alonzo continued but the words barely penetrated his awareness. "Everything appeared fine at five p.m. yesterday. Whatever happened, it happened overnight. This morning, email complaints, some of them weeks old, were suddenly released by the server and flooded the accounts payable inbox all at once. Outgoing payments were debited from our accounts but never made it to the creditors. There is no trace of where the money ended up. The banks are working on it, but…"

"Stop. I don't have time for this crap. Just take care of it. Fix it!" Bruno slammed the phone on the desk. The screen cracked and he hurled it against the wall. "Goddammit!"

No money in Porcelli Industriale or Panama. He was left with option three.

The Collective met quarterly. As chairman, he controlled The Collective funds, but loans required approval. That meant calling a special meeting, explaining the risk, selling the potential reward. Some members would insist on a taste of the profits. No way. He had to secretly take the money, buy the eleven, sell all twelve, and replace the cash before the next shipment arrived. It was a small window.

Chapter 22

"Alice, it's not complicated. Just forget that the buyer's in Japan, forget that he will only work directly with me. You don't have to do anything differently. Just write the contract and I'll handle getting it signed."

"Why? Why would you even help me? You must hate me for going behind your back. What's your cut?"

"You were desperate, I get that. And I don't want your money. I admire how you've pulled this all together." He laughed. "You always land on your feet. I told you this kind of work was up your alley. Just make sure you come out clean enough to get off Bruno's radar when it's over."

"Okay." She chewed her lower lip and thought. "Tell Japan we insist on three hundred million for all twelve. Bruno's not going to be happy below two hundred, but the absolute minimum he'll accept is one hundred eighty."

"The buyer will insist his own people verify the authentication. That could mean a quick review of the data and the accreditation of the labs, or could mean sending someone to obtain samples, stretching this out for months."

"Bruno's not going to sit still for that. He wants it now. Where does your work stand?"

"Better than I had thought. There is only one result left to obtain, but it's a new test and they are repeating it. That's why we're still waiting."

"That means all the other tests passed?"

"Absolutely. And this last test, the new one? Not to brag, but it's patent pending for the developer, who happens to be yours truly."

"You developed a test?"

"I can even do it in my studio at the hideaway, but it's better to have an accredited lab do it. It's slow, but it's foolproof. In the future, everyone will have to use it and I'll make a fortune. But you're getting it free. It is the first time it's ever been used for an important sale."

"Wow. I owe you."

"Damn straight. And you're welcome."

"Please, please, please, just make sure the buyer accepts your results. No delays."

Chapter 23

Porcelli Investigation, Interim Report

The risks people take, the games they play while assuming no one is watching them, nor listening to their conversations, nor monitoring their electronic communications. With no legal expertise, she writes a contract for the sale of twelve antique paintings, sale amount to be filled in following negotiations. She emails the contract to her "authenticator". He emails her back 19 hours later that the Asian buyer agrees to 210 million euros pending authentication, but insists no contract, no paperwork, no names. It all rests on the authenticator's impeccable reputation. The money will be wired to the sellers account following the buyer's agent's cursory examination of the merchandise in Milan. The merchandise will be immediately surrendered upon the seller's acknowledgement of receipt of funds.

She reads the email and calls the authenticator. An embarrassingly undignified soliloquy of gratitude follows.

She calls Bruno; says she has news that must be delivered in person. She drives two hours to Villa Gazza, tells him he can count on 210 million for the 12, that it is now just a matter of buying the 11.

The trap is set.

Chapter 24

The Collective existed because Mario, Bruno's father, had convinced the regional families that peace was more profitable than conflict. The organization of six families, representing over five hundred sectors, now controlled the street drug trade in northern Italy roughly west of a line from Milan to Florence, extending to Monaco. Porcelli Import/Export, later Porcelli Industriale, became their exclusive supplier of street drugs.

Porcelli's global shipping network made them ideally suited to operate as the wholesale distributor of narcotics to the group, however, not all members of The Collective were thrilled. They understood the advantages of having a local distributor with international connections, and the buying power of the group meant Mario could offer lower wholesale pricing. The sticking point for some members was Mario's insistence that he receive payment at least ten days before the scheduled arrival date of each shipment. Actual arrivals could be delayed by two weeks or more due to weather, tides, strikes, customs, and capacity bottlenecks. This meant the delivery of goods could be a month after payment had been made, an inconvenience the members grudgingly accepted.

In the forty-plus years since the explosion, street demand had gone from ninety percent heroin to eighty percent cocaine plus a dozen designer drugs. The ten-day advance payment terms had been applied to those products as well. Through it all, after a rocky start, Bruno had served as an immaculate manager of the business. No problem ever went unresolved, and the prices Bruno could offer were appreciably below any other wholesale supplier in Italy. Initial hard feelings about the terms were long forgotten. The sectors respected how flawlessly the system worked. Volume had increased tenfold, and Bruno reveled in how much money there was to be made by capturing both the transportation and the distribution profits. Markup of the entire farmer-to-street value supply chain was two thousand percent, of which he garnered two-thirds. The Porcelli family never involved themselves at the street level. They didn't need to.

The drugs were brought in concealed among various legitimate shipments of auto parts, heavy industrial equipment, and non-perishable consumer goods. These were stored in seventeen warehouses in six cities across the region. From there, the families repackaged the product for street sale and distributed it to all the sectors. The pre-payments, cash only, were kept in a single safe in an armored shipping container near the docks in Genoa, awaiting the arrival of the next shipment.

Today, Bruno knew the exact sum in that safe. It was Collective money earmarked for the next shipment of product, forty-seven million euros, which was eight million less than what he needed to purchase the eleven paintings.

There was once a time when Bruno also would have known the exact contents of his personal safe at the villa—his "never-touch" stash. Today, he counted it and removed eight million, leaving behind less than one mill.

His eight million euros combined with forty-seven of The Collective's advance money, all in five-hundred-euro notes, weighed one hundred twenty-one kilos—over two hundred sixty-six pounds. It fit nicely in eleven large metal briefcases. Without asking what was in the cases, Vinny stacked them in the rear of an armored van.

****

Alice had explained to Bruno that they were waiting on one final test to verify the eleven paintings were fifteenth century. Everything else—no less than seven other tests—had passed. Those same seven tests had been the basis of authenticating The Angel. The plan was strong, but she cautioned that the buyer might insist on running his own tests. If that happened, it could be months before he could sell the twelve. She thought that was unlikely because the buyer had a long relationship with her authenticator and could be expected to trust his report.

Bruno listened with uncharacteristic patience and finally announced that that was good enough, he had wasted enough time. He told her to modify the contract for the purchase of eleven, rewrite it to remove the authentication clause, and to buy them *now*. She advised against it, said it should be only a few more days for the final test, and argued as strongly as she dared. He asked how her finger and toe were feeling and reminded her she had eighteen more. Okay, she would rewrite the contract but wanted a separate one, an agreement indemnifying her. He stopped talking and stared.

What good was a contract with this man anyway? She made the call to Federico, discussed the new terms, and set up an appointment to complete the transaction.

The drive from Genoa to Federico's estate was ninety minutes. Alice rode shotgun. Vinny, two armed guards, and the money sat behind her in the van. No one spoke, no one turned the radio on.

It was late by the time they arrived. Fairy lights decorated the trees, and soft spots turned the pastel stucco of the villa luminous. Federico was standing in the open doorway when the van stopped at the top of the semi-circular drive. While a distant part of her brain registered how wonderful he looked, she was focused on what he was holding, a printed copy of the revised contract she had emailed him. He signed it in front of her without comment, then led her to an all-heart redwood wine cellar in the basement. The paintings were in individual cartons which Alice opened for a superficial inspection. She nodded to Vinny. While one guard remained at the van, the other transferred one painting at a time to the van and returned each time with a briefcase. The entire transaction took less than twenty minutes. It was anticlimactic. No pleasantries, no celebratory drink. Alice was climbing back into the van when Federico called her.

"Alice, you have a minute?"

She managed to walk, not run, up the steps. He took her hands and backed into the foyer, out of view of the van.

"You look worried. Actually, petrified. I've thought something was wrong since the way we left it after finalizing the initial agreement—"

"You mean the way I left it. I practically ran away as soon as you signed."

"Yes. It seemed we had, well, I thought there was something between us worth preserving. When you left so quickly, I felt a bit used, if I'm honest. Manipulated."

"I am sorry. I was confused with what I was feeling toward you. And I was overwhelmed with the enormity of the deal, with all that was at stake." Tears welled in her eyes.

"It is a lot of money."

"I only wish that was the extent of it. And it's worse now. So much worse, you can't imagine. Maybe one day I can explain and you can forgive me."

"There is nothing to forgive." He squeezed her hand.

Before she could stop herself, she tiptoed up and pressed her lips to his. The moment she grabbed the fabric of his shirt, her tension flowed away, her dizziness stopped. Her mind was clear—this was where she belonged.

The driver tooted the horn.

She opened her eyes but didn't let go. "Federico, if this all works out, promise you'll give me a chance. I have so much I want to say."

He kissed her forehead so lightly she wasn't sure it happened. "I can't wait to hear from you. My door will always be open."

****

Bruno had trusted the transaction to Alice without wanting to. He knew Vinny was too stupid to try a double-cross. He hoped that Alice was too smart to try. What choice did he have? All twelve paintings would soon be his, to convert into enough money to recover from the Swiss bank theft and pay off Il Martello. A single deal netting one-hundred-fifty-five million was a once in a lifetime opportunity.

In anticipation of receiving the eleven, Bruno had moved The Angel from Monaco to Villa Gazza. He opened the safe now and gazed at it, imagining himself owning all twelve paintings, if only for a day or two.

It was almost dawn when the van arrived back at Villa Gazza. Alice and Vinny found Bruno asleep in a chaise lounge by the pool. She woke him gently and whispered that the paintings were ready for their new owner to view. As his eyes opened wide, he groaned, plucked two pills from his shirt pocket, and downed them with clear liquid from the glass beside his chair.

Alice led him into the ballroom. Two guards stood like sentinels at the entrance. The eleven paintings were displayed on easels along the back wall. On Alice's cue, Vinny carried in The Angel and placed it on an empty easel in the midst of the eleven. Even unframed and with only a cursory cleaning, the eleven held up well compared to the one that had, for centuries, been beautifully framed and lovingly cared for. Bruno stood dead still when he saw them, all twelve legendary works of art, together for the first time in over five hundred years. He wept openly.

Alice was touched. She wanted to place an arm around his shoulders. "Is two-hundred-ten million euros enough?" she said.

His eyes were red-rimmed. "I have no choice. Get these out of my sight before I change my mind. Vinny, you boys, put them all in the vault. Remove whatever you need to if there's not enough room."

Alice frowned. "You'll have to explain why The Angel is no longer on display in Monaco."

"I don't have to do anything! You have to finalize the contract to sell these."

Alice coughed to cover a gasp. *I haven't told him the buyer refused to sign anything.* "Um, the sale price of two hundred ten million has been agreed, if you remember, but…"

He had had little sleep, was on pain meds, probably alcohol as well. She recognized the precipice they were both on, the plunge into the pit of

Bruno's wrath that one wrong word might trigger. "We, uh, as you know, we just need the final authentication."

His eyes focused on her. "Tell Asia we have the paintings. Show them photos, all the photos they want. Give them every test result that you have so far. Then you get the cash in my hands the minute those final results are available. I'll give you forty-eight hours."

Chapter 25

Juliano Jacaruso (Jack) was in the container-office in the shipyard. He had been The Collective's enforcer for a number of years, holding on to the job after a string of the men had failed to meet expectations and were never heard from again. Jack was the first to be as effective as Dante had been. What he lacked in finesse, he made up for in brutality. Operations had been running smoothly for as long as anyone could remember, but now some of The Collective's dons were starting to grumble about running low on product. Jack had been trying to speak with Bruno for two days but his calls were not being returned. He was about to reach for the phone when it rang.

"Bruno, where the hell have you been?"

"Sorry, Jack. It's Alonzo. I'm looking for Bruno, too."

"Hey, moneyman. You know anything about a late shipment?" Jack knew Alonzo primarily handed accounts for Porcelli's legitimate businesses but kept a hidden set of books to track The Collective's transactions as well.

"More than I'd like to know. It's why I'm trying to find the boss. I was looking into some problem with the main company's accounts, and I came across a waybill for the container that has The Collective's shipment on it. It's been at the dock for a week and no one's done anything. Maybe Bruno didn't know about it, but that's never happened before. Anyway, I scheduled an exchange with the seller's rep for this morning."

"Good. The dons are getting antsy."

"No, not good. The money vault is empty."

"What the—" Only three people could access that safe. Jack, Alonzo, and Bruno. Bruno, who had been AWOL for at least two days. "You're positive about that?"

"Are you kidding me? There's not even a candy wrapper in there."

Jack blew out a breath. "You keep poking around. Don't say anything to anyone. I'll take it from here."

"What are you going to do?"

"Only one thing to do. Talk to The Collective."

Jack hung up and immediately called Bruno again. Voice mail again. "Bruno, a special meeting's been called. Tonight, eight-thirty. It's important. See you there."

Fat chance, he thought.

Jack arrived fifteen minutes late, deliberately. Bruno, as he had anticipated, was not there. The dons were talking about one thing only, running out of product. The mood had turned hostile.

"Gentlemen. Thank you for coming on short notice."

All six dons started talking at the same time.

"Where's Bruno?"

"He told me a week ago the shipment was due the next day."

"He told me there was a mix up at another port but everything was under control."

"He stopped returning my calls."

Jack held up his hand and waited for silence. "The container is in the dock." He raised both hands now to quell the cheers. "The money is not in the safe. Someone's taken it."

The silence that followed was brief. Two members leapt to their feet. Shouts of "I knew it" and remarks about Bruno's lineage built into an uproar, the consensus of which seemed to be to hang him.

Jack let the men rant long enough that, when he finally stood, the dons all stopped and waited for him to speak.

"Gentlemen, none of us need an advanced math degree to figure out that Bruno is behind this. And I hear you. You want your money, you want your product, you want blood. I advise each of you to keep your hands clean and let me handle it. It's my job. I'm very good at my job."

He took out his cell phone then—in front of the heads of the most powerful families in this part of the world—put it on speaker and punched in Bruno's private number. It went straight to voice mail.

"It's me. Missed you at the meeting tonight. You can expect to see me soon. We need to talk about the future."

Chapter 26

Bruno was at Villa Gazza, screening his calls. He listened to Jack's message twice before erasing it. This shit was getting out of control; it was time to disappear until things were fixed. He stuffed his go-bag with every pill bottle from the medicine cabinet, plus his passport and all the cash he could find, and walked out. He left the front door standing wide open. He might never come back.

The car was new, and he loved everything about it, everything except the quirky falcon-wing doors. It was an experimental all-electric crossover Ferrari, and he was one of five beta testers in the world. Computers might be satanic, but the technology in this machine was from heaven.

The cockpit consisted of exactly four devices: steering wheel, accelerator pedal, brake pedal, and a touchscreen, none of which he ever touched. Responses to his voice commands were flawless, even with his speech slurred as it now was.

"Start. Navigate to Genoa Harbor. Temperature twenty-one degrees."

The acceleration was stunning, seamless, and head-snapping—performance no combustion engine could approach. Once on the highway, he closed his eyes. It was hot.

"Twenty-one degrees!"

The fan continued blowing warm air. The car spoke.

"You have a call with Alice Stevens."

It had been two days. The Asian buyer had authorized his agent in Italy to complete the transaction upon his verbal approval. Alice reported that the lab had been given the forty-eight-hour deadline, and the manager promised results no later than midnight tonight. That would be seven o'clock tomorrow morning in Japan. The buyer's probably in Japan, Bruno thought. I'll have my money tomorrow.

The screen beeped and displayed a picture of Alice.

"This better be good news. So, let's hear it."

"I, um, I didn't call. My phone just rang."

"Goddamn technology. Do you have the results or not?"

"I, uh, well, Bruno, it sounds like you're driving. You might want to pull over."

"Tell me."

"I'm serious, Bruno. They finished the test, but…."

He waited a beat. "The goddamn car is driving itself. I'm not going to wreck. Tell me now!"

"Okay! The eleven paintings, all eleven, they're no more than twenty years old. Probably no more than five."

"What the… That's impossible. Where are you?"

"Do you want me to have The Angel tested?"

"No! Are you f—"

"Phone call ended."

"Call Alice Stevens!" His spit splattered the wheel.

The computer did not respond; the temperature was now stifling.

"Open driver's window."

Nothing.

"Maximum safe speed."

The car continued to cruise at the speed limit.

"Acknowledge command!"

A voice repeated, *"maximum safe speed"*, but the intonation was different now, not the sweet southern Italian female voice he had chosen. It was a computerized growl, neither male nor female.

"You can go faster than this!"

"We will not risk attention from the police."

"Pull over. Stop. Now!"

"Change of plans. You might as well relax."

Bruno stepped on the brake pedal, then stomped it. He jerked the door handle, the steering wheel, all to no effect.

"What the hell is going on!"

"What the hell, indeed. What the hell did you do with my money?"

"Wh—" The blood drained to his feet. "Your money?"

"You have both my money and my painting."

The car signaled, eased onto an exit ramp, glided through a residential area, then turned right, picking up speed as it climbed a steep hill. Bruno's seatbelt unclicked and retracted into the holder. The car continued to accelerate. He cursed and demanded and yelled, but there was no response. He looked for something to smash the window glass, he pounded it with his fists, he pivoted onto his back and kicked the glass once before the pain in his spine almost paralyzed him.

"What the fuck do you want!"

"You. To watch as your death greets you."

Bruno grabbed the wheel and pulled himself up. The car was on a quiet stretch of roadway. There was no shoulder on the right, only steep cliffs. Centrifugal force tossed him left and right as they accelerated through curves and switchbacks. At the crest of the hill, going much too fast, the car fishtailed and loose gravel pelted the undercarriage. As it turned suddenly into a large, deserted parking area, an overlook designed for tourists, he braced with both feet on the brake pedal. The vehicle accelerated toward a wooden guardrail, the only thing between the car and the cliff. Time mysteriously slowed until the abyss crawled toward him. His eyes remained helplessly open, watching the moonlit valley ooze forward, certainly the last thing he would see. A thousand memories, mostly regrets, flashed across the windshield, all the years of living that he had traded for money. So much loss. His mother's smile, his father's guidance. Even Dante, a constant source of friction, but unmatched for getting the job done. Finally, Madeleine…

The brakes locked, the tires squalled, and Bruno's forehead slammed the steering wheel. A burst of stars and then black. When he could see again, he realized the bumper had hit the railing and pushed it half over. Blood pounded in his ears. That was the only sound. No, his Rolex ticked. His life was not over.

The interior lights came on.

Bruno forced air into his lungs. "Il Martello. I know it's you!"

"Check the mirror, Signore Porcelli. Look long. If you want to see your ugly face again, tomorrow you will have seven million euros cash ready for my instructions."

"What do you mean, seven million? Tell me who you are!"

"I ask the questions. While you have my money and my painting, your life is mine."

The same message written on the photograph of his bedroom. "It will take days to get that much cash. You can have the painting back—"

"This is not a negotiation. Tomorrow. The price of The Angel is double, or you pay with your life."

"Tomorrow is not possible. Someone has—"

The lights went out, the doors unlocked, and the engine started.

"Where would you like to go?"

The sweet-sounding southern girl was back.

"Call Alice Stevens."

She must have been sitting by the phone the entire time. "Bruno, I didn't hang up on you. I'm sorry. I don't know what to—"

"Shut up. Meet me at the villa."

"But I'm in—"

"End call. Navigate to Villa Gazza." When the car started, the whirr of the electric motor chilled him. "Stop!" His heart was in his throat. He was not going anywhere in this cursed car. He almost wept when the door opened at his touch, and he leapt out. The pain in his leg was buried beneath the fear in his mind as he limped across the parking lot. At the edge of the roadway, thirty meters from the car, a shock wave of sound slammed his back. The car had erupted in a ball of smoke and flame.

He picked himself up from the pavement and searched the star-packed sky. He realized the ordeal had cleared his mind, as if the jungle of refuse there had been slashed and burned. His messy, complicated life was reduced to a pinpoint of clarity.

Disappearing was not enough. Until the world thought he was dead, he would never be safe.

As he walked down the mountain road toward Genoa, the wind whipped his hair and cooled his skin. The solution came to him, an answer so obvious it seemed to have been there all along, waiting for him to look it in the eye.

Paraguay.

He had a doomsday account there he had not touched in over twenty years, not even to check the balance. With compounded interest, the principle should have at least tripled, enough to keep him comfortable for the rest of his life. He said the memorized account number and code aloud, to assure himself. He would call as soon as he got back to the villa and check the balance. For now, formulate the plan.

The first move was obvious. Buy enough time to execute the plan. As he reached the bottom of the hill, his phone made a sound. He had cell service again. He texted Jack.

Sorry I missed your calls. Having phone issues. We need to talk. Someone is trying to kill me. Will be back in Genoa tomorrow night around eleven.

See you then.

Step one, done. Step two, eliminate the loose end that would otherwise haunt him: Alice. Step three, fake his death.

He stopped as the thought struck him. Steps two and three would be part of the same scenario.

Chapter 27

Alice called Russell as soon as her call with Bruno ended. "Where are you?"

"Oh, somewhere in Asia."

"Bruno is going to kill me."

"Really? It's five o'clock here and I'm ready for a drink."

"Did you hear me? I said Bruno is going to kill me!"

"You mean, literally?" He laughed lightly. "You don't believe that. Look, none of this is your fault. You told him not to buy the eleven before authentication."

"Russell, you are a rational human being. You think he's going to look at it that way? I told him all the results so far were good."

"Which was true. And you warned him to wait."

"You don't know him."

"He's a businessman, he has to—"

"A businessman with crazy mood swings, who already had me beat up once. He demanded I meet him at his villa."

"So go."

"Are you listening to yourself? Are you listening to me? He is going to kill me!"

"Not if he's asked you to his home. That would be sacrilege. He's probably already got some new scheme and just wants your help. Remember what I told you, you are a survivor. Right now, you feel threatened, I get that. You must continue to play the game. Just back up a minute and get a little perspective."

"Okay." *Breathe.* "You really think—"

"You really think you have any options? What are you going to do, go to the police? You're the queen on his chessboard until he solves his money problems. If you can help him do that, all the better, but regardless, the sooner that happens, the sooner you'll be forgotten."

She plopped down on the sofa. Russell's sofa. He'd somehow managed to calm her down enough to think. "You're a great friend, Russell. Why do you put up with me?"

"I look at the world, mostly I see potential. A tube of paint, a rundown villa…"

His Texas accent was beginning to color his words, another soliloquy on the meaning of life was in the queue. She was about to interrupt when the germ of an idea demanded her attention. His voice faded and she saw a window open, a hand reached toward her, Russell's hand….

"Oh my god! I know how to do it! It's so simple. You just have to help me. I know you'll help me."

"Alice, what the hell are you talking about?"

"First, there's no provenance to prove, everyone agrees they were simply dug up a few weeks ago."

"Right, but—"

"And we're not claiming they're the work of some famous artist, or even by the same artist as The Angel. There are no opinions involved, nothing subjective about it. *Everything* is based on the age, the analytical tests."

He shook his head. "And the latest test proves—"

"Stop. Who knows about those results?" She pumped her fist in victory. "You, me, and Bruno!"

"The lab, dear. The manager and the technician at a lab in Switzerland. They're discrete, but they know—"

"They know what, exactly? Do they know where the samples came from, what you were actually testing, didn't you keep that secret?"

"Of course, but…damn, Alice. You want me to lie about the results?"

She could hear him thinking, considering it. "Does the buyer, or anyone else for that matter, even know about the new test?"

"The patent office," he said. "The patent office knows. The application's been filed, which means it's public, searchable. But…okay it's true no one knows it's been used for the eleven."

"So, the fact that we've all been waiting on some unspecified test to be completed…." Her emotional main spring continued to tighten. "And even if, someday, someone does find out, who could fault you because initially you said you thought your test was unproven and shouldn't be relied on yet? Today, you just tell Asia all the reliable tests have been done, and that everything passes. No mention of this patent pending test."

He snapped. "You're talking about my reputation."

"I'm talking about my life! About walking away unharmed from a situation that you assured me was just what I needed."

"Alice, I think we've had this conversation, and I admit—"

"Just think about it. I know you'll come to the right decision. I'm going to meet Bruno, tell him the new test results are invalid, and you're contacting Asia this morning that everything is a go."

She hung up and turned off her phone before he could throw out another objection. Then she remembered his words. It's five o'clock here. She counted forward seven hours. He was in Japan.

Chapter 28

She saw two, and only two paths forward. She could either get back in Bruno's good graces, which meant the twelve paintings had to sell, or she could go into hiding before the sale fell through, meaning she had to collect her commission now.

For path one, three things had to happen: Russell had to lie to the Asian buyer, the buyer had to accept the results, and the sale had to be completed quickly—the sooner the better, before suspicion about the real age of the paintings emerged. The guts to gamble on path one? Not something in her DNA.

That left path two, meaning she had to summon her best poker face ever—lie to Bruno, convince him the deal with Asia was going through, and collect her commission on handling Bruno's purchase of the eleven, before the house of cards could tumble.

Once she decided to do it, she was somehow able to move forward without trembling, as if something this frightening was beyond scary. Self-preservation as anesthetic. She would wake up on the other side, hidden in a different world, one where she was a ghost to everything she knew and everyone she loved.

****

The front gate at Villa Gazza began to retract as soon as her car rolled to a stop. She didn't need reminding there were eyes everywhere. Beatriz led her into the sunroom where Bruno glanced up from his phone. The scowl on his face looked calculated to intimidate.

"What the hell are you smiling about?"

"I have great news." She turned to make sure Beatriz was gone, then whispered. "The report will be buried. No one will know. The authenticator is in Asia right now, telling the buyer the eleven are certified as fifteenth century. No mention of this last test. Bottom line, the deal is going through."

She waited. Five seconds ticked as that information sank in. He still looked like a barely contained volcano, but maybe now he wasn't sure what to be angry about.

"Start talking."

She felt like a professional liar. "I was too quick to tell you about the initial conclusion. With so much at stake, I insisted the lab contact the authenticator and review the data. But before they were done with that, you called, or my phone accidentally called you, and I panicked. I told you what the lab had initially reported."

"And now?"

"Once the authenticator discussed the results with them, got into the nitty-gritty details, both parties agreed it was inconclusive. It's a new test. It's meant to be better than the old ones, but now they're questioning it. The certification will be based on all the other tests."

He slowly shook his head, then laughed. "This is incredible. Wonderful. The lab changed their mind. You stared them down and you won. We won. You are a crafty little thing. When does the sale happen?"

"Day after tomorrow, at the latest."

"Wonderful news. You seem to have a magic charm young lady. And, you are sorely overdue to receive your commission on my purchase of the eleven."

Like he read my mind.

"No use delaying that now. Three-point-five percent of fifty-five million euros. Cash all right?"

Cash? Alarm bells. "I guess I would rather—"

"It was a rhetorical question. No more banks for the time being. I think you can understand that. We'll just sail to a little island I know, someone there will deliver us a hefty little package, and then I'll take you wherever you like."

"Are you sure?" Two million U.S. dollars. Freedom. But getting it meant getting on a boat with him? "I could wait until you have the money on hand, pick it up here."

"You seem to think this is a negotiation. You want your money, you meet me here, sunset tomorrow. Sweetheart."

Chapter 29

Porcelli Investigation, Interim Report

Analysis of latest interaction (Bruno/Alice)

BRUNO - Vocal assay for prevarication, probability >99%.

Interpretation:

1. *He does not believe the 12 paintings will be sold.*

2. *With no money to pay for The Angel, he believes Il Martello will pursue him to the death.*

3. *He believes The Collective will have him eliminated for taking the advance money.*

4. *Alice is a loose end.*

Prediction: He will kill Alice (72% probability) before faking his own death (84% probability).

9:10 PM, he searches internet for homemade incendiary devices and finds one using components available at villa.

11:28 PM, he moves a propane canister from the grill to the trunk of the Dino.

11:40 PM, he moves one bag of ammonium nitrate fertilizer and small can of diesel fuel to the trunk of the Dino.

11:52 He packs a travel bag

Revised probabilities: attempt on Alice's life 78%, faking own death 96%.

ALICE - Flight risk, probability <3%. Following conversation, she drives from Genoa to Williams' residence in Milan. Tail manages to be spotted. Instilled fear of surveillance apparently successful: no computer searches conducted. One phone call placed from outside the house. Rambling message left for Federico, crying, she loves him, doesn't know if she will ever see him again.

Next day, she departs residence approximately two hours before sunset. Drives to Genoa.

Chapter 30

Bruno was sitting in his old Dino with the window down, engine running, just inside the front gate.

"Leave your keys in the car and get in. Please."

An omen? Alice could not recall hearing him say please before.

She had hoped they would take the new Ferrari—self-driving technology seemed like the safer option. Before getting in, she had the nerve to ask him if they could take it. He mumbled something about the goddam prototype car needing service. She slid in and fastened her seatbelt. He seemed sober enough to drive, but with him, who knew?

She was anticipating a long ride to Monaco, but twenty minutes later he turned into the enormous Port of Genoa.

"Is the *Madeleine Too* here now?"

"No, we're taking the company boat. I can pilot it solo."

It was half dark by the time he parked. Lights from offices and high-rise apartments ringing the harbor fractured yellow, white and blue in the choppy water. Every slip in the yacht marina held a yacht, none of which seemed to be occupied. She saw no signs of life but kept checking over her shoulder—sounds and smells were all foreign and eerily familiar at the same time.

"The company keeps a yacht here?"

"She's a little beauty, thirty-two meters. I had her custom built ten years ago. Just small enough they don't require me to use a harbor pilot to take her out."

"Where is everyone?"

"Wednesday night there's no party scene. Pity for you, maybe next time." He pointed to a gleaming white vessel waiting in the last slip. "There she is. The *Profitti Porcelli.*"

It was a beauty but certainly not little. Bruno stopped at the stern, lifted the dock line and dropped it in the water, then walked thirty meters to the bow and did the same.

Alice stepped off the pier onto the gangway. It dipped, and she clutched the rail. The sounds of the water slapping on the nearby hulls triggered something—this was the boat where she had been tortured! A tiny squeal escaped her throat. Every instinct told her to run, but her legs were useless. Bruno grabbed her wrist. She tried to pull away. He squeezed until something popped, and a bolt of electricity shot to her elbow.

"You should calm yourself, my dear. Just think about all that money coming your way. And there's a nice bottle of your favorite waiting for you. You'll feel better once we're underway."

With each step up the gangway she felt more lightheaded. The dense gray clouds seemed to move close enough to touch. At the top, she looked over her shoulder again. There! A tiny CCTV camera was mounted on a lamp pole, eyelevel with where they stood.

She pointed with her free hand and managed a small laugh. "I guess the whole world will think we're headed out for a romantic evening."

"The whole world has a wonderful imagination."

Despite the clamp on her arm, his charming side was still in play. From the top of the gangway, he led her to the middle of the main deck where a wide staircase led up to the next level, the owner's deck. From there, looking aft, a lounge area with tables and benches and a semi-circular bar occupied the rear half. The front half was covered by the cantilevered wheelhouse above.

Bruno pointed forward. "We have a kitchenette and breakfast nook past the stairs there, and the owner's suite beyond that."

He walked her up the next flight which landed them in the enclosed wheelhouse, surrounded on three sides by smoked glass. On the center console he pressed a button to open the side windows. A cool breeze washed across them and Alice's skin puckered. He pressed another button and the navigation touchscreen rose out of the console.

"I love the *Madeleine Too*, but it takes a crew of three. This little peach is much more romantic, don't you think? Just you, me, and autopilot." She was too distraught to reply. He touched the screen and the motors gurgled like they'd been stroked by a lover. He had the yacht to the breakwater before he spoke again.

"It may be a bit rough past the break. I hope you brought your sea legs."

"I don't have any sea legs," she said. "Never did." The motion of the boat was already making her queasy.

"So, just keep your eye on the horizon." He set a course and selected autopilot. "Less than an hour now. Keep an eye out for sea monsters. I'll be right back."

Being alone increased the sense that she was trapped. To her right, starboard she remembered, the western sky offered a soft, dying glow of rose and violet clouds, but staring at the horizon did not settle her stomach. After thirty minutes of waiting, she found a small bottle of Evian under the console and cracked the seal. Sipping it, willing her nerves to calm, she gingerly sat in the captain's seat. The boat's pitch and roll had increased, as had her queasiness. She thought about the contents of her stomach, seeming to inch their way upward. The nearest railing was on the deck below. She closed her eyes. She had to move. She had to get to a railing before she made a mess all over—

"I think this lady should be ready about now," Bruno shouted. He climbed the stairs behind her and then set a silver bucket in the dry sink on the console. He pulled a bottle of QB from the ice and handed her two glasses. "You better hold these while I pour."

She took one in each hand. It was a welcome distraction, and she concentrated on slow, easy breaths while he ripped the foil and popped the cork, letting it sail through one of the windows. Alice watched him fill the glasses until foam flowed over the rims. Something was not right. He had changed shirts. And was that cologne?

He took one of the glasses, clinked it against hers, and tipped it into his mouth. The front of her mind was whispering *no no no*, but she could not think why. The bottle had been sealed. She had watched him open it, heard the pop. She raised the glass to her lips.

The glasses! They had been wet, like he'd just rinsed them. She stared as he poured wine down his throat and refilled his glass.

"You look a little green, my dear. The carbonation might settle your stomach." She shook her head. "No? Well, it's too good to waste." He lifted the glass from her hand and drained it. She let out a breath.

"Worried I was going to poison you?"

"Of course not."

"Would you prefer some hot tea?"

She blinked. "Some tea. Yes. I'll make it. And could we slow down? I think I would feel better going slower."

"As you wish. Three-quarter speed. Make it so, Captain." He touched the screen and the engines droned down to a lower register. "Just below us, in the kitchenette, you'll find a hot water dispenser, cups, and tea bags. Try the lemon ginger." She turned back toward the main staircase. "Use the spiral stairs." He nodded forward. "Takes you right to it."

The lemon ginger was a good recommendation. Her stomach settled with the first few sips. She returned to the wheelhouse cradling a heavy ceramic cup which she sat on the console. "That's a beautiful design. *Porcelli Industriale*." Bruno was bent over the control screen. "Is that a new logo?" He looked up and she pointed to the teacup.

"That was our original logo, during my father's time, before shipping became our principal activity."

"And now? You have a logo for the shipping company?"

He was frowning, scrutinizing the map, clearly unhappy or confused about something. "What?"

"The shipping company. You have a separate logo for that?"

"There should be a booklet in the drawer to your right."

She pulled it open and dug through a jumble of pens, papers, coasters, and koozies. Her fingers touched something hard and cold. It was a small, black handgun. Ice ran down her spine. She jumped when Bruno spoke again.

"If it's not in there, try below."

Without thinking, she slammed shut the drawer and squatted to open the cabinet. She found a glossy brochure beneath a stack of magazines.

"Is this it?"

"Yes. Porcelli Spedizone."

She stood and lifted her cup from the console. Her hands trembled. She finished the tea, glancing at the brochure. The few words of Italian she could make out were all promoting the merits of his family's shipping concern.

Her mind was in overdrive, scheming. As soon as he was distracted, she would slide open the drawer, grab the gun, and, then what? She never got the chance to decide. At that moment all sound from the engines stopped. She scanned the water around the boat, expecting an island. With the moon peeking through the clouds, it was obvious—*there was no land!*

Bruno was muttering in Italian.

"What's going on?" she said.

"I'm not sure. Something with the NAV system. I'm rebooting it." His focus shifted to her. He took her hand and rubbed his thumb along her wrist where a bruise was beginning to show. "I hope I didn't hurt you earlier." His expression was pleasant, relaxed. "Tell me again about the agreement with Asia."

She tried to extract her hand, but he applied more pressure. What was he doing? Where were they? Where was the island?

"What did you say?"

"Asia. What's the next step?"

"Um, sure." *Breathe. Back to the script.* "The sale will go through tomorrow or the day after. My authenticator is certain the—"

"You're lying," he said, smiling.

"What?" She pulled away but he grabbed her arm and pinned it against the console.

"It's a good story, Alice, but that's all it is. And if it happens to work, if the deal somehow magically goes through, then everybody's happy. But I don't buy it. You're hiding something."

"What are you talking—" He clinched her hand with the broken pinky. Panic swept her from crown to soles.

"You're going to be asleep for a couple of hours little lady, starting in about two minutes. Five milligrams of lorazepam work fast." He pointed to the empty tea cup. "After that, maybe you stay asleep forever," he cut his eyes to the open windows, "or, maybe you wake up and walk away with your commission. It depends on whether you stop lying. Now tell me about the deal."

"Bruno, trust me, it's better if you don't know the details. Ow, shit! Stop! What do you want to know?" Her pulse throbbed in her ears.

"Who put you in contact with this wine baron who sold me the eleven paintings?"

"Nobody. I met him at a party a few weeks ago. Federico. He's famous."

"And he told you what?"

"Nothing. He mentioned he had some works to be authenticated, I asked how many, he said eleven, and I just put two and two together." Some of the tension drained from her face; this was his fault, not hers. "I told you not to move on them until the testing was complete."

"And now the testing is complete, and I'm screwed."

"No. I mean, yes the testing is complete, but you're not screwed." She had rehearsed the story over and over on the drive to his villa, but now it sounded desperate. "I told you. You're not screwed because I've worked it all out! We just ignore the last test. It's never, ever been used before, literally no one knows about it yet."

"Literally no one? You, your authenticator, the lab…"

"I said the same thing. But the truth is the lab has no idea what they were testing. They reported the results, and the authenticator, he lied and told them it was a blind test. To see if they could detect the one sample out of eleven that was genuinely old. But all eleven came out as new, so, he discredited the test. He told them to destroy the results."

"But he still knows the truth."

"He's getting a third of my commission, which is more than one percent of two hundred million! Plus, he's complicit in the fraud. That's enough to buy *anyone's* silence, no?"

His face relaxed. He was considering it! She cocked her head and grinned, like a flirt. Where did that come from? Her concentration was slipping.

He laughed and patted her cheek. "You're funny when you're sleepy, and it's harder to tell when you're lying. But I can still tell. It's all just a bit too convenient. And even if your little story's true, I don't like loose ends."

"I'm a loose end?" Her voice cracked. She had no more cards to play. She started to moan. Wait a second. She shouted, "What about the camera, at the pier? They'll know that we're out together."

He laughed, and it was not charming Bruno. "No one knows we're here. Who do you think controls all those sweet little cameras? Let's go."

Anger blazed across her face. "Why are you doing this? All I did was try to help you! Just let me go back to the States, go back to being an artists' rep." Tears spilled as her words began to slur. "That's where I should be. Back in New York…back home…"

He cupped her chin and held it until her droopy eyes met his. "You have nothing to go back to. Nothing. I told the gallery you were fired for fraud and gross negligence. They've been instructed to make sure every gallery in the world knows it. Your reputation is ruined."

"My repu…." It was the oddest feeling. She was angrier than she'd ever been, but at the same time, the drug made her willing, eager even, to let go of everything. She was a ragdoll being led down the main staircase to the owner's deck, through the kitchenette, and into the owner's suite.

"You'll be comfortable here."

They sat on the bed and she slumped against him. "I liked you you know. Greedy and cautious. Innocent but feisty at the same time. We could have done a lot together, until you divided your loyalties." He was talking more to himself than to her. "I was half tempted to take you with me. You'd like Paraguay this time of year."

Alice murmured. "Paraguay? We're going to…"

"I still have one offshore account that bastard Il Martello hasn't found. Eighteen million dollars U.S., untouchable thanks to Alonzo. He set it up and made sure the account info was never written down anywhere. He made me memorize everything. Even he doesn't know the codes."

"Paraguay?"

"Not you, dearie. End of the line. It's just a matter of whether or not you wake up before the explosion. For your sake, I hope you die in your sleep."

"Hmm? Sleep…" Her eyes closed and she felt him guide her back onto the mattress. A voice was coming from nowhere and everywhere.

"Hey, not yet." He slapped her lightly, twice on each cheek. "What's the name of your authenticator?"

She was gone nighty-night but dreamed someone slapped her.

Chapter 31

Muttering to himself, he left her on the bed and closed the door. "As if I don't already know you're sleeping with one of the top authenticators in the business. That Russell Williams character. And you spent at least one night with your wine baron buddy. Women deserve what they get."

He accepted the fact that his future had narrowed to a single option. Nowhere would be safe until Il Martello and The Collective thought he was dead. He had researched bombs, selected a simple option, and gathered the materials. He then packed a tote with essentials: pain meds, change of clothes, fake passport, two untraceable phones completely charged, both with GPS. And enough cash to get him to his ultimate destination.

At the marina, last night, he had carried it all to the yacht. Then he had inflated the escape raft on the swim deck and inspected it. It was larger than he'd expected, but was still a better option than taking one of the full-sized lifeboats stored on the main deck—he had to come ashore somewhere unnoticed.

Then he'd moved two days of provisions from the kitchen pantry and placed them along with his tote bag in the raft's waterproof compartment. The four marine batteries were fully charged, enough for twelve hours running at four knots. He left the raft inflated on the swim deck, concealed beneath a tarp.

Then from deep in the engine room, he opened the door to an alcove just forward of the electrical panels. There, the yacht's ten-thousand-liter fuel tank lay beneath sheets of removable decking.

He placed the propane gas canister upside down above the tank. In a large plastic soda bottle, he mixed a thick paste of diesel fuel and ammonium nitrate, producing two liters of initiator. He wedged the bottle securely atop the inverted gas canister, just like in the diagram he'd found online. He taped the smart phone to the canister and pushed the bare ends of the severed headphone wires into the bottle of paste. The only thing left was to set the timer. When the current was triggered and the wire sparked, the instructions said that heat from the exothermic reaction in the accelerator paste would detonate the propane. That surely, he thought, would detonate the main fuel tank… BOOM! He could almost hear it.

Working with his hands like that, he had felt alive. How long had it been since he'd done something physically demanding, rather than delegating it? The plan would work. He would stop looking over his shoulder, enjoy life for a change, a new life, new friends, in another country, no responsibilities. He would frequent the casinos, swim, surround himself with people who expected nothing of him, eat all the foods his doctors said to avoid. When was the last time he'd felt this good?

Now that he was at sea and Alice had been dealt with, four items remained on his mental checklist: tether the raft to the railing, confirm the yacht's location, set the bomb's timer, and vanish into the night.

Sliding the raft into the sea proved to be almost beyond his capability. After removing the railing, he found the non-skid top of the swim deck gave too much friction. He hosed down the surface, which compromised his footing. Then, in his haste, he pushed the raft into the water before tethering it to the yacht. He grabbed a line an instant before the waves sucked it away. Check one.

Item two, confirm his location. He climbed the stairs back up to the wheelhouse. A thought stopped him. What if the electric motor on the raft did not start? He added another item to his checklist. Test the motor before setting the timer, just to be sure.

He took a final, sentimental look around the wheelhouse. The brochure Alice had found caught his eye. The shipping company, the enterprise he had expanded ten-fold following his parents' death. He considered it a monument to them. He would miss it all, but now that the plan was in motion, he could not wait to leave. The world had changed beyond recognition. Technology he couldn't begin to grasp had brought him to this low point. Eighty million euros of his personal money was gone, stolen from a system that had operated securely, flawlessly, for decades. People could bypass his state-of-the-art security system. Take a photo of him asleep in his own home for God's sake! He'd been held hostage by an assassin who took control of his car, nearly drove him off a cliff, to coerce an exorbitant payment for a painting he'd already paid for.

It was too much. He had been bested, and he was too tired to fight any longer. He rubbed his eyes and then looked down in disbelief at his hands. They were wet with tears. He told himself again, time to go. Time to confirm his location.

The yacht would have drifted, and he wanted to be sure it was still less than two miles from Cinque Terre. He flipped up the cover on the navigation screen. The glitch had struck again; the map indicated he was in the United States, in the middle of Falcon Reservoir Lake near Laredo, Texas. He hit the power switch and waited for the system to reboot, but the screen blinked and went dark. Then every light around him dimmed, flickered, and died. A few emergency lights clicked on. The power was out. One more thing to deal with. Think. Did he need electricity? Surely it was just a breaker. The electrical panels were in the engine room. He could set the timer by flashlight. If he could find one. Easier to reset the breaker. Go.

He felt a driving need to get off the yacht now. With barely enough light to see, he made his way to the spiral staircase, which he despised, but it was a more direct route than the main staircase. He ignored the voice that said never run—the slow motor response in his left leg made running risky. Near the bottom of the first flight, the toe of his right shoe caught the back of his left ankle. He smacked the tile floor in the kitchenette. His bad hip took the bulk of his weight, and the familiar pain stole his breath for a moment. His left leg felt paralyzed. He needed help. Alice was asleep in the cabin behind him. He almost shouted to her. Stupid!

He half limped, half crawled to the stairway, down to the main deck, and rearward to the engine room access hatch. He pressed the control, expecting the hatch to retract. No power. He strained to manually crank it open. Mercifully, emergency lighting in the engine room was enough for him to make out the treacherous vertical ladder below him. Nine rungs. With one leg half working, he winced in pain on every step to the bottom.

Two long gleaming tubes, the engines, sat in the dim light, like twin behemoths waiting command. He turned and ran his fingers down the electrical panels on the wall. Damn it! None of the breakers were tripped. He opened the door to the fuel tank alcove and stepped inside. The emergency lights were on there as well, and the bomb appeared the way he had left it. To hell with confirming the yacht's location. To hell with verifying the raft motor worked. He had to do this now.

He set the timer for sixty minutes, said a quick prayer, and turned back toward the engine room.

60:00

At that moment, a siren triggered. The screaming burst of sound pierced his ears like knives. A voice blared over the speaker system:

Warning. Smoke detected in the engine room.

The accelerant must have— No, impossible. In the alcove, the bomb sat as he had left it. He turned in a complete circle, scanning the room. No smoke. No odor. He shut the door to the alcove. The siren stopped and the sudden emptiness caused his skin to prickle.

The voice on the speakers again:

Fire extinguishers will discharge in ten seconds.

Pulsed blasts from a warning horn erupted and the voice counted down.

Ten.

He stumbled to the ladder, but his left leg would not support his weight.

Seven.

He fought to climb with his hands and one leg, so much harder than descending the ladder had been.

Five.

Halfway up, the power came back on.

Three.

The hatch above him slid closed, sealing the engine room from the rest of the vessel.

One.

The beeping stopped and was replaced with a shriek of white noise. In seconds, a bank of four carbon dioxide cylinders emptied twenty-two cubic meters of gas. All oxygen in the engine room was displaced. Bruno landed on his back and his head bounced hard.

Chapter 32

46:00

Bruno woke with a start. His first thought: I'm alive.

No memory beyond slipping from the ladder. A violent headache. The pain in his leg and back.

How had he gotten here, sprawled on the owner's deck near the aft railing? How long had he been unconscious? The bomb. He checked his phone. Forty-five minutes to go. How much longer would Alice be out? He truly wished her to sleep through the explosion.

He fished in his pants pocket. Two lint-covered pain pills. The rest were in the waterproof container on the escape raft.

He swallowed the pills dry and tried to focus. Get off the boat now, no time to wait for his pain to ease. He forced himself onto all fours. The wind had picked up and the deck was rocking. Think. The electricity was back on, so the fans would clear the air in the engine room and alcove. The accelerant paste would burn. This would still work.

Board the raft, power out to five hundred meters, and watch the yacht erupt. That's it, that's all. Except, something else niggled his mind. The NAV system, haywire. The electricity, off, now on again. What had tripped the siren. What had activated the fire extinguishers?

Mother of God, just like in his car. Someone had remote control of the yacht!

It struck him then. The voice on the speaker system, warning of smoke in the engine room. It was the same voice that spoke when he was carjacked. Mechanical sounding, neither male nor female.

That feeling in the nape of his neck that someone was watching. And now, like some mad illusion, a human voice, behind him, shouting over the storm.

"Have a good nap, Mr. Porcelli?"

"Alice?"

"No. Any other questions you would like answered?" The voice. His heart stopped.

A woman sat at the table, mid-deck next to the staircase, under the cantilevered roof, just out of the cold drizzle that was blowing in gusts. She was plain looking, almost anonymous. Thirtyish? Fortyish? Medium-length gray hair, medium build, medium…everything.

"And, bonus time, I have answers to questions you don't even know to ask yet. This will be fun. Get up. Take a seat."

He did not get up. "You, you did this! *And* you hijacked my car!"

"If you mean *car*-jacked your automobile, then yes. You know it's basically a laptop with motor and wheels. What else can I clear up for you?"

"Why are you doing this?" He screamed, then wiped the spittle from his lips.

"I can tell you *how,*" she said. "But why? Someone else will explain."

"Who? Who the fuck are you working with? Il Martello? Call him! Now!" A vein on his forehead throbbed.

"Time to accept the facts, old man. You're not in control anymore, and like it or not, we're going to share an amusing story before you go."

"*Who is we?*"

"Well, first, me. My name is Ivy. Ivy Ricasoli."

"Ricasoli." He blinked, then studied her. "Like the wine baron."

"My brother!" She clapped her hands and giggled.

Bruno kept a wary eye on the woman and forced himself to move. He crawled to a bench opposite the café table where she sat and hauled himself up onto it. Strangely, a chilled bottle of Grey Goose VX and one glass sat between them on the table.

The moon was now packed away behind multiple layers of thick clouds that had begun rolling across the western sky earlier, leaving the yacht in near darkness. A massive wave crushed itself against the port side and the vessel pitched starboard.

"Hit those lights. There's a switch just beside you," he said. She did not move. "Lights!"

"We'll go with the lighting as it is for now."

"I can barely see."

"You should have had that cataract surgery."

"How do you…" He glared at her.

She stared back, in no apparent hurry, speaking only after he broke eye contact. "I've been keeping tabs on you for a while now, longer than you might imagine. Listening. Watching. For example…." She opened her hand and a collection of tiny electronic devices tumbled out, rolling on the table. "While you were napping, I gathered these back up. Too expensive to leave behind." She giggled again as she re-pocketed them. "Who do you think controls all these sweet little cameras, hmm? Sound familiar?"

The exact words he had said to Alice about the marina. He slumped back on the bench.

"I will say, you are one interesting guy. Lots of people depending on you, lots of people popping in and out of your life. You made a shitload of money, and lost all of it—"

"I never lost it! Someone moved it. But I don't need it. I've got enough left, enough for a hundred years."

"Really? The eighteen million in your so-call doomsday account? When was the last time you checked?"

He glared at her. "You tell me."

"This morning at 10:06. Interesting, exactly twelve hours ago. What are the odds, hm?"

His stomach dropped. "How do you—"

"Does the password MARIOdinoBRUNO sound familiar? And account number A44740003KR6? I had that info today, the moment you entered it."

His jaw moved, but his voice was gone.

"You're having trouble articulating your questions, so let me save you the trouble. Yes, *I* moved your money out of Switzerland and Panama. I temporarily bankrupted your company. And today, everything is gone from your secret reserve. The photos of you sleeping? I controlled the camera drone, I digitally added the shadow of a person, and, to reiterate, I carjacked you and demanded payment for The Angel."

It was clear to him now. "You're working for the assassin Il Martello."

The woman ignored his comment and stared, a satisfied grin on her face. But Il Martello isn't on the boat, or I would be dead already, he thought. What was this ridiculous woman doing? She knew nothing of the real world. She lived behind a goddam computer screen. Anger and adrenaline swept through his veins, and he could feel his strength return. The pain pills had kicked in. He was ready for a fight.

He filled the glass with vodka and drank it in two gulps, oblivious to the burn. The woman watched him coolly, the woman who'd stolen his fortune. Two seconds. Two seconds and he could have his hands around her ugly little throat. She was frail and unarmed. He slid his legs from beneath the table, shifted his weight to the deck, and—

She touched a button on her watch. Bruno screamed as fifty thousand volts discharged from the ring around his left ankle. The ring was snug, the humidity was high, and the effect was instantaneous. He collapsed on the deck. It was a few minutes before he fully remembered how to breathe.

"Back up on the bench as soon as you're able Mr. Porcelli. There's a lot more of the story to come."

"What do you want?"

"I don't want anything. I'm just helping a couple of sisters get what *they* want."

"Sisters?" He stuttered, "Il Martello is a woman?"

She giggled again. "No, no, no."

"They're working with him then. What do they want?"

"I think we can let one of them explain that now."

From the deck, propped on one elbow, Bruno followed her gaze as she turned and looked toward the staircase.

Chapter 33

42:00

Alice woke. Dreams upon layers of dreams wrestled to pull her back into the stupor. She remembered something, not a dream—she had been aware of a siren, a vague emergency. It had soon stopped, replaced with a gentle rocking motion, and she had surrendered back to the fug of sleep.

Now. The rocking was no longer gentle. The darkness was complete, except for a small nightlight near the floor. With no idea where she was, she opened the cabin door and found herself in a breakfast nook. She remembered. The yacht. She heard Bruno's muffled voice. It was coming from the lounge area, immediately aft of the breakfast nook. The doorway was to her left and a wall blocked her view of the lounge. She crept to the spiral staircase that went both up and down—below, two levels were visible, first the main deck, and continuing from there to below decks. Above, she could see into the wheelhouse. The revolver! She could sneak up the spiral stairs without being seen. With the gun, she could return to the nook, spring through the doorway, take him by surprise.

A short minute later she was back in the nook, holding the gun. Not enough light to tell if it was loaded. Surely it was. She held it in both hands, thrust in front of her. Wait. She could sneak past him if she continued down the spiral stairs to the main deck. But, then what? She didn't even know how to use the radio to call for help. With the gun, she would force Bruno to take her back.

She heard his voice again, rising over the crescendo of waves and wind. Who was he talking to? She crept to the edge of the doorway and stopped, trying to understand the words.

She heard him cry out, then nothing. It was time to confront him. She peered around the door. Bruno was writhing on the deck. In the near-dark, she could make out someone sitting, facing away. Thunder crashed and lightning flashed at the same instant, and in that momentary strobe Alice saw a profile. She pulled back into the nook. A woman's face—common, ordinary, but familiar. Her arms trembled and she lowered the gun. It was the woman from the auction.

She slumped against the wall and tried to think what it meant. A new gust of wind whipped through the nook and chilled her. The adrenaline, the weight of the gun, and now the cold—she was shivering beyond control. She slipped back into the owner's suite and found a thick woolen sweater. She pushed the sleeves to her elbows and returned to the doorway between the nook and the lounge.

She could hear two female voices now, speaking Italian, shouting over the moaning wind. She lacked the focus to make out any of the words. The boat made a sudden lurch, knocking her off balance.

She swallowed a cry as her shoulder smacked the door jamb.

Chapter 34

37:00

Bruno struggled to pull himself back up onto the bench. His vision was blurred, his head was splitting. In fact, everything hurt. The scene before him swirled and pitched. The woman, Ivy Ricasoli, turned toward the stairs. He followed her gaze, and saw, ascending…. It looked almost…. No, he shook his head. He was hallucinating. The night was dark and mist washed over the deck. He scrubbed his fingers across his eyes and looked again. The image, transparent white, wafting in the wind, moved—floated?—toward him. He gasped, and the air escaped his throat in a raw howl as he staggered backwards, back across the deck, into the aft railing. As the specter approached, his arms windmilled like a terrified child.

He shrieked, "NO!"

The woman, the specter Bruno saw, was tall, elegant, in her mid-sixties, with soft platinum hair to her shoulders. She wore a floor-length, semi-shear white coverup that whipped and twisted in the wind. From the top step she leveled her gaze at the man stumbling away from her. Ivy grinned and wiggled her fingers hello. In bare feet she padded to Ivy, placing a hand on her niece's shoulder.

Ivy said, "I believe you've frightened him. I hope he doesn't have a heart condition."

"Oh, he has a bad heart. Make no mistake about that."

As he backed away, she walked toward him, closing the gap. He crossed his wrists as if to block a blow. A moment of confusion, possibly of recognition, flickered across his face before his arms sank to his sides.

"You're not, you're…. She's dead!"

She slapped him so hard her palm burned as if she had touched a hot stove.

"And that's the way it is, Orsone." The irony of her old pet name for him.

He tried to speak again, tried to say her name.

"You're…an ombra. You can't be alive."

"You superstitious old fool, of course I'm alive. The only thing dead is any love I had for you."

He sank to his knees.

"Well, that went well," she half-whispered as she strode back to the table. "Bets on what he does next?"

The drizzle was now steady rain, and waves were building, rocking the boat. Ivy caught the bottle of vodka as it skated toward the table edge. "I would just be taking your money. Ninety-seven percent chance that within three minutes, he's over here, looking scared, angry, and defeated."

Ivy would have won the bet. In two minutes, Bruno had limped back, looking as she predicted. He stood behind the bench, keeping his distance.

"I searched for years to find who had blown up the—"

"Cut the bullshit, Bruno." Madeleine's tone started out cool. "You blew up the boat, but I escaped. Then you murdered our father. And Syrina's husband!"

The confusion on Bruno's face lasted only a second. Silvan had been collateral damage in the hit on Antonio. So many years ago. So much had happened since, it was another lifetime. He looked like he wanted to beg forgiveness.

"And you killed our half-brother—"

"Your half-brother?" He shook his head. "What are you saying?"

"Dante!"

Uncertainty, then horror played across Bruno's face. Madeleine struck the table with both hands. "Antonio was Dante's father. And you had them all murdered. Gunned down in cold blood!"

Bruno staggered back, his eyes wide, confronted by demons only he could see.

"You tried to kill me for some imaginary sin, but Dante warned me to get off the boat. And I survived. I thrived. Syrina and I hid in America, wallowing in misery. But what you did only made us stronger. The idea of revenge was a drug. We dedicated our lives to destroying yours, using only our family members to take away everything you valued."

"How…." Bruno had only enough breath for a whisper.

Madeleine relaxed back onto the bench. "How?" She almost smiled. "I knew you would remember Portovenere, that first night we ever spent together, and the legend you were so interested in. The story of Giuseppe, the carpenter-apothecary, and the lost paintings of the prostitutes. With your sentimentality, your greed, your *ego*, I knew how to ruin you. It was an ideal ruse."

She caught the bottle of vodka as it slid again across the table. She pulled the cork, but immediately slapped it back in. "I raised my son to love art as much as I did. He studied analytical chemistry, art history, economics. He learned to paint like an old master, learned to produce works that even the best analytical techniques could not distinguish from antiquities. And Syrina's daughter?" She placed a hand on Ivy's arm. "Ivy became an expert in computer science, electronic banking, espionage, with one goal, to bring you to your knees. It all started with The Angel."

Bruno stared defiantly at Madeleine, as if he suddenly had the upper hand. "You're lying. Your scheme did not involve only family. Il Martello bought The Angel at auction. He wants to kill me. Who else could it have been? Even Aristotle, my security expert, he said so."

Ivy shook her head. "Try to get a grip on reality, old man. I told you I'm the one who took over your car. *We are not working with Il Martello*. Any problems you have with him are on you. You're alive because we are not murderers. What don't you understand?"

"But the gallery owner, Madame Areni? She had to have been part of it. She's not family."

Ivy started to answer, but Madeleine held up her hand. She called down the staircase. "Russell? Join us, please?"

Chapter 35

28:00

The man who appeared on the stairs wore jeans, cowboy boots, and a plaid, snap-front Western shirt with rolled-up sleeves. His grin widened as he kissed Madeleine's cheek and then Ivy's.

"So, it comes down to this," he said. "The great man brought low by a couple of pretty faces from Milan." Ivy giggled. Russell said, "Sorry Ivy, I meant Mother and Aunt Syrina, but you're pretty too. When did you dye your hair gray? It's…nice."

Ivy's face colored.

Russell continued. "Bruno, on the other hand, you look like you're on your last leg. No pun intended. You probably ought to sit down to hear what I have to say."

Bruno checked the time on his phone. Ivy said, "You got someplace you need to be, old man? You seem awfully interested in the time."

Russell saw the desperate look on Bruno's face. "Let's get this over with. Sit."

Bruno grabbed the bottle of Grey Goose VX and poured a quarter of it down his throat. He caught his breath and said, "Chemistry? Business and finance? Art forgery? And the world's foremost appraiser? It's not possible for one person."

"Sure it is!" Russell laughed. He seemed relaxed, unconcerned by the wind, the lightning, the rocking of the boat. "You could put it down to good genes," he winked at Madeleine, "but all it really takes is hard work and dedication to the cause."

"You expect me to believe you painted The Angel, which was appraised by a team of experts, not including yourself, and they were all fooled?"

"Yep." He spoke quickly. "The walnut board I used really is over five hundred years old, so carbon-14 dating shows it to be genuine. Paint is more difficult. The mineral salts used for pigments don't change with time. But the smoking gun of fake antique paintings is the drying oils used to make the paint. The UV to visible absorption spectra as well as the X-ray fluorescence of drying oils change as they age, because they slowly react with oxygen. Modern instruments can measure the changes and pinpoint the age of the paint. Understand?"

Ivy was hanging on every word, but Madeleine raised an eyebrow at her son. "Russell, is this going to take long?"

"Almost finished. Not to give away all my secrets, but what no one has ever done before is synthesize a new oil that has the analytical properties of ancient drying oil. Not right out of the reactor, because the oil would be solid, you couldn't paint with it. But after painting, expose it to just the right wavelengths of UV and gamma rays for a few days, then let the volatile initiator sublime, and voila! The tests can't tell the difference."

Bruno grasped the implications. "So, now anyone can do this. We'll never know the true age of a painting."

"Except! Except I also invented an analytical technique that *can* detect the difference. Patent pending, and worth a small fortune. Soon, no one will authenticate a painting without licensing my new test. It's how we showed the eleven sisters paintings are new. Not that we didn't already know. I painted them as well."

Bruno looked at Madeleine. "The Angel was sold at a legitimate auction. Then stolen. Then returned. You're telling me that was all you."

"Our team, yes."

"Then I bought The Angel."

"Which," Madeleine said, "gave us the key to the whole project, the access codes to your Swiss account. You're such a creature of habit. We knew exactly when you would be unavailable for the sale and planned it for then. You sent your bank info to Alice, encrypted, which was a cakewalk for Ivy. We also planted all those news stories of The Angel's escalating value, and the hysteria surrounding the eleven companion pieces."

Ivy said, "That was fun. The media can be such a wonderfully unwitting accomplice. By the way, The Angel was never stolen, simply hidden in the gallery for a few days."

Bruno roared. "I am right! It wasn't just your family. Madame Areni was in on the scheme."

Russell laughed. "You're right in that she was crucial to many steps, creating the illusion of the mysterious Florence family who supposedly owned The Angel—"

"But you're wrong," Madeleine said. "She is family. You don't remember her?"

"I've never seen her. She doesn't even put her photo on the gallery website."

"Oh, you've seen her all right, over forty years ago at her wedding. Still don't remember? I was her bride's maid."

He swallowed. "Syrina?"

"Syrina is Madame Areni. Before she remarried, she moved to the States for a while. I knew no one there. She took care of me—*when your baby was born.*"

Bruno growled. "My baby? You dare call it *my* baby!"

Madeleine pointed straight at his face. "I was never unfaithful to you! Who do you think would have dared be with me? All my friends were shunning me. Every man I knew was petrified of you."

"Puttana! You were *never* home, constantly traveling or working. How did you get pregnant? Miracle birth? It could not have been mine."

"You don't remember."

"Remember what?"

She bellowed. "The drugs. The booze. Smashing my face with your fist! You raped me, you bastard. Ripped my clothes, then forced yourself on me. It happened!"

Madeleine lunged. Russell grabbed her around the waist and pulled her back to the bench.

Bruno stared, glassy eyed, considering the possibility. It hit him, if it was true, what it meant, all he had missed. "I have a child?" He swiped at his eyes. "A boy? A girl?"

"Boy," Madeleine said.

"Does he look like me?"

She deliberately glanced at Russell. "No, breve orazione penetra."

"God hears small prayers," Russell said.

Bruno shook his head. "No. You're too young!"

Russell snarled, an ugly expression, the first time he showed this encounter was anything more than a game to him. "How many years since you blew up your first yacht, Mr. Porcelli? Just subtract seven months. That's exactly how old I am."

Bruno ripped a cushion from the bench and threw it across the deck. "This is not possible!"

Russell pushed him back down. He leaned in and half whispered. "You did give me one thing of value. My DNA. My claim to all of your legitimate businesses."

Bruno grabbed the collar of Russell's shirt and shoved him out of his face. "If that's what you're after, why not just kill me?"

"For the last time, we are not murderers," Madeleine said. "All we've done is strip you of everything you've dedicated your life to, reduced you to a pauper."

"A pauper? Never! Where is my money!"

Madeleine shouted him down. "I'm finished explaining. Here's what's going to happen now. Three simple facts. You are going to live in seclusion, you will be given a subsistence allowance, and you will contact no one."

Bruno sneered. "What's to keep me from—"

"Any deviation from our instructions, and Il Martello gets a little whisper in his ear about your precise location."

"You can't keep me forever. I'll disappear on my own, somewhere *no one* will find me."

Ivy did not miss a beat. "You really want to play hide and seek with me, old man?"

He met her calculating eyes and wilted. Then suddenly he snatched the bottle of vodka and cocked his arm. Ivy reached for the watch on her wrist. Bruno stopped, took a full breath, then turned and hurled the bottle into the sea.

"How do you think you're going to pull this off? What's next?"

Madeleine said, "We're going to sink this boat. The water is at least four hundred meters here. That's right, thanks to Ivy, we're a lot farther east than you thought. The boat will never be found, and everyone will presume you're dead."

"That was my goal anyway. What's the rest?"

"You'll be taken to a tiny, undeveloped island in the Caribbean, population less than one thousand. They speak nothing but their strange patois. There's only one way off the island, a three-hour ferry from Guadeloupe that arrives once per month. You'll receive an allowance, enough for essentials, nothing as luxurious as internet, or vodka, or healthcare. And we'll be watching, twenty-four seven."

"I'm a prisoner."

"Let's call it a controlled exile. Something I'm very familiar with."

Russell added, "In all fairness, you were right about one thing. To make this work, we involved Alice Stevens. She had no idea about the plot, but she is the one player not part of the family." He winked at Madeleine.

Bruno said, full volume, "You may not be murderers, but you bastards are all hypocrites. You involved Alice, and now she'll never work again, no matter what you try to do for her. An innocent life ruined." He shouted, like it was the last word. "She's ruined, I made sure of that, I completely destroyed her reputation!"

They all turned at a sound from the doorway.

Chapter 36

19:00

The *Profitti Porcelli* was drifting freely. With no engine to keep it oriented into the swells, it pitched and rolled at the mercy of the waves. Still woozy from the sedative, Alice could not maintain her footing. She dropped the handgun into the pocket of the wool sweater and gripped the doorway with both hands.

When Russell had entered the lounge, some of the conversation switched to English. They were shouting to be heard over the increasing storm, and at times screaming with raw emotion. She understood it had all been an elaborate game, played by filthy rich people with no regard for her safety or her future. But she had the gun. She would force them to return, turn them in for kidnapping and extortion. And there could still be one saving grace to come out of this sickening disaster, if her intuition was correct and one of the players in this game still wanted her.

When the waves momentarily subsided, she took the gun in both hands and steeled her nerves, prepared to step coolly through the doorway. But she heard Bruno shout. *"Alice will never work again, no matter what you try to do for her. She's ruined, I made sure of that, I completely destroyed her reputation!"*

A memory flickered. It was what he'd said just before the sedative knocked her out, something about her reputation. The bastard! Rage swept every thought away except one. Revenge! She pulled back the hammer on the revolver, thrust it in front of her, and ran into the lounge.

She shrieked. "Destroy me? I did nothing but try to help you! You're dead Bruno Porcelli!"

The gun fired, ten times louder than the rumbling thunder. The flash from the barrel momentarily blinded her. With the next streak of lightning, she saw Bruno hunkered under the table. Madeleine and Russell were running for the staircase. Ivy had not moved, perhaps immobilized with fear. Alice stumbled and the gun discharged into the deck. Bruno made a hobbling dash to the side railing. He snatched at a lifebuoy, but it remained lashed to the rail.

Alice yelled again, "You. Are. Dead!"

Aiming for the middle of his back, she fired at the same instant he threw himself overboard. She ran to the railing and blindly emptied the gun, four rounds into the black waters where he must have landed.

Madeleine and Russell were crouched on the top stair. They heard the trigger click once, twice. Out of bullets. Alice had one leg over the rail now. She cursed and flung the gun into the waves. "I'll kill you!" Russell ran, leapt, and touched the back of her shoe as she dove headfirst into the roiling water.

"Alice!" He unhooked the lifebuoy and heaved it overboard. It was swallowed by the darkness. He stripped off his boots. Madeleine bellowed, no! Without thinking, Russell leapt.

Ivy ran to the wheelhouse. She swept the searchlight across the waves.

Madeleine screamed, "There he is!" He was being washed farther and farther from the boat.

Ivy started the engine and steered the way Madeleine pointed.

Minutes ticked as the vessel slowly turned into the storm. Madeleine held her breath every time she saw Russell dive…three, four, five times. "She's gone! Save your strength!"

Ivy continued to play the light across the surface.

Madeleine yelled, "The last time he dove I didn't see him come up." Then suddenly, "More to port!"

He appeared completely spent now, gulping air and water. She seized a second lifebuoy. "We're close. Kill the engine!" She threw the ring to within an arm's length of him. "Ivy! Find a line!"

Madeleine saw him put one arm through the ring. From the wheelhouse, Ivy dropped a coiled, neon-orange grab line down to the owner's deck. Madeleine tossed a third of the coil, and it landed perfectly. Russell, barely moving, managed to tie it to the buoy and wrap the remainder of the loose end around his upper arm.

Madeleine's mind raced. Pulling him up the side of the yacht would be impossible. Move! If she stopped to think what was at stake, panic would paralyze her. She shouted to Ivy, "Let's work him back to the swim deck.

Go down and I'll toss it to you."

Ivy ran two flights down the spiral stairs. Madeleine dropped the coil over the aft rail onto the main deck. Slick with rain, fighting the heave of the boat, she moved as fast as she dared to the main deck, past Ivy, and down the last set of stairs to the swim deck. No more than a meter above water level, wave after wave crashed over the surface. Her experience breaking broncos, a lifetime ago, came back to her. She dropped to the decking, wrapped her legs around the corner rail post, and snatched the end of the line as Ivy tossed it.

Decorative lanterns provided the only light; visibility out into the storm was negligible. Even when lightning lit the sky, she could not see her son. By now, all fifty meters of the line were played out—fifty meters of sea surged between her and her heart.

Praying that Russell could hang on, Madeleine pulled hand over hand, vaguely aware that Ivy sat behind her now, using the incoming rope to tether Madeleine to the post.

"You're doing great Aunt Maddie. Twenty-seven meters of line still out, one meter per pull every three seconds. Eighty-one seconds to go!"

As the boat heaved, wind driven sea spray seared the rope burns forming on Madeleine's hands. Her life, beginning with Russell's birth, flashed as she closed her eyes. The ranch in Texas, his grade school rodeos, girlfriends, first truck, off to college....

Boom! Lightning flared and a wave broke at the same instant. She saw a spot of color!

"There he is! Russell, hang on—" Her throat clinched as she realized he was unconscious, or dead. Eyes closed, jaw slack, head flailing with every toss of the buoy.

"Oh my god! Hang on baby! Ivy, grab him!"

Ivy clamped her legs around a post and extended as far as she dared into the sea. She seized the back of his shirt collar. Madeleine timed the next swell and made a final heave on the rope. Russell's body washed under the bottom rail line and up onto the deck. They dragged him to the forward wall of the swim deck, beneath the cantilevered roof. He was not breathing.

03:00

Ivy cried, "I'm not getting a pulse!"

Madeleine pumped his chest. "I did not play this game just to lose you!" She labored over him, the constant sea spray washing the tears from her face. After an eternity, he coughed. They quickly rolled him onto his side. The quantity of water that flowed from his mouth seemed impossible. More coughs, several shallow breaths, finally his eyelids flickered.

He tried to prop himself on one elbow but collapsed. He pointed aft, trying to tell them something.

Ivy found three dry towels and tucked them around him. Madeleine put his legs up on a bench.

Color slowly seeped back into his cheeks. He filled his lungs, coughed again, and croaked, "Where is the raft?"

Madeleine and Ivy started. They had not noticed the escape raft was nowhere to be seen.

00:00

Chapter 37

By the time Russell regained enough strength to walk, the rain was over and the sea state had improved from rough to moderate. The three of them climbed to the upper decks. Russell worked the searchlight as Madeleine scoured the waves for any signs of life. Ivy reported their radar showed no vessels as small as a raft within twenty kilometers, but admitted the resolution was iffy beyond five. She used the ship's sonar to scan the depths. Nothing large enough to be a body appeared. Their hopes diminished with each passing minute.

When Madeleine realized they had been at it for more than an hour, she reluctantly called off the search.

Russell and Ivy reboarded *The Hidden Mermaid,* the power boat registered to the Areni Gallery and in which they had tailed Bruno's yacht. Madeleine released the tie line as she leapt aboard. Russell piloted them a hundred meters out, and Ivy said far enough. As he held their position facing the *Profitti Procelli,* Madeleine covered her ears and nodded. Ivy pressed the remote detonator.

In less than a blink, the shockwave, a screaming wall of compressed air, rocked their small power boat like a tsunami. Twin fireballs roiling above the yacht lit the clouds and danced patterns on the choppy water.

Madeleine closed her eyes.

Ivy nodded in approval.

Russell coughed as the stench of burning diesel caught in his throat. "My god, Ivy, what the hell did you use?"

"Two hundred grams of Semtex plastered to the fuel tanks, another two hundred in the anchor well. More than I needed apparently."

Five minutes later, the yacht began listing to starboard. When the vessel was below the waves, when a final belch of bubbles erupted, exhaustion washed over Madeleine and she said let's go. Russell entered new coordinates and *The Hidden Mermaid* found its way through the weakening storm, returning to its berth in Genoa with a trio of survivors.

Chapter 38

As Madeleine, Russell, and Ivy drove from Port of Genoa to the family villa in Campione d'Italia, Maddie and her sister exchanged texts.

MADDIE: Mission complete

SYRINA: All safe?

MADDIE: Russell, Ivy and me driving back. Explain then.

SYRINA: Federico here now

MADDIE: Be there in 3 hrs. Don't wait up. Love you

It was pre-dawn when the trio arrived. Federico had a bottle of QB in a bucket of ice, but the five living descendants of Antonio Costanzo were in no mood to celebrate. Nor sleep. Syrina served coffee as the group described, analyzed, and dissected all that had happened before the Ligurian Sea swallowed the *Profitti Porcelli.*

By mid-morning, bleary-eyed Madeleine sat alone on the white, sun-warmed veranda overlooking pristine Lake Lugano. The antique wicker chair that she remembered from childhood was golden-brown with age now, and it creaked as she rocked, an irony not lost on her.

After years of preparation, the sting to bankrupt and exile Bruno had not ended as planned; he had escaped, probably died, on his own terms. But the instant he realized what they had done to him! The play of emotions across his face was priceless. Anger, desperation, impotence, and finally resignation. That moment, that treasure of triumph, was not enough to repay her for the decades she herself had lived in exile, would not fill her emptiness, but it would have to do.

She stopped rocking and listened. There was no breeze, no sound of neighbors or boats on the water, only voices from inside the villa. She rose and went into the skylit two-story sunroom where the others sat at a round table. Ivy was still plugged with earphones, scouring on-line news reports for information about the incident. The others could not stop picking at the details, trying to understand what had happened in the storm. Nothing had been prepared for breakfast; apparently Maddie was the only one hungry.

The three from the yacht had told and retold Syrina and Federico everything they could remember. In Syrina's power boat, they had tailed the *Profitti Porcelli* from Port of Genoa, motoring just beyond sight. Ivy hacked Bruno's navigation system, directing it over a deep trench northwest of Corsica. She then used her electronic magic to control the yacht's power, cameras, alarms, fire suppression—everything needed to confuse and finally render him unconscious. They tied the bow and stern of their craft to the starboard edge of the larger vessel's swim deck. The escape raft, they noted, was tethered with a single line to the port corner of the deck, thrashing in the swell. It had been either taken or lost, sometime between their sneaking on board and Russell being rescued. How that happened, how a raft could vanish without a trace, had been rehashed a dozen times, but they were still at it.

Federico looked at Russell. "Maybe Bruno grabbed the lifebuoy, the one you threw for Alice?"

"Chances are he was sleeping on the bottom before I even tossed it."

"He swam worse than the Venus de Milo," Madeleine said. "Refused to ever learn. There is no way he made it to the raft."

Ivy agreed. "Ability aside, he was intoxicated and crippled with pain. The odds of him making it to the swim deck are less than one percent."

"That means Alice took the life raft then, no?" Federico, more than the others, refused to give up hope.

Russell shrugged. "If she made it, then we should hear something soon."

"Like she trusts any of us?" Syrina was convinced they would never see or hear from her again. "If she's alive, she's as far away as possible. You agree, Ivy?"

"Don't ask me to make predictions on something that involves female emotions. One, given what she overheard, Alice has, at best, mixed feelings about Russell. Two, she probably thinks she's in love with Federico on some level. And three, *if* she still craves the life of the rich and famous, she now fears it in equal measure. There are no formulas for all that."

"I can't believe she's gone," Russell said. "It doesn't seem possible. If Alice is anything, she's a survivor."

Federico again. "Ivy, what do you think the chances are she's alive?"

She didn't hesitate. "Twenty-one percent. She's tough. Resourceful. And we never spotted the lifebuoy Russell tossed. But there are two other possibilities. Bruno and Alice could have taken the escape raft *together*. Admittedly, decimal odds. More likely, the raft was simply ripped away in the storm, unoccupied, and they both drowned." She looked at the ceiling. "Seventy-six percent probability."

It sounded like the final word on the subject. Syrina retreated into the kitchen and returned with mineral water and a pitcher of juice. "I'll say one thing. Maddie, Russell, Ivy, you three are lucky to be alive. If Alice had been a better shot—"

"No, no, no." Ivy laughed and clapped her hands. "I couldn't leave that to chance. The night Bruno stashed his bomb making supplies in the fuel alcove? After I installed all my bugs and cameras I scoured the place, found the revolver, and loaded it with blanks."

"This all sounds like an episode of Mission Impossible." Federico couldn't get his head around how they had managed it all, the planning, the risk assessment, the timing. "You didn't worry he might manage to detonate his bomb before you could intervene?"

"Again, leave nothing to chance. I hacked Bruno's internet search and fed him bomb recipes guaranteed *not* to work. The one he chose, with a propane tank? Even the fuse was a dud. It called for earphones, with the buds cut off, plugged into a smart phone. Fifty measly milliwatts, max. The chance of that mixture igniting was zippo. And even if it had, you can't detonate a propane tank with a bit of fertilizer and diesel."

"Still," Federico said, "Alice was such a nice lady. It's a shame—"

Madeleine bristled. "We calculated the odds of her being harmed and they were in the single digits."

"Six-point-six percent," Ivy said.

Russell added, "But still, I was uncomfortable using her from the beginning. Sure, we had some fun together, but—"

"But nothing," Ivy said. "You were friends with benefits using each other to achieve your own separate goals. You introduced her to QB, but she chose to latch onto Federico."

"I wish I'd had the chance to come clean with her, explain everything."

"Russell, look." Ivy was blunt. "She got greedy. Went off book. Got caught in her own lies. If she had just listened and followed the plan, we wouldn't be having this conversation."

Syrina sat her empty juice glass down hard. "But would the end result have been any different?"

"The plan as scripted had a ninety percent chance of success. But Alice went off the rails and it ended FUBAR. What we have here is a classic second choice. Dead or alive, Bruno is finished. If he survived, he knows I'll find him and make his world even more unbearable. I have programs running twenty-four seven, checking transportation, banking, and communications worldwide. My face recognition software can spot a snowflake at a hundred meters, and I'm running an ongoing backdoor government and corporate scan via the dark web. If he pops up somewhere, we'll know."

****

Two more debate-filled days passed, two more nights with little sleep. It was now breakfast again with everyone fending for themselves. Madeleine was last to make her way to the sunroom.

"Who wants eggs?"

"Who wants an update on the latest news on the disappearance of the *Profitti Porcelli*?" Ivy took off her earphones, and everyone stopped what they were doing. "If you can call what the media spews these days *news*."

She told them a rumor had surfaced that Signore Porcelli had faked his death. Another speculated he committed suicide due to financial trouble. Most believed he had been murdered by rivals, as his parents had been years ago.

The more interesting news was that several boats moored on the north coast of Corsica had picked up a distress call on the emergency channel two nights ago. Authorities verified it was from Bruno's vessel. A recording of the call had gone viral, playing on social media over two million times. A substantial reward had been offered by an anonymous source to anyone who deciphered the distorted GPS coordinates on the so-called Mystery Marine Message. While the coordinates were garbled, the end of the message was clear enough: the *Profitti Porcelli* was taking on water, and efforts to launch the lifeboat had failed. Police believed the voice to be that of Bruno Porcelli.

"Russell," Ivy said, "you may or may not be happy to know that, in terms of electronic analysis, your voice is remarkably similar to your father's."

Russell stood abruptly. "That's it, y'all. I've had enough navel gazing for a while. I actually have a life to get back to. Projects are backed up so far, I may have to clone myself."

Federico agreed; it was time to move on. Kisses were exchanged all around. Ivy stuck the earphones back in and unconsciously wiped the kisses from her cheeks. Madeleine and Syrina followed the men outside for final hugs and vague plans to get together soon.

"It's the end of an era, folks," Madeleine said. "I feel like I just retired."

Ivy bellowed from the top of the staircase. "You have to hear this!"

She ran back inside, picked up her laptop, and kissed it smack on the camera.

"What the hell, Ivy? You win the lottery?"

"Read this! It's from Cap Corse, the extreme northern tip of Corsica." Then she began reading it aloud. "Marine Nationale - Sémaphore du Cap Corse: Un turistu hà trovu i resti di una zattera di 2 persone alimentata da batterie lavata à terra à u latu punente à menu di 2 km da a stazione di semaforu. U raft ùn avia micca cuntenutu o identificazione."

Russell said, "Slow down. Is that Italian?"

"It's Corsican." She paraphrased. "Near a military installation at the northern tip of Corsica, a tourist found the remains of a two-person battery-powered raft washed ashore on the west side less than two kilometers from the semaphore station. The raft had no contents or IMO markings." She typed furiously.

Syrina said, "You think it's Bruno's raft?"

"Seventy percent chance. This brand is not a common one. And the location is roughly eighty kilometers in the path of the storm from where it disappeared, and…. Hold on!" She poked her screen. "The military report includes a photo. I just matched it to a screen shot from the camera I had on the swim deck. Now I'm a hundred percent sure. See the oar strapped to the left tube? Same dent in both pics."

"Was anyone on board?"

"No indication given, but someone must have dragged it. The photo shows it well beyond where the waves break. Could have been anyone."

The speculation started again, rehashing everything from prevailing winds and currents to whether zero, one, or two people had been on the raft.

Madeleine tuned it out and went to rock again, alone on the veranda.

As she tried to put all the unanswered questions out of her mind, she realized that finally confronting the husband who betrayed her had started the healing process. She hoped to lock away those heartaches so she could move on. But other wounds—the loss of her father, Silvan, and Dante—she knew would never heal.

Despite years of meticulous planning and execution, Madeleine understood now that too much had been beyond their control. In retrospect, it was impossible to justify the risks. It was a miracle they had all survived. She closed her eyes, and finally the rocker went still.

She woke when someone touched her. Inexplicably, Ivy had joined her on the veranda. She stood at her side with a hand laid softly on Madeleine's shoulder.

"Life sucks sometimes."

Madeleine patted her hand. "At least we can say that one monster has been removed from the population of human beings."

Ivy said, "Yeah. Just because something doesn't do what you planned it to do doesn't mean it's a failure."

"That's from Thomas Edison. I thought you were a Tesla girl."

And then Ivy bent down and hugged her aunt. "No one ever understands when I'm being ironic."

Madeleine smiled, and her eyes filled with tears.

The woman sits alone. In fact, she is the only patron on the secluded terrace of this exclusive resort. Her faraway stare is focused on the surf that breaks on water-blackened boulders, not on the young waiter who opens her table umbrella. He would love to see her eyes, but large sunglasses conceal them. He notices that the curly, bright auburn hair, scrunched beneath an oversized linen hat, does not match her dark blonde eyebrows. The bits of exposed skin he can see are perfectly bronzed; her cheekbones, nose, and mouth, classically beautiful.

The February sky is cloudless and the breeze is almost chilly. Though the sun is past its midpoint, she has just finished her first coffee of the day. For the tenth day in a row now, he brings her a plate of American cheeses, French pastries, and an icy bottle of Italian sparkling wine. He knows that the Hook's cheddar and three cases of rare Quarzo Bianco wine arrived at the resort days before she did, addressed to "Hold for Reservation No. V250453".

The rumor among the staff is that, once the wine is consumed, the woman will move on to her next destination. At least that is what happened this month last year.

She is not unfriendly, but he learns little about her from their daily interactions. She reads *Arts and Leisure* and offers to share her vast knowledge about financial matters. She says she considers no place home, travels the world solo, visits countries only during the off-season. He guesses that she trusts absolutely no one and that she uses a pseudonym— an online search turns up nothing for "Carolina Gretsch", the name on her Amex Black card.

He knows she is a million lightyears beyond his league. Still, he believes he may be in love with her.

Today, he mistakes her pensive mood for loneliness. He gathers his nerve and risks a personal question.

"How long might you travel the globe before settling down somewhere?"

The question triggers something deep and she looks toward the waves for a long time. The simple answer is, she will continue to travel as long as an obscene amount of money mysteriously appears in her checking account each month. It began with no preamble, and she knows it could stop just as suddenly.

When she doesn't reply, he asks, "Would you be interested in a private tasting at the oldest winery in the country? Or I could show you the Fallen Angel Statue at Saint Rita of Cascia Cemetery. She's supposed to—"

"I've had enough of angels for two lifetimes." She whips off her dark glasses and looks at him as if for the first time. She says gently, "Why would you ask an old lady a question like that, anyway?"

He sees her eyes for the first time, the natural smoothness of the skin around them. She can't be more than forty.

Nothing ventured, he thinks. "Have you ever thought about taking someone with you on your travels? I've always dreamed of being rich enough to do just what you are doing."

"Hmpf." She stands as if to leave but leans closer to him and holds his gaze as she slowly re-wraps her silk scarf. "Some unsolicited advice, perhaps. Be careful what you dream. It just might come true."

THE STORY BEHIND THE STORY

The time was the late 1960's. Don played guitar and sang in the choir; Dave played bass in a rock band. They met in the antiquated, coal-fired halls of Bowling Green High School.

Bonding over the lack of compassion from a mis-careered teacher who could have better served humanity as a solo Antarctic penguin herder, their life-long friendship began as kindred spirits playing local coffeehouses, creating one-minute children's dial-a-stories for a local church, producing silent Super 8 movies, and just hanging out. A secret language developed and included the UAWMF game. Neither is sure who owns the next turn.

As the utopian/dystopian high school bubble burst, Don got married, Dave moved to Tennessee. Families happened. For years it was birthday catch-up phone calls, hometown holiday visits. Then came email. Time passed. Don retired while Dave continued to search for a career from which to retire. Don wrote a couple of novels. Dave played in a few more bands. Then came the pandemic and the December 13th, 2020 email with the book idea: *Locked Behind Walls*.

With Don in Philadelphia and Dave anchored just uphill from Nashville, the plotting began. And although there were no in-person writing sessions, *The Twelve Sisters* is a true collaboration. The answer to "who wrote what?" and "who's idea was that?" is blurred at best. The authors edited as they wrote and found the best parts appeared whenever paths were blocked. They wrote three endings, kept them all, and found minor characters becoming integral to the story. Every effort was made to make sure time, technology and locations were accurate. The finished book bears little resemblance to the original idea, and both Dave and Don will forever treasure each version of every character and plot point they imagined along the way.

So now, after eighteen months of twice-weekly video calls and more than two thousand emails, *The Twelve Sisters* is complete and has landed in your hands. We thank you, hope you enjoy it, and look forward to your feedback. If you like it, please tell your friends!

As to the question that begs for answers: Is The Legend of San Russo real? Of course, it is! The Loch Ness legend is real. But is Nessie?

And that other burning question: What about Madeleine's "lost years" between 1977 and 2018? Let's say Don and Dave think of that as a midquel in need of a few thousand words.

Until next time…

ACKNOWLEDGEMENTS

The authors wish to thank the following individuals for their assistance and support in the creation of this book:

Paige Baird, Cheryl Blakeman, Chris Calderaio, Mary Costanzo, Darcy Cummings*,   Dr. Martha Davis, Barbara Deeb, Nan McElroy, Adrienne McCann, Jason Miller, Dr. William Moss, Dr. Matthew Pierson, Valerie Pierson, Thea Suits, and Gus Woods.

*Pseudonym

ABOUT THE AUTHORS

Don Gordon Pierson is a former technical manager, country music DJ, and ice cream truck driver. He is the author of two previous novels, *Ambiguous* and *The un-Natural Aging Process*. Other credits include singer/songwriter on the Americana music album *Another Man's Treasure* and author of the poetry collection *Eighty-eight Keys*. Between chapters, Pierson continues to pursue other interests including travel, photography, abstract and realist painting, reading, and tai chi. *The Twelve Sisters* is his first collaborative novel. He and his wife live in the Philadelphia area and in the Lesser Antilles island of Montserrat.

David Thompson Dorris is a musician, graphic designer and sound engineer. A former video editor, low voltage tech and government map reader, David was the marketing director for a home builder/developer and managed a music publishing company and an indie record label. He traveled the lower forty-eight and Canada on a tour bus, was a paralegal as well as Nashville's first Planned Unit Development Administrator. Somewhere in there he was a stay-at-home dad, coached over 200 boys and girls in three sports, and became a founding board member of a children and the arts nonprofit. *The Twelve Sisters* is his first novel. Dave and Thea live just outside of Nashville. He currently manages a summer/winter community concert series, is a front of house sound engineer, and yes, still plays in a band.

9 789898 534701